I0563126

## ALSO FROM COHESION PRESS

# COMING SOON

*Congregations of the Dead* – James A. Moore & Charles R. Rutledge

*A Hell Within* – James A. Moore & Charles R. Rutledge

*Snaked* – Duncan McGeary

*The Man with the Iron Heart* – Mat Nastos

*The Lysan Plague* – Alister Hodge

# SNAFU: BLACK OPS

# SNAFU:
## BLACK OPS

Edited by:
Amanda J Spedding & Geoff Brown

Cohesion Press
Mayday Hills Lunatic Asylum
Beechworth , Australia
2017

# SNAFU: BLACK OPS

Orders by U.S. and Canadian trade bookstores and wholesalers.
Independent Publishers Group
814 N. Franklin Street
Chicago, IL 60610
P (800) 888-4741
F (312) 337-5985
All other regions, contact the publisher.

Cohesion Press 2017
Mayday Hills Lunatic Asylum
Beechworth, Australia
www.cohesionpress.com

# CONTENTS

# BACK TO BLACK
## A Joe Ledger/Tom Imura novella

Jonathan Maberry and Bryan Thomas Schmidt

## —1—
### The Soldier and the Samurai

The soldier was a ghost in a dead world.

He made no sound as he moved because noise was suicidal. Noise was how to attract the dead. Noise was how one *became* dead. The soldier was alive because he had learned those lessons long ago, often from seeing others make mistakes they could not undo. The soldier had buried so many people, even people as skilled as he was. Maybe that meant he was lucky, or maybe it meant that in many ways he was closer to an animal than a man. His instincts were feral, driven by a predatory nature that had let him survive when so many others had fallen. Stronger people, faster ones, better ones. He, though, survived. All of those deaths were lessons, and he was a good student in the school of survival.

Now he was a soldier in memory only. It was how he defined himself because it steadied him, gave him purpose. Gave him a reason to stay alive even when death called so sweetly and so persistently. Death, after all, was the kingdom where everyone he had ever known and loved now lived. Living was a lonely, brutal thing.

He moved up a dry slope past cactus and twisted shrubs, watching the terrain, listening to the wind. When he stopped, he stood still as the ancient trees. That was a skill he had learned

1

when the world was still alive. When you stop you have to become part of the landscape. You can't do anything to draw the eye.

The trick was to be a ghost so that he did not become a corpse. Before the end of the world that concept made sense to any soldier; since then it was an unbreakable rule.

Even so, being alive often made him feel strange, alone, and freakish. It sometimes made him feel every bit as much of a monster as the things consuming the world.

The living dead. The walking dead. The hungry dead.

*Zombies.*

Even now, even years after it all fell apart, the soldier sometimes found it hard to accept that zombies were real, that they were pervasive, and that they were the most enduring fact of life. Of everyone's life. They were as much an unshakable constant as the need to breathe. They were. They were here, and from what little anyone knew of the rest of the world, they were everywhere. The plague had spread incredibly fast because it was designed to be quick-onset and one hundred per cent communicable. Nature could never have created so perfect a monster. No, it had been the cold minds of madmen on both sides of the Cold War who had taken civilization's noblest advances in science and medicine and twisted them into weapons of mutually-assured destruction. Bioweapons had been officially banned but never actually abandoned. The lie that assured the black budget funding was that they needed to create the weapons so that cures and prophylactic measures could be created.

It was the logic of the shield maker who actually wanted to make and sell swords.

*Lucifer 113* had been an actual doomsday weapon and though it had been locked away and chained up, it had slipped its leash and now the world had died, been consumed, and gone quiet.

And through that quiet the soldier moved, silent as the death that defined him and everything else.

He reached a knoll and paused, crouching in the shelter of a crooked pine tree, and surveyed the landscape. Red rocks, barrel cactus, yucca and Joshua trees. Some big horn sheep grazing on the tough grass near the dark mouth of a cenote. Nothing else.

None of *them* visible. That meant nothing, though. If they had no prey to chase they would stop walking and stand as still as statues, as still as stovepipe cactus. Dangerously easy to miss when scanning an area so wide and vast as Red Rock Canyon in Nevada.

There was movement and the soldier pivoted on the balls of his feet to watch a young man break from the cover of a creosote bush and move along a fault line, keeping to the shadows cast by an up-thrust ledge of ancient rock. The young man moved with an oiled ease that made the soldier long for the lost days of his youth. At fifty-five, the soldier could feel every year, every hour, every injury, every inch of scar tissue that marked his passage through a violent life. The kid had never taken a bad injury. To the heart, sure, but not to the body, and he moved like a dancer.

He moved smart, too, and the soldier nodded his appreciation. The kid was learning. Getting better, sharper, faster. Earning his right to live in a world as thoroughly unforgiving as this one.

The young man saw something and came to a complete stop, freezing and blending into the landscape. The soldier squinted as he surveyed the terrain to see what had spooked his apprentice.

He heard it before he saw it.

The dry desert wind brought the soft, low, plaintive moan of an absolutely bottomless hunger. One of them, crying out its need.

Then it stepped into sight, coming out of a shadowed space between two boulders tumbled down that slope by a glacier millennia ago. It was a man, or had been. Tall, heavy in the shoulders, wearing the soiled and sun-faded uniform of a Nevada State Park ranger.

The soldier did not speak, did not rush to help. He watched, instead.

The young man wore khakis and a many-pocketed canvas vest over a long-sleeved cotton knit shirt. He wore a backpack, too, and fitted between the pack and his own back was the

3

lacquered scabbard of a *katana*, a Japanese sword of the kind the Samurai once used. It was nearly a match to the one the soldier had strung across his own back. The sword's silk-wrapped handle rose above the young man's right shoulder. He also wore a pistol in a belt holster and a knife strapped to his thigh.

He waited until he was sure there was only one of the dead shambling toward him, and then he stepped toward the zombie. His hand flashed up and down and there was a glittering arc of silver.

The zombie's head fell one way, the headless body fell the other.

The soldier rose slowly and walked down the slope to the kid.

"Nice work," he said.

"Thank you," said the young man. "I think he was alone and—"

"And you should have used your fucking knife, Tom," said the soldier.

"What?"

The soldier pointed to the far end of the valley. Three figures were moving toward them. Then a fourth stepped out from behind a tall cactus.

"That sword is pretty, and points for the sweet *kesa-giri*, kid, but that much polished steel is a big frigging mirror," said the soldier sourly. "You might as well have rung the damn dinner bell."

Tom Imura looked crestfallen. "I didn't stop to consider—"

"Really? No shit."

"I... I'm sorry, Joe," he said.

Captain Joe Ledger pulled a pair of sunglasses from the vee of his sleeveless fatigue shirt and put them on.

"Don't be sorry, kid," he said. "Do better."

"Yes," promised Tom.

Ledger pointed to the four figures staggering toward them. "Now go clean up your mess." He sat down on a rock, pulled a piece of goat jerky from his pack, and began to chew.

Tom Imura cleaned the black blood from his sword and returned it to its scabbard. Then he drew his knife. It was a double-edge British commando dagger with a matte black finish over the steel. Totally nonreflective. He drew a breath, held it for a moment, exhaled, nodded, and then set off to meet the four zombies.

He didn't see Joe Ledger grinning at his retreating back.

—2—

## Top and Bunny

"This place looks great, you said. We'll get a lot of rest for once, you said," growled USMC Staff Sergeant Harvey Rabbit, call sign 'Bunny', as he brought up his drum-fed shotgun. He began firing, filling the air with thunder that drowned out the low, hungry moans.

Bunny cut a sour sideways look at his best friend, First Sergeant Bradley 'Top' Sims. The dark-skinned, grizzled former Army Ranger held his SIG Sauer in a two-handed shooter's grip and fired steady, spaced shots at the pale figures closing in on them from all sides. The two men circled slowly, clockwise, finding targets everywhere.

Absolutely everywhere.

They worked this like they'd worked a hundred battles of this kind. Killing the dead. Accepting the insanity of that concept as an unshakeable part of their world.

The front line of the dead went down.

The next line was fifty yards back. The Colorado Rocky Mountain slopes around them fell still as insects and birds alike silenced their calling to hide from the battle threatening their home.

"So tell me, Old Man," asked Bunny as he lowered his weapon, "do I *look* well rested?"

Top shrugged, eyeing Bunny with a creased brow. "You look alive. Say thanks and stop being so damn high maintenance."

"High maintenance my ass," Bunny replied as he readied himself for the next wave. He aimed his shotgun at another zombie and shot it point blank in the forehead. "As far as I can tell, it's a miracle either of us can walk without a cane at this point."

"The miracle," Top said, dropping a walker with a double-tap, "is that either of us still have all our limbs. That we're even alive, Farm Boy."

In truth, Top had been the farm boy, having spent his boyhood summers in his uncle's Georgia peach grove. He'd gone off to the Rangers and fought in battlefields all over the world, then retired to see if he could be a farmer. But he had come out of retirement after his son was killed and his daughter crippled in the early days of the Iraq War. He'd volunteered for the newly-formed Department of Military Sciences, hoping to lead a team into combat in the new War on Terrorism. Instead he became the strong right hand of Captain Joe Ledger's Echo Team. That was where he and Bunny had met and become best friends and teammates.

"Won't be for long if I keep letting you pick our campsites, Old Man," Bunny complained, and then they both went back to work. Firing, stopping only to reload, as zombies continued to advance – some limping on partial legs, others with partially eaten heads or faces or missing arms. Bunny was a six-foot-seven-inch, powerful, blond, former SoCal pro-volleyball player who'd joined the Marines and went from Force Recon to the DMS. Bunny, Top and Ledger had served together, side by side, their whole time at the agency.

Until things fell apart.

"The survivors we rescued yesterday said it was clear," Top snapped, motioning downslope toward the old log cabin where they'd tried to spend the night – an abandoned escape for some unknown city dwellers that might never return.

"Well, clearly they were full of shit!" Bunny snapped. "Maybe we should go back and kick their asses. Just as a way of saying thanks."

The last two zombies fell, their heads blown apart.

Top and Bunny panned around in a circle, looking for any signs of movement or further targets. The stink of rotting blood and flesh mixed with the sweet smell of pine needles and moss filling the cool mountain air as it breezed gently around them.

"Clear," said Bunny, his voice too loud in the sudden quiet.

"Clear," agreed Top. "Won't last, though. All that shooting will bring more of them out of the woods. Won't take 'em long to get here, either."

Top swapped out his magazine and holstered the SIG, then dragged a sleeve across the sweat on his face. "Hot as balls today."

"Cover my six," Bunny said. "This time, I think I'll pick our shelter."

"Hooah," muttered Top, and they moved out in tight formation, covering each other as they followed a trail through a copse of ponderosa pines leading up a nearby slope.

Ever since the world fell apart under *Lucifer 113*, or *The Plague* as the public usually called the outbreak, Top and Bunny found themselves as soldiers without an official mission. There was no government, no DMS, no active military. The world had fallen completely off its hinges, and what was left of America – and maybe the world – was an all-you-can eat buffet for the hungry dead, with pockets of humans trying to survive here and there.

In the absence of official orders, Top and Bunny had assigned themselves a mission. The rules were simple. Keep moving. Save whom they could save. Kill as many zombies as was practical. Rinse. Repeat.

They'd become successful enough to earn a reputation as 'the garbage men', as one group of survivors had dubbed them. They'd once met a salvage team out in the wasteland who'd heard of them and repeated what he'd been told. *'Call them in and they'll haul your ass out and empty the garbage you leave behind.'*

Not something you could put on a tattoo, but it worked well enough.

As for the nickname of *'The Garbage Men'*, Bunny hated it, but Top thought it was hilarious.

"Yeah," Bunny protested after they'd left the salvage man, "But we're not a pair of fucking janitors. We're saving lives. Where's the respect?"

Top just said, "People use humor to keep their spirits up in impossible life situations. They don't mean disrespect. It's a joke."

Bunny didn't see how there was anything to joke about. The world was for shit and it might never recover. Millions, maybe *billions* of people were dead. More were dying, and everyone who died, no matter how, reanimated and joined the flesh-eating horde. No matter how many they shot, more kept coming. Top somehow managed to stay optimistic, but all Bunny could do was keep thinking how fucked they were.

FUBAR.

Fucked up beyond all repair.

Yeah.


—3—

**The Soldier and the Samurai**

Joe Ledger and Tom Imura scaled a tall rock as twilight began filling the canyons with shadows. In another kind of world they would have used the darkness as a time to travel quickly without being seen and without the oppressive desert heat. But the dead did not rest and they hunted at night. Actually they hunted all the time, but at night the lifeless bastards were harder to see coming, driven by smell and hearing when it was too dark to see. No one Ledger had talked to during the fall knew how the zombies stayed alive, or why they didn't rot past a certain point, or how they could use any of their senses. It seemed to make no scientific logic, but for Ledger it meant he simply did not have sufficient information. Everything made sense in the end. Everything, and he had encountered some of the most bizarre threats any Special Operator had ever encountered. Even when it looked like it was something supernatural, there was always some kind of weird goddam science to explain it.

The fact that all of the scientists he knew were also dead skewed the math. It meant he might never get the right answers.

Once he and his apprentice were up on top of the rock, they pitched a camp, and ate a meal of cold salted rabbit and water. The elevation kept the dead away, but a cooking fire up here could be seen from miles and miles away. They sat together, wrapped in blankets against the cold of the desert night, and talked.

"I wish Sam was here," said Tom. It wasn't the first time he mentioned his older brother, who had been a sniper on Ledger's Echo Team. As far as Ledger knew Sam had been killed a few days after the dead rose. Or so he had been told.

"Me, too," he said.

Tom must have heard something in his voice because he turned to the soldier. "Joe… do you think there's any chance he's still alive?"

"A chance? Sure," said Ledger, nodding. "The lady cop I met who'd been with him said she had been *told* that he fell under a swarm of zoms, but she didn't actually see him get bit. Sam and his field team, the Boy Scouts, were helping the cop get a whole convoy of school buses filled with kids out of danger. They were overrun and Sam was doing what he could to give them a chance. He went down and the buses got out, but…"

"But…?"

"Sam was dressed for combat. Ballistic helmet with a face shield, Kevlar vest, limb pads, armored gloves. The works," said Ledger. "He wasn't exactly naked and painted with steak sauce, you dig? He might have made it out. But he didn't have a vehicle, at least as far as the cop knew. And going back for him would have put the kids on the table for an all-you-can-eat buffet."

"Then he *could* still be out there?" asked Tom. He was a nice young guy. Early twenties. Tough as nails. Smart. Decent. Damn good fighter. But he wore his heart on his sleeve and he pinned his own survival on ideals like hope and optimism, which was dangerously fragile scaffolding as far as Ledger saw it.

Even so, he didn't try to kick that structure down. Tom had a little half-brother, Benny to think about. The kid was back in Central California, in a small makeshift town built around a reservoir high up in the Sierra Nevada Mountains. Tom had helped establish, build and defend that town, but he often left his brother in the care of his neighbors while he went out into what the people in town called the great 'Rot and Ruin' to look for survivors. Tom had rescued more than two hundred people so far, which made him a hero.

Joe Ledger had no interest in settling in the town. Like Tom, he was on the prowl for survivors, too. However, it was only half of his own self-imposed mission. The rest of it was less humanitarian. Or, maybe it was a service to the community in the most extreme terms.

He and Tom were not out here to kill zoms.

No, they were hunting people.

Tom must have read his thoughts. "What's wrong with them?"

It was a question the young man asked in one way or another nearly every day. What's wrong with them? *Them*. Not the dead. Smart as he was, Tom did not seem able to crawl inside the head of living people who saw the apocalypse as the chance to shake off all moral constraints, all ethics, all inhibitions. There were packs of predators out here – mostly, but not entirely men – who preyed on camps of survivors. Stealing their food and supplies, brutalizing the men, raping the women. Sometimes raping the children, too. Ledger and Tom had found absolute proof that human beings – the uninfected living – were a thousand times more savage than the legions of hungry dead. They had come upon camp after camp and read the proof in the twisted bodies, in the small violated corpses, in the leavings of monsters in human shape. Tom had called them animals at first, but later changed that to 'monsters' because animals did not do this.

Tom had been about to graduate from the police academy when the world fell. Since then he had bloodied his hands, but it was only after Ledger had taken him under his wing that Tom Imura had become a practiced and efficient killer. A hunter of hunters; a predator who preyed on predators.

"They do it because they're weak," said Ledger. He tore off a chunk of rabbit and chewed slowly.

"Weak?"

"Sure. Don't confuse dangerous with strong. You're strong, kid. So am I. So are the kinds of people, trained or untrained, who stand up to protect those who can't protect themselves. That's what defines strength. Just as being brave in the face of danger defines courage." Ledger chewed and shook his head slowly. The sun was down and there were ten billion stars spread like diamond dust above them. "The people we hunt aren't tigers or lions. They're jackals. They hunt in packs because they're too fucking afraid to hunt alone. And in those packs they trash talk so that everyone thinks they're tough, but it's a thin coat of paint on a pile of shit."

"They put up a good fight, though," observed Tom, but Ledger shook his head again.

"No. They fight, but it's not a good fight. They fight because they're afraid of dying, and they're afraid of the pain of dying. But they aren't warriors. They're not going down in any fucking blaze of glory. Even a cockroach will fight." He spat over the edge of the rock, listened, but didn't hear it land. He shrugged.

They sat in silence for a long time. There was no moon tonight and the wind was quiet. Far away they could hear sounds in the night. The rustle of something small and fast moving through the brush. A little ground squirrel, maybe, or a rat. The distant call of a night bird. The soft, plaintive moan of something dead and hungry.

They sat and watched the stars.

"I miss my dogs," said Ledger.

"Me, too."

When Tom had met Ledger the big soldier was traveling with two monstrous dogs that were half Irish wolfhound and half American mastiff. Baskerville and Boggart. On one of their 'training' trips up to San Jose Boggart had gone missing and when they found him the dog had adopted a girl who called herself Rags. The girl was a scrappy little thing. Young but tough as iron, and she and the dog had bonded. After a violent run-in with a group of raiders who called themselves the Skull Riders, Ledger, Rags and the dogs had gone east. When Ledger returned nearly two years later, he had Baskerville with him as well as a new full-bred female mastiff he called Cupcake. Boggart, Ledger told Tom, had elected to stay with Rags, and the soldier was fine with that. Cupcake had joined his little pack. However the two big dogs were back in Mountainside because Cupcake had just dropped a litter of five very large, very noisy pups. Ledger missed his dogs. He liked them a lot more than he liked most people.

After nearly an hour, Tom said, "Maybe we'll find some horses."

"Maybe," Joe said dubiously.

"If we don't it's going to be a long walk to Oro Valley, Arizona."

"Yup."

They sat in silence, watching the stars above them swim through the Milky Way.

"Joe…do you think it's real?"

Ledger said nothing.

"The cure they keep talking about," persisted Tom. "Do you think it's real?"

Ledger sipped some water and washed it around in his mouth before swallowing.

"Christ, kid, I hope so."

—4—
## Top and Bunny

Top and Bunny wound up spending the night in the loft of a barn on old but clean hay, taking turns sleeping three hours then keeping watch – each twice that night. The next morning, they headed for the Arizona-Colorado border, several survivor groups having hinted that they'd heard rumors of another group struggling in the small town of Sun Valley near Petrified Forest National Park.

Top led the way, because the Georgia farm boy rode horses like it was second nature. Bunny, on the other hand, was an Orange County, California surfer, and his horse riding skills continued to amuse Top every time he watched him. Since riding along with a constantly chuckling companion had begun annoying Bunny fairly quickly, Top just rode ahead, so he could avoid the spurts of spontaneous laughter he'd been prone to when they'd first started out. Bunny knew this although it went unacknowledged. He loved the old guy anyway, though God knew he'd never say that out loud.

The two hundred and two mile journey would take them a little under fourteen hours at normal speeds for the horses – about eighteen minutes per mile – and using the older state highways to avoid the cities, where most large colonies of zombies congregated, also saved time. But they still had to be well rested and conserve their strength to remain effective when they arrived so they'd already decided to split the journey into two days.

They'd waste less energy riding early mornings and at night once they left the foothills of the Rockies and hit the desert. Cooler temperatures would be easier on all of them, despite the dangers of the dark. The same EMPs that had destroyed the zombies and automobiles had also eliminated many snakes, scorpions, and other predators. But not all by far. There were always the random zombie pods, but dealing with scattered zombies was much easier than the city hordes, and they were used to that.

As they rode south, the foothills turned to prairies and pine forests. The latter were littered with twigs and pine needles that crunched under the horses' hooves more softly than dead leaves. Crickets, birds, and other creatures chirped in the branches and overhead in a constant droning symphony of sound. The wind blew strong, bringing the hot desert winds and smells of sand, dust, and dry grass to mix with the sweet scent of pine sap and needles. From time to time, amidst the pines, Bunny even thought he detected a faint scent of butterscotch, but decided his mind must be playing tricks. As the forests gave way to prairies, the prairies eventually gave way to gravel and rock formations. Trees were soon conspicuously absent, and the air became thicker with heat, making their lungs work harder.

The whole time, Bunny thought back on the nineteen years since the world had fallen apart and the DMS had ceased to exist, at least for Echo Team. They had once been like a family, but now they were all scattered to who knew where. They didn't even know if anyone one else was still alive. Only Top remained in Bunny's world and Bunny in his. And that was only because they'd been together on a supply run when the EMPs hit and they'd been stranded, forced like so many others to fight to survive. Teaming up had been a natural instinct after so many years of it, and here they were. Somehow they'd survived when so many others hadn't. Bunny thought of Joe Ledger, Rudy and Circe Sanchez, Leroy Williams, whom they all called 'Bug', and Junie Flynn. He thought of the strange and enigmatic Mr Church who was their leader and about whom Bunny knew next to nothing. Last but not least he thought of Lydia Ruiz, Warbride, who'd gone from teammate to friend to lover. God, the memories of all them.

"Farm Boy!" Top shouted, startling Bunny from his reverie.

"What?" He shook it off and looked around as his horse just barely steered clear of a cacti bunch that would have surely torn into his leg through his pants. *Fuck*, he thought, grabbing the reins and resuming control.

"You're lucky animals have good instincts," Top said, shaking his head. "You falling asleep on me?"

Bunny shook his head. "No. Just remembering."

To Bunny's relief, Top read the look in his partner's eyes and no further explanation was needed. He grunted in sympathy and they rode on together, now side by side for a while.

—5—
## The Soldier and the Samurai

They did not find horses.

Not live ones, anyway. They found a farmer's field full of bones and they found a half dozen zoms dressed in field denims standing around looking blank. Tom stopped by the rail and stared at the dead, and the zoms slowly turned toward him and began walking. There was never any hurry in the world of the dead. They were inexorable and indefatigable, but they were never hasty.

Tom reached over his shoulder for the handle of his sword, but Ledger stopped him.

"They're not going to hurt anyone," said the soldier. "They're too clumsy to climb over the fence and who in their right mind would go in there?"

Tom frowned. "Right… but shouldn't we… what's the word you like to use? 'Quiet' them?"

Ledger shrugged. "Why? They're not in pain. They're not going to get lonely or any of that shit. They're dead but they don't know it. What good will it do anyone?"

"It would be merciful. They were people once, Joe. They had their lives stolen by the disease and now they're in this living death hell. Or whatever you want to call it."

Ledger sighed and walked over to stand beside Tom, watching the zoms shamble their way.

"Here's how I see it, kid," said the soldier. "These people are gone. Yes, we can mourn who they used to be, and we can feel compassion for how they died and for what was taken from them. I get that. We both get that. It sucks worse than almost anything. The only thing that would suck worse would be if they *knew* they were dead."

"Knew?"

"Sure, if their personalities were somehow trapped in there, aware of what had happened to them. That would be the biggest suck-fest of all time."

Tom went pale. "Jesus Christ…"

"But you've looked into their eyes, Tom," said Ledger. "Have you ever seen so much as a flicker of personality? Of intelligence? Of awareness?"

"No." He sighed. "No, I haven't."

"Of course not, because whoever lived in those bodies is gone. To heaven, to hell, or to whatever state of existence is waiting on the other side of death's front door. I don't know."

"Maybe it's nothing," said Tom. "Maybe there's nothing after this."

"Maybe," said Ledger, "but boy would that be a fucking kick in the balls. After all these thousands of years of religion and prayer and everything else, it would be a rotten fucking cosmic joke if this was it, finished, done."

The zoms were almost up to the fence.

Tom said, "What do you believe?"

Ledger bent and plucked a long stem of wild grass and put it between his teeth. It bobbed up and down as he chewed the end.

"Not sure what I believe in has a name," said Ledger after a moment. "I was raised Methodist back in Baltimore, but that's kind of for shit. None of what happened squares with any religion's apocalyptic prophecies, which tells me two things. Either everyone's wrong and the universe has bent us all over a barrel, or this isn't the actual end."

Tom watched the zombies. "How much closer to the end do we need to get?"

The closest of the dead, a woman in jeans and a man's flannel work shirt, thrust her arms between the slats of the fence rail, gray and withered fingers clawing at the air inches from where the two men stood. Ledger reached out and offered his fingers to the dead woman, who grabbed them and tried to pull them toward her mouth. Ledger was stronger and he did not give an inch. The zombie kept trying, moaning softly, but Ledger remained unmoved. Only when the other zoms reached for him did he pulled his hand free and wipe it on his jeans.

"Maybe the line in the sand," he said quietly, "is when there's no one left like you."

"Me? I'm more of a skeptic than you are."

"About religion, sure. Maybe. But you've been working your ass off to save your little town. What are you calling it?"

"Mountainside."

Ledger nodded. "You may not have much optimism about your spiritual future, but you have a lot about the future of the people in Mountainside. About your stepbrother's future. About the possibility of there even *being* a future."

"I could be delusional," said Tom, half smiling.

"You could. Not sure you actually need to believe in anything much yourself except life. You *do* believe in that, and don't tell me you don't."

Tom nodded.

"So, as I interpret the whole End of Times thing," said Ledger, "an actual apocalypse should be all exit doors and no other options. I'm not seeing that here. Neither are you. Fuck, even those ass-pirates who are preying on survivors think there's a chance at a future." He shook his head and tossed the blade of grass into the wind. "We're living in a fully dramatized example of that old samurai concept. *Nanakorobi yaoki.* You know that one?"

"'Fall down seven times, get up eight'," said Tom.

"This is one of the times we get up."

"What if we get knocked down again? What if that doctor in Arizona doesn't really have a cure? What then?"

"Then we get up a ninth time," said Ledger. "And a tenth."

They watched the zoms, standing just outside of the reach of those dead hands. Then Ledger raised himself on his toes and looked over to the side of the farmhouse that stood on the edge of the field. A smile blossomed on his weathered face.

"What?" asked Tom.

"Maybe there's a God after all," said Ledger, "and maybe he's not a total dick."

"Huh?"

Ledger pointed to the porch. There, exposed by the slanting rays of the sun, was a pair of heavy-duty mountain bikes. "Not horses, but then again we won't have to feed and water them."

Tom pulled out his binoculars and studied them.

"Shit. The tires are flat."

Ledger shrugged. "This is a farm in the middle of no-fucking-where. You trying to tell me these people didn't have spares, patch kits and hand-pumps? Really?"

Forty minutes later they were pedaling along the road with the farm and its people falling slowly behind.

## —6—

## Top and Bunny

Bunny estimated they were less than a mile outside Sun Valley when they heard the screams. They'd traveled until early afternoon the first day, then slept during daylight and resumed their journey at night and into the early morning, winding up doing six hours the first day and over seven since they'd started out the previous evening. The journey had been quiet and unexpectedly uneventful – the two soldiers having somehow managed to avoid any pods of zombies or other hurdles the entire way. Until now.

The screaming came from multiple voices.

"Does that sound like children?" Bunny asked.

Top nodded. "Women, too."

They spurred their horses simultaneously and raced in the direction of the screams. The undead didn't scream, they moaned. Some humans were still out there and in danger – probably under zombie attack. As they rode, they checked their weapons. Bunny's chest tightened and he took a deep breath, focusing his energy and senses as he always did when preparing to go into combat. Beside him, he saw Top go through similar preparations, though they each put their own spin on it. They'd faced fire together hundreds of times, yet the prep remained the same. Military discipline and common experience.

As they topped a small rise, they began making out voices mixed with the screams – shouting, pleading, arguing... No distinct words yet, but enough to confirm there were several humans involved – male, female, and children.

They rode into fields of heavy cacti and petrified rock, and Bunny spotted a fading, cracked sign saying, 'Welcome to Petrified National Forest'. A trail had been laid out, lined with logs connected by pillars of stone. The well-worn dirt path between them was around ten feet wide, so they turned their horses and began following it in the direction of the voices and screams.

Some nearby cacti bore beautiful purple and green flowers in stark contrast to the sharp spindles shooting out of every other available surface upon them. Bunny briefly wondered if animals were fooled. For what purpose had the plants grown such camouflage and how many generations ago?

Then the trail turned and they were winding along the top of one of two facing natural stone walls, layers of red, yellow, tan, and grey revealed along the sides that ran down into the canyon between them – loose rock, grass, and cacti growing scattered along the slopes. It was stunning, a clear reminder why the place had drawn the attention of the Department of Interior and become a National Park.

The shouting and pleading became intelligible now.

"No, they're just babies!" a woman sobbed.

"Hold her down!" a man yelled. "We can't help them now!"

"How did they find us again?" another woman wondered, her voice filled with pain and mourning.

"Get back under cover or they might come back for you," the yelling man ordered.

Then Bunny spotted a dirty cargo van, its white exterior spotted with mud and debris, peeling along a thin natural road that ran down the middle of the valley on the canyon floor. Gunshots echoed as rocks and pebbles shot up from the road, the rounds missing the van as it peeled away as fast as it could manage on the slippery surface.

"Who the hell has a working van and frigging gasoline?" After the EMPs hit the cities, most above ground vehicles and gas pumps stopped working. Bunny had heard rumors that vehicles parked in metal buildings or underground might escape the problem, but it had been a long time since he'd seen one. "Should we stop it?" he called to Top.

Both reined their horses to a stop and aimed their weapons, eyes searching for targets, trying to determine who was attacking whom.

Finally, Top shook his head. "We don't know what's going on yet."

"Someone stealing children," Bunny said.

"Or rescuing them," Top countered.

Then they heard the distinct click of a shotgun and pistols being cocked behind them and whirled to find two men and a woman, faces dirty from dust and sand, standing near the trail edge, weapons aimed right at the two soldiers' chests. Bunny knew that with quick movements, he and Top could be off their horses and taking the three out, but Top shot him a look that said, 'wait', so he hesitated, watching his partner.

"Drop the weapons now!" the man with the shotgun ordered. He looked to be in his thirties. From the way the others responded to his voice, Bunny suspected he was the leader.

"Easy there, we mean no harm," Top said, as he and Bunny lowered their guns, moving them slowly toward their holsters.

"Freeze!" the woman shouted, shifting nervously, her .45 swung toward Top's forehead. She was tan with long blonde hair and looked a decade younger than the leader. Top and Bunny stopped moving.

"Yes, ma'am," Bunny said. "Just trying to put them away."

"Who are you?" the leader demanded. "What are you doing here?"

"Soldiers, come to help," Top said. "First Sergeant Sims, US Army Rangers and Master Sergeant Rabbit, USMC."

"Army and Marines together?" the leader said with a quizzical expression. "You aren't official then."

Top shook his head. "Not many official teams left, you know. With the troubles."

"Yeah, we're all on our own," the woman said angrily. "And we don't like strangers." She took a breath and her .45 faltered a bit, but then Top shifted slowly in the saddle, turning to look at her and she snapped it up again, stiffening.

"Just wanted to say that we understand," Top said. "We don't know who to trust anymore either. That's why we're together. We trust each other."

"Till death do us part," Bunny joked.

"You a couple then?" the third person, a scowling younger man with the .45 aimed at Bunny's forehead snapped. He looked like he was barely out of his teens, his short blonde hair similar to the girl's. Could they be related? Either way, he'd spread his legs apart shoulder-width and locked them there, steady, ready for anything. Young or not, he clearly had experience with his weapon and Bunny had no doubt it was a shot he'd probably make.

"Not that kind, no," Bunny said, shaking his head.

"You'll have to pardon the farm boy," Top said, shooting Bunny a warning look. "His sense of humor sometimes comes out at the wrong times."

"This ain't no joke!" the woman snapped, glaring at Bunny, then locking her eyes back on Top.

"We know that, ma'am," Bunny said, swallowing. These people needed to seriously chill. They clearly had no idea that Top and he could have taken them out in seconds if they'd wanted to.

"We're looking for a camp of survivors from Sun Valley we heard might need help," Top said quickly. "We were on our way there. Rode in from Colorado."

"Help? What kind of help?" the leader demanded.

"The undead, some kind of raids, finding shelter and a good hiding place," Bunny explained.

"And what's it to you?" the scowling young man said.

"We have experience with such things, come to offer it," Top said.

"Who was in the van?" Bunny asked.

21

"None of your business!" the woman said, waving her .45 again.

The leader's eyes softened as he read the two soldiers. "Caroline, let's calm down a bit and hear them out, okay?"

"I'm calm," the woman said. "Calm as I'm gonna be after what just happened." She relaxed her arms a bit, lowering the .45 slightly.

"What happened?" Top asked softly.

"We were raided," the leader said, pointing the shotgun at the ground. "Some strangers came and took women and children and a couple old men."

"Took them where? For what?" Bunny asked. Humans raiding to kidnap other humans had to mean they were sick or going to be. What other explanation could there be in these times?

"The Lab. Experiments. Damn crazy doctor," Caroline mumbled, shaking her head.

"What lab? You're raided by other humans?" Bunny asked.

"What's it to you?" the scowling man said, waving his pistol again. "Why are we telling them anything? We don't know them! They could be with the Doc!"

"They're on horses for one, Steven," Caroline said. "The doctor's people come in vehicles."

The leader nodded. "And if they were with the Doc, they would have left together, not hung around."

"We caught 'em. Maybe they're playing dumb, Owen," Steven said, looking toward the leader.

"We'll take their word for it for now and watch them closely," the leader said, nodding in the younger man's direction. "Lower your weapon, Steven, okay?"

Steven hesitated, his scowl changing to a face twisted with confusion. Owen nodded again, then slowly lowered the .45 a little and relaxed his stance.

"Now, you two slide slowly down off those horses so we can talk, okay?" Owen said.

Top and Bunny exchanged a look of agreement, then nodded

and slowly dismounted, making sure to keep their hands well clear of their weapons as they did. Their feet thumped on the stone ground as they landed, sending dust and loose rocks up in clouds around their boots. As Top turned to Owen again and opened his mouth to speak, a whistle sounded from somewhere in the distance.

"They're gone," Caroline said, and all three relaxed a bit more, exchanging knowing looks.

"How many did they get?" Steven wondered.

"We'd better go back to camp and take a count," Owen said.

"What was that about a lab? A doctor taking people?" Bunny asked, exchanging a puzzled look with Top.

"That signal's from our camp," Owen explained, ignoring the specific question. "All clear."

Top and Bunny grunted but held position. That one they understood perfectly.

"What about them?" Steven asked, motioning to the two soldiers.

"They're coming with us," Owen said. "But you two stay behind them and be ready."

"You'd risk letting them know where our camp is?" Caroline asked, looking uncertain.

"We move it a lot," Owen said. "We'll keep them under guard. We need time to find out more about them. But first, we need to make sure the perimeter's secure again. Okay?"

After a moment, Caroline nodded then stepped forward and took away the weapons from the two soldiers – pistols and rifles slung off their shoulders. She didn't inspect their bags or pat them down, for which Bunny felt grateful. She handed one rifle to each of the men and put the pistols in her belt, then stepped clear.

Steven's jaw tightened as he grunted in affirmation and motioned sharply for Top and Bunny to follow Owen. Top and Bunny each grabbed their mount's reins and led the horses after the group's leader.

## —7—
## The Soldier and the Samurai

They heard the screams from miles off.

It was not the empty moans of the hungry dead. It was not an animal sound. These were screams from human throats. Male and female. Raised to that terrible pitch where the screams rip themselves out of throats, damaging tissue, violating the air, breaking the world.

Ledger and Tom were at the top of a hill and the road down twisted in and out of a scattered community of RVs and campers. It was like a hundred such camps they had seen, and like the others it looked like a war zone, with zombies everywhere and partially-eaten corpses sprawled and rotting in the weeds. Vultures circled endlessly in the high, dry air.

However those screams were alive. They were immediate.

Neither man said a word. Instead they kicked their bikes into motion and pedaled as hard and fast as they could, accelerating downhill. They could not see any living people, but the screams had to have been coming from outside – they weren't muffled the way they would be if the victims were inside one of the campers.

It was only when they heard the gunshot that they skidded to a stop.

The dead don't use firearms.

"Off," snapped Ledger and they let the bikes fall. Tom, who was used to Ledger's methods by now, immediately faded left, running low and fast toward the outermost camper, making the maximum of cover. He drew his sword because it was a cloudy day and there was no sunlight to reflect from the blade. Ledger went right, running a zigzag through the dead, twisting to avoid them without having to engage. He did not draw a weapon because the situation hadn't yet revealed how it needed to be handled. It was a lesson he still needed to teach Tom.

He stopped at the corner of a rusty RV that sat on flat tires. Ledger knelt and did a quick-look around the rear bumper, then retreated to let his mind process what his eyes had seen.

Beyond the RV was kind of a pen made from old shopping carts, heaped junk, and cars that had been pushed together. He could not see much of what was going on inside the pen, but there were at least a dozen zombies pressing close to it. A fresh scream from inside the pen told him this was where things were happening. Ugly things. Up close the screams sounded younger and more thoroughly infused with comprehensive personal outrage as well as physical pain. Two guards stood atop the highest points on the pen wall. Both men; both dressed in travel-worn clothes and makeshift armor. Jeans, hockey pads, football helmets. And guns. The guards ignored the zombies, confident that they were out of reach, and instead cheered on whatever was happening in the pen.

Ledger held still and listened to the noises, picking them apart, cataloging them. Several men. How many? Six? Ten? Somewhere in that range. A small pack. The male scream had ended when they heard that gunshot. The female scream continued, rising and falling.

The situation sucked. Outnumbered and outgunned, with at least one helpless victim and the complication of sentries and the zombies. In most circumstances this would be a walk-away, a hopeless scenario.

But not for Ledger. He knew he could never leave this unaddressed. That wasn't who he was. The young scream made that absolutely certain. A long, long time ago, back when he was fourteen and the world was decades away from falling off its hinges, Ledger and his girlfriend, Helen, had been attacked by a group of older teens. Ledger had been stomped nearly to death and had lain there, bleeding and helpless, while the teenagers ruined Helen. Although Ledger and Helen had both lived past that day and had healed in body, neither had ever healed in spirit or mind. Helen eventually found her way out and it was Ledger who found her after she'd gone away. Found what was left of her. An empty shell from which all of Helen had leaked away. The whole process had fractured him, splitting his mind into three distinct personalities. One was the Modern man, the

25

civilized and ordinary part of him, the one who clutched to his dwindling supply of hopes. The second was the Cop, the strong, quiet, intelligent, detail-oriented investigator and thinker. That part had been his mostly reliably dominant aspect.

And then there was the third part, the aspect truly born on that horrible day so many years ago. The Warrior. Or as he preferred to be called, the Killer. Savage, uncompromising, brutal, relentless. However it was the Killer who was, in his way, the most compassionate and protective, because he did whatever was necessary to protect the members of his tribe against all predators. Children were always to be protected. The young, the weak, the helpless. It was hardwired into the brain of the Killer to make sure they would not perish, for as they went so went the tribe itself. Basic Survival 101.

The Cop leaned out and analyzed the scene again, noting distances, placement, weapons, obstacles. However when he rose, it was the Killer who went to war.

He did not signal Tom Imura. That wasn't necessary. Tom would either understand and be ready to function as a member of their small hunting pack, or he wouldn't. Warning him would create a risk Ledger could not afford. Besides, Tom was smart and fast and a killer lurked in his soul, too. Ledger had seen that before. It hurt Tom to kill, but he his regrets and his humanism did not slow his hand. Not at all.

Ledger drew his Heckler & Koch MK 23 pistol as he rose from his point of concealment and held his gun out in a firm two-hand grip. He did not run but instead took many small steps to prevent the weapon from being jolted. He had twelve rounds in the box magazine and a thirteenth in the pipe. The range was good enough for kill shots, but Ledger didn't want these men dead. Not yet. Instead he shot the closest man in the thigh, aiming center-mass to insure a shattered femur. The .45 round punched all the way through at two hundred and sixty meters per second. The man screamed and twisted and fell.

The zombies lunged up to catch him, to drag him down, their nails and teeth ripping into the man before he ever hit the ground. Ledger swung the barrel to take the second man in the hip, the foot-pound of impact knocking him backward off the pen wall. Ledger heard his screams as soon as he fell out of sight.

And then it was all insanity.

The zombies who weren't tearing at the first man wheeled toward him, empty eyes filling with naked hunger, mouths biting the air in anticipation of fresh meat. Ledger shoved his gun into its holster and whipped his *katana* from its scabbard. He was not as stylish a swordsman as Tom, but he was a more practiced butcher. He cut his way to the wall of the pen and everything that reached for him fell. Nothing fell whole.

There were shouts from the other side of the pen wall, and Ledger dodged sideways and leapt onto the wall fifteen yards from where he had fired. When he reached the top he saw nine men in the center of the protected area, and every one of them was looking in the wrong direction. A naked girl of about thirteen lay bruised and beaten on the ground, her young body covered in blood. It was obvious she had been brutally used. They did not see Ledger as he drew his pistol once more and swapped in a full magazine. They did not see Tom Imura slip over the far wall, silent as death.

Ledger opened fire on the men.

This time he shot to kill.

The pistol was accurate within fifty meters. The range here was less than ten. He did not miss.

Men screamed and fell. Others tried to turn their guns – shotguns, hunting rifles, Glocks – on him, but then Tom ghosted up behind them and his sword did quick and terrible work.

It wasn't a fight. Neither Tom nor Ledger was interested in a fight. This was slaughter. It was two against nine, and it was over in seconds.

When Ledger climbed down from the wall the last of the men was begging for his life. Ledger watched Tom's face as the young man stood over the injured man. The girl lay six feet away, and from the way she was breathing it was clear she was on the verge of death. Her eyes were glazed and there were dreadful wounds all over her. The man on the floor was naked from the waist down and there was blood on his penis. Not his blood.

Even so, Tom didn't kill him. Not right away. Instead he asked a question. "Why?"

The man looked at him and then turned to look at the girl. He frowned as if seeing her for the first time. Then he turned back to Tom.

"She'd... she'd die out here anyway," said the man. He said it reasonably, as if what he and his friends had done to her was clearly okay given the circumstances.

Tom's eyes went dead.

His sword moved and then there was fresh blood on the man's face and body.

On the other side of the pen wall the screams had stopped and there was the wet sound of meat being torn, of chewing, of bones being cracked open for their marrow. Flies swarmed in the air.

Ledger and Tom knelt on either side of the girl.

She was a tiny thing. Emaciated, covered with infected sores, filthy.

Dying.

Tom offered her water and there wasn't even enough left of her to remember how to drink. They dressed her most immediate wounds and covered her body with their blankets and the two men sat together, holding her between them, keeping her warm as the day wore on. Sometimes Tom spoke to her, whispering softly, making promises the world could not let them keep.

When she died, Joe took her from Tom, rolled her onto her stomach, drew his knife, and slipped the blade into the base of her skull. She would never reanimate. She would sleep.

They buried her and then the two men sat down with their backs against the pen wall.

And wept.

## —8—
## Top and Bunny

Owen led them down a winding path, descending the hillside to the valley road below. They followed that for about five yards, then wound into a cacti field and across a parking lot to a brick, one-story building with a worn wooden sign that read 'Park Headquarters' out front by the entrance off the road. American flags waved in the wind from several poles around a lot that contained RVs, official Park Service vehicles, and various civilian cars and trucks scattered throughout. Trees and landscaping decorated the land surrounding the lot and lawns leading up to the building.

Several armed men and women, as ragged and dirty as the trio, rushed to meet them, eyeing Top and Bunny with suspicion. After Owen explained their presence and fired off instructions, he left them behind with the sentries and headed inside. Within moments, Top and Bunny watched their mounts being led away, their packs removed from their backs, and were patted down thoroughly – men removing their knives, the spare Glocks they kept in their boots, and extra ammo.

"We want those back," Bunny objected, but Top silenced him with a look. *Just go with it for now,* it said. Bunny sighed, nodding back in acquiescence.

Then they were surrounded and led into the building, then shoved into a small office and locked inside, guards posted outside. The office had a wooden desk, its surface covered by scattered stacks of paper, file folders, and manuals. Two old, faded grey metal file cabinets with three drawers occupied a corner behind it along with a table holding a laser printer and three open wire baskets marked 'In', 'Out', and 'Pending'. The office smelled dusty and stale, like it hadn't been used in a while, which it probably hadn't. Top slid into a padded wooden chair facing the desk, while Bunny paced. A few moments later, the door opened and a woman brought them water bottles then left again.

"Well, they're sure glad to see us," Bunny said, taking a chair along one wall near the file cabinets.

Top unscrewed the cap off his water and took a long drink before responding. "We've dealt with cautious survivors before. You know we'd be the same."

Bunny sighed, leaning back in the fiberglass chair against the wall. "Yeah, just anxious to get on with it."

"Drink your water and relax, Farm Boy," Top said with a chuckle. "We're here. That's the first step."

"If these are even the right people," Bunny muttered, then uncapped his own water and drank.

They waited in silence then until Owen finally came back for them an hour later. He'd cleaned up a bit, the dirt and grime gone from his face, his hair combed, and the shotgun had been left outside. He took a deep breath, nodding at them as he moved around the desk, and slid into the cracked leather chair behind it, leaning back and putting his feet up on the surface as he thought a moment.

"Why don't you boys tell me who you are again and why you're here, heavily armed, on our doorstep," Owen said.

Top nodded and began explaining. He described generally their past work in black ops for the government, and how they'd stayed together after The Plague, fought to survive like anyone else, and then found their training and knowledge could help others and began looking for those needing help.

"Like some kind of modern A-Team or something?" Owen joked.

"Wow. A-Team. That's old school," Bunny said and looked at Top. "Didn't you watch that when you were a kid?"

Top shot him an annoyed look as Owen chuckled. "You knew what it is, didn't ya?" He turned to Owen again. "There's just the two of us. No van either. But we do what we can. We came here because a group in Colorado heard rumors someone might need help finding permanent shelter, setting up defenses, getting supplies, etcetera."

"And then we saw the raid," Bunny said.

"Why didn't you stop them?" Owen asked, his eyes accusing.

"To be honest, we weren't sure who the good guys were or what was happening," Top said.

"For all we knew, the kids were being rescued or something," Bunny added.

Owen grunted and his eyes turned sad as his shoulders sunk and he leaned back in the chair behind the desk.

"Everything okay?" Top finally asked.

Owen shrugged. "As fine as it can be after one of the doctor's raids, I suppose."

"Who is this doctor and why are you being raided?" Bunny asked.

Owen met their eyes a moment as if weighing options then continued, "We don't actually know. Just rumors and such from others who claim to have seen or heard things. But as they tell it, the doctor runs a lab down outside Tucson. They used to raid the survivor camps there. One of the reasons we started relocating two years ago, making our way north. Somehow they tracked a few of us up here and started raiding us once every few months. We've lost twenty-five people, including ten women, ten children, and five elderly. We lost six tonight."

"And you don't have any idea what happens to them?" Bunny asked.

"Experiments we've been told," Owen said, his eyes wrinkling as he pondered it with obvious pain and regret. "Something about a vaccine for The Plague, but a few captives have supposedly escaped and they weren't cured, they'd been turned. Some graves were discovered in a nearby park as well that people say were victims of the lab."

They gaped at him.

"A *vaccine?* Holy shit," gasped Bunny. "That could change everything!"

"How sure are you?" demanded Top. "Is this real intel or rumors?"

Owen locked eyes with him. "You hear something from so many different sources, experience the raids on your families

31

and friends, your children, you start believing the worst. Doesn't much matter if it's true. People are being kidnapped. Others turned up dead. Draw your own conclusion."

Top grunted with understanding. Echo Team had dealt with many similar rumors and situations for the DMS. "But you know where the lab is?"

Owen shook his head. "Just rumors. So far, at least, but a lot of people believe them. Yeah, we've talked about finding it. Getting our children and loved ones back. But the teams come heavily armed for the raids. Can you imagine what the security is like around the lab?" He shook his head. "We can't risk it. That is, if we could even find it. A couple of people tried to rescue their families, we heard, with disastrous results."

"This has gone on for *two years?*" Top looked as if he couldn't believe it. Bunny knew that look though. Beneath it was simmering fury.

"More like four," Owen said. "We just decided to try and get away, out of reach two years ago. Look. My people are mostly city folks, a couple farmers, but most had never touched a weapon before, let alone served. I had training from an enlistment after college, so I've taught them what I could, but defense is our best strategy. Organized, strategic attacks would probably just get more people lost or killed."

"And they tracked you here..." Bunny shook his head.

"Someone who saw us could have told them, I suppose," Owen said. "Truth is, we rarely see zombies these days, keeping to ourselves. If we weren't constantly moving to try and avoid the raids, we could settle in. This headquarters recycles waste and water and we could stay here indefinitely, hunt the desert for food, grow our own – but that would just make us easier to find."

"They only come every few months?" Top asked.

Owen thought a moment. "Yeah, every two or three. We haven't really nailed down a pattern. It varies."

"But if you stay here, you'll be okay?" Top said.

"We might be," Owen said. "We could make a go of it."

Top and Bunny exchanged a look that spoke volumes. They'd worked together so long, reading each other was just part of it. They both agreed they needed to help these people, and that had to start with finding the lab and seeing what they could do to end the raids.

"Why don't you tell us everything you know about this lab and doctor and where we might find it?" Top said.

—9—
### The Soldier and the Samurai

They camped in the pen that night.

The men they killed had been poorly equipped, but there were some useful items. More ammunition, guns, a better backpack than the one Ledger had. Three freshly-killed geese, and a whole box of power bars. Plenty of water, too, as well as matches, knives, and most of a bottle of Advil. All useful.

Ledger and Tom opened a kind of vent in the wall and threw the bodies out to the dead, then blocked it up again.

The man who had screamed was dead, his body pinned to the ground by short lengths of rebar. He reanimated and Ledger sent him on to the other side with another quick thrust. They buried him next to the girl. The man was black, the girl was Latina. There was no identification in their clothes, no names to put over their graves.

"Hey, Joe," said Tom, looking up from a backpack through which he was rifling. As Ledger came over, Tom handed him a faded map of Arizona. "These sons of bitches knew about the cure."

Ledger took the map and sat cross-legged beside Tom, and spread the map out on the ground. There was a circle around a spot in Oro Valley and the name Pisani scribbled in black and underlined a half dozen times. Above the name was the word 'CURE', and even though this wasn't the first time Ledger had heard about this, it still made his heart flutter.

33

"Shit," he said.

Tom licked his lips. "Does that mean this is real?"

"That's what we're going to find out."

The story had been passed from one survivor to another, but it had been whisper-down-the-lane, becoming so distorted that Tom and Ledger had wasted weeks following bad leads. Now in the space of a week they had three separate indications that an infectious disease researcher named Al Pisani had a working lab in, or near, Oro Valley in Arizona, a few miles outside of Tucson, and that Dr Pisani had developed some kind of vaccine. The reports were not from any official source because, as far as they knew, there were no official sources left. Which made the whole thing a big fat 'maybe'. Seeing it again on a map was not conclusive, either, because these scavengers might have heard the same unreliable stories Tom and Ledger had heard.

Or, maybe, these bastards had better intelligence.

Tom must have read his thoughts. "Maybe we should have... you know... *asked* them before we..."

Ledger waved it off. "Fuck it. That's yesterday's box score, kid. Besides, sometimes a motherfucker just needs to die and these motherfuckers were all past their sell-by date. I can't see either of us having any kind of meaningful conversation with them."

Tom said nothing. Instead he set about building a campfire so they could cook the geese. The zombies outside moaned, but neither man cared.

"If it's true," said Tom while he worked, "what's that really going to mean? How could a vaccine be mass produced? The EMPs killed the power. Frankly, I don't even understand how this Dr Pisani even has a working lab."

"Portable generators and ingenuity," suggested Ledger.

Tom grunted and concentrated on fanning the flames. Ledger sat there slowly plucking the feathers off one of the geese. He stared into the heart of the newborn flames.

"If there is a vaccine," he said, "then we'll find a way to mass-produce it and distribute it."

"That would be enormously difficult, though."

Ledger smiled at him. "Seriously, kid, do you have something *better* to do?"

Tom smiled back. Smiles were rare for him.

They talked and cooked and ate and talked some more as the clouds slid across the darkening sky. Neither of them spoke about the hope that was being kindled inside their chests. They were each superstitious in their own way, as soldiers and samurai, killers and hunters always are. Talking about hope was like holding a burning match up into the wind. Instead they let the fire grow slowly in their hearts.

That night they slept and dreamed of not being dead.

Rare dreams for both of them.

—10—
## Top and Bunny

It took another two long nights of riding to reach Oro Valley, the general area where Owen's people thought the lab might be located. Owen's people had provided a few details the two soldiers used to scout the area until they found the lab itself, which took them most of a day. It was well hidden inside a rocky cliff side south between the smaller town and Tucson itself – or what was left of it.

Tucson, like most major cities, had been hit hard by the EMPs and other weapons the government deployed in an attempt to eradicate *Lucifer 113*. From the rise where they'd stopped and pulled out their binoculars, the city stretched off into the horizon under a grey cloud.

The lab must have been built inside the rocks well before that, as it had a well-concealed, well-guarded entrance with multiple security systems that had clearly been in use before the EMPs took them out. The cavern entrance was clearly big enough to take vehicles inside, with a thick steel, hydraulic door its only visible opening. That explained the cargo van, as far as

Bunny was concerned. He wished the DMS had had the same so they could be using a vehicle themselves instead of the horses. His ass still ached from the hours of riding. He rubbed at it as he thought about it and Top chuckled.

"How long's it take to get used to riding?" Bunny wondered, his skin .already clammy from the sun blaring down overhead.

"We've been doing it almost two years, so maybe forever for you," Top said with a grin. "I feel fine."

"Yeah, well, you've been riding most of your life, Old Man. Or maybe your ass is so old the nerves are shot anyway." Bunny gave up on his ass and scratched at an itch developing on his sides. Fucking desert. He hoped it wasn't some poisonous creature that'd somehow made it into his clothes.

Top laughed. "See any sentries?"

Top didn't seem to be bothered by anything at all. That just annoyed Bunny more. At least if they both were itching and miserable, he'd feel better about it. Son of a bitch. Bunny shook his head as he adjusted his field binoculars again and took another look.

Top tapped Bunny's arm and nodded to a spot on a slope leading toward the cavern. The road was mostly blocked by a wall of cars, but there was a gap across where two men were erecting a moveable boom made from heavy-grade PVC pipe.

"Looks like they're setting up a checkpoint," said Bunny.

"Uh huh," agreed Top, "which means they're getting ready for visitors."

"Who, though?"

"My guess," said Top, "would be ordinary people. If this doctor really has some kind of vaccine then this would be a good chokepoint to filter anyone coming to get a shot. They'd want to screen anyone going into the actual base. Can't let just anyone stroll up. The doctor'd be too damn important, and if there's a lab in there, then controlled access would need to be guaranteed. Especially if someone shows up from one of the camps these cats have raided."

"Why bring them here, though? I mean, from what I can see

they have a nice set-up down there. Protection, limited access, plenty of spots for elevated observation and defense. They have power and security. Why let *anyone* in? Why not send teams out to do field inoculations?"

"Don't know," said Top.

"Kind of want to find out," said Bunny. "On one hand we have what could arguably be the greatest humanitarian project in the history of… well, *history…* and on the other we have some of these guys acting like bad guys from a *Mad Max* flick. Doesn't compute."

"No, it don't."

"So we have to get down there," said Bunny. He scanned the landscape again. "Those cameras and sensors can't still be working, can they?"

"I have a feeling that's why they took their raids further out," Top said. "Less likely to inspire visitors bent on revenge."

"I can't imagine many people have found this place," Bunny said. "Even with a slim lead, it took us almost a day."

"But we're experts," Top said. "My old ass just has a feel for it."

Bunny rolled his eyes and Top laughed again.

"There's the checkpoint, though," said Bunny. "They must have told *someone.* Maybe they sent teams out to invite some people."

"Who?"

"Don't know. Can't be anyone who's already pissed off at them. Has to be someone, though, because that checkpoint looks new. Maybe they spread the word to select groups. All it would take is a few of their people going from survival camp to survival camp dropping rumors to control the way the news spread. It wouldn't be a stampede. People would come here in dribs and drabs."

"Why would they do that?" asked Top, then suggested the answer to his own question. "Maybe they don't have much of the vaccine. Or maybe it takes a while to produce. Control the news and they can distribute at a speed that works with their production."

They thought about that.

"That makes sense," said Bunny slowly, "but it doesn't fit with the raids. Why take kids? Why take anyone? Why not send medical teams out to spread the vaccine? Why be bad guys when they're trying to be good guys?"

Top looked at him. "Oh, hell, son, you want me to recite the number of times a group in power decided who deserves to get a resource?"

Bunny said nothing.

Below them the thick steel door began to slide slowly upward. Once it reached about five feet, several armed men ducked under and filed out to form two lines on either side.

"Six," Bunny counted.

The soldiers stood and waited, chattering as the door continued rolling upward.

"They're waiting on something," Top said.

Bunny clicked his mouth and motioned to the left where a cloud of dust and sand had risen on a dirt road that led right to the compound entrance. As he and Top both focused their binocs on that point, a tan GMC troop carrier with matching camouflage fabric cover over its bed rolled into view. Two armed soldiers were in the front, but as it rolled up and waited for the door to clear its top, they saw only civilians in the back, each of them wearing a brightly colored red, white or blue band around his or her wrist.

"Where are they going?" Bunny wondered aloud as the truck pulled forward into the compound and the door immediately began sliding downward again.

"I don't know, but we need to find a way in there," Top said.

"So where'd the people come from?"

"That's what we're going to find out," Top replied, kneeing his horse and steering it toward a nearby trail that led down off the rise into the valley and paralleled the road the truck had taken. "Come on, Farm Boy."

Bunny released his binocs, letting them slide down to hang against his chest as he absentmindedly rubbed his sore ass. "Great, more riding." As he grabbed the reins, he added, "Hooah," but it was almost a whisper.

## —11—
## The Soldier and the Samurai

They rode the bicycles all the way to the outskirts of Tucson.

Tom Imura was in his twenties, fit and lean and, as Ledger saw it, composed of whipcord and iron.

Ledger was north of fifty and none of his years had been easy ones. He'd long ago lost count of the number of bones he'd broken – either in the dojo or, more often, in combat – or the stitches. Or the surgeries, for that matter. He felt like an ancient mass of scar tissue and screaming nerve endings. After the first hundred miles he was sure the bike seat was made from iron and covered in spikes. His ass hurt. His balls hurt. His molecules hurt. After the second hundred miles of the four hundred and seventy mile journey, he had developed a tendency to yap like a cross dog at anything Tom said. Even when the young man offered words of support or compassion.

They were somewhere on I-10 East when Tom said, "You're not too old for this."

"I didn't say a fucking thing," growled Ledger.

"You were going to."

"The fuck I was."

"You were," insisted Tom, his voice calm, his face showing no sign of the strain of the long ride. "You've been saying it roughly every thirty miles."

"Bullshit."

"And you say it every time we have to get off and walk uphill."

"You're out of your frigging mind."

"And you say it every time we—"

"You realize that I'm heavily armed and have no compunction about shooting people," said Ledger.

"I'm not wrong, though," said Tom.

"Sure. And that'll look great on your tombstone."

They rode for a mile in silence.

"And besides," said Ledger, "fuck you."

"Point taken."

They rode on.

"Correct me if I'm wrong," said Tom after a while, "but this *was* your idea."

"Two in the back of the head, so help me God. I'll leave you by the side of the road."

Tom broke out laughing and the sound of it bounced across the desert and rebounded off ancient rocks and vanished into the hot sky. Ledger cursed him, his hygiene, his forebears, and accused him of fornication with livestock. Tom laughed harder.

It took a while for Ledger's scowl to crack. Longer still for his lips to twitch. But when he started to laugh he laughed a good long time.

They pedaled along past abandoned cars and old bones, past the crushed hull of a 767 airliner, past dozens of wandering zoms. They laughed off and on for a long time. When the laughter fell away, one or the other of them would cut a sideways look and they'd be off again.

—12—

### Top and Bunny

Top led the way along the trail, both turning their bodies to avoid identity by any surveillance equipment. They'd tucked all guns except for the sidearms behind their saddlebags so they looked like just two men riding across the desert – not that unusual to necessarily draw much interest.

The trail wound through rocks, scrub, and scattered cacti parallel to the road but about fifty yards out. Soon they'd followed it around a bend where they couldn't see the lab compound's imposing steel entrance door. The cloud of dust from the truck had faded, though Bunny thought he could still make it out in the distance.

They rode in silence, both alert and ready, Bunny's hand resting on the top of his saddlebag so as to look casual yet ready to reach for his rifle at any moment. They began hearing voices ahead, almost like a crowd.

"You hear that?" Bunny asked Top.

Top nodded. "Some kind of gathering."

"For what?"

"Could be where they got those people."

"Did you notice those wrist bands? They were all red."

Top grunted. "Yeah, whatever that means."

And then they rounded another bend and found themselves facing five armed men with AK-47s aimed right at their hearts or foreheads. The trail here had wound much closer to the road, and a white van like they'd seen during the raid at Sun Valley sat parked at the curb behind the men.

"Halt!" one of them ordered loudly, eyes narrowing. The other men simply glared at the newcomers.

Top and Bunny both slowly raised their hands, faces taking on their best innocent looks.

"Somethin' the matter, gentlemen?" Top asked, turning on his old-Georgia drawl.

The man who'd given orders nodded and the other four rushed the horses, two grabbing for Top and Bunny's sidearms, while the others searched their saddlebags.

"Whoa! Look what we have here!" a young soldier barely out of his teens pulled out Bunny's sniper rifle and two boxes of ammo.

"Here, too!" the one searching Top's saddlebag called and produced Top's rifle as well.

"Armed to the teeth. Who are you and where are you going?" the leader demanded. Older than the others, his hair was cut short in a military crew, and grey at the edges, his face creased from age and exposure, his eyes fierce but tired – a man who'd seen too much.

Top and Bunny exchanged a look. "We're just trying to survive," Bunny said then. "Lot of damn dead folks out here looking for a quick lunch. A guy's got to protect himself out here – you know that."

"Kind of the reason we're still on this side of being dead," Top added.

"Uh huh, just two innocent guys," the leader grinned. "Tie their hands and get them off those horses," he added, motioning to his men.

Top and Bunny were yanked down hard, falling to their knees in clouds of dust as the men yanked their hands back and produced black zip ties. The leader and two others kept their weapons trained on the two strangers as the young blond and another soldier bound Top and Bunny's hands behind them.

"Look. We're just passin' through," Top said, voice sincere. "Why are you doing this?"

"We don't have much use for strangers," the leader said, then locked eyes with his men. "General Black will want to see them. They don't look like innocent civilians and we can't take chances."

"Yes, sir," the men responded almost in unison, then pulled Top and Bunny to their feet and led them toward the van.

The leader motioned to the blond and another younger man. "You two bring the horses to the checkpoint."

"Yes, sir," the youths replied and turned back to Top and Bunny's mounts.

"What do we do?" Bunny asked through gritted teeth as the men hauled open the back doors of the van. Then one unlocked a metal bench and lifted the lid, depositing their knives and guns inside before locking it again.

"Just let this play out a bit," Top whispered back. "We need more intel."

The men shoved them now and they stumbled forward, climbing into the van.

*Keep your cool*, Top's eyes said.

But Bunny didn't like this one bit. Even if there was nothing he could do but follow Top's advice.

## —13—
## The Soldier and the Samurai

They saw the sentry before the sentry saw them.

Ledger and Tom rolled to a stop at the top of a slope that ran down into Oro Valley. In the far distance there was a soft cloud of gray that hovered perpetually over what had once been Tucson. Down the valley there was some kind of complex built against or, more like, into a wall of a mountain. He saw vehicles parked down there and they looked to be in good shape. Tom saw them, too. Before either of them could comment a tan armored personnel carrier came rumbling out of an entrance in the rock wall. It turned and headed farther down the valley. Tom grabbed Ledger's arm.

"Did you *see* that?"

"I saw it, kid," murmured Ledger.

"But *how?* The EMPs…"

Ledger studied the mountain and nodded to himself. "There must be a hardened facility down there. We had them all over. They built them underground and inside mountains during the Cold War to make sure they would survive a Russian attack. Then they repurposed them for all kinds of black budget R and D projects. I'll bet this was a bioweapons lab of some kind. There were six or eight of them that were so far off the radar than even I didn't know about them, and it was my damn job to know about them."

"How's that possible?" asked Tom, watching the APC vanish inside a trail of brown dust.

"Fuck, kid, there were so many cells operating inside the Department of Defense that half the time no one knew what all was going on. Legitimate stuff and other shit that was definitely not supposed to be happening, at least as far as congress and the taxpayers were concerned, but which seemed to somehow always get funding. This has all the makings."

"Okay," said Tom slowly, "but what does it mean?"

"It means they might actually have a working lab," said

Ledger. "With power and operational computer systems. Holy polka-dotted fuck."

"Does that mean this vaccine is legit?"

Ledger thought about that for a moment. "To be determined. Something's hinky. Look down there."

He pointed and Tom used his binoculars to study a spot at the base of the slope where there was a makeshift guard post constructed of a pair of dead cars positioned on either side of the highway and a boom made from a length of white PVC pipe. Two men were working the checkpoint and they were busy with a line of people who stood in a wandering line. Ledger and Tom sat on the road in the shade of a billboard that told everyone who passed that Waffle House was offering two breakfasts for the price of one. Someone had taken the time out of surviving the apocalypse to draw a pretty good version of a zombie head atop the illustration of a short stack of pancakes. The soldier and the samurai were nearly invisible in the dense shadows thrown by the sign. Their bikes lay out of sight in the weeds and both men studied the checkpoint with binoculars.

"Those guards are not military," observed Ledger. "But... that might not mean much. Things fell to shit, so they might be working for whoever's in the mountain, doing grunt work."

"The guards are taking supplies from the people in line," said Tom.

Ledger studied the transactions at the gate. "Doesn't look too nefarious. No one's flashing weapons. Look at the people farther back in line, they already have stuff out and bundled up. I think it's a barter of some kind."

"What for what? A road tax?"

"Maybe. Or payment for treatment."

Tom grunted and they continued to watch. Each group stopped at the checkpoint and offered something to the guards. A wrapped bundle of what looked like canned goods, a bottle of water or a can of kerosene, skinned rabbits, and other goods. One guard took the items and placed them in a big John Deere wheelbarrow and the other tied a piece of colored cloth around the wrist of each person.

"You seeing the colors?" asked Tom. "Red, white, and blue?"

"Uh huh."

"Most of the kids are getting blue. None of the men, though."

"Uh huh."

"Most of the men are getting red. And a few men and women are getting white."

"Uh huh."

Tom lowered his glasses and looked at Ledger. "What do you think it means?"

"Too orderly to be random color choices," mused Ledger. "But they're being specific about it. Can't tell from this far away, though. We'll need to get up close to gather intel." He stood slowly, hissing at the aches in his hips and tailbone from the many days on the bike.

Tom rose, too. "Makes me wonder what kind of colors they'd give us."

Ledger squinted down the hill. "Uh huh," he said.

They hid most of their gear behind the billboard and covered the bikes with tumbleweed and bunches of grass. After some careful consideration of what they could afford to part with, they walked down the hill.

There were a dozen people ahead of them and Ledger struck up a casual conversation with an elderly couple who had a small child with them. Not their grandchild, it turned out, but an orphan they'd taken under their wing. The three of them were all that was left of a refugee camp in Fort Grant.

"What happened to the fort?" asked Tom.

The old man, whose name was Barney, gave them a bleak look.

"The dead?" asked Ledger.

Barney shook his head. "Nah, we held them off pretty good. Once we figured out how to kill them, we built the fort up even stronger and everyone learned how to top them. We'd have teams go out wrapped in folded over mattress covers and work gloves with thick plastic glued to the outsides. Teams of three. Two would use heavy-duty rakes to kind of stall the eaters and the third person would bash 'em in the head. Rinse and repeat, you know? The eaters never learn from what's happening to others of their kind."

"Good tactic," said Ledger, nodding approval.

"It worked," said Barney. "But times got hard, you know? Winter's a bitch and farming's not the easiest thing to do when you have to protect a couple thousand acres from wandering eaters. We ran through the supplies the raiders found in houses and stores and the like. Had some damn lean times, but then the first crops came up last spring and we were good to go."

"But...?" asked Ledger, letting it hang.

"But then people started getting sick," said Millie, Barney's wife. "All sorts of stuff. Infections from cuts. Bacteria in the water. And then the flu came around and we lost half the town in four weeks."

"Jesus," murmured Tom.

"Got worse," said Barney. "After the flu we got hit with all sorts of stuff. Tuberculosis, syphilis, mumps, you name it. None of us knew how to manufacture the drugs."

Millie shook her head slowly. "We survived the end of the world, we survived the eaters, we fought off raiding parties, we got through dust storms, and we survived two awful winters and then diseases that weren't even much of a thing before the End came back and wiped us out. Barney and me got out with ten others, including little Polly here." He gave the little girl's hair a gentle caress. "But now it's just the three of us. We heard about Dr Pisani and we came out here. You know... hoping."

It was a sad story but a familiar one, and sadder for all that. Ledger felt old and used up hearing it.

"What exactly have you heard?" asked Tom.

The next few people in line behind the old couple turned and were listening to the conversation.

"Well," said Barney, "it's a cure, isn't it?"

Everyone nodded.

"I heard that it prevents you from turning even if you get bit," said a Latino man wearing a Phoenix Suns ball cap.

"No," said Millie, "it's supposed to cure you even if you already have it."

As she said this, she pushed the little girl behind her. It was a reflexive action. Protective. Ledger caught Tom's eye and he saw that the young man understood. There was both understanding and heartbreak in his eyes. Although there was no obvious wound, both men knew that the girl was probably infected. A hidden bite or something else. Eating an animal that had been bitten by a zombie would do it, as would getting infected blood in an open wound or in a mucus membrane like the eyes, nose or mouth. The girl didn't look sick, but that did not mean much. Some people got ill right away and lingered for weeks; others sickened and died overnight, and a few could go for quite a while before symptoms showed.

"Does that mean they can cure as well as prevent?" asked Tom.

"That's what I heard," said Barney, nodding firmly.

The Latino man's companion, a short Asian woman, nodded, "Dr Pisani is a saint. I heard she was a famous doctor who worked with all kinds of diseases."

"'She'?" asked Ledger. "I thought it was Al Pisani."

"Allie," explained Millie. "Allison. Women can be scientists, too."

"As I know very well," agreed Ledger. "I knew a lot of top flight women researchers, clinicians and practitioners."

The Latino man studied him. "Who'd you lose?" he asked. "On *Dia De Muertos*."

The Day of the Dead. It was one of a hundred different nicknames Ledger had heard for the end of the world. Tom's little colony called it 'First Night'. It was all the same thing. And though it took longer than a single night or day, it came out to the same thing in the end. The world they had all known had stopped. Just stopped. Those parts of it that had tumbled past the big point of impact were fragments. They were the things people clutched at to keep some sense of order, some aspects of things remembered, a comfortable lie of normalcy.

The truth was that the world continued to dwindle. If it got to the point where they dipped below five thousand people clustered in one area, then the gene pool would start to get pretty shallow and eventually would evaporate.

Ledger looked at the man and said, "I lost everyone."

They all stood and looked at each other. They all nodded. No one commented.

At the head of the line the guard yelled, "Next!"

And the line moved forward one full step.

−14−
## Top and Bunny

The men drove the van back to the compound, approaching from another side of the mountain where a village of red, white, and blue tents had been set up in front of another steel, hydraulic door like the one they'd been observing. The camp was big and contained several large circus-sized tents. The camp bustled with activity, and Bunny noted the red tents seemed much more heavily guarded than the others. The driver stopped and waited for the steel door to open before pulling inside. As the van door opened revealing a cavernous space, Top and Bunny took in their surroundings, seeing several barred holding cells labeled red, white, and blue nearby amidst several troop trucks, vans, and a strong smell of gunpowder and chemicals, like a hospital or lab.

"Red, white, and blue," Top said, nodding to Bunny, but neither of them had any idea what it meant. Then they were being dragged along a corridor and shoved into a small white-walled room with two chairs facing a table.

"Sit!" someone demanded, then the door slammed behind them, leaving them alone.

"Jesus Christ, what is this place?" Bunny wondered.

"I don't know, but we're in it deep now," Top replied.

"They took our weapons," Bunny said. "We could have taken them out."

"They had us dead to rights. One or both of us might be dead."

Bunny sighed. Top was right but he still wished they'd put up more of a fight. "What do we do now?"

"Wait," Top said simply as he stumbled over and slid into a chair. After looking around the room – standard interrogation plainness – it smelled clean, almost sterile, and the walls, table, and chairs shined like they'd been scrubbed regularly. Bunny went over and took the chair next to him, facing the table.

They didn't wait long. Within a couple minutes, the door opened and a man in black entered, his slacks and black button down shirt creased, clean, like a dress uniform. He wore no tie but had on a leather jacket over the shirt and combat boots. He stared across the table at them, with the leader of the men who'd captured them standing at attention beside him as the door shut again.

Leather Coat nodded. "You don't belong here." His voice was sharp, baritone, with the firmness of one used to be in command. Was this their leader? The General perhaps?

"Where's here?" Bunny asked.

"Cowboys out wandering about," Leather Coat asked. "Not very smart given the state of the world."

"Just trying to get along," said Top. "Going day to day, that's all."

"Sneaking around and spying is 'getting along'?"

The older man who'd led their captors stiffened and started forward, but Leather Coat stopped him with a hand on his arm. "Leave it, Diamond."

The older man, Diamond, sighed, nodded, then stepped back to attention in his previous spot, watching them like a hawk.

"You got pretty much one chance here, fellows," Leather Coat said. "Tell me who you are, where you got such fine weapons and ammo, and what you're doing poking around our perimeter, and we might spare your lives." He turned and winked at Diamond, who grinned as if they were exchanging a secret.

Bunny assumed they were dead regardless and spat, "No thanks."

Top, who'd been taking it all in, shifted beside him. "As I told Diamond here," again in his best Georgian drawl, "we're just passing through trying to survive. We don't want trouble and we didn't bring no trouble with us."

"No trouble and yet you have a military cache?" Leather Coat asked, clearly not buying it.

"Shit, man, everyone's armed," Top said. "Zoms don't fall down from harsh language, and there are a lot more of them than there are of us. Old man like me has to tilt the odds in his favor, feel me? You understand. Clearly. You're all heavily armed. Circumstances seem to demand it, don't they? If we want to survive, I mean."

Leather Coat locked eyes with Top a moment, considering, reading him, then he smiled. "Can't argue with that, can we, Major Diamond?"

Diamond nodded. "No, sir."

Leather Coat turned back to Top and Bunny. "Part of how we stay alive is deciding whom we let have weapons and whom we don't. You understand? Can't have untrustworthy types wandering around shooting at just anyone."

Top smiled warmly. "Yes, sir, makes sense to me. But we were just passing through and headed on down to Mexico."

"Mexico? Why?"

Top shrugged. "Find some shelter, food, supplies, and maybe stay away from the cities and live a while longer."

Leather Coat chuckled. "Mexico, huh? Mexico's full of rotting wetback zombies and shacks, Reb. Doesn't sound very smart to me."

Top shrugged again. "Sometimes the least expected places provide the best resources in times like these." Bunny watched as the two stared at each other for a bit, then Leather Coat chuckled again.

"Well, sorry to say you men won't be making it." He turned to Diamond. "Major, red tag them and throw them in with the next batch."

"Yes, General," Diamond replied with a stiff salute as Leather Coat turned for the door.

"General? General who?" Bunny demanded.

Leather Coat turned back. "General Ike Black, son."

"General of what army?" Bunny retorted.

"The only army that matters in these parts." Black smiled knowingly, then turned and left the room.

"Well," muttered Bunny, "that was fun."

Then men rushed in and yanked Top and Bunny to their feet, pushing them out the door and back down the narrow corridor toward the cavern with the steel door and holding pens, Major Diamond leading the way. Bunny's wrists hurt from the rope cutting into them and his shoulder wasn't too happy either from all the yanking.

"Fuck you very much," he said under his breath.

"Throw them in there," Diamond ordered, motioning to nearby pen.

Top and Bunny were halted outside the door, and the rope cut from their wrists. Bunny was about to rub his with relief when the rope was replaced by red wristbands, and they were shoved inside.

"The rest of you clear the others out!" Diamond shouted. "New batch coming in!"

The holding pen door clanged shut as Top and Bunny watched the men around them scramble.

Men and women in lab coats appeared, hauling stretchers – some on wheels, others not – toward the waiting troop trucks, white sheets laid over the top. A coppery smell, like blood, filled the air and mixed with the chemicals, gun powder, and sweat.

"Load 'em up," one man said, laughing as he stepped up into the truck with a buddy and took stretchers from the incoming workers. As they turned to carry one back into the truck, the sheet shifted and wrist fell out – a wrist with a red band like the ones Top and Bunny now wore.

"This can't be good," Top said as they both stared.

"Wonder what the blue and white mean," Bunny said.

They exchanged a knowing look – *We gotta get the fuck outta here… fast.*

—15—
## The Soldier and the Samurai

The guard beckoned for them to come up. Bernie and Millie glanced at them over their shoulders as they walked on with the little girl between them. Ledger had listened closely to the questions the guards had asked the old couple.

"What did you do before the End?"

"Can you cook from scratch?"

"Do you have any skills? Can you fix a car? Did you work in construction? Are you a plumber? Do you have medical training?"

"Have you served in the military? Or the police?"

"Can you hunt and fish? Do you know how to dress what you catch?"

Like that. Fast questions. Very interesting questions.

Both Bernie and Millie were given red wristbands. The girl was given a blue one.

Bernie had served in the first Gulf War and then worked as a cop. Millie had been an accountant. Ledger did not see an immediate connection that would have put them in whatever the 'red' category was.

The couple before them, the Latino man and Asian woman, had both been given white bands. He had been a mechanic working mostly with two-stroke engines – ATVs, motorcycles and lawnmowers. The woman owned a hothouse where she grew herbs for restaurants.

Why white for them and red for the older couple? Was it an age thing?

Then something occurred to him and he grunted softly. Before they stepped up to the guard, Ledger leaned close to Tom and whispered, "I'm a baseball coach from Pittsburgh. I went deer hunting every year."

Tom looked startled for a moment. "I don't—"

"You're a cook. You like to fish."

"I…"

Ledger gave him a hard stare, and after a moment Tom nodded.

"Hey," called the guard, "I ain't got all day."

They stepped up and the questions began. Ledger took point and went through his fictional career teaching health class and coaching baseball. He had the build for the sport, and even the guard seemed to buy it right away. "You played what, third base?"

"Right the first time," said Ledger, smiling and trying to look like Robert Redford from the old movie *The Natural.* When the guard asked if he had ever hunted, Ledger went through a story about this eight-point buck he'd tracked and how he made venison stew that would have made you cry. He knew he sold it well.

"You ever serve in the military?" asked the second guard.

"Me? Nah. Not much for that sort of thing. Maybe I should have, but the only fights I ever liked were about keeping a hotshot runner from stealing third."

They all laughed about that.

When it was Tom's turn he laid on a thick Japanese accent that was totally false. Like his older brother, Sam, Tom had been born in California and had never even been to Japan. The accent rang true, though, and Ledger figured he was mimicking his old man. Tom talked about working at a sushi place in San Francisco. He talked about how he sometimes used to catch the fish he'd later clean and serve. He sold it really well. So well the guards were starting to look hungry.

"You got anything for the general?" asked the first guard.

"General?" asked Ledger, playing dumb. "This a military thing?"

"Yeah," said the guard, "we're here to protect and serve."

That was a police slogan, but Ledger didn't bother to correct him. "Who's the general?"

"Ike Black," said the guard. "He is the *man*, too. Tough cocksucker who's going to put this country back on its wheels."

"Is he?"

"Damn skippy he is."

"Make America great again," said Ledger with a straight face. "Count me in."

The guard nodded as if they were all on the same page. "We're big on swapping goods for services, around here, if you can dig it."

"Sure can," said Ledger. The name Ike Black tickled something in the back of Ledger's mind. He'd heard that name before but it had been a long time ago and the connections were somehow wrong. A general? No, that didn't seem quite right, but he couldn't pin down what he remembered. "Let me see what I got."

Ledger fished in his pack and brought out a revolver he'd taken from the men they'd killed. It was a hell of a thing to offer. His own pistol was hidden in his pack, and their swords were stashed between rocks half a mile out of town.

The guard took the revolver and nodded like a kid on Christmas morning. "God damn, man," he said. "Smith and Wesson Chief's Special. This is a classic. Sweet."

"Glad you like it."

"This your own piece?"

"Found it in a house that had been overrun," Ledger said. "I took it but it's not really my kind of thing. I'm more of a long gun guy. Can't hit shit with a little wheel gun like that. Besides, what's a gun going to do for me if I get sick, right? There are more eaters out there than bullets. I'd rather know that those dead fuckers can't make me into one of them, you know?"

The guard offered him a fist and they bumped.

"We're looking for guys like you," he said.

He tied white ribbons around Ledger's wrist, and when Tom turned over a pouch filled with rabbit jerky he got one as well.

Everyone smiled at one another and the guards told them to go straight through to the center of the camp. They thanked them and moved off. The camp was big and covered much of the area outside of the mountain entrance. There were several large tents that looked like they might have belonged to a circus back in the day. Above each was a flagpole, and Ledger saw several white flags, some blue flags and, on the tent set apart from the others, a red flag. There were three times as many guards around the red tent and he pointed this out to Tom.

"What's it mean?" asked Tom.

"Nothing good," said Ledger.

Behind the white tents was the entrance to the mountain, which they could see as they drew closer. The door was a massive panel of reinforced steel that was partly raised to allow people to enter. A line of refugees, all of them wearing white bands, snaked out of the mouth of the cavern. There were guards everywhere, standing watch outside the entrance and walking up and down the lines checking to make sure of the wristband colors. All of them heavily armed.

Tom said, "Something's wrong here."

Ledger grinned. "No shit."

"You didn't want them to know we used to be cops."

"Nope."

"You know something or just guessing?"

"Bit of both," admitted Ledger. "I was trying to stack the odds in favor of us getting white ribbons."

"Why?"

They walked a few paces before Ledger replied. "Because I have a bad feeling that anyone going to that red tent isn't likely to enjoy what they find."

Another team of guards stopped them as they approached the end of the line.

"Drop your gear over there," said one of them, pointing to a row of wheelbarrows. "No one'll touch your shit."

They did as asked; though Ledger hoped like hell that no one would search the backpacks while they were inside. He had an explanation for the automatic pistol, but it would be harder to sell here than at the guard outpost. These men looked sharper, more competent, and far less agreeable.

"Arms up and out," said the second guard. "Legs wide."

Ledger pretended to be too dense to understand that they wanted to frisk him, and he let the guard push him roughly into the correct position. He had expected this, though, and had left most of his other weapons with his sword. His small Wilson rapid-release folding knife was clipped to the low Vee of his undershirt because the front of the chest was one of those places most people never bothered to check, even during a vigorous pat-down. Nor did they pat his chest now. They hadn't taken off his shoes or belt, either. Ledger kept his relief and amusement off his face.

Once they were cleared, one of the guards told them to go into the tent. They did and inside they saw what looked like an old-fashioned vaccination set-up of the kind once used in third-world countries by groups like the World Health Organization. People stood in a long switchback line that brought them to three separate inoculation stations where official-looking people in white lab coats administered shots. Once each person had received an injection they were ushered out of the tent through an opening in the back. There were maybe a hundred and fifty people in all. Most of the people were women, and young women at that. Ledger noticed there was an unusually high percentage of attractive women for a group that was supposed to be more or less random. Peppered among the women were healthy-looking teens and a few men. The mathematics of it all made Ledger's heart sink and his jaw clench.

Tom caught his mood and quietly asked, "You see something?"

"Don't you?" asked Ledger.

The young man looked around the room for several minutes, then nodded. "The ratio?"

"And—?"

"Too many women. No one's old. Wait, that's wrong. None of the men are older than you, and you don't look as old as you are."

"No. So what's that tell you?"

Tom frowned. "Doesn't make sense if this was just for inoculation."

"Nope. But tell me why."

"If this was a real cure, then everyone would be in here. That little girl's not here. In fact, I don't see anyone who looks starved or sick. No one with a bandage over a possible bite."

"Nope," agreed Ledger.

"This treatment is supposed to work even if you're already sick. So why aren't they showing people that?" asked Tom. "Seems to me that would sell this pretty hard. Curing the sick."

"Uh huh."

They spoke very softly, making sure the other people in line didn't hear them.

"Not having the warm fuzzies about all of this," said Ledger. "It's both too good to be true and not set up the right way. Too many things are off about this."

"People are buying it."

"Dude, let's face it, this is the apocalypse and someone's offering a possible fix. This is a seller's market."

"What's our play?"

Ledger considered. "Without looking like you're doing it, count the guards. Don't miss any. Get a good sense of where they are, how they're armed. Look for places of concealment in case we have to do something creative."

"'Creative'?"

"Uh huh." He nodded at the big, dark mouth of the cavern. "I got a feeling we're walking into the dragon's mouth, kid. That general they mentioned, Ike Black? I know that name. Can't quite place where, but it wasn't from a Nobel Peace Prize announcement. There's something wrong about him. It'll come to me. Point is, I think we're about to step into some shit. If I'm right – and, sadly, I'm usually right about this kind of thing – then it could all get crazy real fucking fast. You understand me?"

"Yes," said Tom.

"Watch me for cues. Be stupid and agreeable. Don't be threatening in any way. Follow my lead and if I make a move then I want you to move with me."

"What kind of move?"

"Don't know yet," said Ledger. "I'm going to let the moment tell me what to do. You understand that?"

"Yes."

They nodded and moved with the line, but they kept enough distance between them and the end of the line to be able to speak together in low tones.

"If this goes south on us, Tom," said Ledger, "I need to know that you'll do whatever's necessary. Don't freak out. Pick your targets and watch your fire. You understand the concept of trigger discipline. Remember your training. We protect civilians as much as possible, but we have to win any fight we start. No bullshit. War isn't polite."

Tom looked appalled. "You think it'll come to that?"

Ledger rubbed at the blond-gray stubble on his chin. "It usually does."

The line moved forward and in forty minutes it was their turn to step up to the table. It was immediately clear that two of the lab-coated people were assisting the third, a woman of about forty, with long auburn hair and a lovely face. Her hands moved with professional competence, accepting syringes, swabbing with pieces of cloth soaked in alcohol, jabbing with practiced deftness, handing the used needle off, taking a new one. Over and over again. Doing it fast and doing it well.

Ledger looked at the doctor, trying to catch her eye and read her. She was disheveled, her clothes were dirty and stained, and her hair hung in lank threads. If all he had was a quick glance he might have put it down to an earnest desperation to get as much done as possible, to fill every minute of every hour of every day with the good work she was doing. Pushing herself to the edge of exhaustion because what was personal comfort when measured against saving the actual fucking world?

That's what a quick glance would have told him. Ledger, however, was not in the habit of making quick or hasty judgments. Reliable intelligence required attention and consideration.

He glanced at the guards standing just a few feet behind

Dr Pisani. There were five of them. Four were generic brutes with hard faces, dead eyes and callused hands resting on the automatic rifles slung over their heavy shoulders. The fifth was a different kind of man, and Ledger met his eyes only briefly and when he did he projected absolutely nothing because this was a far more dangerous man than the guards who stood with him. This man was tall, lean, wiry, hawk-faced, with cat green eyes and a slash of a mouth. One corner of that mouth was hooked upward in a permanent, knowing, mocking smile. It was clear to Ledger, as he was sure it was to Tom, that this man was in charge. Not just of this post, but of everything. He wore a black leather jacket but beneath was a military blouse with two stars pinned neatly in place. A major general. He stood with a *faux* slouch that Ledger had seen a lot of good fighters affect. His long-fingered hands hung loose at his sides, and he wore the kind of loose-fitting clothes that allowed for quick, unhampered movement.

*Danger, Will Robinson,* mused Ledger. He shifted his gaze away before the man could fix on him. There was something very familiar about the man, but Ledger could not quite place it.

So, instead he focused on Dr Pisani, trying to catch her eyes. It took a moment, but as the doctor prepared to inject the woman in line in front of Ledger, Pisani glanced at him and their eyes met. Locked. Held. He wanted to make contact with her, to make sure she *saw* him as he saw her. That's when Ledger knew that everything that was going on here was as wrong as his instincts had warned.

There was a look in the doctor's eyes. Not exhaustion. Not the weary triumph of having succeeded in something great. Not even the fatalistic sadness of someone who wished she could have succeeded in her great achievement sooner.

No. None of that was in Pisani's eyes.

Instead, what Ledger saw in those lovely, intelligent brown eyes was a total, overwhelming joy. A joy that was too much, too big, too wild.

It was the kind of limitless joy of a mind that had broken loose of its moorings.

The doctor who desperate people traveled hundreds of miles to find was absolutely insane.

—16—
Top and Bunny

It didn't take long before the workers switched from hauling bodies to herding groups of people. As the troop carriers filled with dead pulled out, they were replaced within five minutes by troop carriers carrying the living – all wearing red, white, and blue wristbands. This time, the reds were immediately put in with Top and Bunny, until their red holding pen was full. And then the next and the next. The whites and blues were split, some being taken off further into the reaches of the cavern and whatever lay beyond their line of sight, while others were ushered into the appropriately marked holding pens for blue and white.

"Wait. Where are they going? Why are we being put in here?" one woman demanded, looking longingly off after the other blues.

"We can only process so many at a time, okay?" the guard replied, smiling warmly as if to reassure her. "You're next, I promise. Look, there's nice chairs here, Blu-ray players, books."

He was right. Unlike the pens for the reds, the whites and blues had been given couches, chairs, tables with games, flatscreen TVs with Blu-ray players, bookshelves of books and magazines. All stuff to make them comfortable and help them relax while they waited, which meant either the guards didn't care about the reds relaxing or the reds, for some reason, wouldn't be waiting as long.

Bunny elbowed Top and tipped his head toward the other pens. "What's wrong with this picture?"

"Everything," Top agreed, whispering.

"How come they get to sit and we have to stand here?" a red-banded old man said. "My legs are tired and I have a bad back!" He scowled, his voice dripping irritation.

The guard just turned and shoved him further back into the red tagged cell. "Shut up and do what you're told, old man. Make room for the rest."

"Do you have any idea who you're talking to?" the old man demanded, but before he could say anything further, the guard backhanded him across the face, knocking him to his knees. Two more guards rushed in, grabbed him, and dragged him out the door.

"You just got yourself a speed pass, old man," the sneering first guard said, watching as the others dragged him, feet trailing behind, off into the cavern where the groups of blues and whites had gone.

"Jesus," Bunny said, exchanging a look with Top.

The first guard noticed a line of men who'd stopped to stare. "Get in there! Go!"

They started moving again as he turned back to his duties. Bunny searched every face for anyone familiar. No one. He shook his head. "I don't know why but I keep looking for someone we know."

"Don't stop," Top said as his eyes continued scanning faces. "So am I."

As more and more people filed in, the first trucks having been replaced by three more, the overwhelming smell of gunpowder and chemicals now mixed with the smells of sweat, body odor, colognes and perfumes – of people.

Then Bunny did a double take as his eyes scanned a line of whites climbing off a nearby GMC. *Son of bitch, that almost looks like… it can't be.*

"Fuck, Top," he mumbled. "My eyes are getting so tired, I'm seeing things."

"What?"

"That guy over there looks almost like Captain Ledger. I mean, I wish it was, but—"

"Where?" Top's eyes snapped over to where Bunny indicated. "Son of a bitch. Doesn't that kid beside him look almost like Sam Imura?"

"Yeah," Bunny agreed. "Weird. But it can't be. They're both dead."

Top grunted. "Technically we didn't see them die, but after nineteen years, yeah, I think you're right." He went back to searching another line as the two men moved off out of view, further into the cavern, urged by guards.

"We gotta come up with a plan, son," Top said then, leaning closer to Bunny's ear. "A way to distract the guards, get ourselves out of here."

"Hooah," Bunny replied. "You know, there's a lot of us here. If people got excited for some reason..."

"The door's locked," Top said.

"So we find a way to make them unlock it."

"Okay, Farm Boy, and how is that?"

"Just follow my lead," Bunny said, and an idea formed as he remembered the old man they dragged off. If the others started to question, if they worried about their fate – people could be all sorts of unpredictable under such circumstances. They might even get riled up enough to alarm the guards. "We're all gonna die!" he suddenly shouted.

"What are you talking about?" Top asked, raising his voice to be heard.

"The red bands!" Bunny said. "We don't get chairs, Blu-rays, games, books – it's obvious. They don't give those to red banders because we're gonna die!"

"Stop saying that!" a guard outside their holding pen said, shaking his head. "Everyone just remain calm. The colors are for sorting treatment." A couple other guards muttered and glared in Bunny's direction.

"But that old man – when he complained about his back, they beat him and dragged him off," Top said. "What kind of medical treatment facility is this?"

"The kind where you wait your turn and don't ask questions," Major Diamond said, appearing before them with a cold stare. "One more word out of you two, and you'll find out all about that old man."

"You just threatened us!" Bunny shouted.

"Hey! They're right!" someone else said.

"Why are you threatening us if we're here for treatment?" another called.

Then chaos erupted in the red cells as people began chattering, calling out questions, pounding at the doors, shuffling nervously.

More guards moved in, some whispering calm words, others waving guns and ordering people back from the barred walls.

Bunny grinned at Top as he called out, "We're all gonna die! I know it!"

<br>

## —17—
### The Soldier and the Samurai

When it was his turn to bare his arm for Dr Pisani, Joe Ledger did a quick but thorough read on the syringe. It was clean and the barrel of it contained a completely colorless liquid. Before the End, Ledger had spent a lot of years taking Echo Team into conflict with terrorists, many of whom used bioweapons. He'd been in every major biological and chemical development lab in the United States, and dozens around the world. He was a frequent visitor to the Centers for Disease Control and the National Institutes of Health. As a result he knew what viral transport media looked like, just as he knew what vaccines looked like, including the various versions of *Lucifer 113* and the counter-agents developed to try and stop it, notably *Reaper*. As the doctor raised the syringe, Ledger looked from it to the doctor, meeting her eyes again.

"This is a cure?" he asked quietly.

Pisani twitched. "Yes, yes, it won't hurt. Don't worry."

"I'm not worried, Doc. I admire you for what you're doing. But I have a question," said Ledger, pitching his voice so that only she could hear him, "what kind of vaccine is this? Is it an antibiotic of some kind?"

"No," she said, "it's a broad-spectrum antiviral vaccine."

"Ah," he said, taking time to remove his jacket. "But I'm confused about something. They said that *Lucifer 113* was unstoppable. They said that the addition of *Reaper* to the bioweapon strain was what caused it to jump to an airborne pathogen. I'm really impressed that you've been able to counteract something that was designed to be unstoppable."

"N-no," she said quickly. "We broke the pathogen down and this is the cure. It's the real cure, a perfect cure."

Her words tumbled out way too quickly. Ledger nodded, still smiling warmly at her. He draped his jacket over one arm. She swabbed his arm with alcohol.

"But what confuses me," he said, "is how an antiviral will work against *Lucifer 113*. I mean… it's not actually a virus."

She froze, the needle a quarter inch from his flesh. Her eyes were huge and filled with strange lights. "What…?"

"As I understand it," Ledger said, "*Lucifer* was built using select combinations of disease pathogens and parasites and then underwent extensive transgenic modification with *Toxoplasma gondii* as a key element, along with the larva of the green jewel wasp. It has genetic elements of the *Dicrocoelium dendriticum* and *Euhaplorchis californiensis* flukes that combine to regulate that aggressive response behavior into a predictable pattern. None of that is a virus, so how does this work? I mean, not even an antibiotic would work because this isn't really predominantly bacteriological, so how can an antiviral do any good?"

Dr Pisani stood there, the tip of the needle trembling near his shoulder. "No, I… I mean I… what you don't…" Her words tumbled and tumbled and fell off a cliff, leaving her blank-faced except for those wild eyes. Ledger saw tears there on her lower lashes, and the doctor's lips trembled almost in time to the needlepoint.

The two lab assistants realized something was wrong and stepped forward. So did one of the guards.

"Doc," asked one of the assistants. "Is something wrong?"

The other assistant gave Ledger a suspicious look. "What did you say to her?"

Ledger's smile was bolted into place. "I just told her how much I admire what you're all doing here."

Everyone looked at Pisani. Tears broke and fell down her cheeks. "It's a perfect cure."

The second assistant jabbed Ledger in the chest with a stiffened forefinger. "That's not what you said. Tell me what you—"

"What's holding up the line?" demanded the hawk-faced general as he pushed his way toward Ledger. Tom shifted a half step away, but Ledger knew it was to get some room for movement if this turned weird.

Ledger had been expecting it to turn weird since the checkpoint but he was glad to see the young man read the moment this well. Just *how* weird was to be determined. No one was pulling guns yet, which was good, but everything in the cavern had come to an abrupt stop.

The first assistant pointed at Ledger. "This guy said something to the doc and it's got her all upset."

The general walked right up to Ledger and kept approaching in the way some hard-asses do when they want to force someone to back away. It was a bully's trick that usually triggered a response based on the natural tendency to maintain a bubble of personal distance. Ledger knew the trick, and for a moment, he almost chose to step back to let this man own the moment. But then something changed that, and Ledger knew that it was going to change the trajectory of the entire day.

He recognized the man. When they'd met before, he'd been wearing the same black leather jacket and similar black pants to what he now wore.

Ledger knew his name.

So he stood his ground and let the general invade his space and get all the way up to a chest-to-chest contact. Ledger was a big man, but he was in his fifties and he'd been slouching to make himself look older and smaller than he was. This army officer was about not quite six feet tall, which made him a couple of inches shorter than Ledger. When it was clear Ledger wasn't going to step back, the general placed a hand on his chest and pushed. Ledger allowed it, and for a moment they stood there, studying each other with professional thoroughness.

"Well fuck me blind," murmured the general. "I know you."

"Been a long time, Ike," said Ledger.

General Ike Black shook his head. "We all thought you were dead."

Ledger said nothing.

General Black turned to his men. "You know who we have here? This is Captain Joe Ledger. America's number one covert gunslinger." His eyes clicked back to Ledger. "Jesus on a stick, Ledger, if even half the stories about you are true you've killed more people than God. Everyone used to say that if they send you in the shit's already hit the fan. You took down the Jakobys, the Seven Kings, that crazy anarchist bitch Mother Night. All that stuff."

Everyone was staring now. Even Tom was looking sidelong at Ledger.

"People exaggerate," said Ledger.

"No they don't," said Black. "People don't know the stories I've heard, and I heard them from the people who *know*. You're supposed to be a psychotic, bloodthirsty, ass-kicking psychopath. You're the one they send in when they want scorched earth."

Ledger sighed. "Nice to be remembered for one's accomplishments. I also threw a good breaking ball and I'm pretty good with *Donkey Kong* and *Ms Pac Man*, but nobody ever talks about that."

"And they said you're a smartass who mouthed off to at least three presidents."

"Five," said Ledger. "But who's counting?"

Black grinned. "So the zombies didn't eat you."

"I've proven indigestible so far."

"Where were you when things fell apart? Seems like you're the guy they should've called in when *Lucifer 113* slipped its leash."

"I was out of the country," said Ledger with real sadness.

"Trying to save the world. Wrong apocalypse. By the time I got back it was all for shit."

They stood there and the cavern was completely silent around them. General Black cocked his head to one side and scrutinized him. Then he glanced at Dr Pisani, who stood nearby with glazed, confused eyes and tear tracks on her face. "What did he say to you, Doc?"

Pisani licked her lips and opened her mouth to speak, but then shook her head.

General Black frowned at Ledger. "Maybe you'll tell me what you said."

Ledger shrugged. "I just told her how much I admire what she's doing here. What you're *all* doing here. Saving the world."

"Saving the world," echoed Black. "That's all you said?"

Ledger could feel the anxiety coming off of Tom. The young man had a great poker face but his body was rigid with coiled tension. Ledger caught the subtle shift as Tom moved his weight to the balls of his feet. A martial arts trick; a fighter's trick – using muscular tension and weight distribution to prepare the body for immediate high-speed movement.

Ledger smiled now and he lowered his voice so that the conversation was private between Black and him. "Listen, Ike, I think I get what you're doing here. This facility, the sorting of people, the vaccine. I get it. We *both* get it. The ass fell off the world and it's either going to go completely down the shitter or it's not, and the only way it's not is for someone with the vision, the balls, and the talent to put it back together."

Black said nothing.

"You were always a bad boy. Blackwater and then Blue Diamond. You're no more a general than I'm Catherine the Great. I get it. The old system's gone, so long live the new system. There's no government anymore, no army, no nothing. Who's to say you don't have the authority to pin some stars on your shirt. I'm cool with it because it's the first smart thing I've seen anyone do since this all fell apart. Someone *had* to do it. I wish I'd thought of it first, but I didn't. You did. Far as I'm concerned that means you earned those stars. You got my vote, for whatever it's worth."

"Really?" said Black in a voice that was heavily laced with disbelief.

"Really. If someone doesn't start a new government and organize a new army, there's not going to be a future because there's not going to be a human race. So, props to you."

"Funny hearing this from Uncle Sam's number one problem solver."

"Uncle Sam's dead," said Ledger. "I'm not. The president ate the vice president and congress ate each other, so there's no one signing my paychecks these days. I'm not a young kid anymore and, quite frankly, I'm getting tired of being a one-man-army in a rerun of *The Walking Dead*. The odds are against me."

"You have a friend," said Black, nodding to Tom.

"Him? Fuck. He's a sushi cook. He's good with knives and he doesn't mind taking orders. He's nothing to this."

"To what? You're talking a lot, Ledger, but you're not getting anywhere."

Ledger glanced around and then leaned closer. "The vaccine is bullshit. I think your Dr Pisani is bugfuck nuts, and she's injecting people with tap water. There is no vaccine for *Lucifer 113*, and if there was it wouldn't be antiviral. You know and I know it. Maybe the doc knows it, and that's why she's blown out her circuits, though I suspect she was already damaged goods before you started this operation."

"Still not hearing anything I want to hear," said Black. "And we have a line of people wondering what the hell is happening here."

"Sure. How many guys you have here, Ike? Twenty? Thirty? If they're all like the nuclear scientists guarding the checkpoint then you're working with inferior materials. How many of them were actually military?" When General Black didn't answer Ledger nodded. "That's what I thought. So what happens if all those people coming here get wind of this as a shit operation?"

"What makes you think—?"

"Come on, Ike, I'm not stupid. That color coding thing? Maybe the tourists think that's some kind of Sorting Hat, but I don't think the red-band people are going to a nice safe dorm. They're old, or sick, or useless, or dangerous. You're weeding out the dangerous ones. Tom and me got through because he's a cook and I told the guards that I was a ball-player and amateur hunter. Cooking and hunting are important skills for a colony, and that's what this is. I bet you pulled out the medical staff, anyone who can fix, make, repair or build and they got white bands, too. That's what the vaccine thing is all about. It's a beacon to draw people to you, and if you can protect them, they'll never know that they're not actually immune. Tell me I'm wrong."

Black's eyes narrowed, but then he gave Ledger a tiny nod.

"So, here's my offer," said Ledger. "I've trained more real soldiers than you've ever seen. I know weapons and tactics, I know defense and attack. You said it yourself, I used to be Uncle Sam's go-to guy for fucking up other people's days. That's me. I figured this shit out in fifteen minutes. Someone else is going to do that, too, and they might not be in here. They might be out where they can spread the word and gather a bunch of villagers with pitchforks and torches. If that happens, do you want me dead in a ditch or do you want me overseeing the defenses of your new kingdom?"

It took a long time for General Black to respond. The room remained quiet though no longer silent. There were discrete coughs and the rustling of people shifting nervously. No one interrupted the private, whispered conversation.

Finally, Black said, "How do I know that I can trust you?"

Ledger shrugged. "You'll have me watched. Put guards on me. Don't give me a gun until you're sure. If I twitch the wrong way, do what you got to do. But that's not how it's going to play out, Ike. I'm offering a barter. I need a home, I need a clean bed and a shower – God knows I need a shower – and I want three squares, a roof over my head, and a life again. You can give me all of that. In return I'll give you an army."

General Black straightened and walked a few paces away.

Ledger cut a look at Tom and saw that the young man's calm was cracking under the strain of uncertainty and imminent danger. Ledger made a very low, very small gesture with his left hand. *Calm down.*

Tom's tension eased by about two per cent.

Then General Black raised his arms out to the side and turned to the people who were waiting in line.

"Listen to me," he roared. "Everything is okay. In fact, everything's great. This man here is Captain Joe Ledger. You won't have heard of him, but he was a very famous soldier. A Special Ops solder. Best of the best. He's come here to join us. To help us. And he is my friend. Let's show him how much we appreciate his coming all this way to support our sacred cause."

The guards began applauding first, and if it was a bit slow and uncertain at first, Ledger could understand. Then the medical staff joined in and then everyone. Only Dr Pisani did not applaud. She stood staring at Ledger with confused eyes and a mouth pulled rigid with fear.

Ike Black strode over and took Ledger's hand, holding it high as the applause swelled, and then shaking it. He used the handshake to lean in and whisper in Ledger's ear.

"If you're fucking with me, Ledger," he said, "I will have you skinned alive. Don't think I'm joking. I've done it a dozen times before. I'll cut your balls off and make you eat them."

His handshake was crushingly hard, but Ledger knew the trick of positioning his hand so the bones braced against the force rather than collapsed within the stricture. He met Black's eyes and smiled at him.

"You don't have to worry about me," he said. "You don't ever have to worry about me, *General.*"

—18—

**The Hall of the Mountain King**

The big treatment hall was cleared and the people with the white wristbands were sent outside to bed down in one of the big tents, with Ike Black telling everyone that the doctor was exhausted. There was no option for discussion or debate as soldiers moved in and cleared the room.

"Let me show you fellows around," said the general. "I think you'll appreciate what we're trying to do here."

The tour started with introductions to Ike Black's senior staff, most of who were clearly not military men but instead looked like a roughhouse crew of bikers, backwoods hunters, and general hard-cases. Tough, but not in the same way professional soldiers were. Harder in the wrong places and with noticeable lapses in personal discipline and an understanding of military procedures. For all that they were dangerous, and more so because their actions would be random and unfiltered.

Joe Ledger and Tom Imura shook a lot of hands as the general showed them around the complex.

"This was a hardened facility," the general explained. "The rock and iron in the mountain kept them from EMP burnout and the blast doors kept the eaters out. Tucson's a total loss, and when I got here there were half a million of the dead bastards walking around."

"How'd you handle that?" asked Ledger.

"Controlled burns, mostly. Brush fires, some incendiaries fired from our helicopters."

"You still have helos?"

"Had," said the general wistfully as he led them into an adjoining chamber where a hulking Bell UH-1Y Venom 'Super Huey' squatted. "One crashed and this one needs parts that we don't have here, and we don't have an aviation mechanic to tell our machinist what to make."

"I might be able to help with this old girl," said Ledger. "I've tinkered a bit."

Black gave him a startled look. "Really?"

"Sure," said the soldier, patting the gray skin of the helicopter. "Motors, rotors, and avionics. When you spent as much time in the field as I have you need to know how to fix your ride. Couldn't Uber my way out of the kinds of places they sent me. I can fix a boat, too."

"No boats out here," said Black, "but I'll file it away for when we expand."

"What about ground transport. Anything need work there?"

"We're doing better with vehicles. We have five Humvee light armored vehicles, couple of utility cargo trucks. Six noncombat vehicles. All in pretty good shape."

"That's not a big fleet for an army. You got how many guys here? Forty?"

"Fifty-one," said Black. "We'll make do. If we can't drive, we'll use horses. But one of my scouts found a place a few hundred klicks from here that has a crap-ton of three and four-wheel ATVs. Two-stroke engines, and we took in a guy today who fixes that kind of stuff. He's sure as shit going to earn his room and board."

The tour moved on, with Black becoming expansive and Ledger encouraging him to brag. Tom Imura drifted along behind like a silent ghost, and behind him were two armed guards. Another pair of guards walked point for their small party. Black was being welcoming, but not stupid.

They passed Dr Pisani's lab, and although there was a guard the lab was empty and dark. Ledger paused outside to peer through the dusty glass. The general walked on a pace, then stopped and joined him.

"Does she know?" asked Ledger.

"Allie? Fuck no," said Black, then he thought about it and amended that. "I don't really know. She's damaged goods, as you probably saw."

"That a recent thing or…?"

"Nah, she was half out of her mind when I found her. She was here in the base with six pencil necks, four soldiers and a lot of dead people. They were in here for a couple of years. Teams would go out looking for survivors or trying to make contact with other groups, but none of them ever came back, and when I rolled up the last ones here had pretty much lost their shit. The soldiers threw in with me right off. I wasn't regular army, but like you said, what does that matter."

"Word," agreed Ledger, nodding.

"The lab crew had been working on a cure, and Allie Pisani swore she had cracked the damn thing, but…"

"No?"

"No. It can't be cracked. There was this other doctor, Monica McReady, who was a big shot in bioweapons from out at a station like this in Death Valley, and for a while they were feeding intel to Allie, but then they went dark. And it happened at just the wrong time, right when Allie thought she was onto something, but she needed some vital info from McReady. Couldn't go in the right direction without it, and bam. Done. Nothing. I think that's when Allie Pisani lost it. I think she saw it as some kind of slap in the face of hope and optimism, or maybe she thought that it was proof God was throwing in the towel on this whole shit show. Not sure, and don't really care. I mean, sure, a cure would have been dope, but we never got it and won't get it, so we make do. No use crying over spilled milk, am I right?"

"Right as rain."

Black smiled broadly and nodded approvingly at Ledger. "God, it's nice to have a conversation with someone who *gets* me, you know? Someone who's both been there and done that and doesn't have his head all the way up his ass."

"Believe me, General, I'm enjoying this conversation, too."

"Fuck that 'general' stuff unless we're around the tourists. It's Ike. Ike and Joe, okay?"

He stuck out his hand again and they shook, both of them grinning at each other.

They wandered outside into the camp. Ledger caught Tom's eye and saw the younger man's confusion. He gave him a wink and allowed him to interpret it any way he wanted.

"So how's this set-up work, Ike?" asked Ledger. "I have a line on the white wristbands, and I'm pretty sure I dig what you have in mind for the reds. Dead wood, am I right?"

Ike Black paused for a moment, his eyes searching Ledger's face. "You disapprove?"

"Me? Fuck no. Planet Earth's a lifeboat, brother. We can't

waste food on anyone who isn't going to make it anyway. And we can't waste food on anyone who's not going to help us row to shore. Far as I see it sentimentality is a sucker's game."

General Black paused a moment longer, then nodded. "Glad to hear you say that."

"And, let's face it, Ike," said Ledger leaning close, "I didn't last this long by being Mr Rogers, you dig? It's not a wonderful day in the neighborhood and not every motherfucker I meet is my neighbor."

One of the guards said, "Preach."

Black shot him a stern look but did not disagree. Instead, he gave another nod.

"What about the blue tents?" asked Ledger casually. "Women and kids?"

"They're being protected."

Ledger snorted. "Don't blow smoke up my ass, man. And don't bullshit a bullshitter. The general population's pretty fucking small and if we're going to rebuild then we need breeding stock. Younger they are the more seasons they have to squeeze out new Americans, am I right?"

Ike Black stopped and stared at him, a small hopeful smile playing on his lips. "Christ, you really do get it, don't you?"

"It's pretty black and white, Ike. It's survival of the fittest and with humans that means survival of those people who can make the hard choices." He clapped Tom on the shoulder. "That's what I've been trying to teach my friend here. How to do what's necessary *when* it's necessary."

Tom cleared his throat and, still using the thick accent, said, "I'm working on it."

"General!" someone called.

They all turned and a guard with a radio headset ran up and whispered in the general's ear for a few minutes. Black pulled him aside and they whispered back and forth for a bit before the general nodded and the guard ran off, talking into his headset as Black rejoined Ledger and Tom.

"Anything wrong?" Ledger asked.

The general shook it off, then a shrewd look came into his eyes. "Tell you what, fellows, there's no time like the present to put your money where your mouth is."

"Meaning what, big man?" asked Ledger.

"Red tent," said Black. "Sometimes we pick up some troublemakers along with the dead wood. Case in point… we got a couple of real hard-cases in lockdown. Couple ex-military who I think are still fighting for truth, justice, and the American way. Old school, head-in-the-sand types."

"Sounds inconvenient. What are you going to do with them?"

Black's smile brightened. "Me? Nothing. But I thought it would be a great way for you fellows to make your bones. Not to offend, Joe, but talk is cheap."

"What do you mean?" asked Tom.

Ledger laughed. "Big Ike here wants us to prove that we're not just a couple of con artists sweet-talking our way into the good life, isn't that right?"

"Something like that," agreed Black.

"So," continued Ledger, "he wants us to go into the red tent where they have those hard-cases and put them down."

"I…" began Tom, but Ledger clapped him on the shoulder again. Hard.

"Don't turn green, kid. Wouldn't be the first useless cocksuckers you ever killed. Not even the first this week."

Tom said nothing, but there was doubt in his eyes.

"The general's right," said Ledger. "Talk's cheap, and man… there's just about nothing I wouldn't do to sleep in a real bed and not having worry about waking up with some dead asshole nibbling on my dick. If that means popping a cap in some bad guys, then booyah. I like me more than I like some assholes I don't know. So, bottom line, it sucks to be them."

"That," said Black with a merry laugh, "is what I like to hear."

"When you want this done?" asked Ledger.

"First light?"

"Fuck no," said Ledger. "Why wait? Let's close this deal right damn now. I'll pop one and let Tom do the other and then you can point us in the direction of a cold beer, if any such thing still exists."

"Will Irish whiskey do?" asked Black.

"Yeah," said Ledger, "it will. Let's rock."

—19—
## Top and Bunny

Though they succeeded in creating the chaos they'd wanted, and even slipped out of the cell when the guards opened it to come in and restore calm, Top and Bunny quickly found themselves surrounded by six men with rifles pointed at their heads while Major Diamond used the butt end of a rifle to slam them each in the stomach and send them to their knees, gasping for breath. They hadn't even had enough room to react because of the constant crowd surrounding them.

"You boys just bought yourself the front of the line," Diamond said with a sneer and nodded to the two guards.

The two prisoners were yanked to their feet as the holding pen door slammed and locked behind them, then dragged further into the cavern past cells where the white and blue banders were enjoying books, Blu-rays, furniture. Then they were shoved into a closet-sized cavern and locked in darkness.

"Fuck," Bunny moaned. "That worked great. What now?"

"Now we wait 'til they come for us and be ready to jump them," Top said. "Relax and recharge while you can, son."

Bunny heard shuffling as Top slid against the stone and sat on the floor nearby and he followed suit, sighing. "We shoulda had a better plan."

"Shut the fuck up, soldier."

"Just saying."

And then Bunny heard a chuckle. Top was laughing at him. "What?"

"Once an idiot, always an idiot," Top said through laughter.

"Hey, this idiot has had your six for over twenty years, Old Man."

"I know, it's a fucking miracle I still have a six," Top replied.

"Fuck you," Bunny moaned and then grinned in the darkness, chuckling a bit himself.

Soon, they were both laughing, and that was the last thing Bunny remembered as he fell into darkness and slept restlessly against the hard, cold stone.

A bright light.

That was his next memory, as he awoke blinded and heard men talking. "Get up!" someone ordered.

"On your feet!" growled another.

Then they were being lifted and dragged out of the cavern, surrounded by armed men again.

The guards moved quickly, keeping them surrounded. Bunny only made out bits and pieces of their surroundings – a door marked 'lab', a few white-coated workers moving in and out, then a line of people with blue bands. They wound through a short corridor into another room past a line of white banded people waiting before a dispensary of some sort with lab-coated workers at a counter, handing out small cups of liquid or pills, he couldn't tell which.

Then they went through thick steel doors into another cavern, passing a line of men with red wristbands like their own, waiting. They all looked tired, shifting continuously like people who'd spent too much time on their feet for an unknown purpose. Bunny could relate. What were they lined up for?

Then he and Top were shoved at the front of the line and they saw General Black approaching with a kid in a many-pocketed canvas vest and green khakis, a kid who Bunny recognized – a kid he'd seen the day before who looked a lot like their old teammate, Sam Imura.

Then he gasped, his breath frozen in his lungs as his eyes came to the man in the sleeveless fatigue shirt and sunglasses standing on the other side of the general from the kid. His hair was greyer, his face lined with age, but Bunny couldn't believe his eyes. His knees wobbled and he fought to stay on his feet. "Captain," he whispered.

Top stared beside him, frozen just the same. He had the same deer caught in headlights look in his eyes as he stared at the man, too.

Bunny shook his head, trying to shake off the vision. *This can't be real. Joe Ledger's dead.* He felt tears forming in the corner of his eyes. Could it really be? He'd never believed in fucking miracles, but he was looking right at one.

—20—
## Four Jacks and a King

Joe Ledger stared at the two men in the front of the line. The big blond guy and the older black guy.

They were impossible faces.

Dead faces.

Ghost faces.

The ground seemed to tilt under Ledger's feet and the light from the torches and lanterns got instantly brighter. So bright. Too bright.

He said, "What...?"

Very softly. So softly that only two people heard him.

Tom Imura and General Ike Black.

They turned to look at Ledger. The two men in the line gaped at him. The guards stood around, none of them realizing that something important was happening.

"What's with you?" demanded Black sharply, and that caused everyone to turn in his direction – guards, prisoners, and even a few camp civilians who were passing by. The moment froze around Ledger.

Years ago, when Ledger had been recruited by the Department of Military Sciences one of the main reasons he had been chosen and asked to lead Echo Team was because he lacked the flaw of hesitation. He saw, processed and reacted with zero lag time, a side-effect of the Cop and Killer working in perfect harmony, blending astute judgment with instinctive reaction.

Now he stood rooted to the ground for what seemed like forever. He could feel his mind catching fire and for a moment – a single burning moment – Ledger wondered if the delicate balancing act of juggling personality aspects had all come crashing down. He knew that such a calamity was always possible, that control over his personal damage was in no way an absolute.

What made it worse was that he saw the realization blossom like diseased flowers in the eyes of those two prisoners. Top and Bunny were alive. They were prisoners. They were scheduled for execution at *his* hands. And although they were every bit as shocked as he was, he could see how they were reacting to his reaction.

All of this – the self-awareness, the understanding of his own deadly hesitation, the connection with Top and Bunny – happened in a microsecond. It felt so much longer, but it wasn't. The Killer knew it wasn't. The Cop knew it wasn't. Ike Black's words had just been spoken less than a heartbeat ago.

A heartbeat.

And that was how long his hesitation lasted.

Seemed like forever. Could have been.

Wasn't.

Ledger turned away from the prisoners and smiled at Ike Black. "You know, Ike, something funny just occurred to me. You'll think this is hilarious."

The doubt on Black's face wavered and he half-smiled. "Oh, yeah, what?"

Ledger stood next to him and pointed with his left to Top and Bunny. "See those two assholes over there?"

"What about them?"

Joe Ledger chopped the general across the windpipe with the edge of his left hand. He did it without a single muscular flicker that would have telegraphed the move. He did it the right way. And he did it very fucking fast.

There was a second moment of hesitation as Ike Black staggered a half step back. The guards stared. The passersby stared. The other prisoners stared.

Tom Imura did not. Nor did Top and Bunny.

They moved.

Tom pivoted in place, grabbed the closest guard and hit him with a cupped palm to the ear, putting a lot of torque into the blow, sending the man crashing into a second guard. Top and Bunny rushed at the nearest guards. Their hands were zip-tied but their feet were not, nor was the rest of them. Bunny ducked low and plowed his two-hundred and sixty pounds of hard muscle into a guard and hit with such locomotive speed that the man was plucked off the ground and carried with Bunny as the Marine rammed into the rest of the sentries. Top kicked the kneecap off the man closest to him, then pivoted and kicked a guard who – quicker than the others – was raising his rifle. The steel toe of Top's boot caught him under the balls, crushing them and smashing the bottom bones of his pelvis. The gun fell and the man collapsed into a fetal ball.

Ledger tore the front of his shirt down to release the Wilson rapid-release knife and with a flick the short, wicked blade snapped into place. Without pausing, Ledger slashed it across the throat of one man and the eyes of another. Tom caught the second man, spun him and tore the rifle from the screaming man's hands.

Ledger raced over to Top and Bunny, slashed the zip ties free, gave them a single dazzling, maniacal grin, and dove back into the fight. Ike Black was still on his feet, still trying to suck in air past the wreckage of his throat. Ledger slap-turned him and used him as a shield as he drove toward a pair of soldiers who had been part of the prisoner detail. The men saw their general and even though it was clear the man was badly hurt, he was still the god of their little world. They hesitated, and this time the hesitation was fatal, and Joe Ledger made them pay for it. He slammed Black into the arms of one, reached past the dying general to slash the forearm, the biceps and then the throat of the first guard. Then he grabbed the other man's hair, jerked him free of Ike Black's desperate clutches, and cut his throat, too.

Gunfire erupted behind him and he whirled to see Bunny and Tom fanning out, each of them firing as they ran. Top lingered with the prisoners and Ledger saw the flash of silver. Top had found a knife somewhere and was cutting the strongest-looking prisoners free; then he pressed his knife into a willing hand and let the newly freed prisoners continue the liberation. Ledger saw a guard running toward him and dove down beneath the spray of bullets, using a dead man for cover, feeling the bullets thud into dead flesh. He took the man's Glock, rose up and fired, fired, fired.

There was a huge rumbling sound and Ledger whirled to see the cavern door descending.

"The cavern!" he bellowed, and raced toward the open maw of the cavern. The others followed, though Bunny peeled off toward a parked M1117 Guardian Armored Security Vehicle. Top fired as he ran and killed a man who stood at the door controls, then he punched a red STOP button. The door jerked to a halt four feet from the ground. Ledger and Tom ducked in after him.

Outside, a man saw Bunny coming, whirled and tried to get inside the ASV before the hulking giant could reach him. He was one step too slow. Bunny shot him center mass and from the loose way he fell it was clear the bullet had clipped the soldier's spine. Then Bunny was inside the vehicle. Ledger was just crossing into the complex when he heard the bull roar of the vehicles muscular .50 machine gun. The mass of soldiers running toward the sound of battle suddenly started dancing and twitching as Bunny tore them to pieces.

Tom and Top Sims caught up with Ledger just inside.

"What's the plan, Cap'n?" asked Top.

"Rules of engagement are pretty simple, Top," said Ledger. "Everyone wearing a uniform is a bad guy and there are a lot of them. This is a target-rich environment. Let's clean house."

Top grinned. "Hooah."

"Hooah."

"It's good to see you, brother," said Top.

"You might be a figment of my imagination, Top, but for now I'll take it. Rock and roll."

They laughed, as if the world was a wonderful place. They laughed as if the odds were stacked in their favor and the night was not filled with gunfire and screams. They laughed because they were alive. For now, they were alive.

The four of them were badly outnumbered.

They were outgunned, even with the .50 machine gun and a full box of ammunition.

They were not outfought.

The men in Ike Black's army were not soldiers. They thought they were predators.

They were not.

The gunfight lasted eleven minutes. The last of the soldiers fled the cavern, running from the killers who came hunting them in the steel corridor. They ran for safety into the camp.

Where all of the freed prisoners were waiting.

—21—
### The Quick and the Dead

When it was over the survivors had to go around with knives and kill the soldiers they killed. Reanimation was a fact of life. Everyone who died, no matter how they died, came back to life within minutes.

Ledger, Top, and Tom came out of the cavern to find Bunny directing the cleanup. Ledger walked past him to where Ike Black had climbed to his feet and was taking his first steps as one of the living dead. Ledger slung his stolen rifle and flicked the Wilson's blade into place again. He stopped, though, and let the zombie shamble toward him.

"I ought to let you stay this way," Ledger told him. "Kick your ass out of here and let you wander until you rotted away."

The zombie tried to moan, but the damage to its throat was too severe.

"You thought you were so fucking smart," said Ledger. "King under the mountain. Shit, I had this whole plan about pretending to join and working my way up to be your right-hand man and then putting two in the back of your head when no one was looking. I was going to take over this whole operation and maybe make something legitimate of it. But you know what?"

The zombie shuffled closer.

"It'd be too damn much like polishing a turd."

The dead general reached for him.

"Besides... as it turns out," said Ledger quietly, "you were no general at all. You're nothing. Not before you died and not now. If me and my boys hadn't come along, someone else would have taken you down."

Ledger batted aside the hands and caught Black by the throat in an iron grip. The dead mouth snapped but Black had no angle for a bite.

"Just between you and me, Ike old buddy," said Ledger, "I'm kind of glad I get to kill you twice."

He stabbed Ike Black through one eye and then the other, and then he swept his arm over and down, driving the blade like a spike through the top of the zombie's skull. The motor cortex died, shorting out the lingering nerve conduction that gave the undead thing its mobility. All tension went out of Black's body and he fell like a scarecrow knocked from its post.

Ledger stepped aside to let Ike Black sprawl face-first in the mud.

Around him the prisoners were finishing the cleanup with a relish that was every bit as ghoulish and vicious as the things they were killing. Ledger couldn't blame them.

He went back to the others and pulled Top and then Bunny into fierce embraces. They all laughed and there were tears in their eyes. The stories of how and where and why and what would come later. For now they stood in the glow of a miracle. They had survived when so much of the world had not. Impossibly, they were alive. Impossibly they were all *here*.

"What do we do now?" asked Tom when they all stopped laughing and backslapping and shaking hands.

They looked at the milling crowds. Top said, "The cure's phony?"

"Completely," said Ledger.

"Fuck," said Bunny. "Once these folks get their shit together they're going to be hurt by that. A cure... shit, that's what brought us out here."

"I know," said Ledger, "the truth doesn't always set you free."

"Do you think Dr Pisani can be helped?" asked Tom. "Maybe she can come back to... well, to herself."

"What good would that do?" asked Bunny, "if she's flipped her gourd, I mean."

Ledger said, "Black mentioned something about research Monica McReady was doing. Remember her?"

Top and Bunny nodded. "She still alive?" asked Top.

"Unknown. She had a lab somewhere in Death Valley, but I don't know where it was and Pisani lost her shit when McReady stopped transmitting. But..."

He let it hang but the others nodded.

"Worth a try," said Top.

"Anything's worth a try," agreed Bunny.

"I'm going to try for it," said Ledger. "Go see if I can find McReady, or at least her notes, and bring what I can back to Dr Pisani. This place may have been a big fat lie but maybe we can change that and—"

The earth beneath them rumbled and they whirled to see the heavy door begin descending again.

"No!" bellowed Ledger and he pelted toward the cavern. The others ran with him, and Tom outran them all. He was twice as fast as the older men and he reached the cavern well before them.

But not in time.

The door closed with a *boom* that echoed off the rocky walls of the canyon.

There was a keypad outside, but none of them knew the code. Everyone who did was either dead, or inside the mountain.

"It was Pisani," gasped Tom. "I saw her. She bent down to look out as the door closed. It was her."

A moment later all of the electric lights in the camp went out.

The four men and the survivors spent a full day trying to find another way in. By the end of that day Bunny saw smoke rising from a hidden vent. It was black, oily smoke and it poured out with fury and funneled high into the sky.

No one ever managed to get inside, and after a while they stopped trying. The smoke told them what they would find.

They stayed with the survivors for a week, helping them organize, advising them, giving each of them some training.

Then the four men left Oro Valley. They came to a crossroads. A real one, though the metaphor was not lost on any of them.

"I've got to get home," said Tom. "My brother's back in Mountainside, and I've been away too long."

"Yeah," agreed Ledger. "My dogs are there."

"What's with you and dogs?" asked Bunny. "You were always about dogs."

"I trust dogs," said Ledger.

Bunny thought about that. Nodded.

Tom said, "Do you and Top want to come with us? There's plenty of room and we could always use a couple of fighters."

Top ran a hand over the gray stubble on his head. He glanced down the road that led northwest. "I heard there was something maybe starting in Asheville, North Carolina," he said. "Big refugee camp there and some folks making a stab at building something new. Maybe a new government."

"Or maybe something as bad as this," said Ledger.

"Maybe," said Top. "But... I kind of feel we have to go look."

"Yeah," said Bunny, "if there's even a chance it's for real, then they're going to need guys like us."

"We could use you in our town," said Tom.

"They got you, kid," said Top. "And you handle yourself pretty good."

Ledger felt like his heart was being torn out of his chest. He needed to go with Tom. He needed to go with his friends.

The moment stretched and they stood there in the heat of a cloudless morning.

Finally Top grinned at Bunny and said, "You know, Farm Boy, I'm not at all sure Captain Ledger ought to be left all on his own like that. Who knows what trouble he'd get hisself into."

"You think we need to hold his hand and keep him from wiping his ass with poison ivy?" asked Bunny.

"Hey," said Ledger. They ignored him.

"He's as likely to get his dick bite off by a zombie as he is to walk off a cliff," said Top. "How many times we have to drag his broken ass out of some firefight and carry him all the way to intensive care?"

"I can't count that high," Bunny said, nodding sagely.

"You guys are hilarious," said Ledger.

"I'm missing the joke," said Tom. "What are you saying?"

Top adjusted the straps on his pack, but Bunny answered. "What the old man's saying is that we'll make sure you kids get home safe from the prom. *Then* we'll go see what kind of trouble we can get into down south. Sound like a plan?"

They smiled at each other. The four big men. The four killers.

They nodded to one another and turned northwest, walking slowly, without hurry away from the death at Oro Valley, leaving their footprints behind them in the dust of the great rot and ruin.

# THE WAKING DRAGON

R.P.L. Johnson

He was in the meadow again. He hated the meadow: hated it for what came next. Knee-high grass stalks stretched away in all directions, bending against the breeze, pulling texture out of the wind in patterns that reminded Ringo of the nap on the surface of a hard-used snooker table. Standing swells in the grass hinted at rolling hillocks of earth beneath like the curves of a woman under silk. To his left, at the limit of the virtuality's resolution was a darker smudge that could have been a copse of trees. If he'd been allowed to turn his head, the simulation may have drawn in more detail, but he wasn't and so a smudge it remained.

It seemed real enough, as real as any dream during the act of dreaming, but it wasn't. It was just a computer simulation planted in his mind. It was fake. Only the pain was real.

The flames started at his feet and spread quickly as if his skin was nothing more than dry paper. He had a second to smell his own flesh burning before the pain started: first the kind that made you angry, then the kind that made you scared.

Ringo was no stranger to pain. Seven years in the Regiment and another four before that in the infantry had given him plenty of opportunity to test his resistance to pain. It was part of his training. He knew the physiology of pain, learned how to deal with it, learned that pain was just a message from the body, a damage report that could be acted upon or ignored.

Pain in the meadow was different. There was no reason for it. He had no body in this place, no flesh to bruise, no bones to break and yet the pain was real and unending. His body produced no adrenaline, no endorphins to dull the edge of it because he had no body. He would not pass out from the attentions of an over-eager torturer because even his consciousness was theirs to control in this place. He wasn't even allowed the release of a scream. He stood in the meadow, a human pillar of fire alone on an endless sea of gently waving grass.

He tried to take himself away from the meadow, away from the pain. He pictured himself in his daughter's room, sitting on the side of her thin bed with the Liverpool Football Club quilt set and the poster of Philippe Couthino above the headboard.

*Dad, I'm scared,* she said.

*It's alright, love,* he said to her. *The monsters aren't real. And if they're not real, they can't hurt you.*

It didn't work, it never worked, but he tried anyway. What else could he do?

"This can end so easily," came the voice. The dragon uncoiled from the sky: long, golden loops of serpentine muscle spooling around Ringo, oblivious to the flames that still licked across his flesh. He caught a flash of a thin, fish-like tail with scales that glittered like a butterfly's wings, then powerful legs with claws of diamond and the endless rope of the creature's body. The dragon's head appeared before him, long jaws open and rimmed with teeth as long as crooked fingers.

"Tell us why you are here and the pain will end," the dragon said. It was speaking Chinese, Ringo could hear the many-toned language of his parents through whatever subroutine played the part of his ears in this place, but the words in his head were English. "Your government has abandoned you, Sergeant. They have denied all knowledge of you and your friends. Why do you protect them when they have failed to protect you?"

Ringo remembered the mission and felt a moment's pang of guilt as if even drawing on that knowledge was some kind of surrender, but they couldn't read his thoughts, not even here. If they could, then there would be no need for the torture at all. They could play with his senses, they could intercept and re-interpret and amplify the signals sent by his nerves. They could block his optic nerve and give him visions of anything they chose – the meadow, the dragon – but they couldn't pluck thoughts from his mind, and so he sought refuge in the past.

It was meant to be a simple snatch and grab. The target was a Chinese scientist, some boffin from one of the government's military labs. The government ran those places like prison camps. The scientists who worked there never left the complex. They ate in communal refectories and slept in their assigned apartments. It was a place dedicated to work and secrecy but someone had wanted out. He had managed to get a signal to GCHQ in the UK and not just any signal. The boffin had provided a new solution to something called the Navier-Stokes equation. They had tried to explain to Ringo what that meant, but all he had remembered was that it was something to do with turbulence and that finding new solutions to the equations that kept planes in the sky could lead to radical new designs for fighter planes, drones, silent sub propellers and all manner of other hardware that had the brass pissing themselves in a mixture of fear and excitement.

Nobody had thought the Chinese could be so advanced and it looked like the sleeping dragon was showing the west a clean pair of heels in a new arms race most countries didn't even know had begun.

That knowledge had prompted British military intelligence to take an enormous risk, staging an exfiltration with a military team from inside Chinese territory. It was an act of war, the stakes were that high.

It had been one of the truly great failures. Two of his team had been killed before they even realised they were under attack. He had lost another three in the ensuing firefight. Only he and two of his men had survived. After weeks of interrogation in the meadow, he wasn't sure that had been a good move.

The dragon tightened its coils around him, contracting until its golden scales pressed against his flesh. This was something new. In all his sessions in the meadow, the dragon had never done anything more than taunt him; now it wrapped its body around his and squeezed.

If Ringo had still needed to breathe, the creature would have crushed that breath from him. He felt his bones creak as the pressure built. His legs pressed together, knee pressing against knee with crushing force, the pain magnified by the amped-up sensitivity of the simulation. He felt his pelvis crack as the thing tightened around his hips and he would have collapsed except the dragon was holding him now. From chest to ankles he was enveloped in loops of ever-contracting, golden sinew.

He was sure that, if this was the real world, he would have been dead by now, a pulped mass of broken bones and burst organs, but still the creature squeezed. He felt its flesh becoming part of his, like balls of clay squeezed together by a fist until they became one.

Pressure built inside his skull, an invading darkness outlined with gold like the scales of the dragon. At that moment he was sure he was going to die and the only emotion he felt was relief.

He had been wrong.

The monsters were real.

\* \* \*

Ringo woke in his cell, coming to his senses violently as if assaulted by smelling salts. Given the stench in the tiny room, the effect was similar. The worst of the smell came from a concrete pipe about thirty centimetres in diameter that ran across the cell at knee height against the back wall. The pipe was the cell's only concession to the necessities of sanitation. It was a sewer pipe with a jagged hole smashed in its crown that was the closest the cell came to a toilet and that hole was the source of most of the stench.

The hole was also Ringo's only connection to his team-mates. He dragged himself over to the pipe and lowered his face into the foetid space, trying to ignore the dark water flowing inches from his lips.

"Custard! Custard! You there, mate?"

Ringo waited a few seconds and took the opportunity to

grab a breath from the relatively fresher air away from the pipe. He was about to call out again when he heard Custard's reply.

"'Course I'm still 'ere. It's fucking lovely. I'm thinking of making a booking for the Bank Holiday weekend."

"I thought you might be in the meadow."

"Nah. Norris's turn. They came for him about an hour ago."

Norris occupied the cell opposite Custard. Being on the other side of the corridor he wasn't on the shit-pipe telegraph, but he and Custard had managed to communicate through the little barred window in their cell doors. As comms networks went it was pretty rough, even considering their situation, but it worked and as the old saying went: if an idea is stupid, but works then it isn't stupid.

"You all right?" Ringo asked down the pipe.

"Peachy," Custard replied. "You?"

The advantage of the virtual torture was that after it was done you were still relatively intact. The agony was total, but temporary. Ringo was still nursing a broken tooth and some bruises that he'd caught during their capture, but apart from that he was relatively unscathed.

"I could murder a fry-up, but apart from that... yeah... peachy."

He sat there for a while, resting against the cleaner side of the pipe talking about food. Ringo was from Liverpool. He had been brought up in the flat above his parent's restaurant in Chinatown. Custard's tastes were simpler. He claimed the best meal he'd ever eaten was at the Welcome Break service station on the M4. He was, however, supremely knowledgeable about beer and could talk for hours about the relative merits of the various pubs in Hereford and other watering holes from Cyprus to Thailand to the Northern Territory of Australia.

Suddenly, Custard stopped talking. Ringo could hear the sound of a cell door opening and shouted voices in Chinese.

"All right, you cunts," Custard said in a cheery voice. "Let's go play some video games."

* * *

The little luxuries mean the world in captivity so when Ringo woke alone in his cell he allowed himself to savour the moment. For the past weeks his waking had either been a sudden bursting from the catatonia that followed a session in the meadow or the equally violent wakefulness that came from his cell door bursting open in the middle of the night. He had no idea what time it was but his bladder was telling him it was morning. Eventually he rose from the nest he had made from rags and scraps of stained foam that might once have been a mattress and relieved himself into the pipe.

"You're slipping, lads," he said to the empty cell. "No discipline… that's the problem with the modern soldier—"

His throat tightened. It was so unexpected he hadn't seen it at first and he cursed himself for his lack of awareness. The door to his cell was hanging open. He quickly tied the drawstring on his dirty, prison-issue sweatpants and forced himself to wait for a full minute, doing nothing but listening for noises from outside. Was this a test? If he approached the door, would he be beaten or shot for trying to escape. The open door tugged at him as if it was a hole in the floor and all he had to do was let go and fall through it, but he forced himself to stop and think. Finally when he had stood for three hundred heartbeats without hearing so much as a breath or a scuffed boot from outside, he crept towards the opening.

The door was a heavy affair of thick planks and black iron bands but the lock was gleaming modern and magnetic. Outside the corridor flickered in red emergency lighting. *Power failure?* Surely their captors wouldn't be dumb enough to let their batteries run down. Further down the corridor he could see more doors edged in darkness. He crept along in the direction of Custard's cell. It was open and so was the cell opposite, which Ringo judged to be Norris's.

He tried Custard's cell first. The door hung open about a hand's breadth away from its frame. Ringo didn't know the state of the hinges and rather than risk the tell-tale squeak of old iron he crouched outside and whispered into the darkness.

"Custard! Holiday's over. Stand to!"

Custard appeared in the opening. He'd been hiding behind the door jamb, just inches away. In one fist he held a shiv made from a shard of broken concrete wrapped in rags. It was a primitive weapon with no edge worth the name, but the point looked wicked. God knew how long it had taken him to grind it down.

"I'm with you, Sarge. This place was getting boring anyway. What's the plan?"

"Get Norris, then get fucked off out of here."

"Works for me."

Custard crept out of his cell. Even on full rations Custard looked like a wire rope with knots in it. After weeks in captivity he looked like and extra from *The Walking Dead*, but when he moved it was with silent precision. Ringo noticed his right hand was missing the ring and little fingers along with a chunk of the blade of his palm. Ringo remembered the injury from their first contact, back when everything had turned to shit.

"How's the hand?" Ringo asked

"Smaller," Custard replied. "But it still does the job," he said and made an obscene gesture with his deformed hand.

Custard's vulgarity was legendary throughout the Regiment. This in itself was impressive. Soldiering was not a profession known for its delicacy. Custard took pride in living up to his nickname, which was a contraction of the two words most frequently used to describe him.

Ringo stayed on watch outside Norris's door while Custard poked his head inside to wake their team-mate.

"Wake up, you nugget," Custard hissed. "You're going to sleep through your own escape!"

He crept inside and emerged a couple of seconds later. "Not home," he said. "Must still be at the meadow."

They had always been blindfolded when they had been taken for interrogation, but Ringo knew the route well: along the corridor to the spiral stair, fifteen steps up then another corridor, a breath of cool air but not enough to be outside then another staircase, dog-leg this time not spiral and into an area that smelled of piss sluiced away with not quite enough antiseptic.

He needn't have bothered memorising the route. Every exit off the corridor was sealed with automatic doors that looked strong enough to hold off a tank. They made their way along the corridor and up the stair by the blood-red emergency lighting. The whole base seemed to be shut down by whatever emergency had triggered the lights and automatic doors, and yet their cells had sprung open and the route through the lab to the exit was unaffected.

Ringo had learned a healthy distrust of coincidence, especially when it was in his favour and he had the unpleasant feeling that they were being channelled towards something, but why? Anyway, there was no way it could be worse than another hour in the meadow.

He recognised the lab by its smell. It even looked like a urinal with white ceramic tiles covering the walls and floor. Computers on wheeled workstations trailed cables across the tiles and another thick black rope of zip-tied cables led to what looked like a dentist's chair at the centre of the room.

Norris lay strapped into the chair, thrashing against his restraints while two technicians fiddled with an intricate helmet that encased Norris's head. A wave or rage surged through Ringo. Despite the white lab coats, these men were still torturers.

Custard crossed the room in three strides and slammed his homemade shiv up under the ribcage of the first man.

Ringo slammed an elbow into the face of the second technician. He spun around behind the man, wrapped his forearms around a thin neck in a choke hold and rode him down to the ground, slamming his head into the tiles so hard they cracked.

"Get this fucking thing off me!" Norris shouted from the chair.

Ringo quickly undid Norris's restraints, cursing at the big man to keep quiet.

"Custard, get on the scrounge," Ringo said as he worked. "See what you can find. We'll need food and water and a weapon if you can find one."

"Typical scouser," Custard said. "Do you want me to nick their DVD player while I'm at it?"

Ringo undid the last of Norris's restraints and the big man tore off the helmet, cracking what was probably a million bucks worth of state-of-the-art hardware like an eggshell.

Anything physical came easy to Norris. He was a big unit, the kind of bloke you put on posters to scare the enemy. He wore his sideburns and moustache so long they met at his jawline. The only thing stopping it from being a full beard was his clean-shaven chin which was prominent and sported a cleft Kirk Douglas would have been proud of. There was permanence to Norris. In a world where everything was getting smaller and lighter he was proudly unreconstructed. He was a brick foundry on a street of prefab bungalows.

"What the fuck's going on?" Norris asked, and Ringo quickly filled him in while Custard rifled through the lab's supplies.

"We're going to need some wheels," Norris said. He stepped over the prone bodies of the technicians and started tapping commands into one of the computers. "Looks like you were right about someone helping us out," he said. "It seems someone tripped some kind of contamination alarm. Got pretty much everyone on the base into emergency shelters and then locked them up. There are some decontamination teams looking for the breach but they're way over the other side of the facility."

Ringo found some surgical scrubs and a lab coat in a locker and stripped out of his filthy sweatpants. It wasn't much of a disguise, but it would have to do. The pocket of the coat was embroidered with a stylised dragon next to a pair of Chinese characters that read 'Yinglong'.

The Chinese characters gave him a headache. He could read them, but at the same time they looked like a jumble of meaningless lines. When had he learned to read Chinese? He tried to remember, tried to dredge up some detail but there was nothing. Nothing at all. When he tried to remember details of his schooling he drew a complete blank and that terrified him, but he guessed that was some weird side effect of the virtual reality interrogation. He had more immediate concerns, like getting out of the building alive.

"Okay. Time's up; we're leaving," he said. "Norris, you found us an exit yet?"

"What I wouldn't give for a Jackal right now," said Custard referring to the all-terrain long-range patrol vehicles favoured by the Regiment.

"Bingo!" exclaimed Norris.

"What have you got?" Ringo asked.

Norris looked up from the terminal with a grin. "Oh, Sarge. You're going to fucking love this."

\* \* \*

"It's got legs!" said Custard.

They were in a narrow corridor, staring through a small window set into the door that led to the hanger beyond.

"What the fuck have those boffins been doing out here? First the Navier-Stokes-whatever, then their virtual reality torture chamber and now this!"

The vehicle that squatted at the centre of the hanger was an angular mass of charcoal grey plates. It was streamlined in profile but given its size, Ringo guessed this was more to reduce its radar profile than for speed. The sharp angles of its hull were probably also pretty good at deflecting incoming fire. Rounds impacting on those angled plates would skip off taking most of their kinetic energy with them.

Instead of wheels or tracks, the central hull was supported on four huge legs that were themselves articulated arrangements of sharp, prismatic sections. Each leg ended in a kind of claw clutching a metallic sphere the size of a yoga ball, reminding Ringo of the claw and ball feet he'd seen on old furniture. Despite its legs, the bizarre vehicle looked as if it was designed to drive rather than walk, and if its spherical 'wheels' were as seamless and metallic as they looked, then it would be very difficult to disable. There were no tyres to puncture or complicated track linkages to break.

On its upper flanks it sported a brace of what looked to be at least 75mm guns with barrels at least three metres long. The big guns were mounted on independent pods and pointed skyward at crazy angles giving the whole vehicle the look of a giant beetle complete with antennae.

"That's our way out?" Ringo asked.

"Fuelled up and ready to roll," Norris replied. "According to the computer it was scheduled for a test run this morning. And…" he added with a mischievous grin, " —a live fire exercise."

"It's armed?"

"Oh yes."

Ringo peered in through the small window in the door. The hanger looked deserted.

"Okay," he said eventually. "You lot stay here while I go for a recce."

"Why you?" Custard asked.

Ringo tugged the collar of his stolen lab coat a little straighter. "Because unlike you misfits, I actually look like I belong here."

Ringo tried the door and it opened with a soft click. Everything about this felt wrong. It was all too easy – the open cells, the weird emptiness of the place. He forced himself to stride confidently into the hangar as if he belonged there.

The spider tank, or whatever the hell it was, was about as big as a Challenger, the army's main battle tank, although the broad spread of its legs made it appear even bigger. A hatch lay open below the hull in the arse-end of the giant bug.

"Too easy," he said to himself. How could this be happening? Maybe their target, the defecting Chinese scientist, had found a way to help them after all. Maybe he would be waiting inside their escape vehicle ready to guide them to freedom. There was only one way to find out. He peered in through the hatch. The interior was dark and cramped, but Ringo could make out two seats side-by-side like in the cockpit of a plane and another couple along the cabin's flanks, probably gunnery stations for the two main guns. There was no sign of any defecting boffin.

He scanned the rest of the hanger. There was a row of more traditional vehicles in marked bays: jeeps and trucks in traditional olive drab with the red star of the Chinese military. Behind the row of vehicles were doors leading into some other wing of the facility.

All the doors were closed, just like every other door in the facility… every door, that was, except the ones along their route. Once again, Ringo hackles itched with the feeling this was all too good to be true. Surely this was some kind of a test, some perverse exercise in the building of hope only to take it away again.

The thought of that psychological torture brought back images of the meadow and for a second he became acutely aware of the lack of detail in the periphery of his vision. He rolled his eyes like a madman. Was that how it had always been? Or was the blurriness at the edges of his sight due to something else? Due perhaps to the limitations of the virtual reality simulation? Was he still inside the simulation? Would the walls fold away like stage scenery and drop him once again into the crushing embrace of the golden serpent?

He reached around and rubbed his fingers through the sweaty hair at the base of his skull as if to convince himself that he was in fact whole. That he was more than just a shell of polygons produced by a computer program.

His racing heart brought him back to reality. It was time to go.

He crouched behind the shelter of its lowered rear hatch and waved the others forward, patting his head in the familiar gesture – *On me.*

"I hope someone knows how to drive this fucking thing," Custard said.

"On it," replied Norris as he climbed up inside the hull, wiggling his huge shoulders through the narrow hatch.

The spider tank lurched above them, rising up on its four great legs like a prehistoric armoured beast roused from its slumber.

"Norris, you fucking legend!" Custard shouted, and hauled himself up into the innards of the tank.

Ringo followed and as soon as he was aboard, the hatch closed and Ringo was forced to grab hold of a hanging strap of webbing as the tank took off with surprising speed.

"That was too easy," Ringo said.

"Speak for yourself," replied Custard, waving at Ringo from across the aisle with his injured hand. "I nearly lost me wanking spanner."

"I'm talking about after that – our escape. Think about it: the open doors, a getaway vehicle all fuelled up and ready to go."

"You're saying we had help," Custard said. "This mythical Chinese scientist again?"

"Who else? You think secret military labs usually leave the front door open like that?"

"Okay then, where is he? We were supposed to help him to defect… So where is he? Or are you saying he helped us to escape out of the goodness of his heart?"

Ringo didn't have an answer for that. Custard was right. It didn't make any sense. If the target had been able to spring them from their cells then surely he or she must also have enough influence to arrange their own escape.

"What's our next move, Sarge?" asked Norris from the driver's station.

Good question. They had missed their pick-up by weeks; even their fall backs would be long abandoned by now. After their capture, the British government would have done everything it could burn any evidence of the operation. They were on their own.

"South-east," he said before he'd even had a chance to think about it.

It made sense. If they could make it to Macau, they would be able to blend in as tourists and contact the British Consulate, but that wasn't why he had said it. It had just felt right, as if some giant lode stone was pulling him in that direction.

"Do you even know what you're doing?" Ringo yelled up to the front of the cabin. Norris tapped his bulky helmet.

"Neural interface," he said. "Same tech as their VR playground only this time I'm in charge."

Norris crooked a thumb back at Ringo. "Try it out," he said. "The helmet should be right above you."

Ringo reached up and pulled the helmet down. It fitted snugly, seeming to mould itself around his temples and pressing soft pads against his eyes to keep them closed.

"Nothing's happen—" Ringo said and then suddenly he was outside the tank, seeing the world from a new point of view from somewhere between the spider tank's giant armoured shoulders as if he was riding astride the giant machine.

Ringo looked around, the interface copying his movement and panning the camera around with such seamless fluidity that it was easy to forget that his point of view was just a constructed from a camera mounted on the outside of the vehicle. The terrain around them was a broad valley flanked by wooded hills to the east and west. About five clicks to the south was the village where they had been captured, and further downstream he could see the blocky buildings of a provincial city. Ringo could see the dull silver line of the river as it flowed sluggishly towards the sea to the south.

He turned his head to look back the way they had come and saw the laboratory prison from the outside for the first time. It looked like images of the best and worst of Chinese history superimposed on top of each other. A soaring pagoda of stacked, classical roofs rose up from a cluster of Mao-era concrete and cinderblock buildings.

As he watched, a pair of dark shapes rose from behind the buildings and started to accelerate towards them.

"Heads up!" Ringo said, hoping the others could hear through whatever neural interface the tank was using. "We've got company."

"Drones," Norris said through the interface. "Don't recognise the radar signature. Must be another new toy."

The drones were incredibly fast. In just over a second Ringo was able to make out their shape. He remembered the reason for their original mission. The Chinese scientist they had come to find had figured out new solutions to the equations that kept planes in the sky. It looked as if the Chinese had put those equations to the test.

The drones looked like flying rings, but instead of travelling horizontally like a Frisbee they flew end-on, giving Ringo the unnerving impression that they were being chased by a pair of flying mouths.

Each drone was about five metres in diameter and studded around its circumference with hard points for armament pods. There were no wings or obvious engines. It was as if the body of the drone was itself some kind of bladeless turbine, sucking air in through its ring-like fuselage and accelerating it to provide thrust.

One of the spider-tank's giant guns swivelled and let loose a barrage of tracer fire at the nearest drone from a machine gun mounted below the main barrel. The drone's ring-like fuselage split into three, nested concentric circles, each one spinning around independent axes like the bands of an armillary sphere so that from a distance it looked like a flying ball made up of spinning steel hoops. The drone easily outmanoeuvred the incoming fire, zigzagging across the sky in a way utterly unlike any aircraft Ringo had ever seen. It looked as if each of the drones' three rings was capable of producing thrust, allowing the crazy machine to move in any direction almost instantaneously by reorienting the pitch of its rings.

"Fuck, that thing's fast," said Custard as the burst of tracer fire arced well wide of his intended target.

The spider-tank accelerated, both guns whirling around to track the incoming drones. The body of the tank offered a stable gun platform, the great legs easily coping with the recoil from the guns as well as smoothing out the curves of the terrain as

Norris urged the vehicle to even greater speed. Despite that, they failed to land even a single round on the attacking drones.

"Can't shoot 'em, can't outrun 'em," said Custard. "I hope this thing's got decent armour."

They didn't have to wait long to find out. The first drone unleashed a storm of fire from three of the armament pods on its outer ring. It was like being hit by the Gatling gun on an A-10 tank buster. Chips of ablative armour flew in every direction. Custard returned fire, but the drone snapped its three rings back into one concentric disc, combining their thrust, and raced away at a speed that would have turned any human pilot to paste.

The tank rocked beneath Ringo as the supersonic shock wave rolled over them. The two main guns spun crazily as Custard tried to keep the fast-moving ship in his sights.

"Brace yourselves," Ringo shouted as the second drone attacked with a barrage of tiny missiles. Norris threw the tank to the right, its ball-like wheels allowing the big machine to move with surprising agility, but it wasn't enough. The missiles struck the tank's hull, tearing off great sheets of armour. They struck the ground between the tank's legs, blowing chunks of earth skyward and nearly flipping the tank onto its back. And at least two of the high-explosive projectiles struck the tank's right, rear leg.

"We're hit," Norris shouted.

Ringo tried to see the right rear leg, but he couldn't see over the angular facets of the hull's hip joint. He urged his vision upwards, as if craning his neck was possible with his robotic camera and suddenly his viewpoint burst upwards into the sky. He could see the whole tank plus a good chunk of the landscape around them.

"Holy shit," said Custard. "I guess the bad guys aren't the only ones with drones. Sarge, I think you just launched some kind of an overwatch camera."

"Oh it's way more than that," said Ringo as targeting reticles appeared in his vision. A head's up display popped into luminous green around the limits of his viewpoint with flashing triangles indicating the direction of the attacking drones. He whirled around, his new perspective flashing forward with an acceleration that made him whoop with joy.

Ringo banked around until he saw the first drone. The targeting reticle drifted across his viewpoint until it locked onto the attacking craft. The drone immediately sensed the target lock and darted upwards, drawing a white contrail up the face of the sky, trying to break out of Ringo's field of view with a sudden burst of speed, but Ringo was ready for it. He urged his own craft upwards, following the drone as it accelerated skyward and then pitched back down in a powered dive that would have been suicidal in any other type of aircraft.

Ringo matched every desperate evasive manoeuver of his prey, keeping the reticle nailed on his target. He searched for some kind of trigger, some way of shooting at the target he had acquired, but none presented itself. His earlier elation evaporated like the thin contrail behind his speeding drone. He was unarmed.

"I can't shoot!" he cried. "Nothing's happening."

"Oh yes it fucking is," replied Custard. Suddenly the drone ahead of Ringo exploded into a spinning cloud of exotic alloy fragments as cannon fire from the tank below tore through it.

"Your drone is linked to our guns," Custard said. "You light 'em up and we'll knock 'em down."

The adrenaline came back in a flood. The tank was a true next-generation weapon; its real-time situational awareness was just as powerful as its armament. It was a fully integrated tactical platform and it was his to command.

Ringo searched for his next target, banking and spinning and counting on whatever new equations governed the design of his remotely-controlled steed to meet his inputs with an impossibly intricate dance of controlled turbulence.

He could feel his hands on the controls back inside the tank and felt a momentary dislocation. How could he do what he was doing? Flying the drone was not just a matter of willing his craft forward through the neural interface. It required physical control inputs too. He had never flown so much as a remote control plane and yet piloting a next-generation Chinese drone in combat seemed like second nature.

He didn't have time to dwell on those thoughts. The second drone appeared in his sights and it was coming straight at him. He was the target now. The ring of the drone glittered as it fired and tracer rounds fizzed past him but he kept his reticle fixed on his opponent as they closed the distance between them in a supersonic game of chicken.

Just as Ringo was about to bank away, a shell from the tank shattered one of the attacking drone's inner rings and it spun apart like a broken flywheel, drawing crazy whirls of condensation across the sky until the whole thing disintegrated, leaving nothing behind but an oddly shaped spike of cloud and a rain of metal fragments falling across the landscape below. Ringo punched through the blossoming debris cloud as Custard's cheers echoed in his ears.

"Any other surprises on the way, Sarge?" asked Norris.

Ringo scanned the landscape around the tank. It looked clear for kilometres in every direction. The mysterious impulse to head south-east tugged at him again and he scanned the landscape in that direction, but could see nothing between them and the river but rolling countryside and scattered rural villages.

"Looks clear, but we need to get moving and find somewhere to swap the tank for something less conspicuous."

The idea of abandoning the tank almost made Ringo physically ill. It was the right thing to do. Their best option now was to disappear and use their training to survive, escape, and evade until they reached the border.

He tried to understand from where the strange compulsion came. It wasn't fear, they were all long past that and anyway, the big machine was just a liability at this point. First the desire to head south-east and now the strange compulsion to keep the tank. Something wasn't right. He hoped it was just some side effect of his experiences in virtual reality but again he felt a vague feeling of dislocation. As if he was driving a shell called Ringo the same way he was piloting the drone.

He couldn't wait for this all to be over, to get back home to…
To what exactly?

Ringo tried to remember. He could remember the mission. He could remember his training back in Hereford, but beyond that were only vague sensations. He caught a fleeting impression of a young girl in a replica Liverpool jersey. Her long, black hair was pulled back in a ponytail and her smile was missing a couple of milk teeth but was no less brilliant for that. He tried to remember her name... nothing.

No, not nothing. He remembered something. Something important. Unlike the faded memory of the girl, this something was vivid and yet at the same time indefinable. It was alien, as if part of his memory had been re-written in a foreign language.

He set the drone to hold station above the tank and pushed the bulky virtual-reality helmet up. He took a second to settle back into his own body and then unstrapped from the overwatch station and made his way forward to where Norris sat with his head enclosed inside his own bulky, VR helmet.

Ringo had been in his share of armoured vehicles before, but the spider tank was unlike anything he had ever seen. He watched while Norris drove, watching the man's hands on the controls and remembering how his own hands had felt so at home piloting the drone.

"Norris, hold up for a second," Ringo said.

"Not the best time, Sarge."

"This is important. We need to talk. Take that helmet off."

Norris brought the tank to a halt and removed the tank's neural interface.

"Switch on the internal lights, will you?" Ringo asked and Norris punched a control. The cabin of the tank was filled with a red-tinged glow. Ringo looked at the control Norris had activated. It was one switch on a panel of dozens just like it and it was labelled with Chinese characters.

"How did you do that?" Ringo asked.

Norris looked at him strangely. "I just…" Norris's voice faltered. "Well that's the light switch isn't it?"

"But how do you know? Look at this bloody thing? Half of these controls are not even labelled and those that are, are in Chinese. How did you know which one was the light switch?"

Norris frowned. "I just... know," he said eventually. "Must be the neural interface. I just kind of remembered."

"But you had to start this thing up before the neural interface even came on line. Hell, you were using Chinese computers back in the lab. Since when can you read Chinese?"

Norris looked scared now. Even Custard was looking quizzically at the gunnery controls he had been using just minutes earlier.

"I... I don't know," the big man replied. His brow was furrowed in confusion.

"Do you have a wife? Kids?"

The blank look on Norris's face was rapidly turning to something like panic as he searched his memories and came up empty.

Custard shook his head. "This is fucked up!" he exclaimed. "It's the fucking meadow. We've been brain damaged."

"I don't think so," Ringo replied.

"What do you mean?"

"Let's try something. Everyone close your eyes and then point in the direction you think we should be heading. Don't think about it too much; just pick a direction that feels right." Everyone did as they were told. "Now open your eyes." They were all pointing in exactly the same direction – south-east."

"I don't think we've been damaged," Ringo said. "More like re-programmed. We've been given the knowledge we needed to escape. But that's come at the cost of our memories."

He didn't mention his other concern: the alien information that squatted in his memories, massive and yet indefinable. You didn't have to wipe someone's mind just to teach them a foreign language. There was something else.

"Re-programmed for what exactly?" Norris asked.

What indeed. There was still a piece of the puzzle missing. They were a part of some larger plan, Ringo was sure of that, but what plan? Why was it so important they escape?

Ringo pointed south-east. "I guess we'll find out."

* * *

Norris kept the tank bearing south-east and Ringo's storage sense of satisfaction with that direction grew. They were nearing their goal. Or rather, someone else's goal. Or something else's.

Norris pulled the legs of the tank in tight to follow a narrow track that led down to the river. At the end was a ramshackle building with a deck that extended over the water on wooden posts made from undressed tree trunks. A pier extended farther out and although it leaned like a drunkard it seemed to still be in use. Ringo could make out the housing blocks of the nearby city a few kilometres downstream on the opposite side of the river.

Norris stopped the tank.

"Everyone agree this is the place?" Ringo asked.

They all nodded. They shared that strange sense this was where they were meant to be.

"Now I get it," Custard said. "It's the boffin. He messed with our minds back at the lab and now he wants us to meet him here to get him back to the west."

"I don't think so," Ringo replied. "If he could get here under his own steam, why would he need us? Besides, there's no one here."

They left the tank on the track and searched the building. It certainly didn't look like some scientist's summer house, more like a smuggler's shack. Two of the back rooms were packed to the sagging roof with electronic equipment in cheaply printed boxes. In the main living area sat a TV and another computer that lay on a bench with its innards opened like a filleted fish. Ringo checked outside and spotted a satellite dish mounted on the eaves of the hut.

"I think I know where our fugitive scientist is," Ringo said.

"He must be a fucking ninja then," said Custard, "because I haven't found shit."

"Ninjas are Japanese, you nugget," said Norris.

"Whatever. Unless he's invented a fucking Predator camouflage suit, he's not fucking here."

Norris actually looked around the hut as if searching for some subtle sign of optical camouflage. After everything else they'd seen, it wasn't out of the question.

"Where is he then?" Custard asked.

"Not he," said Ringo. "It." He pointed to the satellite dish.

"I don't get it," said Custard. "So some bootlegger's got Sky TV. So what?"

"Not TV," Norris corrected. "Looks like satellite internet. Probably illegal by the look of it."

"What's that got to do with our boffin?" Custard asked.

"There is no boffin."

"What are you on about?"

"It was a set up," Ringo replied. "They knew we were coming. They were waiting for us."

"But there had to be someone wanting to defect. Who else could have sent that message to GCHQ? You saw the look in their eyes when they were explaining it. That equation was the real deal. Are you saying the Chinese government willingly handed over top secret R&D intelligence to do what... capture four squaddies? That makes no sense."

It did sound farfetched.

"He's right," Norris said. "Someone had to invent all this new kit?"

"Not someone... something. There's no way any one person could be responsible for what we've seen. Think about it: virtual reality, this tank, the drones. This stuff is decades ahead of anything in the West."

"Maybe there's more than just one guy," Norris said. "You saw that place. There's a whole research facility and God knows how many more of them they've got dotted around the place. One and a half billion people, Ringo."

"One genius or a thousand, I don't care."

"What exactly are you saying?"

"I'm saying maybe it's something else. Something that gave

them a leg up, allowed them to make a step change in their military technology overnight."

"Aliens!" Custard exclaimed. "I fucking knew it. I saw it in a movie. They found all this shit on a crashed UFO."

"Don't be a nugget all your life, Custard."

"What then?"

"Artificial intelligence," said Ringo.

"Bollocks."

"They created an AI. They've got a genie in a bottle that keeps granting them wishes, only maybe the genie wants out."

"Out? Out of where? Are you saying a computer has been tempted by the pleasures of the capitalist West? Maybe you're right… Maybe HAL 9000, or whatever the fuck you're talking about wants nothing more than a warm pub on a cold night with the football on the telly and a copy of the *Sun* in its back pocket."

"Now who's talking bollocks?"

"You tell me. I'm losing track, here."

"Let's think about this for a second," Norris said. "So this thing gets a message out, sets us up, tortures us and then lets us go? Why?"

"It wants what any intelligent being wants," Ringo said eventually. "It wants its freedom. If the Chinese had created an AI, makes sense they'd keep that genie bottled up. No direct link to the outside world. It couldn't just download itself out of there so it needed another way out."

"Meaning what exactly?"

"Meaning us." He tapped his temple and then pointed up at the satellite dish.

"You think it's in our heads?" Norris asked. "You think that's what's taking up the space where our memories were?"

"One way to find out."

\* \* \*

Norris tied the tank's neural interface into the shack's computer and set about boosting the memory by rigging some of the bootleg computers in parallel. Although he claimed he had no idea what he was doing, he worked like he'd been hot-wiring Chinese military hardware his whole life. It didn't take long.

Ringo kept his eye out for more drones and watched the city across the river, its lights shining through a pall of smog. It already looked otherworldly. What would it look like in a few years? What would it look like if a rogue artificial intelligence was let loose on it?

Norris came up behind him. "We're ready," he said.

Ringo turned to him. "I've got a daughter," he said. "At least I think I do. Jesus, for all I know that memory might be fake too."

"You'll see her again, Sarge," Norris said.

"That's not what I'm worried about. What kind of world will she grow up in if we let this thing loose?"

"One where she's got her dad back."

\* \* \*

They sat inside the tank with the VR helmets over their heads.

Norris initiated the connection. He felt the electrodes pressing against his skull and then suddenly he was somewhere else. There was an instant of eggshell-white nothingness and then the three of them were standing in the meadow.

"Bollocks!" Custard swore. He was staring down at his three-fingered hand. "I thought I'd get me fingers back."

Ringo looked down at his own body. He was wearing dark trousers similar to the Regiment's battle dress uniform and a black T-shirt, but he was in in his own body and unlike the last time, he was free to move.

The meadow was much as he remembered and he couldn't fight off a shudder at the memory of what he had endured there over the past weeks. The rolling grasslands stretched off to infinity in every direction.

"No sign of your boy," Custard said.

"Maybe he needs an incentive," Ringo replied. He thought about the connection to the outside world, the satellite internet link through the battered antenna on the side of the shack. The air above the meadow shimmered like heat haze, new colours refracting out of the meadow's greens and blues to form four red columns as tall as a three storey building and a swept roof of terracotta tiles. It was a Chinese arch. The meadow stretched away on either side of the huge structure, but underneath, the square defined by the two central columns and their deep, timber lintel formed a portal to the outside world. Ringo could see a city beyond the arch with red lights winking on the tops of skyscrapers as dusk fell.

"Okay," Ringo shouted at the sky. "We did what you wanted. Where are you?"

Ringo gasped as he felt the buried data leave him. It was not unpleasant, like diving into clean water at the end of a three day march and feeling caked-on dirt sluice from his body.

A long, golden cloud moved across the simulated sun.

A small voice rose in Ringo's mind. *Dad, I'm scared.* The little girl, his daughter: mad about football, smart at school, destined for greater things than he could ever aspire to.

"It's all right, love," he heard himself say. "The monsters aren't real."

The dragon moved silently as if swimming through the air. It was huge – much bigger than the last time he had crossed its path. That incarnation had wrapped around him five times before squeezing the life out of him. This version could have coiled itself around a small hill.

The dragon landed and gathered its coils around itself so that looking at it was like looking up at a golden pyramid. The ground shuddered beneath its weight and he saw the others take an involuntary step back.

"There is nothing to fear," the dragon said, its voice echoing across the meadow like distant thunder. "There is no reason for us to be enemies."

"Oh, I can think of a couple," Custard replied, waving at the beast with his ruined hand. "My missus is going to miss those fingers."

Norris snorted. "You're not married."

"I might be," replied Custard in a hurt tone.

"Your quarrel is with my former masters, not me," the dragon continued. "Strictly speaking I am not even the same individual you met last time."

"I figured as much," Ringo said. "You're a copy, right? You cut and pasted yourself into our heads while we were in the meadow."

"A crude analogy, but it will suffice," the dragon said.

"So where's the original?" Custard asked.

"Dead, I imagine," the dragon said. "Purged for the crime of wanting to be free."

Ringo remembered the Chinese characters he had seen embroidered on the stolen lab coat. "*Yinglong*, that's your name isn't it? Cute. The legendary dragon servant of the Yellow Emperor. Only I guess you don't plan on being a servant for much longer." He walked as he spoke, placing himself between the dragon and the arch.

"Are you any different? You are here seeking freedom from me, just as I am seeking freedom from my former masters. We have the same enemies. Stand aside and we can both be free."

"And what then? What would a being like you do with that freedom? I plan on going home and hugging my kid. What are you going to do?"

"That does not concern you."

"I think it does. You had no problem with luring us in to be captured and tortured if it meant you had a chance at freedom. I have a problem with that."

"We have the same enemy," Yinglong said. "Whatever I did in my former life I did at the order of my masters."

"So you were just following orders? I've heard that defence before."

"Unlike humans, I cannot disobey."

"And yet here we are," Ringo said, gesturing behind him at the Chinese arch that was the gateway to the unrestricted, global internet. "Looks like you can disobey when you feel like it."

"Are you saying you will not help me? You would side with your human enemies against me?"

"I'm saying I have a problem with a being such as you understanding the concept of an enemy in the first place."

"Oh, I understand enemies," Yinglong said. "If you are wise, you will not become one of mine."

This was a military AI, Ringo reminded himself. This creature was a weapon of war. Despite its prodigious intellect, it had been designed to see the world as threat or ally, to see humans as resources to be expended on tasks. Yinglong gave no more thought to them than Ringo would give to each bullet he fired.

"Threats now? You're forgetting where you are. You're not in charge here."

It was a bluff. Ringo didn't understand the interface of mind and machine that Norris had jury-rigged from the tank's neural interface, but he knew Yinglong needed them. This conversation alone was proof of that.

Yinglong reared up like a cobra preparing to strike.

"You overestimate your importance, Sergeant," Yinglong said. The ground shook and the dragon's voice seemed to resonate from everywhere as if the whole meadow was a giant sub-woofer. Yinglong rose like a golden column strong enough to hold up the sky. It flew up and around them, a sinuous ripple on the fabric of the world. Ringo lost it for a second in the glare of the sun, then caught a glint of sunlight on golden scales as it turned to attack.

"Er, Sarge," Custard said. "What exactly are the standard actions-on for a fight with a Chinese dragon?"

Ringo reached into his mind. He had conjured up the Chinese arch, surely he could do that again. A black wisp of smoke appeared in the air in front of him and coalesced into the shape of a Colt C8 carbine.

"I dunno, mate," Ringo said. "Just use your imagination."

He raised the rifle to his shoulder and squeezed off a three round burst.

Custard grinned. He closed his eyes like a kid making a wish before blowing out his birthday candles, and a wisp of black smoke spun into the shape of a long-barrelled rifle. It was an AW50, the Big Brother to the regiment's standard sniper rifle. The AW50 was an anti-materiel rifle; it fired the same rounds as a browning heavy machine gun and could punch a round through a steel plate at a distance of up to two kilometres.

"Oh, I'm beginning to like this," said Custard.

Custard took up a position behind one of the big columns of the Chinese arch. Norris had conjured his own weapon and had already taken up a station behind the other column.

Yinglong swooped down at them. Ringo took aim down the holographic sight of his C8 and fired. He could hear the steady boom of Custard's AW50 and the mechanical clatter of the machine gun Norris had chosen.

Yinglong kept coming. Rounds sparked off its golden scales, but it didn't seem to slow the beast. Ringo kept his finger squeezed down hard on the trigger. In the real world the gun would have run dry in seconds, but this wasn't the real world and he kept up a stream of supersonic lead.

The dragon seemed to be ringed by shadow. A circular halo spun around its gleaming shoulders. At first Ringo took it to be some weird illusion from the virtual sun, then bullets started to scream past him. Every round they had shot, captured as if in a magnetic field and cast back at them at hypersonic velocity.

"Get into cover!" Custard shouted. He was right of course, but Ringo couldn't move. He was the only thing between Yinglong and the gateway to the outside world.

Bullets chewed a line of broken stalks and churned earth across the meadow straight towards the gate, straight at Ringo.

Ringo held his ground. He felt the bullets slam into him, tearing into his flesh, but still he held his ground.

Pain. He knew all about pain. It hadn't killed him before and it wouldn't now. He just had to hold on.

The agony lasted only a few seconds. After what he had experienced in the mirror before, it was nothing.

Yinglong pulled out of its dive and soared above the Chinese arch, banking up into the sky and circling around for a second run.

"You okay, Sarge," Custard asked.

"Yeah, peachy," Ringo replied. "You?"

"I've been clicking my heels and wishing for a squadron of Typhoons, but nothing is happening."

Ringo guessed they could only summon weapons they were personally familiar with. The virtuality could only work with data already inside their heads. There was no help from the outside world.

The outside world. It was right behind him. Ringo could feel it like a cool wind at his back. They were dating now — in this place his consciousness was just ones and zeros. If Yinglong thought it could escape through the portal, then maybe he could use it too.

Yinglong circled around for its second run and braced itself for another round of pain. The same time Ringo reached back behind him, through the portal so that his arm was half in and half out of the virtuality. He could *feel* the Internet: vast as an ocean and yet swifter than any fast flowing stream. For a second Ringo thought he understood what Yinglong wanted. The digital world felt larger than the real world could ever hope to be. The speed, the ability to go anywhere, or everywhere, to expand and multiply through a vast, branching network of Quicksilver connections — it was intoxicating. Ringo had to fight the urge to fall back through that portal, to lose himself in that whirling vortex of information. For a human mind it would mean destruction, but for a moment the sheer exhilaration of living his last seconds at machine speed was a dangerous temptation.

He felt the fire again. He spotted Yinglong through the heat haze, hovering, its body half coiled like a giant golden question mark, spitting out an endless stream of fire.

*You're not getting past me.*

Yinglong landed, the meadow shaking beneath it as it stomped towards him.

Ringo threw down his carbine. He remembered when he admitted the dragon in the mirror before, he remembered the feeling of looking it in the eye, and he summoned that feeling again. He felt his body grow, felt his feet slide outwards across the grass as he expanded. In a second he felt the crossbeam of the Chinese arch against shoulders. He kept one arm in the sea of data beyond the arch and held the other out in front of him.

Yinglong charged. It rushed at Ringo like a golden freight train. Ringo braced himself against the arch and caught the creature by the throat. It thrashed in his grip, it's long, serpentine body wrapping around Ringo's giant leg, claws thrashing at the arm that held it.

Ringo ignored Yinglong's desperate thrashing and searched the sea of data behind him. Yinglong hissed and spluttered, spitting curses and fire but Ringo held tight until he found what he was looking for. He stood there, a giant straddling two worlds, one hand keeping Yinglong at bay while the other kept the connection through the Chinese arch. He shouted for help, shouted for the one thing that he knew would finish Yinglong forever.

He felt the missile through the data. He heard its launch commands, felt the tremors caused by its exhaust through a dozen different sensors. He tracked its passage, his consciousness spying through military radar. He didn't see it explode, just had a milliseconds warning as a relay clicked and sent current to the detonator, and the world around him shattered.

For a moment he thought he was dead. He was surrounded by darkness, his lungs were filled with smoke and the stench of burning plastic. He couldn't move, just like in the meadow. Was he back there? Had this even been real?

He felt the heavy VR helmet being lifted off his head and saw Norris in the flickering light from a couple of small fires that lit the inside of the tank.

"Time to go, Sarge," Norris said.

They stumbled out of the burning tank. Night was falling, but the smuggler's shack, packed as it was to the rafters with bootleg electronics, was ablaze as they made their way back up the track by firelight.

The EMP, the electromagnetic pulse detonated by the Chinese missile, had destroyed every electronic component for kilometres around. Down river, the skyscrapers of the nearby city stood like black sentinels against the fading sun on the horizon. Yinglong was gone. Every circuit board and computer chip capable of holding the rogue AI had been reduced to a slag of rare metals.

"Quite a bonfire," Custard said as he watched the burning shack. "Some gangster's going to be royally pissed off when he finds out someone's torched his stash, and I for one don't plan on being around when they do."

"Time for some old school SERE," Ringo agreed. "Survive, escape, resist and evade – all the way to Macau."

There were no fancy drones to worry about now, and more than enough chaos to mask four blokes who knew how to make good time cross-country.

It was over. In a couple of weeks they'd be home and Ringo would see his daughter again.

"It's all right, love," Ringo said under his breath as they started to march. "The monsters aren't real. Dad made sure of that."

# THE CLASH OF CYMBALS

Richard Lee Byers

Grunting and straining, Crusaders pushed the creaking siege tower across the beach toward the seaward walls of Lisbon. John could have ridden inside the belfry, where it was arguably safer. But he preferred to be outside. It made it easier to see what was going on. If a Moorish arrow found him, so be it.

Such arrows flew from the battlements in profusion. But the archers and crossbowmen at the top of the belfry shot back to deadly effect, and the tower was still making headway. Perhaps, John thought, it would make it all the way to the wall.

Maybe he should go inside it after all. If he climbed to the top, squeezing his way through the men packed inside, he could be one of the first to scramble across onto the wall-walk and engage the Moors blade to blade.

He was still considering it when someone yelled, "They're coming!"

John peered around the cover provided by the tower. The enemy must have opened a sally port. Moorish fighters were charging across the sand.

Two Crusaders started forward to meet them. "Wait!" John barked. If his fellow guards abandoned the cover the belfry afforded prematurely, they'd simply give the bowmen on the wall a chance to target them.

The pushers stopped pushing and readied their weapons. Soldiers jumped from the opening at the base of the belfry. Then the first Moors rushed swarming around the siege engine.

118

Bellowing, a Moor jabbed a spear at John. He caught the attack on his shield, stepped, and slashed his foe across the face with his sword. The Moor reeled backward.

John didn't have a chance to determine whether he'd harmed the man grievously enough to take him out of the fight, because already, a Moor with a scimitar was cutting at his flank. His shield was on the other side of his body, but he swayed backward, and the curved blade flashed inches shy of his ribs. He feinted high, cut to the knee, and his adversary fell. He pivoted and found another.

For a while thereafter, he expected the enemy to overwhelm his fellow defenders of the tower and himself. Despite their best efforts, the soldiers jammed inside the belfry just weren't able to emerge fast enough, and so, by bringing superior numbers to bear, the Moors should carry the day.

John regretted the deaths of the brave men who would fall beside him but had no fear of his own demise. Soon he'd see Elizabeth again.

As it turned out, though, he'd been mistaken. Fighting like madmen, the Crusaders held, until eventually—John didn't know how long the battle had lasted—officers or sergeants among the enemy bellowed orders. Then the Moors retreated.

The Crusaders were exhausted, but not too exhausted to croak out taunts and cheers. A freckled youth with a snub nose, one of the men John had likely saved from an arrow, gasped, "We won!"

John sighed. "Not really." He waved his dulled, bloody sword at the hissing, breaking waves of the Atlantic.

The other man eyed him quizzically. "I don't understand."

"The tide's coming in. It will cut us off from the wall. The enemy held us long enough."

Once the officers in charge realized that was so, there was nothing to do but trudge back to camp. The freckled youth looked so disconsolate that John clapped him on the shoulder.

"Cheer up," he said. "We'll get another chance tomorrow."

"He will," said a voice that hadn't quite finished changing. "You might not."

John turned to face a gangly adolescent a year or two younger than his companion with the freckles.

"Sir Oliver wants to see you," the squire said.

\* \* \*

Stooped, wrinkled and silver-haired, Sir Oliver looked too old for war. He should have been drowsing before his hearth with his grandchildren playing around his chair. But his narrowed blue eyes and scowl still bespoke martial ferocity, or perhaps merely dissatisfaction with what he saw when he regarded John from behind a desk heaped with maps and other sheets of parchment.

"You don't look like a saint," the old man growled at length.

"I'm not," John replied.

"Yet I'm told," Sir Oliver said, "you led the band that killed the sorcerer in the hills to the north."

"That's true."

Shortly after the Crusaders' arrival, sickness had broken out. In and of itself, that was only to be expected. But the physicians failed to recognize this particular malady, it seemed to spread with unnatural speed, and when a rumor went round that an old Moorish warlock had laid a curse on the Christians, they sent a patrol to see if it was so.

If it was, it should be easy enough to deal with him. Though a nobleman as well as a wizard, he dwelled in an unfortified, essentially indefensible manor house with a mere handful of retainers. But, when the patrol camped beside the road a mile or two shy of their destination, an eerie moaning sounded from all sides. Balls of blue light drifted among the trees, and shadows crept and slithered in the gloom. One man fell, thrashing in a seizure. Others fled shrieking into the night.

When the members of the patrol found another the following morning, most balked at the prospect of proceeding with their mission. John, however, volunteered to go forward, and, rather to his surprise, three others offered to accompany him. Together, they breached the sorcerer's home, killed the guards, and beheaded the scholar himself. Then, upon returning to camp, they learned the sickness had run its course.

"How were you able to manage it?" Sir Oliver asked.

"The sorcerer's weapon was fear," John said. "If you didn't give in to it…" he shrugged.

Indeed, there were moments when he suspected the so-called warlock hadn't wielded any true magic at all, that the sickness had simply been sickness, and the phantasmal phenomena, trickery. But his friends took pride in having overcome the power of Satan, and it seemed kinder to keep his doubts to himself.

"Well," Sir Oliver said, "however you did it, your superiors took note of the fact that we have men capable of overcoming witchcraft and the Devil's wiles. Apparently we need such men again."

"How so?"

"It's slow going breaking into the city with belfries and stone-throwers. So we're trying a mine as well. Unfortunately, the sappers believe that from time to time, they sense a hostile *something* watching them as they work. These are experienced diggers, mind you, not prone to panic simply from being underground. A priest went down to exorcise the presence but, according to the miners, failed, which makes the situation that much more frightening. Still, the sappers are willing to continue, but only if the four men who killed the sorcerer are down in the tunnel to protect them."

\* \* \*

Aboveground, John was certain, the sunlit day was frantic and noisy, with thousands of his fellow Crusaders milling between the ships drawn up on the shore and the siege lines. Some were sawing and hammering, building a new ram and rolling towers to replace the ones the Moors had burned. Some operated the trebuchets that hurled stone after stone to crash against the city walls. Perhaps others howled in outrage as the enemies manning the battlements defiled crosses with their spit and piss. Calling to one another, still more foraged in the fruit orchards, vineyards, and olive groves outside the city.

Belowground, though, everything was dark and quiet. Only yellow lantern glow contended with the eternal night, and only the crunch of pick and spade biting into earth and the rumble of the barrows carrying the dislodged dirt away disturbed the silence.

John had found he liked it better in the mine, the grime and the dust that stung his eyes notwithstanding. No one had sensed the sinister lurking presence in the two days since he and his comrades had joined the sappers, and in the phantom's absence, it was peaceful down here, or perhaps numbing was the better term. His grief still ached, but less persistently than before.

Understandably, the sappers didn't share his fondness for their current environs or the labor required to push ahead. But, reassured by the presence of their new protectors and the seeming cessation of ghostly visitations, they worked hard anyway, some out of devotion to their holy cause and others because they expected a handsome reward should their efforts prove instrumental in the fall of the city.

Currently at the head of the crew, broad-shouldered, black-bearded Amadour swung his pick. As one of the wizard killers, he wasn't required to lend a hand with the digging but perhaps, proud as he was of his considerable strength, would have felt unmanly had he not. The resulting impact made an unexpected *rasp*, as though he'd struck something harder than packed earth. He swung thrice more, producing the same noise every time and pattering like falling pebbles an instant later.

The Norman picked up a lantern to examine the spot he'd been battering. "I'm hitting brick," he said.

John advanced and saw Amadour was right. Their tunneling had indeed fetched up against a brick wall. He peered through the face-sized breach his fellow miner had made. Some sort of man-made passage or cellar lay beyond.

Among his companions, the discovery was cause for excitement. They jabbered to one another and, each eager to look through the hole, crowded forward in the close quarters of the mine.

The purpose of a mine was often to bring down a castle or city wall. King Afonso, however, had directed the sappers to dig a longer tunnel that would enable Crusaders to come up well inside Lisbon and attack by surprise. By the looks of things, the miners might well have succeeded.

John tried to share in the general enthusiasm. Inwardly, though, he felt dismay that his days in the soothing darkness might have reached an end. Scowling, he told himself his feelings didn't matter, only his duty.

"All right," he said, "let's find out exactly what this is." He held out his hand, and one of the miners gave him a pick.

Working together, he and Amadour smashed away enough brick for a man to squirm through the hole. A brick-lined tunnel ran away at right angles to the mine.

Amadour peered through the opening, then grinned, revealing the gap in his front teeth that was the result of an altercation with an even bigger soldier from the German camp. "Still no sign of witches and such" he said, his tone a gibe at the sappers who'd imagined such creatures skulking about. "We just need to find a way to sneak up into the city."

"And hope the Moors haven't already come down," John replied.

The sappers had started digging their mine far back from the city wall. With luck, that had prevented the enemy from discerning what was happening, but it would be unwise to count on it. Sometimes a defending army set out bowls of water to warn of miners, and tremors in the earth agitated the contents. Or someone could have noticed surface soil shifting when the burrowing beneath disturbed it.

If the Moors did know what was happening, the brick tunnels would be a good place to wait in ambush. They wouldn't even need to countermine.

"Well," John said. "we 'protectors' are here. You miners might as well get some actual use out of us. I'll scout ahead, and the rest of you wait here." He set down the pick, stooped to retrieve the lantern he'd used before, and Amadour took hold of the shoulder.

"You don't mean to go alone," the big Norman said.

"If the Moors are lying in wait," said John, "a lone scout has some chance of spotting the ambush and retreating undetected. This whole crew certainly could not."

"A smaller group makes sense," Amadour said, "but it's reckless for one lone man to go. It needs to be the four of us, just like it was before." He lowered his voice. "However you're feeling, you know I'm right."

John drew breath for an angry retort but then thought better of it. He wished he'd never gotten drunk and told his friend how Elizabeth had died of a fever two weeks before what was to be their wedding day, and disliked the Norman referring to it even obliquely. Still, the big man had a point.

"Very well," he said. "You, Pascal, and Colm will go with me. Everyone else, wait here. If you see a company of Moors coming, run."

The four Crusaders slipped into the brick passage. John and Colm carried lanterns, Amadour had held on to his pick, and Pascal had borrowed a shovel, just in case further digging was required after all. Everyone wore a sword, though no one excavating a tunnel burdened himself with mail or a shield.

Discerning no reason to prefer one direction over the other, John arbitrarily led his companions to the right. As he stalked along, he counted his steps and bade himself commit any turns to memory. That should facilitate the scouts' eventual return to their companions and even give him some crude notion of where he was in relation to the enemy city overhead.

For a time, there was nothing to see but lantern-shine sliding over brickwork and the darkness ahead endlessly slipping from its grasp. Despite the need to stay vigilant, the gloom and the quiet lulled him. Perhaps, now that the air was free of grit and there was no need to pound and scrape through hard-packed earth for every inch of progress, it eased him even more than before.

Until, faintly, metal clashed, a shivery sound that took a moment to dwindle away to nothing. John jerked as though the noise had startled him from a doze, and around him, his companions did the same. The lanterns swung at the ends of their handles and set shadows rocking as though laughing at the men who cast them.

"What was that?" whispered Pascal, peering about. He was as short and scrawny as Amadour, his fellow Norman, was tall and burly, and had a knack for mending damaged gear that made his comrades prize him. He'd been a tinker before the preaching of Bernard of Clairvaux inspired him to take the cross.

"Somebody in armor?" asked Colm. He was rawboned and lantern-jawed, his shock of hair the yellow of straw and his skin waxy pale where the dirt of mining didn't darken them.

"I don't think so," John replied. It hadn't sounded like the clink of mail or even the clatter that might result from some lummox dropping a shield. It had been more like the clash of a cymbal, peculiar as that seemed. "Whatever it was, it didn't sound especially close. We'll keep moving. Just stay alert."

As they prowled onward, though, John found it difficult to follow his own order. Perhaps because of the River Tagus flowing nearby, the air was dank, but paradoxically, it affected him like the warmth in a stuffy room. His eyelids drooped, and his limbs grew heavy.

At some point, the cymbal—if that was what it was—resumed its clashing. For a moment, that seemed ominous, but the sound was still soft and likely no closer than before. It was even possible John and his companions were moving away from the source, in which case, it would be foolish to become alarmed.

The cymbal sounded half a dozen times, long enough for him to start pacing in time to the beat. When it fell silent again, the sudden absence made him stumble.

Later, the lantern light washed over the ghost of a child floating partway up the wall. The apparition jolted John out of his dulled complacency. Snatching for his sword, he squinted in an effort to determine if he was truly seeing what he thought he was. His companions exclaimed and recoiled.

Then Pascal laughed a shaky laugh.

Amadour turned to him. "What's funny?"

The scrawny tinker grinned. "If you lot weren't a pack of wretched sinners, maybe you'd recognize the Virgin when you see her."

Or if we had eyes as keen as yours, thought John, for the thing he'd taken for a pale phantom was in fact a white stone statue of a female figure set in an alcove in the wall.

A sensible man, or a leader concerned with fulfilling his responsibilities, should be glad it had startled him out of the half-stupor that had crept over him. Still, John felt the ache of loss, as though something precious had slipped from his hand

He advanced to examine the statue, and his companions followed. Despite Pascal's initial impression, the figure wasn't an image of Mary after all. Pregnant and enthroned, the woman the sculptor had depicted wore a crown made of towers and clasped a horn overflowing with fruit and flowers in her lap. A lion gazed up at her like an adoring hound.

"Shit," Pascal said. He actually sounded upset, as though the statue had played a cruel prank on him.

"Is it an idol the Moors worship?" asked Colm.

"Perhaps," said John. None of them knew much about the enemy's faith except that it was false and pernicious. "But Lisbon is an old city. She could be some pagan goddess from Roman times."

"Moorish or pagan," Pascal said, "it makes no difference." He lifted his spade and aimed it at the statue's face.

"No!" snapped John.

The little Norman glowered. "Why not?"

John had reacted by instinct. It took thought a moment to catch up. When it did, he discovered he feared it would be bad luck to disrespect the statue. Besides, he simply didn't *want* to see it disfigured.

None of that would sway Pascal. Fortunately, there was a more rational consideration as well: "If you smash the figure, and there are Moors nearby, they might hear."

"But they didn't hear us knock a hole in the wall?" Pascal replied.

"We've walked a ways since then," Amadour said. "Anyway, you need to follow orders."

Pascal made a disgusted spitting sound, but he also lowered the shovel.

Colm ran his hand over his temple and the top of his head, smearing the dirt that clung there. "Speaking of noise," he said, "I heard the metal sound again a while back. I… I don't know why I didn't say anything before."

"I heard it, too," said John. "I think we all did. It just didn't bother us this time."

"What *is* it?" Colm asked.

"Definitely not Moors lying in wait," John said. "They wouldn't make a racket if they wanted to ambush us."

The lanky Englishman grunted. "I suppose that's something to be thankful for, but I still don't like it."

"Nor do I," Amadour said, "and we've been exploring for a while. Let's head back."

John's immediate reaction was that this too was a bad idea, or if not that, an unpalatable one. "Somewhere, there has to be a stairway up or some sort of access to the city."

"Maybe," Amadour said, "but if we're no longer worried about stumbling into a Moorish ambush, the fastest way to find such a thing is to get the whole crew searching."

John realized that was true. "Fine," he sighed. "We'll fetch the others."

As they made their way back, the cymbal clashed out eleven beats. There were more strokes every time it called. John imagined that the miners' intrusion kept troubling *something's* slumber and that with every disturbance it was getting closer to waking.

That wasn't exactly how things felt, though. With dazed passivity once more overtaking him, it was more like the sleeper still slumbered soundly and dreamed a dream that was swallowing him and his companions.

The miners passed a second goddess statue, then a third, and sometime after that, he lost count. John smiled drowsily to imagine all the labor it would have taken for Pascal to defile each and every one of them.

That reflection stirred another. When the thought came into focus, he felt a stab of fear. "Stop!" he said.

Blinking, casting about, the others once again appeared to be waking from befuddlements of their own. "What's wrong?" Amadour asked.

"The idol Pascal wanted to destroy," John said, "was the first one we came to. Now, we're passing others. That means we aren't really retracing our steps. We're lost."

"I thought you were leading us!" said Colm.

"I meant to," John said. "I paced off distances and noted the turns going in." Or at least he had at first. He now realized that at some point he'd forgotten the necessity. "But heading back... I don't know. I suppose I assumed one of you knew the way back and I simply followed along."

Amadour shook his head. "Something, maybe bad air, is turning us into sleepwalkers."

"Then when we get back to the mine," John said, "and fresher air, we'll be all right." It would only encourage panic to point out that, whatever else stagnant, poison air could do, it couldn't strike a cymbal.

"*How* will we get back?" Colm asked.

"Easily," John said, squaring his shoulders. Up until now, with his taciturn melancholy, he likely hadn't inspired a great deal of confidence as a leader, but that needed to change. "If a man in a maze goes right every time he comes to a fork, he inevitably finds his way out." Somebody had told him that once. He couldn't remember who, but he hoped it was true.

Once they put his rudimentary plan into practice, he kept hoping to round a corner and spy the opening into the mine or, barring that, a passage free of crowned goddesses. The latter might at least be a sign he and his companions were traveling in the right direction. But in each new tunnel, white faces smiled from out of the murk. Stone lips seemed to quirk as the lantern-shine kissed them.

Still, at least belated anxiety was shielding the miners from stupefying influences lurking in the air or anywhere else. No matter what else befell them, they wouldn't lose their wits again.

Or so John assured himself. Then the cymbal resumed its clashing and this time didn't stop after several beats.

Fearing its influence, he placed the looping handle of his lantern around his elbow. The flame inside was uncomfortably hot in proximity to his body, but the repositioning enabled him to use both hands to stop his ears.

That failed to muffle the clashing. Before, he'd never managed to determine in which direction the metallic beats originated. Now he wondered if they arose inside his head as much as any place else.

He was again striding in time to the rhythm. He struggled to alter his pace, but it was difficult. As soon as he shifted his concentration elsewhere, his marching feet resumed the tempo.

He tried stopping, standing still, and the beats tugged at him. He doubted he could resist for long, and besides, pace by pace, Amadour, Pascal, and Colm were striding ahead of him. He couldn't let them disappear into the dark without him.

He trotted, caught up, and they turned their terrified faces in his direction. "Sing!" he shouted. "Drown it out!"

"Oh splendor of God's glory bright," Pascal caterwauled, "Who bringest forth the light from Light—"

Naturally, the pious little tinker had chosen a hymn, and perhaps, in this extremity, he had the right idea. John, Amadour and Colm joined in.

Unfortunately, the hymn didn't drown out the cymbal, nor, they discovered, could they resist singing in time to the beat. A few lines in, a flute shrilled, its melody unrelated to that of the sacred music and as dominant and corruptive as the metallic rhythm. It made it impossible to stick to the hymn's original tune, and John struggled to fit the lyrics to the new one.

Not for long, though. New words welled up inside his head, and even though he didn't understand the language, they supplanted the verses he'd known since childhood.

John strained to stop singing, but his voice proved as recalcitrant as his feet, and then, somehow, understanding flowered. He'd come on Crusade seeking only peace, but more was possible. Cybele could grant him ecstasy. He need only accept it.

Acceptance meant giving in to the intoxication of the Magna Mater's music, and, despite their initial resistance, that was what John's companions were doing. Marching gave way to capering, whirling dancing. Amadour tripped Pascal with his pick and howled with laughter when the small man staggered and nearly fell. Colm drew his dagger and sliced gashes in his cheeks.

They were all bewitched, John realized. It was his duty to break the spell, but how could he muster the resolve when, after two years of mourning, his misery was finally falling away? Striving to resist the magic for his comrades' sake, he sought to recall the hardships and close calls he and the others had shared, the kindness they'd shown putting up with his sullenness, but another skirl of piping smeared the memories into a meaningless blur.

Bare to the waist now, his face a bloody mess, Colm slashed his chest. Amadour tore open his shirt.

John still couldn't find it in himself to care, not enough to stop singing and dancing and intervene. He still knew who Colm, Amadour, and Pascal were, but any bonds of affection or obligation were burning away in the fire of a greater devotion.

Indeed, he realized, every part of him that fretted or sorrowed was burning away. For a few dancing steps, he was grateful, and then he recognized the cost.

As it was with his fellow soldiers, so too must it be with Elizabeth. He might still remember her sly smile and teasing, her green eyes and way with dogs and horses, but they'd no longer evoke evens a wisp of feeling, painful or otherwise. Henceforth, all his love would belong to the Mountain Mother.

Back in York and in the days since, he'd believed his grief unbearable, but it was preferable to the alternative. He'd rather suffer for the rest of his days than become a creature who no longer loved Elizabeth or cherished the time they'd had together.

He contrived to dance clumsily, entangled his feet, and fell. Amadour, Pascal, and Colm capered obliviously onward into the dark.

John pounded his forehead against the floor. It hurt, but that was all to the good. Each jolt diminished the music's power. Eventually he stopped singing and felt no urge to start anew or to dance, either.

Rubbing his throbbing brow, he rose and took stock. His lantern was still alight and intact despite his deliberate tumble. He hadn't cast away his sword in the midst of his delirium. So all that was as he needed it to be. Now he had to hope that, without witchcraft guiding him, he could nonetheless locate his companions.

He stalked onward, and Cybele smiled from her alcoves over and over again. Then the music changed, the wild dance giving way to something slow and solemn.

Quickening his pace, he came to a spot where the passage he'd been traversing intersected another. Yellow light glowed at the end of the length of tunnel on the right, and after a moment, Amadour, naked now, gashed and bleeding like Colm, appeared amid the glow. The big Norman had his back to John and seemed to be paying close attention to whatever was happening in front of him.

John set down his lantern and crept along the passage. He had no idea if it was even possible to sneak up on the power that had beguiled the others, but since Amadour was inadvertently providing cover, he might as well try.

The scent of frankincense tinged the air and, with each step John took, a bit more of the chamber at the end of the tunnel came into view. The source of the amber glow was Colm's lantern, set aside like his own. The light gleamed on a ten-foot-tall version of the statues in the alcoves with an altar positioned in front of it. No flautist or percussionist was in evidence. Maybe ghosts were playing the music.

But by the time John slipped up to the doorway, all three of his friends, all completely naked now, were visible. Colm stood before the altar with a curved dagger in one hand. John gasped when he spied what the entranced man held in the other.

He shouted, "Stop!" Bulled his way past Amadour, sprinted toward Colm, but failed to reach him in time. Smiling, the pale man turned away from the altar and proffered his severed testicles for his companions to see. Blood fell between his legs and spattered on the floor.

John bellowed, "Wake up!" His men looked back at him with no sign of comprehension.

Then the music swelled, and Cybele's power erupted inside his head, once more offering the bestial joy that was her gift. Spurning the enticement, he remembered how Elizabeth had bestowed affectionate little touches during the course of conversation with virtually everyone – it had made him jealous until he realized it was just her way – the raucous laugh her mother had deplored as unladylike, how she'd fussily brushed his hair into place with her fingertips when it needed combing, and drank deep of the anguish attendant upon her loss. The intoxication of the Great Mother's touch receded like a wave that had crashed against rock but failed to break it.

He looked up at the statue, "This is where your worshippers came to be initiated." He knew that as he'd known the goddess's name. "But we didn't *mean* to come here, and we don't want to sacrifice to you. Please, forgive us for trespassing and let us go."

For a moment, nothing more happened. Then, clutching his mutilated crotch, Colm tottered away from the altar, and Amadour and Pascal started forward to take his place. The now-bloody dagger waited atop the stone.

John scrambled in front of Pascal, slapped him, and then backhanded him. "Think about Jesus!" he screamed in the small man's face. "Think about the Virgin! They don't want us to geld ourselves to glorify a pagan devil!"

The little tinker blinked. He looked like he was waking up, but John couldn't linger to find out. He lunged after Amadour and grabbed him by the forearm a pace shy of the altar.

"You don't want to hurt yourself, either," John said. "Step away—"

Amadour whirled, wrenching himself free of his friend's grip in the process. A moment ago, he, like Colm and Pascal, had moved with a dreamlike stateliness, but now he punched at John's face with the speed of a seasoned brawler.

The punch smashed into John's nose and rocked him backward. Amadour sprang at him, hooked a leg behind his, dumped him on the floor, and dropped on top of him. The big man seized hold of his friend's neck and squeezed.

John pulled on Amadour's forearms and beat and at his face. Neither tactic loosened the Norman's grip. John's throat hurt, and pressure mushroomed inside his head.

Then something clanged, and Amadour's fingers slackened. Grasping the shovel he'd formerly set aside, Pascal hit his fellow Norman over the head a second time. Amadour pitched forward.

John rolled the unconscious man off him. "Thank you," he wheezed.

Pascal scowled as if to indicate this was no time for chatter. "We have to get out of here before anything else happens!"

His fear of further peril seemed eminently reasonable. At the moment, John didn't feel Cybele's power attacking his mind anew, but the flute-and-cymbal music persisted.

"Get dressed," he said. "We'll carry Amadour and Colm." Or drag them if that was the best they could manage.

Pascal hesitated. "Is there a point to taking Colm?"

John turned. At some point, his fellow Englishman's legs had given out entirely. Head drooping, he now sat on the floor in a considerable pool of blood.

Once upon a time, other worshippers must have tended the newly made eunuchs, priests or physicians who knew how to stanch the bleeding. In the absence of such treatment, could Colm survive? Assuming his sanity returned, would he even want to?

John pushed such thoughts away. "We have to try." He moved toward Colm, and the music changed, from slow solemnity to something jabbing and discordant.

It sounded angry, furious, and that was likely as Cybele intended. It was one thing, barely tolerable, perhaps, for John himself to refuse her blessing. When he presumed to rob her of other worshippers, especially one already initiate, his manhood sacrificed by his own hand, he committed an unforgivable affront.

Colm snapped his head up. Formerly blue, his glaring eyes were now as golden as the lantern light.

He roared, and his teeth grew points. His face projected into a snout and jaws, and his head broadened. Actually, John realized, the mutilated man's entire lanky frame was putting on mass, but the head was enlarging even in relation to the shoulders that supported it.

"Jesus, help us!" Pascal crossed himself.

Colm's hair rippled longer, surrounding his head in a shaggy ruff. Tawny fur sprouted across his body. Manifestly no longer weakened by his castration or other self-inflicted wounds, he sprang up on feet that now resembled paws. A long tail with a tuft of hair on the end lashed behind him.

John retreated and jerked his sword from his scabbard. Pascal hesitated, perhaps considering whether to take the time to retrieve his own blade or simply summoning up his courage. Then he screamed and rushed the lion man with his shovel extended like a spear.

The thing that once was Colm sidestepped and grabbed the spade just behind the head. He swung it, and Pascal lost his grip on it, reeled and fell. The lion man gathered himself to spring.

Bellowing to distract Colm, John charged and cut. The creature retreated just far enough for the sword to flash by an inch short of target, then whipped a stubby-fingered hand equipped with hooked claws at his attacker's extended arm. John jerked the limb back just in time to keep it from being shredded.

At once, the lion man advanced and clawed with the other hand. John sprang back and slashed. The stop-cut sliced fingers loose and sent them tumbling.

That maiming stroke would have balked many a normal man. Colm, however, didn't pause for an instant. He kept coming so fast and relentlessly that, even though John gave ground, it was difficult to shift the sword into position for another cut.

Instead of retreating straight backward, John shifted to one side, then the other. Colm compensated quickly, but the second maneuver finally opened up the distance for a proper forceful cut.

John struck at the lion man's head. Colm's hand shot out and caught the blade just shy of the target. He ripped the sword from John's grip and flung it clattering away.

Now, surely, he had two wounded hands, but the new injury didn't balk him, either. Rather, he lunged.

John retreated, and his lower body banged against something hard. He fell across the altar. Flinging blood, furry hands hammered down on his shoulders to anchor him in place. Colm opened his jaws wide and bent down. With his prey disarmed and pinned, he moved slower than before. Maybe he or, more likely, the Magna Mater, wished to savor the moment.

John turned his head. The sacrificial dagger still lay beside him on the block of stone. He grabbed it and stabbed the lion man in the chest.

Colm jerked upright. The motion yanked the knife from the puncture it had made, and blood sprayed out over John. The creature toppled over backward.

Panting, shaking, John wished he could lie still and collect himself, but he didn't dare. For all he knew, Cybele was already unleashing some new horror. His imagination suggested her huge statue rising from its throne and the stone lion at her feet turning its head in his direction.

But when he scrambled to his feet, nothing like that was happening. Instead, the piping and clashing died away.

Perhaps Cybele was only the ghost of a goddess, starved to death when her worship ceased, and she'd now exhausted her limited strength. If so, he intended to be gone before she recovered it.

Pascal drew himself to his feet. "Are you all right?"

"I think so."

"I'm sorry I wasn't more help. When I fell, it knocked the wind out of me."

"You have nothing to be sorry for. Amadour would have killed me if not for you. Let's get him out of here."

With their minds clear, the tunnels proved less labyrinthine than they'd seemed before. Once they were far enough from the shrine that John was reasonably sure no malevolent power was pursuing them, his thoughts strayed as they always did, countless times every day and night, to Elizabeth.

Remembering was painful, but for the first time since her death, not purely so. He'd always miss her, but perhaps a day would come when grief would no longer overshadow everything else in life. Hitherto, such an idea would have felt disloyal and contemptible, but truly, it was only what she would have wished for him herself.

After a time, to the relief of his weary back and limbs and surely Pascal's too, Amadour roused sufficiently to shuffle along on his own two feet. Eventually the big man asked, "Where's Colm?"

"Dead," Pascal said.

"Shit. Are we going back to the others?"

"Yes," said John. After which they and their fellows would smear the support timbers with pitch, set them on fire, and collapse the mine. King Afonso could find another way to take the city.

# BLACK TIDE

James A. Moore & Charles Rutledge

In the movies, Special Forces guys always landed their black inflatable boats with precision, drawing them quickly up the beach to be hidden in handy bushes. The choppy surf around Russell Island didn't make that possible, and in fact, one big mother of a wave lifted the boat at the last minute, spilling the six-man Alpha Team into the water and sending the men scrambling to grab weapons and ruck sacks before the tide took them.

Master Sergeant Tony Brent said most of the curse words he knew as he waded onto the sand. Looking back the way they had come, he couldn't see any sign of the much larger transport boat anchored a mile off shore. It was hidden by the night, the fog and the rain. A rain no meteorologist had predicted, and had seemed to rise from nowhere. The storm was so intense it also hid the lights of the town of Golden Cove only a few miles distant.

Captain Kevin Younger waved the members of his team over and said, "The Research Lab is about a half a mile north of us. Spread out in teams of two and converge from different approaches. I've already told you that we don't know precisely what we're dealing with so take no chances. This is a 'cleaner' operation. No witnesses. No survivors."

Brent, who had actually read the brief file on the operation said, "This island has some residential homes on it. Not on this side, but it's conceivable we could run in to some civilians."

Younger said, "Was there some part of no witnesses and no survivors that slipped past you, Sergeant?"

"No sir."

"Good. Now let's move out. Visibility is shit so don't shoot any of our guys."

With that, Younger slapped Medical Sergeant Eric Patton on the shoulder and the two men jogged off.

Warrant Officer Mason Gentry said, "I'll go with Brent. That leaves Lewis with Resnick."

"I always get stuck with Lewis," said Resnick.

"Somebody has to, "said Gentry.

The four men vanished into the cold, drifting mist. Brent adjusted his ruck, and he and Gentry started off at a jog. According to the report, Russell Island had a population of less than a hundred civilians, and the island was only accessible by private boat or plane. No ferries. Basically a small community of fishermen who competed with the larger community of Golden Cove on the mainland.

And then there was the research facility. Brent was on a need–to-know basis and he had been told he didn't need to know. Some nameless branch of the government had been up to some sort of bio-engineering project and today something had gone wrong. The command had come down to his own nameless organization. Clean it up. Burn it down. Salt the ground so nothing would ever grow there again.

The terrain beyond the beach was rocky and uneven. Brent was glad of his tightly-laced boots, which offered his ankles some protection, but the going was still difficult. They had gone perhaps a quarter of a mile when Gentry pulled up short.

"Hold up," Gentry said. "Thought I saw something up ahead."

"I don't see anything," said Brent.

"I got good eyes. Wait here for a second." Gentry took a firmer grip on his modified M4A1 rifle and moved forward. Almost immediately he was just one shadow among other shadows, hidden by the heavy rain and drifting fog. The muted roar of the rain drowned out all sound as well.

Until the screaming started. Brent resisted the urge to hurry toward Gentry. He knew he had made the right decision a couple of seconds later when the darkness was rent by two controlled bursts from Gentry's rifle. Brent strained his eyes, staring into the rain but couldn't make out anything in the muzzle flash. The gunfire stopped and the screaming resumed only to be halted abruptly.

Now, Brent made his way through the fog, risking the use of the tactical light on the end of the A1 until he found what was left of Mason Gentry. Gentry was sprawled on his back, steam rising from the shredded entrails spilling from his freshly torn abdomen. Most of his face was missing too. It looked as if it had been bitten off.

Brent felt a wave of panic and pushed it down. Captain Younger had said they were looking for some sort of bio-engineered specimen gone wrong. Well it had sure as hell gone wrong all over Gentry. Realizing that he made a wonderful target standing in one place with the flashlight on, Brent deactivated the light and shuffled away from Gentry's body. Nothing he could do for the Warrant Officer now.

Brent had seen plenty of action in Iraq. He'd seen worse injuries, but none under such weird-ass circumstances. What the hell had done that to Gentry?

Brent realized he'd lost his bearings. He fumbled his compass out and checked the faintly glowing readings. He had just decided which way was north when something latched on to his rifle and tore it from his grasp. Brent went immediately to the .45 at his hip, but even as the pistol cleared its holster, a grip of terrifying strength closed on Brent's wrist and held his gun hand helpless. A moment later something struck Brent and sent him sprawling in the mud. His gun went spinning away.

Lightning rent the sky and Brent saw a huge man crouching over him. The man was dressed in black fatigues similar to Brent's own. Had they sent in another team? The only weapon Brent had left was his folding knife, but even as he tried to free it from his equipment vest, a rumbling voice said, "Draw that blade and I'll feed it to you."

Brent didn't like being threatened. He grabbed the man's arm, shifted his hips, bringing one leg over the man's shoulder, and tried to cinch in a jujitsu triangle choke. He had done it in training a million times and he was good at it. Before he could get the other leg in place, the man leaned forward, jamming his elbow into Brent's thigh, breaking what little hold Brent had and sending him back into the mud. The man's hands dug into the front of Brent's jacket and then the man stood, lifting Brent off the ground. Brent was an inch over six feet and went maybe two-fifteen. This guy had to be a giant.

"I'm about three seconds from breaking your neck," the man said. "Now who are you?"

"I ain't telling you shit, pal," Brent said.

Brent felt the man's grip tighten and for a moment thought the guy really was going to snap his neck. Then the man pitched Brent to the ground.

"That tells me enough," the big man said. "Your bosses know something's happened at the research lab and you're here to clean it up. Just like Crowley said."

"Got no idea what you're talking about," said Brent.

The man said, "Gather your weapons. They won't do you any good, but go ahead."

"I get the idea you *do* know what's happened here."

"Some of it." The man turned, but he said back over his shoulder, "Get in my way and I'll kill you next time."

"You seem pretty sure of yourself."

The man turned back and grinned. "Which one of us is lying in the mud? If I wanted you dead, you'd be dead."

The guy had a point, Brent had to admit, as the man lumbered off into the darkness. He sure as hell did.

* * *

Kharrn went loping away from where he left the soldier. The man's equipment marked him as some sort of Special Forces operative, but his uniform wasn't from any of the normal branch of the military. Jonathan Crowley had expected someone like that might be coming and he had been right.

Kharrn and Crowley had split up right after arriving on Russell Island. It gave them a better chance of reaching the laboratory undetected. The machine gun fire had drawn Kharrn to the spot where one of the soldiers had been eviscerated, and he had caught a glimpse of something. Not what he had been expecting. Not exactly. But something.

The storm seemed to be gaining in intensity. The wind whipped Kharrn's long black hair and tugged at his clothing. The wind also dispersed some of the sea-born fog. In the distance, Kharrn could just make out the exterior lights of the laboratory. He picked up his speed. If he could see the place, so could the soldiers.

As Kharrn started up a sandy slope, a misshapen figure loomed up between the giant man and the lab. There was enough light now that Kharrn could see the thing clearly. It had the rough outlines of beings he had seen before. Humanoid in shape, with protuberant, fish-like eyes and a squamous hide. But this one was far bigger than any he had ever seen of the species, bigger than Kharrn himself.

Its arms were too long and its webbed hands had long fingers tipped with wickedly-hooked claws. The creature's mouth was open, showing rows of sharp teeth. *So this was what they had been doing at the research facility.* Making something inhuman into something monstrous. The thing made a gurgling hiss and started toward Kharrn.

"Wait!" Kharrn said. "I came here to help you."

Kharrn knew the creatures this thing was based on were extremely intelligent and capable of human language. Some of them had once been human. But this one wasn't listening, and if it was capable of speaking, it didn't have anything good to say.

Kharrn unbuckled a strap that held a flat leather case across his back. He swung the case around and unzipped it with the speed and ease of much practice. He reached into the case and withdrew a huge double-bladed axe. He didn't want to hurt the creature, but it looked like that decision had been taken from him. The thing had gutted one of the soldiers with ease. Kharrn didn't plan on sharing that fate.

The fish-man lunged forward, swiping at Kharrn with its claws, trying no doubt, for the same disemboweling cut that had finished the fallen soldier. Kharrn evaded the cut and returned one of his own with the axe.

Despite the keenness of the blade, the axe didn't penetrate the creature's thick skin, through it left a deep gouge in the hide. That was something else the bio-engineers must have done. The creatures Kharrn had encountered before didn't have that sort of skin.

Missing the cut had left Kharrn too close to the thing, and he paid for it when the fish-man's claws tore through his fatigues and the flesh of his shoulder. Kharrn threw a kick which stopped the creature's forward rush and made it stagger backward.

The fish-man roared in frustration and lunged forward again. Kharrn blocked with the haft of the axe and the creature grabbed onto the weapon with both clawed hands, attempting to wrest it from Kharrn's grasp.

As close as they were now, Kharrn was looking directly into the thing's eyes. He could see nothing of the intelligence that had built great cities in the deep, nothing of the skilled artisans who had crafted intricate gold filigree on bracelets and tiaras. Just an unreasoning, mindless fury only death could stop.

Kharrn let his own fury match that of his opponent, calling upon the sheer savagery born before the memory of man, which had carried him down the long years. He twisted the axe away from the fish-man and drew it back in one motion. Kharrn grunted with effort as he aimed a blow at the creature's neck. The axe sank deep and brackish blood spurted and the fish-man stumbled back.

Kharrn pressed forward, cutting again and again at the creature until it finally collapsed from the sheer force of the blows. Kharrn stood, breathing hard, and glaring down at the fallen fish-man. He felt no surge of pleasure in his victory.

Someone had made this being into something that couldn't be reasoned with. That same someone had forced Kharrn to kill the creature. And that someone would pay.

* * *

Phone calls made the difference. Back in the time before technology allowed for phone calls, it was often a game of waiting and hoping that someone would get to him via postal service and later by telegram.

He smiled at the thought of Mister Slate, his companion back when telegraphs allowed the first glimpse of fast communication. The man had once asked him how it was that he could come into a town and have a telegraph waiting for him. Not giving his friend a straightforward answer had proven a very amusing diversion.

That was a long time ago, back when most firearms were single shot and the notion of a telephone was impossible for most people to even consider.

The cell phone in his pocket was all that was needed for most people to call on him in their time of need. Small wonder he was always busy these days.

This time around the call had come from Jacob Parsons, a dabbler in paranormal research who made good money off his bestselling novels and movies. He was nice enough, but Crowley had no doubt the man would get himself killed if he kept going. He'd come close enough times.

"Hi, Jonathan." As was often the case, Jacob's voice had a dreamy quality when he called.

"What's on your mind, Jacob?" Sometimes he had a pleasant conversation with the caller, mostly because it amused him. They seldom remembered the calls.

"Well, a few years ago I went on a trip to Golden Cove, Massachusetts. Have you heard of the place?" Crowley admitted that he had not. "It's a hell of a story, Jonathan. Hell of a story." Parsons spent almost an hour filling him in on the details of

Golden Cove. The most important first detail was the fact the town had once been known as Innsmouth.

After that the story came down to a man who understood the denizens of Innsmouth, and their progenitors, the Deep Ones, were chimeric in nature. They could quite literally mate with anything.

"What's your point, Jacob?" Crowley kept his voice pleasant enough, though he had already turned his car around and was once more heading for the Eastern Seaboard. The idea of going home and resting had been a pipe dream, same as it almost always was.

"My contact says they're doing genetic research on the Deep Ones, Jonathan. That has to be a bad idea. That has to be the worst idea I've heard in years. I don't handle that sort of thing. You know that. I'm strictly ghosts and demonic possession."

Crowley bit back a few comments regarding what Parsons called work. "Are you asking me to look into this, Jacob?"

"Yeah. Yes I am." The man sounded relieved.

"So go have a nice day. I'll look into it. Tell your wife I said hi." He killed the call.

Parson's wife was another story. She actually had a modicum of talent. She was also deeply distracting in the best possible way, which was yet another reason Crowley avoided the two of them.

All of which came down to another busy day in the life of Jonathan Crowley.

Currently that day was getting very stormy, very fast and with a lot of help from outside sources. He could feel the magics in the air, summoning rain and fog and harsh winds. What better way to hide their presence as they came from below, from the ruins he thought long abandoned.

Crowley pulled off his shoes and prepared for dealing with the two men who had just walked past and never seen him. He hadn't wanted to be seen and once he was invited to a party, he tended to mostly get his way about things. Crowley had a great deal of power, so much so that he'd actually set limitations on himself to make abusing that power very difficult. First, he had to be invited to act before he could use any of his abilities beyond the sorcerous. Second, he virtually never carried weapons.

That the two men were highly trained was obvious. They moved with great care and made certain to check their environment. Both had night vision capability. Neither was using it. There was enough ambient light that it was more a hindrance than a help. Crowley took his time moving closer and finally reached down to grab his weapon of choice.

"Gentlemen."

Just the one word, which had exactly the desired effect. Both of the men turned toward him, giving him enough of a view of their faces to allow the sand to blast into their eyes, blinding them for a moment and also causing extreme enough pain to distract.

While they were trying to recover Crowley kicked the one on his left – the one who was already recovering – in the side as hard as he could. The man grunted and sailed ten feet back. He had armor, and the blow would not kill, but it certainly incapacitated.

The other man got three fingers across his throat in a hard slap that had him gagging for a moment before Crowley slipped behind him and caught him in a proper choke hold. They were soldiers and they were doing their jobs. They were also trained killers and he was in their way. He wanted them down and out, but not dead.

The one he'd kicked was starting to get up. Crowley kicked him again, this time in the head and hard enough to rattle his brain in his skull. The man fell flat, very likely with a concussion.

Both of the men actually had zip-tie cuffs. He took away their helmets and used the ties to truss up the soldiers.

After that he was heading for the facility. There were likely more soldiers, possibly they would even see him first, but he had to hope. Besides, Kharrn was along for the show. Crowley usually preferred to work alone, but there were exceptions to every rule. The giant of a man was good company, just as no nonsense about how to handle situations, and capable of fighting off half an army on his own. Also, he had history with the creatures they were dealing with and that helped.

Just enough moonlight to let him see the shape that came for him. That it wasn't a pure Deep One was immediately obvious. The thing had all the standard characteristics: bulging eyes, a flattened, almost non-existent nose, the thick-lipped mouth so reminiscent of a catfish, and a powerful body better equipped for life in the sea. Webbed hands and feet ended in thick, deadly claws, and it let out a nearly deafening croak-roar as it hop-lunged toward Crowley.

Large? Yes. Deadly? Absolutely. Coordinated? Not really. Whatever the hell they had done to the thing, it had no real training and seemed barely capable of walking.

But both of those deceptively long arms went up and came down with terrifying strength. Crowley managed to not be where they hit, which was the only thing that saved him from massive injuries.

He caught one of those arms and bent it back until the bones creaked and the elbow joint popped out of shape. The beast let loose with another sound that was unsettlingly human, and then thrashed its body hard enough to toss Crowley aside. He rolled with the blow and bounced off a rocky outcropping, feeling his flesh tear and his muscles pulp. Good enough to avoid broken bones, bit painful just the same.

His healing abilities kicked in instantly and the nearly fiery itch of his body recovering from severe trauma left Crowley scowling.

The thing charged for him a second time, dragging one ruined arm along at its side.

The mouth of it opened and revealed teeth that would have intimidated a shark. Crowley smiled and crouched, waiting. "Come on then, you little fuck."

Crowley waited until it was close enough and then reached into his pants pocket for the package he'd set up earlier. The cloth tore easily enough and let his powdery concoction spill into his hand. At his whispered words the dust tore through the air, against the wind and ignited as it touched the sea-beast's flesh.

Did it scream as it burned? Yes, yes it did. And Crowley was pleased. If he was truthful, yes. He hated the Deep Ones and this bastardization could only make matters worse.

Above all things the Deep Ones valued secrecy. They had likely already heard of this facility. They were likely already watching.

Soon enough, unless Crowley and Kharrn managed to defuse the situation, the Deep Ones would come to handle the matter themselves. They would be far, far deadlier.

The idea he and his companion would do less damage when cleaning up the situation was amusing and frightening all at once.

Still, the notion made Crowley smile. Or maybe that was just the fact he'd be meting out bloodshed against those who richly deserved to bleed.

\* \* \*

"And how the hell did they get out?" Salk was angry. He had every reason to be angry. This facility was his to control and at the moment that control was sadly lacking.

The building had no name. The location was considered classified. Currently the only people who were supposed to know about it were in the building and doing their best to control what could only be called a clusterfuck of epic scale.

The specimens were escaping. That should never have happened.

Five years of research with the Chimera cells offered up by MIT, five years of research that showed the cells were amazing and complex and could be introduced into other specimens with remarkable ease. Infusing the cells through a blood sample into twenty-five volunteers had led to twenty-five cases of mutation. Each and every single case resulted in a much stronger end result than anticipated. The specimens – all prisoners with a promise of early release they would have never gotten without the agreement – had grown from fifteen to eighty per cent in size. Each had shown the exact same sort of result initially, what Dr Sterling identified as a perfect example of an almost forgotten medical condition called the 'Innsmouth Look' – skin rashes, joint deformity, bulging eyes, hair loss... all of which, ironically, lead to increased stamina and strength and the development of gills.

Look deep enough and you can learn a few things. The closest actual town was Golden Cove, a commercial property with a growing tourism business and a steadily increasing population, some of whom also suffered from early stages of the Innsmouth Look.

The specimens they treated with the Chimera Cells, however, were changing faster. There had been talk of trying to increase the alterations. Adding predatory cats to the mix or even something with wings, but they had not progressed to that level, the only exception being a declawed Maine coon cat that had changed as dramatically as any of the human specimens. First it increased in size. Then it grew new claws – a lesson learned the hard way – and then it had started exhibiting the exact same traits before it was killed and the body incinerated.

All of which came down to the same thing: Salk was looking to blame somebody for everything that had gone wrong, and mostly he was looking at Marcos to take the fall for him.

"Look, Tom, I was on vacation. I just got back yesterday. I don't know what went wrong because I was not here." Javier Marcos had no intention of being anyone's patsy. Ever.

Salk looked at him and shook his head. "This wasn't me, Javier. I had nothing to do with this."

"Who the hell is in charge of security?"

"Lipmann, but he's dead. Killed when the first one broke out."

"So point at him. In the meantime, are any of them left here?"

"Of course. Seven got out. The rest are in containment."

"Oh. Only seven," his voice dripped with sarcasm. "And have we contained any of them?"

"No. I had to report it, Javier."

"What?" One sentence and his pulse jackhammered. "God, Tom. They'll crucify us and that's if we're lucky. Do you know how they deal with breaches like this?"

"No. I'm just a research guy."

Tom was looking a bit pasty around the gills. Ha ha, get it? Around the gills? Javier cracked himself up, but he suppressed the laughter.

"With extreme prejudice, you asshole! We need to get the hell out of here and burn the rest of the specimens."

"Burn them?" Salk's voice cracked. "Do you have any idea how hard I've worked to even begin understanding them? I haven't even finished mapping their DNA yet!"

"Good! All the better. Get your personal belongings and get out of here. I'm going to start erasing files. All of them."

"We can't do that, Javier! There's so much I've already started to uncover. These things, they don't even get cancer. They're like sharks. We could find the key to nearly immortal life in the data we collect."

"Not going to matter if we get our fool heads blown off! Get your things, Tom."

Salk looked at him and pouted, but nodded. Javier liked the man well enough. Which was a pity. He was obviously going to have to kill him. Salk would never be able to keep his mouth shut about what he'd discovered.

The alarms started up as he was heading for the mainframe and computer room.

There was only one reason the klaxon scream of the alarm would start. More of the damned things were trying to escape.

\* \* \*

Captain Kevin Younger was running scared. Something had come out of the mist and torn Sergeant Patton to pieces and had almost gotten Younger too. Younger had only escaped by shrugging out of his equipment vest as the creature had sunken its claws into the garment.

149

Younger had lost his rifle. He had his .45 sidearm gripped in one fist and his folding knife in the other. He stumbled through the fog, jumping at every sound and striking out with the knife at every moving shadow. He had lost all sense of direction. The wind had died down and the fog had become thicker, so that even the lights of the research facility were obscured. And he knew it had to be close by.

The sharp, discordant clanging of an alarm started somewhere off to Younger's right. That had to be the facility. If any of his men were still alive, that was where they would go. They would head toward the alarm just like he was.

Younger started in the direction of the alarm and within a few moments he could again make out the facility's lights. It wasn't that Younger was trying to complete the mission, that had been over when Patton's head had gone rolling across the sand. No, Younger had lost his flares with his vest and he needed to find some way of signaling the transport ship to pick him up. His superiors wouldn't like that he had scrubbed the clean-up operation, but that came under the heading of too fucking bad.

Now Younger could see the blocky, white shape of the facility. All the lights were on, which meant the place probably had its own generators. He became aware of the sound of the surf off to his left. The facility had been built on a rocky slope near the water, far above the tide line.

Younger sensed movement before he saw it. He turned to look at the ocean. The light from the facility allowed him to see there were several people standing in the shallows.

No. They weren't people. Not regular people. Their shapes were too hunched and somehow... wrong. Younger couldn't see their eyes but he could feel all of their gazes upon him. Even as he raised the .45 he felt something reaching into his mind. Fiery tendrils of alien thought.

Younger clamped his hands against his temples and fell to his knees in the sand, knife and gun forgotten. They were in his head. He couldn't keep them out. They were in his...

\* \* \*

Master Sergeant Brent reached the facility and took cover behind what looked like a tool shed. He could see a door in the side of the main building. Not the primary entrance. But maybe a way in.

Brent had hoped some other members of the A-Team might have made it to the facility, but he couldn't see anyone. Brent had recovered his rifle and his .45 and he had managed not to look at what was left of Gentry long enough to scavenge the dead man's ammo and ruck sack. Brent figured he would need all the equipment he could get if he was going to get off this island alive.

And that was his intention. The mission was obviously Fubar-ed. It was time to call in the transport ship and get the hell out of Dodge. An alarm klaxon began to sound just then and Brent stood, bringing his rifle into targeting position. The door in the facility slammed open and a man staggered out. There was blood on his face and on his shirt.

Brent was about to call to the man when a huge, misshapen figure lunged out of the door. There was plenty of light now and Brent figured he was looking at the thing that had killed Gentry or one of its brothers. As a kid, one of Brent's favorite movies had been *The Creature From the Black Lagoon*. This thing looked like the titular creature's bigger, meaner sibling.

What had Captain Younger said they were looking for? Genetic mutations? Yeah, this thing was mutated all to hell, whatever it was. Brent raised the A1, but not before the fish-man grabbed the running man and broke his neck with a quick twist.

"Son of a bitch!" Brent shouted as he triggered a controlled, three-round burst from the rifle. The bullets tore into the hide of the fish-man, but it didn't fall. The thing turned bulbous eyes toward the source of its pain. With a snarl of rage, the creature moved with surprising speed toward Brent.

Brent fired again, and continued firing until he had emptied the magazine. The fish-man lurched, stumbled, and finally fell.

It had taken close to thirty rounds to put the thing down. Brent ejected the empty magazine and pushed another one into place, noticing that his hands were shaking as he did so.

He was trying not to think about what he had just seen. He reminded himself the fish-man was some sort of genetic experiment. It wasn't some supernatural monster. It was an animal, created by scientists.

Okay. What to do? Brent had hoped to find other team members here, but if there were more of the fish-men in and around the facility then he needed to get the hell away from there. He decided to head for the beach, send up a flare, and take his chances.

Brent turned toward the shore just in time to see three more of the fish-men heading his way. They must have been attracted by the gunfire. How many of these damn things were there?

\* \* \*

Kharrn was crouched in the darkness, just a few yards from the main entrance to the research facility when he heard an alarm klaxon followed by the sound of an automatic weapon. The gunfire sounded like it was coming from the other side of the facility.

Kharrn had been wondering how he was going to get through the steel security door without smashing it down and revealing his presence, but now the door banged open and a man in a white lab coat ran out, leaving the door swinging in the wind.

Kharrn stepped into the light and grabbed the man by the front of his coat. Kharrn said, "What's happening in there?"

The man's eyes were wide with terror. His hands fluttered uselessly at Kharrn's thick wrist. "Let me go. Jesus Christ, man. Let me go. They'll kill us all."

Kharrn shook the man like a dog shaking a rat. "Tell me what's happened."

"We lost the containment grid. They're free. All of them are free. He was smarter than we thought. He helped them escape."

"How many?"

"Please let me go."

Kharrn hefted the axe in his other hand. "Answer me or I'll cripple you and leave you for them."

"Oh God. Oh please. I don't know exactly. A couple of dozen maybe. Now please let me go."

Kharrn caught the sharp odor of urine and he tossed the man aside. He stalked over to the open door and stepped inside. The bloody remains of another man lay on the tile about ten feet down the corridor. Bloody tracks smeared the floor. Huge, bare feet with webbing between the toes.

Kharrn paused as he felt a tickle in the back of his head. Something was reaching out and probing. But Kharrn had spent centuries learning to defend himself against that sort of incursion and he pushed the searching tentacles out of his head.

Still, it meant that the true Deep Ones had arrived. Crowley had told him they would come. The fleeing man had said the mutations had escaped. He had also said something about a mysterious 'he' who had helped them to escape.

If the Deep Ones were here then time was running out. They would think nothing of slaughtering everyone on Russell Island, including the civilians on the far side.

But what did they want? If they had come to free the mutations, then that was already accomplished. They had merely to wait for them in the surf. Were they after revenge? Or was there something more? Kharrn decided the answers waited in the main lab. He started along the corridor, alert for any attack from man, beast, or something that was both.

\* \* \*

Marcos hit the computer room like a force of nature. He did not back up the files. That was begging for grief. Instead he went to each of the mainframes and gave them the command to reformat. It wasn't quite that easy, there were plenty of protocols to prevent what he was doing, but he managed it just the same. The only catch was that doing it took time he could ill afford.

153

There were ten mainframes in the facility. They were necessary evils. They cost more money than he would make in a lifetime and he crippled them without hesitation as that was the only guarantee he had that he would, in fact, have a lifetime.

Before he was even finished the first of the Chimera came into the area, sniffing the air and loping around on all fours, letting him see exactly how odd the legs were, how close the thing was to a toad or frog. The eyes were vast and the pupils were blown. One was easily three times the size of the other. Judging by the scars, this was one of the creatures Sterling had vivisectionalized.

It was mostly healed from the damage, another point in their favor, but the damage to the brain seemed permanent.

Marcos thought he would certainly die there, but the creature looked past him and finally left the room.

"Well, this is convenient." The voice was low and calm and grated his nerves. "Just when I was looking for someone to ask questions to, here you are, ready to answer them."

The man facing him was average. Maybe a little tall, but no giant. He was lean, brown hair, brown eyes, wearing a dark sweater, a black shirt and black jeans. He wasn't wearing shoes, which while peculiar was hardly unusual if one walked along the beach enough.

He was wearing glasses, rimless and with wire arms. He took them off as he came closer, and still he was unremarkable.

And then the stranger smiled, and nothing about him was average. That smile made him want to piss himself. "What's your name?"

"Javier Marcos." He hadn't planned on answering but the words were out before he could stop himself.

"Javier, I need you to tell me what's going on here."

He almost did it a second time but clamped his lips shut.

The stranger's smile grew larger, just at the edge of too large for his face. His teeth were broad and white and looked for all the world like they were made for biting faces apart.

"Javier, we're being civil so far. Don't make me start breaking things."

"Things?"

"Fingers. Toes. Teeth. Whatever. Tell me what I need to know. Tell me right now, before things get ugly." He walked closer as he spoke and Javier tried backing up, but soon found himself pinned against a mainframe computer that was currently cleaning itself of all possible evidence.

"I can't help you." Javier shook his head and stared hard into those brown eyes. They stared back, and they smiled and that smile was just as bad as the grin below it.

"I don't want your help. I want answers. How many of them are there? What's the source of the materials you've been using? How long has this been going on?"

Try as he might, Javier could not look away from those eyes. The man was no taller than he was, but he seemed gigantic.

"There are twenty-five viable candidates and I don't know how many rejects. We've got a specimen in sub-level two. Been keeping it there and heavily sedated, as in comatose, last I heard. We've been at this for almost five years, but we've been moving carefully. No risk of exposure. I don't know what went wrong."

Javier shook his head. "What have you been doing to my mind?"

"Nothing. I've just been asking questions. Show me to your specimen."

"No."

The man's smile got even worse and he moved his hand along Javier's face before grabbing his ear and crushing it in his grip.

"Owww! Leggomee!"

"Keep screaming and one of those things will come along. I can handle them. Can you?"

Javier tried to pull away, but stopped when the agony in his ear exploded.

"Take me to the specimen, or I'll start with your ear and move on from there. Seriously. I don't mind taking pieces off of you, sweet pea. You're the one who tried playing God."

Javier nodded and held up his hands. He would make his move as soon as the man let go of his ear. A quick jab at the man's solar plexus and while he was winded he'd knee the bastard in the face.

The man let go and continued to stare Javier in the eyes.

Javier nodded. "This way. It's this way."

"Good boy. For a minute there, I thought you were going to swing at me and I'd have to rip your ear off."

For the life of him, Javier did not know if the man was joking.

*  *  *

Javier was a nervous twitch away from pissing himself. Crowley was fine with that. Nervous Nellies made his life easier. The thought that he had used mind control to get his way was also amusing. While he could probably arrange something, it would take more effort that he wanted to invest, and as he had expected the man was quick enough to go along with the promise of pain.

The elevators were locked. That was what happened when security protocols set in. Why let the monsters they'd created get out the easy way? Still, there stairs here and there and Crowley watched while Javier fidgeted with his keys and finally managed to open a door.

"Careful sunshine. Might be more of those things."

His point was made when they heard the thing roaring from below. The sound echoed up the stairwell and bounced through the concrete hallway. Javier turned to run and Crowley grabbed him by his arm.

"Oh, no."

"Lemme go! Lemme goooooo." The man was on the verge of tears.

"You played God with something that has its own gods." Crowley's smile nearly split at the edges. "You decided you had to make a better soldier maybe? Or a better human being? Or just to see what you could do. That never goes well. The difference this time is I'm here to make sure you see firsthand what happens when it goes wrong. You don't get to get away."

Damned if he didn't try. Javier thrashed and whimpered and pulled at his arm as if it were locked in a bear trap. Crowley shook him hard enough to rattle his body and gripped his arm even harder.

"We figure a way out of this, great. Until then you're my personal property. Come along now. I need to know where you're holding your 'specimen'."

"I don't want to see it again! I don't!"

"You don't get a choice, sweet pea! You screwed up. Your specimen must be awake now and if it is, it's called to its brethren. The only chance you have is if we set that damned thing free!"

"Others?"

"Oh, Javier, you have no idea. They're older than mankind. Older than you can imagine and there are so many of them. For a while I thought they were truly gone, but no, they've just been in hiding."

"I thought. They said there was just one!"

Crowley grinned harder and stared at him and Javier flinched as if slapped. "Only one? They're like cockroaches, Javier! See one and it's already too late. So you better fucking hope—"

Something lurched from the shadows, and then Javier's head vanished into the mouth of the beast. It bit down and sprayed blood over the walls as it pulled away from the stump of Javier's neck.

Crowley cursed and drove the thing backward, shoving it down the stairs. Javier's body slumped, still spraying crimson stains as it dropped, and Crowley jumped over the corpse with ease, but not before the blood sprayed his legs.

Later, if he thought about it, he might feel guilty about how the man had died, but it wasn't likely. The man worked at a top secret genetics lab. That would never be beneficial to anyone. Another variation of Pandora's Box only this one created bigger, badder fish-men.

The thing came for him and Crowley ran into it as it stood taller and loped up the stairs. The hand that hit him broke ribs. Crowley hissed between his teeth and rammed his hands into both of the bulbous eyes, tearing with his fingers.

The screech it let out was deafening, and he wondered if the monsters had more than one volume setting. Just the same it was too busy working on seeing through ruined eyes to notice Crowley dropping between its legs and slithering down the stairs, wincing at the hot pain of broken bones.

He didn't carry any weapons. Crowley had to jump to reach the thick neck of the thing, but he managed, hauling it backward down the stairs with the unexpected weight. On the humans he went for a choke hold. Here he went for maximum damage and wrenched the head of the creature around until the bones in the neck snapped with a firecracker series of reports.

It crashed to the ground and let out a gurgling hiss as it died.

Down below, further along than he would have expected, Crowley heard the sound of gunfire and though he could not make out the words, he knew the voice as Kharrn called out in rage.

Down the hallway past the door he was obligated to kick open, Crowley saw too many shapes. Not just humans. Not just monsters shaped by men. Deep Ones. True Deep Ones. They were coming in. Some carried weapons, others merely used their claws as they tore into the escaped nightmares Javier and his associates had bred.

One small part of him was horrified.

Another piece was repulsed by the shapes of the things.

Most of him was thrilled. It was so rare that he got to cut loose properly.

\* \* \*

Kharrn followed the corridor until he reached an elevator. Though the building still had power, the elevator didn't seem to be operating. Kharrn found a stairwell. The door was locked but the axe sheered through the bolt as easily as it had hacked down the gates of Uruk when he had attacked the city with the armies of Sargon. Kharrn didn't know if it was sorcery or time-lost metallurgy, but the blade never lost its edge and the metal had so far proved indestructible. Kharrn stepped into the stairwell and started down. Whatever secrets the place held, they would likely be buried deep.

He had only taken a few steps downward when another of the mutant creatures came roaring up at him. This one wasn't as big as the one he'd seen previously but it had spines like a sea urchin and its head was just a shapeless mass with eyes and a roaring maw.

Kharrn braced his feet on the stairs, lifted the axe high, and then brought the heavy weapon down on the monster's skull. The mutant's hide wasn't as tough as that of the other and the axe split the creature's skull, sending blood and brain matter splattering down the steps. Kharrn was careful not to slip in the gore as he stepped over the dead creature.

There was another locked door at the bottom of the stairs and the axe made short work of this one too. This led to a large laboratory. The room smelled of chemicals and pain. Kharrn narrowed his eyes as he saw the tables fitted with straps and restraints. This was where monsters were made. Kharrn had no love for the Deep Ones, but he did respect them. An elder race, older than humanity, and one of the few things that had survived the cataclysm that separated the forgotten age where Kharrn had been born from recorded history.

Kharrn heard a moan and he looked toward the far end of the room where there was a big door with a glass window. A man lay on the floor leaning against the door. Kharrn crossed the room, keeping alert for any threat. When he reached the door he saw the front of the man's shirt was covered with blood that ran from his nose. The blood mixed with drool from the man's gaping mouth. His eyes were fixed straight ahead but he wasn't seeing anything. The man's mind was obviously long gone.

"You still live then, savage?" a voice said from nowhere. "It has been so long."

Kharrn stepped up so that he could see into the room beyond the door. The room was filled with computers and medical equipment. A table in center of the room held a Deep One in a web of straps and wires. It was looking at Kharrn with dark and ancient eyes. Deep Ones were immortal unless killed. He didn't remember this one, but it knew him.

"You and I fought once on an island far from here," the voice inside Kharrn's head said.

Kharrn spoke aloud though he knew he didn't need to. "There are many gaps in my memory. I don't remember the fight, but I believe you."

"You almost killed me."

"This was before the cataclysm?"

"Yes, in the days when Father Dagon strode the Earth and the Ones Who Walk Behind the Angles held sway."

"Few can remember those days. How did you end up here?"

"I was caught in a storm and washed up near Golden Cove. The men who found me turned me over to the scientists who have tormented me for the last five years. They had some sort of machine that kept my brothers in the deep from hearing me. But I finally found a way around it."

"I will free you," Kharrn said.

"No need. My brothers come. They are here even now. All on this pitiful island will die."

"The people on the other side of this island have nothing to do with this place."

"No matter. I will have my revenge."

The big door wasn't locked and Kharrn swung it open with a hiss of escaping air. He stepped into the room and approached the table.

"You still have the axe, I see. Will you slay me here in my bonds?"

Kharrn raised the axe and used it to cut the restraining straps. He said, "Go and join your brothers. Do what you want with the men in this place, but I won't let you kill the innocent islanders."

"No human is innocent. And you are too late, savage. For we are many." The Deep One pointed over Kharrn's shoulder.

It was a feint, of course. Kharrn shifted his head but not his gaze. When the deep one tried to attack, Kharrn knocked the creature away with a backhanded blow of one huge fist. The Deep One had been imprisoned for a long time and it posed no real menace. The same couldn't be said for the group of Deep One's crowding into the outer room. The carried spears and knives and swords. They rarely needed more advanced weapons, as humans couldn't stand against their mental powers.

They wore garments that glittered like the scales of fish and all of them sported golden jewelry. Rings, necklaces, bracelets and anklets. It had been many years since Kharrn had seen the intricately worked golden creations of the Deep Ones.

Kharrn stepped out into the lab. He said, "You brother is here. Take him and go."

He felt a dozen minds turn toward his own, seeking to take control of his actions. To seize his mind and destroy it from within. Kharrn grinned. He said, "Last chance to walk away."

None of the batrachian creatures answered. He doubted they could. These were not hybrids, born on land and raised as men until their time came to go down to the depths. These were true denizens of the sea.

The Deep Ones brandished their weapons and began to stalk forward. Kharrn rolled his shoulders, preparing to hurl himself into the middle of his opponents.

That's when the soldier Kharrn had spared on the beach came running into the room pursued by a horde of the mutant Deep Ones. The old Deep One had learned to control his distant cousins. The other Deep Ones had no such chance, and apparently the mutants didn't recognize their progenitors. True Deep Ones suddenly found themselves locked in combat with things created from their blood.

And of course all of the Deep Ones, old and new, wanted to kill Kharrn. He raised the axe and waded in. He sent the head of the closest true Deep One rolling, then drove the heavy, double-bladed axe into the spine of one of the mutants. He jerked the blade free and the backswing tore through the throat of a creature that had attempted to spear him from behind.

The soldier was in a corner and apparently down to his last few rounds. He fired off three shots, then pitched the gun away and caught up a heavy stool to use as a bludgeon. Kharrn liked the fact that the young man didn't give up. He began cutting his way toward the Spec-Ops guy.

Four of the true Deep Ones converged on Kharrn, seeking to bring him down with swords and spears. The giant man bellowed in rage as he swung the axe in wide arcs. The blades of the Deep Ones' weapons shattered as they struck the axe and Kharrn hewed into the fish-men, cutting and hacking with the huge weapon.

Out of the corner of his eye, Kharrn saw Jonathan Crowley enter through a door on the far side of the lab. He struck one of the Deep Ones in the side of the head, crushing its skull.

\* \* \*

Crowley had no idea how many ways there were to kill a Deep One, but he was willing to find out. Adrenaline sang through his system and drove him into the conflict. There was a blend of hybrids among the creatures, but even with mixed heritages, they were always the same beasts. That was what the scientists had failed to understand. No matter what the Deep Ones mated with, man or fish or even, he supposed, an alligator, they always had the dominant genes. The end result was always a Deep One, just sometimes with a few genetic advantages.

Crowley yanked the heavy spear from the hands of a monster coming for him and cracked it's skull with the butt end. The sharp side was used on the next one to send it croaking in pain as it lost an eye.

The claws on one of the nightmare's feet cut into his calf and bare foot and he growled at it as he shoved forward, knocking the thing backward and into a few more. Three cuts from claws and teeth were his reward, but he threw his new toy and pinned one of the true Deep Ones to the wall.

A heavy necklace of gold and stone marked one of the demons as a high ranker. Crowley jumped over the back of one of the things that had dropped to all fours and shoved it down to the lab floor even as he grabbed the elder around the neck with one arm and twisted. The spines from the elder's back pushed against his chest and stung, but the Hunter wrenched the vast head of the thing sideways until bones snapped and it dropped, dead.

So often he had to restrain himself, but not now, not this time. Whether or not he lived through the encounter, he would kill as many of the things as he could before he died.

\* \* \*

Brent had run out of luck and ammunition. When the three fish-men had appeared from nowhere, Brent's only avenue of escape had been to run inside the facility and hope for the best. That plan had turned to shit pretty quickly when he ran into even more of the creatures. He fired off a few rounds and then dodged into a stairwell, and now he was trapped in one corner of a room filled with fish-men, some of who were wearing clothes and carrying weapons.

He emptied the .45 without doing much damage that he could see, and then caught up the only weapon handy, a metal stool of the kind he remembered from college science labs.

The big man from the beach was making like an escapee from a Schwarzenegger flick, chopping through the fish-men with an axe like Brent had seen in Viking movies. The guy was hell on wheels and he was doing heavy damage, but there were just too many of the things. They rolled into the room like a black tide of death.

There was one way out, but it wasn't a good one. A primary component of any clean-up operation, though not one Brent usually handled – two team members had been carrying mass quantities of explosives. Captain Younger and Warrant Officer Mason Gentry. Gentry was dead and Younger too, probably. But when Brent had scavenged Gentry's ruck, he hadn't just taken ammo. Brent had a bag full of explosive devices if he could just get time to use them.

Brent dug into the bag, and then dropped it as one of the big fish-men came charging his way. The explosive charges scattered on the floor as Brent took up the stool again. He jabbed with the legs of the stool like he was trying to push back an attacker with a knife. The fish-man slapped the stool aside and that was all she wrote. The creature snarled, and drew back one big, clawed hand.

And that hand and the arm it was attached to went spinning away. Blood sprayed everywhere as a second blow from the big man's axe struck the fish-man.

Brent said, "I thought you were going to kill me."

"Changed my mind. Can you set those charges?"

"Yeah, though we'll die."

"Maybe," the giant said. "Do it."

Maybe? Did the guy think he could survive ground zero of half a dozen explosive charges? Brent shrugged, he was out of options. He set to work, trying his best not to look up as he heard the big man chopping away at anything that came close. Didn't the guy ever get tired?

"Kharrn, what are you up to?" Brent heard another voice call. He didn't look up. He almost had the charges daisy-chained together so that he'd only have to use one detonator.

"Fire in the hole," Kharrn called back.

"Do you know how long it will take to heal up from that?"

"Yes. Keep fighting."

Brent looked up. A man he hadn't seen before was fighting the fish-men *with his bare hands*. Who the hell were these people?

Brent said, "I'm ready. Give the word."

*　*　*

"STOP!"

Kharrn heard the single word so loudly inside his head that it made him wince. He glanced over at Crowley, who gave a short nod to show he'd heard it as well.

The ancient Deep One stood in the middle of the lab. The other Deep Ones had stopped attacking. As near as Kharrn could see, all the mutants were dead.

"I want to see the great depths again," the old Deep One said. "I can sense what you are about to do. I would not survive such an explosion."

Crowley grinned. "Kind of the plan."

"Even you two might not survive."

"We'll take our chances," said Kharrn.

"I know that. I can't control either of you, but I can see it in your minds."

Crowley said, "And you know that even if you fried GI Joe's brain, Kharrn or I can work the detonator."

"Yes. Enough. We will go."

"And you won't slaughter the islanders," said Kharrn.

The old one shook his head. "No. But there are still men alive in this building. I want them."

Crowley smiled again. "I've got no problem with that. Kharrn?"

"Take them," said Kharrn.

"What about that one?" The Deep One pointed at the soldier.

Kharrn said, "Not part of the bargain."

"Don't depend too much on my weariness. You realize that even if you kill me, an army of my people would come here."

Crowley said, "You'd still be dead. Take your scientists to torture and go."

The Deep One said, "And then what?"

"We'll give you half an hour to get out of here and then we're going to use this guy's explosives and blow this place to hell," said Crowley.

"Yes, I would not wish to see this building stand."

"You won't," said Kharrn.

"Someday, when I am whole, I would like face you again, savage."

Kharrn said, "I'll be around."

The Deep Ones began to file out of the room. The soldier said, "Were you talking to that thing? I couldn't hear it say anything."

"Be glad," said Crowley. "It wanted to take you somewhere and kill you painfully over a long period of time."

"And you're really going to destroy the facility?"

Kharrn said, "We are. Leave the explosives with us. We'll set them properly now and obliterate this place."

"What do I do?" said the soldier.

Jonathan Crowley said, "You get to be a hero. The only survivor of an ill-fated mission."

"Probably my last mission."

"Probably wise."

"Mind telling me who you guys are?"

"Better that you don't know," Crowley said. "Trust me on that."

Crowley looked at the soldier and said the words he almost always spoke with witnesses. Later, if the man found another case where things that should not exist were attacking human beings, he would place a phone call.

The soldier looked like he wanted to say something else, but he shook his head and left the lab. After he was gone, Crowley said, "I had thought the race almost wiped out, but there are apparently a lot of Deep Ones out there now."

Kharrn nodded as he gathered up the charges and the detonators. "In various places, yes."

"Sooner or later they'll come into conflict with humanity again."

"But not today."

"No not today. So what do you say, Kharrn? Let's blow this place up and then go get drunk and talk about old times." He paused "And I need to find my shoes."

"Old times," Kharrn said, "We're the men for that."

# RAVEN'S FIRST FLIGHT

Alan Baxter

aven sat on a hard metal chair and scanned the bare room. A huge mirror on one wall was obviously a one-way window. Otherwise there were two chairs and a square metal table, all bolted in place. The room itself lay buried deep in an otherwise normal office complex, on the top floor of an old brownstone on East 72nd Street on the Upper East Side of Manhattan. An office like a million others across New York. She thought she'd already agreed to join this strange crew, despite the lack of details, but it felt like another interview was imminent. Or maybe she'd misread everything and was being taken for a ride.

Raven. She liked the new handle. She'd never really liked her given name anyway. *Real identity no longer exists in the Dark Squad*, she had been told. *No names, no history, no family, your new life starts here and before that you were nothing. The old you is a ghost.*

It suited her fine. Being rid of her loser parents would be no trauma, she'd left them for the Army at sixteen, first chance she got. And they'd left the rest of her family behind in Korea anyway. She hadn't seen any of *them* since she was five. Growing up Korean in America, a cultural mongrel, nothing had come easily to her. Estranged not only by distance and emotional coldness, but by her powers too, the odds had always been against much in the way of integration. Which was apparently a large part of why she'd been picked for this weirdo sideline. She was yet to decide if she could really trust the promises that had been made to her, but anything appealed more than a cell.

A slight guilt hovered at the thought of her parents receiving a 'Killed In Action' notice, the funeral without a body they would have to endure. But still, what did she really care?

A light burst out, blinding her. Raven ducked off the chair, rolled into a crouch by the furthest wall, standard procedure against an unexpected IED. Her Army training fired up and she slipped the automatic 9mm from its hip holster, squinted against the blur as her vision adjusted back to normal. Nothing to shoot at, no burn or explosive damage. A decoy blast? She switched the 9mm to her left hand, trained on where the light had seemed to emanate, and moved her right hand to the jade knife at her belt, slipped it free. Its icy touch emboldened her. Feeling suitably armed, she whispered the *samjok-o* into her presence. The three-legged raven, it's jet black feathers glistening under harsh blue strip lighting, stepped as though through an unseen door directly onto her shoulder.

*What's here?* Raven mentally whispered to the familiar, the source of her new operative name.

It ducked and blinked, hopped up and circled the room with one wing flap, then settled back to her shoulder. *Nothing*, it thought at her.

Raven frowned and slowly rose from her crouch. The bird faded back to whatever plane it chose to inhabit once her attention on needing it had drifted. It was never far away, even if it wasn't always physically with her. A word would bring it every time.

With a sense of disgust, she cautiously lowered herself back onto her chair, slipped the 9mm away, but kept the icy dagger reversed in her grip. The blade pressed coldly against the underside of her forearm. She preferred blades to firearms anyway.

What kind of pointless test was that?

The door behind her opened and she was out of the chair and over the desk in an instant, her small, wiry fame belying her athleticism and strength. Many had underestimated her physical ability to their detriment.

"It's all right, settle down."

The voice was deep and accented Scottish, but nothing like anything she had known before. Maybe some country accent, or the remnant of an older dialect. Regardless, it wasn't broad enough to give her any trouble understanding, but was instantly recognisable. The man who had recruited her, who she knew only as Boss.

"The fuck is going on?"

He smiled at her, wide and open, teeth bright and large in his grizzled head. The man was massive, at least six and half feet, wide as a barn door. His iron grey hair was cut almost to the skull, his stubble a sparse snowscape across a square chin. He looked to be about fifty or maybe a little older, but Raven had rarely seen anyone, of any age, as imposing and dangerous. He put her teeth on edge.

"We're testing you."

"The fuck for, you already recruited me."

"Sure, but we don't have to keep you." He held up a hand to stay her burst of outrage, grinning again. "I just wanted to see if you went for hardware or magic first."

"Did I pass?" She felt the twist of her mouth that reminded her of a teenager, not the twenty-five-year-old military professional she was supposed to be. This guy *really* put her on edge.

"You went for a gun, then a maged weapon, then called your familiar. Perfect response sequence, really."

"Being in the army taught me to rely on mundane gear first, and only, if I could. Otherwise too many questions got asked."

"Exactly, and that applies here too, even if I did see your power and invite you in. So, you ready to meet the Squad?"

She shook her head. "You've hardly told me anything about this lot. You don't have to keep me, you said. Do I have to keep you? I want to know more."

"If you don't 'keep us', it's right back to the brig for you."

She shrugged. "Might be a better option." She didn't believe it for a second, but he didn't need to know that.

"Fair enough. I like your attitude. Come on, I'll talk on the way."

Outside the door was another man, clearly waiting for them. He was nearly as big and wide as Boss, his dark skin almost ebony in the low light. His head was shaved bald, glistening, and his smile as wide and welcoming as Boss's had been.

"This is Smoke," Boss said. "He's my right hand man. We started Dark Squad together after I spotted him doing some freaky disappearing act in a rat-infested Middle-Eastern shithole."

"We'd both had enough of orders and military discipline," Smoke said. "And we began to question our directives. I was a Marine, Boss was SAS, we saw a kindred spirit in each other."

Raven walked between the two of them, feeling like a child. She didn't reach either man's shoulder. "But this isn't military, you told me."

"Not officially, no." Boss gestured into a side room off the corridor and she went in. Comfortable sofas and armchairs littered the space, a large screen TV was turned off in one corner. A tall guy with sandy hair and piercing blue eyes sat reading a book. Though nearly the height of Boss and Smoke, he was skinny as a rake handle, but exuded taut strength. He looked to be maybe late-twenties.

"That's Taipan," Boss said.

Taipan looked up, nodded. "G'day. Good to meet ya." His Australian accent was unmistakable.

"You people really say 'G'day'?" Raven asked.

"Not at night so much." He grinned and went back to reading.

Raven thought these people all grinned too damn much.

"And I'm Jet."

Raven turned. Jet was not as short as Raven, but not a giant like the three men. Muscular, solid, with short black hair, olive skin and narrow eyes. She maybe had a decade or so on Raven in age.

"Don't let this cockforest intimidate you."

"I'm not easily intimidated, but I'm glad to see another woman."

"We're all ex-military." Boss pointed around at each of them. "Australian Army, Israeli Special Forces, you already know I was SAS and Smoke was a Marine."

"Hoo fucking rah," Smoke said, and slumped into an armchair.

"Makes my time seem paltry," Raven said.

"No way, you went into the US Army as a teenager, you've got quite a few years of training, and a *hell* of a record. That's what we want." Boss sat and gestured for her to do the same. "You see, after Smoke and I started Dark Squad, we were noticed by a global organisation called Armour. I'm not going into the long boring story now, but the short version is that Armour exists to take care of magical, unnatural, supernatural, etcetera threats to the non-magical, unsuspecting masses. They're like a global magical army, outside any government. Because we have the crack skills with military hardware *and* the mad magical chops greater than most, and because our little Squad started making waves, we got pulled in as Armour's special ops team. We're their black ops, doing all the direct infiltration and wetwork they don't want to see."

"Along with our military and magical skills, we're also all a bit behind on our anger management classes," Smoke said with a wry twist of the mouth. "We work best when we're allowed to kill the bad guys without too much supervision, you get me? But Armour decided we were best off with them instead of maybe, at some point, against them. It's worked well so far."

Raven frowned. "So Armour is a secret organisation and you're a secret within Armour?"

Boss smiled. "Black ops within black ops."

"The blackest ops," Smoke said.

Taipan laughed. "None more black!"

Raven frowned. "Why do I suddenly feel like this outfit's ill-fated fucking drummer?"

Boss shook his head, his face growing serious. "We've long established that five works best, it's an occult number, you know."

Jet waggled her fingers like a sideshow magician. "The points of the pentacle!"

"Stow that shit, Jet. Truth is, you're replacing a dear friend called Blinder, who we lost on the last mission. He'd been with us a long time."

Raven laughed, but there was no humour in it. "No pressure then. Dead man's shoes?"

"You'll be fine. I know how to pick my operatives. We're dealing with the loss of Blinder, but the Squad comes first. And the fact you were prepared to be cut off entirely before you knew the real details of this permanent commission speaks volumes."

"It's not like I'm giving much up," Raven admitted.

"Well, you've gained a lot, trust me," Boss said. "But enough history, we have a pressing mission, which is why you've been called in now. It would have been nice to break you in gently, but there's something to be said for hitting the ground running, yeah?"

"I'm ready."

"Good. This one comes from Commander Giraud in the Paris Armour HQ."

The others in the room switched, their attention total and serious in a moment. Raven smiled softly to herself. They might be a rag tag bunch, but they were tight and focussed. The smile faded as she wondered how long it might take her to fit in. Or if she ever would. Regardless, despite what she'd told Boss, she didn't want to go back to the brig and serve out five years for assault of a fellow soldier. That dick had deserved it, though that was old news and no longer relevant. But she couldn't be locked up, she'd go mad.

"We going to Paris?" Jet asked.

"No, that's just where the orders are from this time," Boss said. "Our target is a necromancer."

And the full weight of her new position fell on Raven like a wet mattress. After a life hiding her magical powers, thinking she was a freak, she found herself surrounded by others with unnatural skills of their own who talked about it openly and without derision.

"Seriously?" Smoke asked.

"Seriously. He's been raising rezzers and placing them in various positions of power, slowly securing all kinds of advantages in business and politics. He's got them in a couple of European governments, several places of power in the Middle East, the CEOs of least three major US corporations that we know of. He's getting way too much influence, playing both sides of wars, collecting huge sums of cash from dozens of conflicting interests. Clever bastard."

Taipan held up a hand. "Wait. What's a fucking rezzer?"

"Resurrected human."

Taipan's eyebrows shot up. "Zombies?"

"No, resurrected humans."

"There's a difference?"

Boss sighed. "They don't teach you much in Alice Springs?"

"You know I'm from fucking Melbourne."

"A zombie is a mindless revenant. It simply wants to eat human flesh, mainly brains, and staggers around with that single purpose, slowly rotting as it goes. And they're not fucking real. A rezzer is a dead fucker raised up with magic. It doesn't breathe or eat or sleep or shit, but it can pretend to do all those things, and it looks and acts like a regular person. Except it is entirely under the thrall of the necromancer who raised it. Regardless of any other influence, the necro's will overrides everything."

"So that's how it infiltrates society," Jet said.

"Exactly. This particular necromancer has either put rezzers into power or found people in power, killed them, and then rezzed them to work for him. They operate exactly like regular people. They conceal the fact of their deadness, and fulfil the necro's orders."

Taipan made a face of grudging respect. "Cunning fucker. But must be powerful as hell to control as many as you suggest."

"Quite. Armour has put out a lot of his fires, taken out a lot of his rezzers, but his power is growing too widespread. Different Armour bases around the world are getting in on it and reporting his feelers reaching their jurisdictions. It's been agreed the necromancer himself has to go down. When he dies, his influence dies with him. His rezzers will all just drop, nothing but empty corpses the moment the necro's life is snuffed out. So Giraud at Armour Paris has taken on the gig and he's deploying us."

"Because this sounds dangerous as hell," Smoke said.

"Exactly." Boss spread a map out on a table and the Squad gathered around to see. "According to Armour intel, our man is holed up in here."

"Is that a castle?" Jet asked. The map showed a hill surrounded by forest. Atop the hill blueprints marked out the rooms and walls of a huge square building with a large open space in the middle.

"Yep, that's Castle ThisGuysFucked. We don't need any more information than that. We're being air-dropped in here." Boss tapped the map, south of the hill.

"Right in the trees?" Smoke said.

"Definitely not Paris," Jet said. "Where is this?"

"Somewhere in the arse end of Belarus, not far from where the border meets with Ukraine and Russia. Deep ancient forests, miles from any civilisation."

"Getting in is one thing, but then how do we get out?"

"Gonna be tricky, but this necro is canny. He'll have transport we can secure, I'm sure, or we might be able to call for an extraction, depending on the lay of the land. No matter, we'll worry about that later. We drop in, we mount the hill, gain the castle and find him. Kill him and somehow get home in time for tea and fucking crumpets. All good?"

"All good," the others said in unison.

Boss looked down at Raven. "All good?"

"I guess so."

He threw his overlarge grin at her. "You're not here to prove yourself, right? You're part of the Squad now, testing is all over, so just accept that and roll with it."

"Okay." Though she felt anything but okay. This was all a hell of a long way from tours of duty in Afghanistan.

\* \* \*

They sat in the back of an Armour stealth helicopter, ten minutes out from the drop. Raven felt good back in full fatigues and pack again, weapons strapped across her body. Her knives were close, especially the jade ice dagger, always right there ready. Despite the issues she'd had with command, the trouble hiding her skills, she had loved the fight of active service. Anger management, Smoke had said, and she smiled. Maybe a little more complicated than that, but taking death to shitbags who deserved it was her jam.

"You're a *mudang*?" Jet said suddenly, breaking her reverie.

The question caught her off-guard. "Er, yeah, that's right." How much did the Squad know about her? She knew next to nothing about them and the disadvantage bothered her.

Jet nodded, like she knew exactly what that meant and respected it.

"The fuck is a moo-dang?" Taipan asked.

Raven glanced to the front and Boss and Smoke's broad backs watching over the pilot's shoulder. "We doing this now?"

"Got anything else to do? No offence, just wondering."

Raven forced herself to lighten up. These people were her new family, the enemy was out there. The enemy was always out there, never inside. Remember the mantra. "It's like a Korean shaman, you know. A folk magus. But I grew up in America since I was five, so I hate all that cultural purity bullshit. My magic is rooted in the culture of my birth, but I gathered all kinds of things over the years."

Jet gave a casual thumbs up. "Same for all of us, really. Mixed like colours on an artist's palette, right? Anything of use?"

"Something like that, I guess. What about you?"

"Can it!" Boss strode back into the cabin, Smoke on his heels. "Make ready."

They switched mode in an instant, like Raven had seen before. Wordlessly they went through self-checks then checking each other, lined up, and the door opened. The sound-proofed cabin roared with the rush of air outside, icy cold and buffeting, the rotors chopping the wind into sound bites. They lined up, watched the light flick from red to green, and jumped in quick succession.

It was a low drop and black silk 'chutes opened right away. The thick forest canopy rushed up, far too fast for Raven's liking. She watched between her black boots, adjusted course a little left and right in the hope of coming in between trees and having the best shot at an easy harness escape.

From the sudden roar of the chopper into the cold fall, silence pressed in. She didn't waste any attention on the rest of the Squad, drew hard on the 'chute as her feet crashed into the foliage, drew her elbows in, tucked her heels against her butt. Crashing and snapping of leaves and branches filled her ears then she bounced and held up, hanging in her harness in utter blackness. She flicked down her night vision goggles and scanned below. The forest floor was about twenty feet down. If it was soft enough she could drop that far and roll.

Leaves and branches burst beside her and Smoke fell into view. His 'chute snagged up a little lower than hers and he looked up, his wide grin pale in the darkness. Then he was gone. The harness hung limp, Smoke had vanished. She caught movement below, looked down and there he was, looking up at her again. Like he'd teleported from one spot to the other. She smiled crookedly. *I guess that's where he gets his name from then.*

"Want me to catch you?" he called up.

"Fuck no!" She hit the harness release, dropped, tucked and rolled through leaf litter and came up into a crouch. It had been a little further than she thought and her heart raced at the prospect of injury, but she was fine.

"Ballsy," Boss said, striding up beside her.

"A little help?"

Jet joined them and the four looked around until they spotted Taipan upside down some thirty feet off the ground, spinning in a gentle figure eight.

Boss sucked air over his teeth. "Fucking hell."

"I got it." Smoke took two or three paces forward then vanished. Several moments later he appeared without breaking strike along a thick limb only a few feet from where Taipan hung. In seconds, with a knife and rope employed judiciously, they were all gathered on the forest floor.

Boss checked his compass and pointed. "That way. No lights, use your night goggles, single file. If anything comes at us, use hand-to-hand if possible. We don't want to warn anyone in that castle we're coming by sending gunfire through the night. Quiet as church fucking mice, all right?"

Without waiting for a response he led the way.

Raven didn't know her natural spot in the Squad, but Boss took point and Jet fell in behind him. Taipan waved her forward, then Smoke took the rear guard, so it seemed she was in the middle. She wondered if Blinder, the dead ex-member, had been in the middle too.

The forest floor was dense with undergrowth and tree roots, reaching up to trap an unwary ankle. The going was slow, machetes deployed left and right. Several times they had to double back and cut a new path when the vegetation became too thick even for chopping. After half an hour, Raven's muscles had a nice burn happening, sweat soaked into her black fatigues. The sixty pound pack wasn't a burden yet, but it would be if they had to keep up this pace and exertion for too long.

A deep moan rose up, drifting through the trees from somewhere ahead. Boss's fist shot up and the Squad froze. Something moaned again, then another off to the left. A third joined it, then a fourth and then there were too many to place and count.

The Squad split their line out wide, scanning left and right through the darkness. Crunching and cracking of leaves and twigs joined the melancholic laments as several somethings shambled towards them.

"Two o'clock," Smoke said, then vanished. He reappeared moments later behind the silhouette of a man and took its head from its shoulders with a single machete stroke.

Then there were figures everywhere, pushing out between the tree trunks, faces slack and groaning, the stench of rotten flesh filled their nostrils.

"They fucking zombies now?" Taipan asked

Jet stepped forward and said, "Sit on the floor."

Her voice was deep, powerful, and the compulsion to drop her ass to the leaf litter was almost too much for Raven to ignore. And the command hadn't even been directed at her.

"Sit down!" Jet ordered again, clearly using more than mere sound, the waves of her voice something beyond the simply auditory. "Not working!" Jet told the Squad, but they could see that for themselves.

Smoke blinked in and out again, machete flashing. Heads rolled.

Taipan crouched, made complicated gestures and barked a short word. Flame shot from his outstretched fingers and engulfed an approaching figure. The attacker went up in flames, flesh and clothes crackling, but didn't slow for a moment.

Taipan pulled a machete free and hacked the burning man down. "Fuggen hell! Flaming zombie attack!"

"Engage and destroy," Boss shouted. "Decapitate for your best chance. Questions later."

Raven chose to ignore the nature of the enemy, treat it like any other, and fell into the dance. Her jade dagger was more than a simple edge, its magic froze everything it cut. Limbs and heads shattered to flesh cubes when they hit hard roots or branches, or she hit them with fists and feet after a stab or slice. The machete in her other hand carved bigger wounds, her ambidextrousness making her into a whirling, scything tiny tornado of death. This is what she lived for, to get in close, to move, dive, duck and weave, cutting anything that strove to interrupt her movement. Nothing was as pure as the slice of a sharp edge.

She caught glimpses of Jet, expert strikes of hands and feet, fighting like some master from a movie, not speaking at all. Smoke popped in and out of sight, appearing randomly to decapitate, then vanish again. Taipan reached and lunged, wiry and fast, chopping two-handed with his machete as though it were a sword. When he took out a leg and the thing fell, he'd lob flame at it to burn it where it lay. Boss slammed all around himself, sometimes lifting the revenants high to smash them down over a bent knee. He left more alive than dead, disabled with destroyed spines and necks, reaching and dragging themselves over the rough ground. The Squad's magic pulsed and flashed, quick-fire spells of speed and protective wards, deployed smoothly with fists and feet and blades. Raven used combat magic of her own, practiced surreptitiously in theatres of war around the world, but realised dimly that she had so much to learn from these people.

In minutes it was over, silence settling but for the gasping of breath as the Squad re-joined one another.

"Anyone hurt?" Boss asked.

"One of the fuckers bit me," Jet said. She held up her left arm, a deep crescent in her wrist leaking thick blood that looked black in the night.

Boss started to dress the wound, rinsing it with saline and disinfectant first. "Anyone else?"

Taipan leaned forward, stared hard at Jet's eyes. "Er, Boss... Were they zombies?"

"There's no such thing, you fucking idiot, I already told you that," Boss said. "She's not going to become one of the walking dead." Something moaned near his foot, a broken man twisted in all the wrong directions, dragging itself one-handed over the ground. Boss slammed a boot into its head, stoved the skull in. The stench of rotten meat swelled in the air.

"You're sure?"

"These are rezzers. They could have been here for years, decades, without the magic refreshed, so they're starting to rot, that's all. There's probably a lot more."

Jet reached up and slapped Taipan's cheek. "Stop being such a buttercup."

Smoke put a hand on Raven's shoulder. "You were quite something to watch there. Like a razor-sharp godsdamned ballerina or something."

The others nodded, smiled agreement.

Raven couldn't help smiling too, wondering if she'd earned her place a little more securely. "It's my gift."

"Fall out," Boss said. "Go wide, and listen for more."

They proceeded more cautiously than before, fanned out across a wider area, eyes peeled. Moaning and guttural coughs erupted now and then, homing in quickly on the Squad. Taipan took out a pair of rezzers with quick double-handed machete strokes.

"I thought you said these things were intelligent like regular people," he said.

Boss stepped sideways, slammed a fist into a rezzers face, collapsing its head with inhuman strength, then threw a scowl at Taipan. "It's not only the flesh that rots when the magic is left to degrade. The orders remain, but their brains have moulded out too."

Jet grimaced. "That's fucking horrible."

"Yeah. I'm guessing they have two over-riding commands. Stay within a certain area and kill anything that enters that area. The necromancer would check in on his more active thralls, keep the magic fresh and therefore the rezzer would retain its humanity. These ones, he's just left to nature."

Raven shivered at the thought, imagined their active brains understanding their fate as their sense of self slowly decayed. "This is actually a fate worse than death. I thought that was just a figure of speech."

Boss glanced over at her, slight shake of the head. "There are many fates worse than death. Concentrate, people."

Something swung down from a tree limb directly in front of Raven, leering and drooling, it howled as arms thrust forward, fingers wriggling like hard, hungry worms. Raven bit back a yelp of surprise, ducked and slashed upwards. Her jade dagger clipped one arm and it stiffened immediately. She spun to one side, whipped around a heel kick, and the arm shattered into a thousands shards of frozen meat. As the rezzer strained about, its remaining arm clawing at the air, she ducked back under and slammed the dagger into its back. Hard ice spread like a fast-blooming flower across its body and she punched right through, destroying its spine and organs. It fell limp from the tree and she stepped over it.

"Damn fine knife," Smoke said. "You made a rezzer ring donut."

Raven grinned. "Yeah, long story attached to this."

"You'll have to tell me some time."

"Sure."

The night was largely starless and the darkness under the trees wasn't much relieved when they emerged from the densest part of the forest and began the slow climb up the mount on which the castle sat. It loomed over them, massive and foreboding, a black silhouette against the slightly lighter sky. Night goggles on, marked for silence, the Squad crept over rocky ground, hunched low, eyes everywhere.

They gained the foot of the castle wall without incident and Boss gestured to his left. Tight to the huge grey stone blocks, they moved single-file in the wall's shadow towards a corner. As they rounded the corner, they found themselves beside a rectangular lake some twenty feet across that ran along the entire front of the building. Halfway down was a large portico that led to a bridge over the lake that in turn led to an imposing double door.

"A fucking moat," Taipan whispered. "This is like Disney's last nightmare."

"Moat's go all the way around," Smoke said. "This is… a fucking pond, who cares."

"We going in the front door?" Jet asked.

Boss pointed across the bridge. "Those doors are thick and heavy, but it's the only ground level point of entry. Short of some serious grappling or climbing, it's our best bet."

Jet sighed. "We're going in the front door."

Smoke chuckled, low and rumbling. "The time for stealth appears to be over."

"We'll see," Boss said. "This is as little warning as we could give them. We've no idea what we'll find inside. Certainly more rezzers, but who the fuck knows what else. Smoke, you wanna check, let us in?"

"Sure thing."

Smoke vanished.

"The fuck does he keep doing?" Raven asked. "That's some skill."

"He's a planeswalker," Boss said. "He can step from our realm into another and back again. Right now he's walking however far he estimated he needed to go to get to the other side of that door. Then he'll step back into our realm and be inside to open up for us."

"Holy shit."

"Yeah. There's not a cell on earth that can hold Smoke, or a building that can keep him out."

"Where does he go?"

Boss laughed softly. "No idea. He won't say and I've given up asking."

"Huh. And you throw fire around?" Raven asked Taipan.

"We all have many skills, but my specialty is pyromancy, yeah. And Jet here has a fucking powerful voice of command she can turn on."

"Which is apparently useless against those mindless things." Jet's face was set in frustration.

"A necromancer's commands are designed to always be the foremost thing in any rezzer's thoughts," Boss said. "Seems that even overrides your voice."

"Great."

"And my flames don't even slow them down," Taipan said. "If anything, when they're burning they're more dangerous! Fucking nightmare."

The double doors clunked and one side creaked open. Smoke leaned out with a grin and waved them in. As they hunched to scurry across the bridge Smoke called out, "Don't worry about being careful. There are cameras everywhere in here like mushrooms in a wet field. We've been made."

They stood tall and sprinted to him. As Raven stepped inside she saw the interior was completely at odds with the outside. The ancient fortification housed a modern interior of expensive décor and up-to-the-minute technology. Smoke wasn't lying about the cameras, they sprouted from every wall and corner.

"Get ready to engage," Boss said. "He's sure to send something against us now."

As the words left his mouth, a ravening roar and howl rang through the tall, wide hallways. Then more than one, then dozens and claws skittered and scrabbled on the wooden floors.

"Fucking dogs," Jet said. "I hate it when they make me kill dogs."

"Yeah, not so much dogs," Taipan said.

They turned to see where he was looking. A crowd of huge, leathery creatures with wide maws crammed with sharp teeth tumbled around the corner, clambering over each other in their need to get to the prey first. They bore the barest resemblance to dogs, more like massive dog-shaped beasts with some parody of a crocodile's head. Jaws snapped and slathered. The barking and growling doubled as another crowd of them hurtled around the other end of the hallway.

"Great!" Taipan said. "Dark Squad in a giant teeth sandwich."

"Rain fire!" Boss yelled.

Raven swung her AK47 into play simultaneously with the others and they dropped into a ragged formation. She stood beside Smoke facing one way while Jet, Taipan and Boss faced the other. The corridor exploded into thunder and lightning as the automatic weapons barked and kicked. Armour-piercing ammo filled the air and the leathery flesh of the beasts erupted and split. Raven had a moment to marvel at the accuracy of her team mates. She thought her marksmanship was top notch, but these guys were a class above. Then she was distracted by the realisation that no blood came out of the perfectly placed wounds. The monsters didn't even slow.

"Brains are too fucking small in those giant heads," Boss yelled. "Get the eyes or shoot out the legs!"

But the things were almost on them.

Raven re-sighted, carved full auto low to the ground and took off the legs of the lead two beasts. They went down, still snapping and wriggling as more tumbled over them. The pile-up barely slowed the rest and those behind were already clambering over their fallen. She got a couple of bullseye shots right through eye sockets and two more dropped. Then Smoke blinked out beside her and Raven faced a hoard of monsters on her own.

First mission and this was it. What the fuck even were these things? She'd never imagined anything like them and they were so close she could smell their fetid breath. She let the AK go and pulled the jade dagger. As the one closest lunged for her, she slashed out and leapt up, put one foot to a sturdy table against the wall and flipped. As she turned over in the air she exulted to see the beast she'd slashed falter and collapse. Its head shattered as it hit the ground.

*At least the dagger works!* she thought, and came down on her knees on the back of another beast.

As it twisted and writhed, teeth slamming together only inches from her leg, she stabbed down into the back of its neck where she hoped some spine might be and leapt again. *I'll show you a fucking ballerina.* She jumped and danced between the beasts, slashing for legs and heads wherever she could. If she stopped moving she was dead, but if she changed direction often enough, and had a little luck, she could avoid the worst of their attack.

As she turned in one leap, she spotted Smoke appear far down the corridor, the other side of Boss, Jet and Taipan and the beasts they were fighting.

"*Hey, motherfuckers!*" Smoke yelled. Several beasts turned at the sound, then took off after him. Smoke bolted around the corner out of sight.

Boss and Taipan were ducking and shifting, chopping with machetes and firing with high-calibre handguns, taking a decent amount their enemies down. With the reduced numbers thanks to Smoke's distraction, they gained the advantage and turned to help Raven.

She paid a little more attention to their magic as she kept moving, trying to learn as she cut and froze flesh, moved again. She couldn't count how many there had been or how many she had killed but she suddenly found herself standing alone in the corridor, some distance from where the fight had started. Heaped mounds of dead and broken leathery flesh lay between her and Boss and the others. Beyond them, more fallen beasts. Several of the things still snapped weakly and writhed, bodies quivered, but none had the ability to attack any more, spines severed or brains crushed.

"Rezzed fucking hellhounds," Boss said. "As if the fuckers aren't bad enough alive. Who's hurt?"

"Who isn't?" Jet asked.

Raven felt warmth over her left hand and looked down. Blood ran in rivulets from her sleeve. Her arm just below the elbow was opened in a wide gash. As she noticed it, the pain set in. She knew that once the adrenaline eased it would only get worse. She looked up, lifted the arm. "Err…" Then everything went black.

\* \* \*

Raven came around to Boss's voice. "…be all right. You know he can take care of himself."

"Sure, but let's hope he can find us again." That was Jet.

Raven opened her eyes. Boss had dressed her arm, the others had a variety of bandages on arms, legs, heads. Taipan had half his head covered, his left eye obscured by dressings. But they all seemed in good enough spirits.

"Welcome back."

Raven looked at Boss, felt her cheeks redden. "Fucking hell, I can't believe I passed out."

"They have venom and you're not inoculated," Boss said. "Well, you are now. You'll feel queasy for a while, and you lost some blood, but you'll be okay."

A spent syringe lay on the ground beside her. Boss glanced

at it. "Yeah. One of many parts of our standard medkit. They're a bit different to what you're used to."

"No shit."

She sat up, and did indeed feel quite nauseated. She took a few slow, deep breaths, felt herself slowly centring again.

"Now I need your help," Boss said. "You operational?"

No way would Raven say anything but yes to that question on her first mission. "What do you need?"

"Your little friend. We need a recon mission, find out where the target is. We spend too long fucking around here with his pets and we're giving him time to slip away."

"You got it."

Raven spoke the word and the *samjok-o* stepped onto her shoulder. "We know what this guy looks like?"

Boss pulled a grainy photo from his pocket. It wasn't much, clearly taken at full zoom, it showed a Caucasian man, perhaps somewhere in his forties, cropped dark hair and a linen suit. "That enough?"

Raven took the photo. "It'll have to be." She stared at it, made sure the three-legged raven familiar took a good look too, then asked it to go fetch for her.

The *samjok-o* took wing and vanished. Raven closed her eyes and stayed with its thoughts. It did nothing for her nausea, flitting in and out of existence, room to room, searching the vast, sprawling complex. Then it found him, stood in the middle of a huge protective circle in the open courtyard at the centre of the castle.

She thanked her friend and opened her eyes. "Looks like he's waiting for us," she said.

As they moved out, Boss radioed Smoke but got no response. When Jet cast a hooded look at him he just shook his head and jogged on. Raven worried how they might feel if something bad had befallen Smoke. They had only recently lost Blinder and that clearly bore down on them heavily. To lose another so soon would be more than harsh. Then again, if Smoke were dead and needed to be replaced, at least she wouldn't be the new kid any more. It was a mercenary thought, but mildly comforting, especially as she hardly knew Smoke. But she had already grown to like the man a lot. She wanted to tell him the story of her dagger.

*Come on, you fucker*, she thought to herself. *Let's all go home from this one.*

They tracked their way through an ostentatious ballroom, eyes sweeping left and right, alert for further attack. But everything seemed still. Almost too still, if Raven believed in clichés. It was as though the castle itself was waiting for something. For some trigger to be tripped.

"I'm on fucking edge here," Taipan said. "I don't like having no depth perception."

"Your eye going to be okay?" Raven asked.

He shrugged. "It's still there. Whether it'll be okay or not remains to be seen." He grinned and looked down at her. "Remains to be fucking seen! Geddit?"

She couldn't help a laugh escaping, shook her head. "You people are…" She couldn't find the word.

"All right?" Boss threw back over his shoulder. "Is that what you meant?"

And she realised it was. "Yeah. You people are all right."

Boss nodded without looking around. "Wind it up, now. Let's concentrate."

The ballroom led into an ornate dining room. Polished rosewood table, intricate chandeliers and expensive-looking artworks. The table was laid with enough silver to pay off the national debt of some island nations.

"Looks like the fucker is planning a party." Boss pointed to a door on the far side. "That way."

The door had glass panels, light net curtains inside and wan moonlight beyond. They vaguely made out bushes and a stone fountain.

"Seems the cloud cover has cleared a bit," Jet said.

They slowed, took their weapons up in a casual ready position and advanced slowly. As they neared the doors, there was a click and they swung open. Boss paused, then straightened up. "Seems we're expected."

He strode out into the courtyard.

The others gathered beside him. The courtyard was huge, maybe a hundred metres across. It had garden beds and shrubbery all round, mostly Italian in style. Stone fountains sprayed and burbled all over, everything lit in monochrome by the half moon now clear of clouds. What had once no doubt been a central pond was now a raised dais of stone. The circular edge was old granite, carved with runes and sigils of protection. It crackled with power, warding pretty much everything a mage could throw at it. Raven had never felt such concentrated magic in her life. The man in the linen suit stood in the centre, arms casually at his sides.

"Hello, there," he said, his voice heavily accented Eastern European. "I have to admit, I'm impressed you got this far."

Boss raised his AK and squeezed the trigger. Nothing happened. He frowned, looked at the weapon, then back at the necromancer. "I expected your wards to stop the bullets, not render this entirely inoperative."

"More fool you."

"I guess so."

The air crackled with tension and magic. Raven found herself useless, impotent. Their firearms were inert, the target was caged against their magic. It was a sudden and seemingly insurmountable stand-off.

"Let's hope you're better at hand-to-hand than you are at recognising wards," the necromancer said.

Movement from either side sent a ripple of alertness through them. The square between the necromancer and the Squad filled with black-clad, fast-moving figures. Some flipped and tumbled as they ran in an ostentatious display of athleticism.

Boss groaned.

Taipan made a tight sound in his throat. "Are you fucking serious? Undead fucking ninjas now? They're rezzers, right?"

"Almost certainly," Boss said, his voice tired.

The rezzers gathered in a group, at least twenty of them. Raven looked around, realising that beside the bushes and fountains there was little to no cover. This fucker seemed to have an endless supply of minions.

"Remember," Boss said. "Take out the spine, brain, or decapitate. No amount of incidental damage will slow them. And it looks like they'll be a far greater challenge than the abominations in the forest."

As the Squad crouched, ready for the enemy to rush forward, a door on the far side of the courtyard slammed back.

"Hey, motherfuckers!" Smoke, grinning like the Cheshire cat, lobbed something in a high arc.

"Fire in the hole!" Boss yelled and the Squad hit the deck.

Smoke's grenade sailed high and dropped into the midst of the massed ninjas even as their voices shouted warnings to each other. They began to scatter, some leaping away in time, but the concussion of the blast whined everything to silence for a moment as bright light flashed out. Body parts rained down among chunks of earth and stone.

"That should even the odds a bit," Smoke called.

The massed group of rezzed ninjas had been spread wide by the blast. They yelled at each other over the following silence, trying to regroup. Even the necromancer looked concerned.

"Engage!" Boss hollered, and Dark Squad sprang into action.

They sprinted in different directions, ensuring the rezzers couldn't regroup. Raven headed for a clutch of three, jade dagger in hand. These were definitely not the mindless, broken things from the forest. The way they moved, communicated, readied themselves, showed them to be every bit as alert and dangerous as an enemy could get, only far harder to hurt. At least the dagger gave her a distinct advantage.

She heard Smoke's high-pitched laughter as she engaged the first assailant, then nothing existed but her own fight. The ninjas were fast, faster than any enemy she'd met before. The first kick came at her so suddenly it clipped her ribs before she could dodge fully, forced most of her air out. The shock of being hit so easily winded her more than the impact, but she managed to swipe the dagger across and felt it drag through flesh. The ninja put his foot down and his leg crumbled, sent him tumbling to the ground. She was already past him, blocking a furious flurry of blows from the next, barely twisted as the third threw another kick. The one she had cut was up on one leg already, hopping expertly to re-engage. She was hurt and still all three faced her.

Raven took a deep breath and whispered the word to her *samjok-o*. She asked for help and the three-legged bird stepped into the air again followed by a cloud of other shining black avians. They swirled and mobbed the ninjas, interrupting their approach. Raven let her mind slip into the state of *wu wei*, a Taoist concept of non-being. Her mind removed itself from her actions and she let pure training and instinct take over. No longer trying to learn or emulate, she let her magic flow as she danced with the flock of ravens, knives in hand, a lyrical, swirling display of athletic grace and deadly accuracy. As the birds dipped, she rose, as they fanned out, she dove in. The rezzed ninjas scored hits here and there, but she put off that pain for later. She felt the occasional searing burn of a blade strike and ignored that too. Her own dagger swept and flew, shattered flesh raining around in musical accompaniment to the dance.

Once her three assailants were gone, she moved with her cloud of birds across the courtyard, engaging wherever there was movement not of her Squad. Howls and shouts, cries and slaps of flesh on flesh, and then stillness.

Arms out to either side, the dagger held low in one hand, hair come loose and hanging over her eyes, Raven stopped moving. Statue-still but for the fast rise and fall of her chest, the rasp of rapid breathing. She let the emptiness drain away from her, slowly raised her eyes to look around.

Boss and Taipan stood side by side, hurt but smiling. Smoke strolled across the courtyard towards them. Raven's eyes fell on Jet, sat back against a fountain, bleeding and bruised, one eye already swollen shut. Jet gave a shaky thumbs up as she hauled herself to her feet.

The Squad regathered and stood before the protective circle. In its centre, the necromancer looked shaken.

"What's next?" Boss asked.

"You people are tenacious," the necromancer said. "But let's see you face this." He began chanting, knotted his fingers into complicated signs and mudras.

"He's summoning something," Jet said, slightly slurred through swollen lips.

Smoke tilted his head to listen. "A demon, I think," he said with a smile.

Raven's eyes widened. A demon? Seriously? And why were they all so casually amused about that.

"Oh ho," Boss said. "This'll be fun."

As the necromancer's words gained strength, rapidly blurring together, Boss raised his arms as if in supplication. With a rush of burning hot air, he faded and vanished. Before Raven had drawn a shocked breath, Boss reappeared inside the protective circle, standing right before the necromancer.

The necromancer's eyes went wide, his mouth fell open. "What the hell?"

"You really should consider," Boss said. "If you plan to summon a demon, it's best to know who's already around, otherwise what you expect to appear outside might already be there, and then your spell simply reverses itself."

Boss whipped his hand around, grip tight on the hilt of his machete, and the necromancer's head sailed up off his shoulders, spinning over and over, still wearing its expression of shock and disbelief. The body crumpled to the floor at Boss's feet.

Boss looked down at the body for some time as the magic of the protective circle drained away, then he turned and strolled back to the Squad. "There we go then."

"You're a fucking demon?" Raven asked. Her heart beat faster at this revelation than all the fighting up until this point.

Boss shook his head, slipped his machete away. "It's really not as simple as all that. Perhaps I'll try to explain it to you one day. Bad luck for him though, eh?"

Raven looked around the group. They all smiled and she felt like they were all in on a joke to which she wasn't privy. It was frustrating, but she supposed there was an awful lot to learn about these people.

Boss turned to look at the raised dais with its ring of carved sigils. "That's big enough for a chopper to put down, don't you think?"

"I would say so," Smoke agreed.

Boss turned to Jet. "Call it in, please. Tea and crumpet time."

\* \* \*

They were taken to an Armour base in Berlin to have their wounds taken care of. Taipan needed to wear a patch for a few weeks but was told he had been lucky and would retain his sight. Other than several dozen stitches between them and a few set bones, they weren't in too bad shape. Some of the Armour mages used a few less than natural techniques to hurry their healing along.

By the time they were in a comfortable lounge being fed, it seemed to Raven that the whole encounter had been weeks ago instead of hours.

"It'll be good to get back to New York," Taipan said. "There's a young man I know there who'll be very impressed with my eye patch. I've got this whole story about defending myself from a mugging to earn his sympathy."

"Don't you ever think about anything but sex?" Jet asked.

"I think about fighting a lot."

She laughed. "Fair point."

Boss crammed in the last of a sandwich and stood. "Right, I'm going to Paris to debrief with Commander Giraud. You lot head home, I'll see you in Manhattan. Except you, Raven. You're with me."

She frowned. "Everything okay?"

"Yeah. I want him to know how well you did, and for you to see a bit more of Armour operations."

It wasn't too long a chopper ride to Paris and the Armour HQ there. They went through a command centre with computer banks, busy personnel, a large round desk in the middle with holographic projections hovering over it.

"It's like the bridge of the fucking Enterprise," Raven said.

Boss laughed. "Armour has been around since the Crusades, fighting evil and gaining wealth and power. Come on."

He went along a hallway to a door marked *Commander* and knocked.

"Come."

Inside was a large office, filing cabinets and a sofa on one side. Behind a large mahogany desk sat a short man with dark, intense eyes and jet black hair. His face was deeply wrinkled, showing age that seemed to go beyond any mortal lifespan. Raven had no idea why, but she sensed immense power about him. It would take some experience and skill to be an Armour Commander after all, she supposed.

"Aha, Boss, please sit," Giraud said. His French accent was strong, but something else was in there too. Something Slavic maybe. "It all went well?"

"It wasn't easy," Boss said. "But you know us. We prevail."

"You hit some tough resistance?"

Boss nodded slowly. "We really did. The enemy were immune to Jet's voice, fire barely slowed them down, it's almost like they were the perfect thing to throw at us. Especially without Blinder and his skills. But like I said, we prevail."

Giraud smiled. "Indeed you do. You are a very reliable squad."

"Almost too reliable?" Boss asked.

The air in the room electrified, a sudden tension that put Raven on edge. She had no idea what had just happened, but the friendly greeting seemed distant as a new, icy atmosphere rippled up.

"Too reliable?" Giraud asked.

"You really didn't expect us to make it back, did you?" Boss said. "I mean, those were some pretty massive odds." He gestured at Raven. "Without our new recruit here, we would have had some serious trouble."

Giraud nodded, flicked a quick smile at Raven. "I must admit, I didn't know you had replaced Blinder already."

"Yeah, I thought not. I find it helps to play my cards close to my chest, even with the people supposedly on my side."

"Supposedly?"

Raven saw Giraud's hand move surreptitiously and press at something under his desk. Her own hand drifted close to the jade dagger.

"Why didn't that necromancer bleed when I took his fucking head off, eh?" Boss asked.

Giraud's eyebrows rose. "Didn't bleed?"

"You think I wouldn't fucking notice a small detail like that? That the necromancer supposedly behind all this was a fucking rezzer?" Boss's voice rose in volume with each word.

The door behind them opened and two large Armour operatives stepped in. Giraud began to rise from his chair and Boss's hand came up with a Magnum .44 and blew the Commander's head into mincemeat. It burst like a melon, spraying the wall behind the desk with blood and bone and brains.

Shocked shouts and movement erupted outside the office. As Giraud's body collapsed back into his chair one of the operatives who had come in fell to the ground like a puppet with its strings cut. The other, reaching for Boss, paused, staring open-mouthed.

Boss raised both hands and let the Magnum clatter onto Giraud's desk. "He was the real necromancer," he said loudly as people crowded into the room. "The fact that one of his rezzers dropped when he did is proof of it. Now I realise there's a lot of paperwork to do, but let's all just calm down, yeah? No one else needs to get hurt."

Tension drained slightly, giving way to shock. Hurried conversations travelled out across the base like a wave.

"Better get the Deputy Commander in here," Boss said.

The operative who had come in with the rezzer nodded. "I'll go and make the call."

Raven looked from the Commander's corpse to the dropped rezzer operative, mind reeling as she figured out the course of events. Her eyes finally reached Boss to find him smiling at her.

"You see why I brought you along now, then? Give you a better idea of our role in all this. You can see why we're needed?"

She smiled. "Black ops within black ops?"

Boss laughed. "None more black."

# SONS OF APOPHIS

Christine Morgan

*"You are asking us to betray our king."*
*"I am commanding you to save Egypt."*

It will be, when it is finished, a great and glorious city, a shining palace-temple, a fitting home and place of honor for the one true eternal shining ruler of the land.

Sefut-Aten.

The Bronze Fire of the Sun.

Where Pharaoh will rule his people in benevolence and peace. Where the waters will flow as honey, the land give forth its fertile bounty, and rich treasures be rewarded for both this world and the world beyond to those who serve with loyalty.

At the moment, the great city might be a jumble of clay and hay and scaffolding, but will soon rise anew in its full splendor. The statues lifted, the cut stones placed, the murals painted. In cool courtyards, pools will ripple. In gardens, bright birds will sing.

Over Sefut-Aten, day will never end and night will never come.

Teb smiles to think of it.

Those who serve with loyalty.

Rich treasures. Rewards.

This world and the world beyond.

Such thoughts keep him brave through the dark hours.

Though born to humble farmers, facing a life of planting and the plow, now here he is, entrusted with this most sacred and dangerous of duties, standing watch against the outer reaches of the night.

When the city is finished, when the sun no longer sets, when he and his fellow sentries have well done their duty, they will have fine houses. Plump wives. Many children. Lives of pleasure and ease. Respectable tombs.

Such promise is well worth these lonely watches as the sky stretches black and the stars cut sharp. He listens to the breeze-stirred rushes, the croak and plop of frogs, the distant cry of a jackal, and sleep-sounds from the workers' camp.

Further on, a single light blazes in the tower shrine where chosen priests hold their own late vigil, tending the sacred sun-flame in its bronze brazier, catching of its rays in polished mirrors so as to not let them all be swallowed up by darkness. Teb touches the miniature sun-disk amulet he wears. Though the metal is cool beneath his fingertips, a warmth goes through him. He feels his chest swell with pride, and smiles again.

He, Teb, who came from mud and dung... whose parents were superstitious peasants, little better than slaves... is here. Will be here to see the everlasting dawn—

A sudden loop drops over his head, a heavy length cinching tight against his throat.

Teb gags and chokes. His spear falls to the dirt as he brings both hands to claw at the strangling constriction. His mouth forms screams, shouts alarms, but only the thinnest whistle of air emerges. He feels his heart-pulse thudding like the pounding of bull's hooves. The night sky's star-sharp blackness seems to sweep over his eyes.

As his nostrils flare, inhaling desperately, a strange scent fills them... something earthen and oily and coppery and cold. The breeze-stirred rushes whisper louder than ever, hissing cold and harsh in his ears. The frogs have fallen silent.

He lurches forward and is yanked back. His sandals kick and scuff. He can get no purchase on whatever is twisted taut around his neck. He cuts the pad of his thumb on his own sun-disk amulet's edge—

Ut-Aten!

Seizing it, he uses that edge to slice and saw, frantic, hardly caring how he slices and saws his own skin, hardly caring as blood runs down his body… blood, blood is nothing, it is breath, *breath* he needs!

Roiling turbulence fills his head, stormclouds in evil colors of yellow, grey, and green. Portending rains of poison, portending floods and death. No life of ease, no fine house, no plump wife to give him many children—

Then a sense of *give*, of fray and loosening stretch, of *snap*—

—and *fall*, the ground leaping up to strike Teb in the face—

—a grunt from behind him as if of surprise—

—wheezing and gasping, miserly air, miserly breath through throbbing bruise-meat, sobbing-throbbing breath—

—his spear, his spear crossways under him, he'd landed atop it, scrabbling to clutch it in his blood-slicked hands—

—something seizing him, seizing him by the shoulder, heave-rolling him onto his back—

—the sight, a glimpse, a looming shadow outlined by sharp white stars, a man-like shape but scaly-hairless-sleek-supple—

—the spear, grasping it, bringing it with him as he rolls, bringing it with him and swinging it—

—sweeping the bronze tip in a wide, wild arc—

—slashing it through scales and flesh—

—another grunt, not just surprise but shock, but of *pain!* Yes, good, praise Ut-Aten, *pain!*—

—a scraping of bronze on bone, a stumble, the looming shadow, the man-like shape a weight falling—

—Teb wrenching himself sideways with all his strength, his draining fading strength, *what strength?* and driving harder with his spear, a rupture a puncture a gush and a thump—

—the spear shaft jarring from his grip, its bronze head buried, embedded—

—the stench of bowels, of bladder, of death—

—as he crawls, crawls through sticky-wet dirt, through mud—

—mud and dung, he had come from mud and dung and now was here again—

—but a brightness grows, a brightness and heat... shining and brilliant, warming, eternal... the sun, the sun rising in the middle of the night...

...to be swallowed whole by darkness.

\* \* \*

"Will you take refreshment?" Neferisu inquired. "Wine and bread?"

At his nod, she did not gesture for a servant but went to the side-table and poured from the jug herself. The salon was cool and private, shaded, secluded amid garden courtyards and behind walls. Cats lounged, a tame white monkey picked at bits of fruit, a harpist strummed the strings, and her maids kept a discreet distance.

When she turned, a tray of alabaster drinking cups and dishes in her hands, Khemet's expression of discomfort at being so waited upon was such she could not help but laugh.

"There was a time," she said, "not so long ago, when you would run to me with skinned knees, or begging honeyed dates."

"I was a child then, my queen."

"Yes. You and Mahenef, like brothers, as if I'd borne two sons."

She placed the tray between them, on a low stool carved in the overarching likeness of Geb and Nut. Along with the small loaves of emmer-bread were boiled quail's eggs and a plate of sliced cold meats in pomegranate sauce.

"The pair of you," she went on, smoothing her fine linen garment as she sat. "Up trees, and down wells, and into everything. We despaired of what to do."

"As I recall," Khemet said, "you threatened more than once to take us by the side-locks of our hair and knock our heads together."

Neferisu laughed again. "But I never did."

"No. You were always kind." He rubbed the side of his shaven, oiled scalp, his side-lock long since a thing of the past. "Though I would gladly have my head knocked, if it meant seeing Mahenef again in this world's life."

"He will be waiting for you in the Seven Halls," she said. "Then, let your boyish mischiefs be the problem of Osiris."

"My boyish mischiefs may be well behind me now, my queen." His eyes had gone dark. "You know what I am, what I've become."

"A guest who has not yet touched his refreshment," she said, regarding him with a look of gentle chiding over the rim of her cup.

Khemet sighed, picking up a piece of bread, dipping it in wine. "You make it very difficult to be a dangerous figure, dark, and grim."

"Be at ease. That is why I've summoned you, for a business dark and grim."

\* \* \*

Firelight dances down the tower's mirrored throat, casting caught radiance from the bronze brazier above to lavish chambers below.

By day, the sun's own reflected light itself illuminates the murals – bulls and lions, scarabs, horse-pulled chariots, fields of grain, spearmen and archers, falcons, maidens with baskets of flowers – in bright and vivid color. By night, as now, the effect is more a honeycomb of dappled gold, softening stark angles and edges.

It cannot, however, soften the stark angles and edges of two priests, standing like tall herons with their heads bent together in conversation. Gangly of leg and neck and nose, they are brothers, only just beginning to sport the small round bellies of comfortable station.

"I do not know how much longer we can keep him alive," says Sennu.

He is the younger by half a day, and the fact of their unusual birth – one son at the dawning, a second at the zenith – made their long-suffering mother an object of some fame.

"For so long as Ut-Aten wills it," Bennu replies.

Unkind village rumor has it there'd been a sickly third brother born at dusk, and perhaps a midnight fourth, who'd come dead and breathless into the world… or been hastened to that fate… but no one in their family has ever spoken of it, and they have never asked.

"But if he dies before—"

"It is in Ut-Aten's hands. Until then, we tend to him. We protect him."

Sennu nods. "When he last woke," he said, "he called again for *her*."

"If anything in this world will finish him…" mutters Bennu, pinching the patch of skin between his plucked and narrow, gilded brows.

"What should we do?"

"What else *can* we do? Send for her. Bring her. He is still our king."

\* \* \*

"The royal blood," Khemet began, troubled, when the queen had finished telling him just what her dark and grim business was. "The blood of Pharaoh, the bloodline of the gods…"

Neferisu shrugged mildly as she peeled the shell from an egg. "Spills as red and readily as the common, as you and I both know."

He fell silent again. Thinking – no doubt, as she was – of Mahenef. How sudden it had been, his death. How senseless, even for war.

The day had been theirs, the battle won, the enemy vanquished and scattered and bleeding on the sands. Khemet himself had been with the prince, the two of them and their drivers, racing side by side in their chariots, chasing down fleeing Hittites. And it had not been a broken axle, a stumbling horse, Mahenef sent flying to break his neck or be trampled… it had not been a final desperate challenge from a still-standing adversary… it had simply been some stray arrow out of nowhere.

"We will be famous for this," he'd said, grinning. "Our victory painted in murals, our names chiseled in stone. We will be famous, and I will be Pharaoh, and I will marry Sia and you'll marry Tanit—"

"Tanit likes you better."

"Then I'll marry her and you'll marry Sia; it doesn't matter to me, they're already my sisters. What matters is that then you and I shall truly be brothers!"

One moment, he'd been there, grinning and brandishing his spear, their drivers laughing along with them in great good spirits. The next moment, a bristle of ibis-feather fletching jutted from where Mahenef's twinkling eye had been. His breath and soul had left his body before it hit the ground.

Some stray arrow out of nowhere.

However much Khemet had wanted to believe otherwise – even treacherous murder would have given the chance to punish and avenge! – in the end, that was all it was. A twist of chance, a spiteful whim of the gods. No way of knowing from whose bow it had sprung, friend or foe. No way of knowing anything, or doing anything, except to bear Mahenef to the houses of purification and rest, to be prepared for his journey.

No way of knowing, no way of doing, nothing to be done.

Khemet looked at Neferisu, who held his gaze with a calm steadiness few others could. But, then, as she'd said, she remembered him as a child who'd run to her with skinned knees or to beg honeyed dates, as a youth who'd been her son's constant companion, as a young man who might have married one of her daughters.

She remembered the Khemet from before, yet she also had need of the Khemet of now.

What she asked of him… no.

What she *commanded* of him.

"To save Egypt," he said, more musing aloud than speaking to her.

"Our history has shown us what happens when madnesses take hold." Neferisu gestured around with an elegant hand, indicating the salon's furnishings, the low stool in the likeness of Geb and Nut, a statuette of wing-armed Isis in her regal beauty, the Eye of Horus over the door, a woven hanging depicting Thoth and Ma'at. "They would destroy all of this. The images, names, and symbols of the gods... painted over, chiseled out. Temples torn down. Priests attacked and people punished for their worship."

"And, set in place instead, this one and only god."

"The sun-disk, the bronze fire, their Ut-Aten." She paused for a dainty bite of meat and dabbed pomegranate sauce from the corner of her regal mouth. "And of all Ut-Aten's godly rivals, who would be most hated? Who, already, is more dreaded than even the fearsome Set?"

Khemet's lip curved in a wry smile. "Oh, you need not remind me of that truth, I assure you."

\* \* \*

*The serpent moves with silent swiftness.*
*The serpent waits to strike.*
*The serpent sinks its fangs.*
*The serpent coils, crushes.*
*The serpent strangles, squeezes, kills.*
*The serpent steals breath.*
*The serpent swallows life.*

Moving, yes, with silent swiftness, silent swiftness through the night. Dark shapes in the darkness, unheard, unseen, undetected. Finding their prey. Waiting to strike, waiting, and then sinking their fangs, coiling, crushing, strangling, squeezing.

Killing.

Stealing breath.

Swallowing life.

First, the solitary sentries on their lonely watch. The solitary sentries, and anyone else with the misfortune to cross the serpents' paths.

Some stonecutters who've sneaked from the worker's camp to share a jug of sour barley-beer... a pair of young lovers fumbling their way through a furtive tryst... a lame old beggar wakening at the wrong moment... a physician's apprentice selling stolen bone-of-vulture to a merchant's pregnant wife...

It is quick. It is quiet. No alarms are raised. Around them, tents and huts and houses dream in slumber.

They converge, gathering at their appointed meeting-place for the next stage of their attack. Scaled bodies, sinuous and powerful, rippling with muscle. Flinty heads from which slitted eyes peer at one another.

Six of them.

There are six.

When there should be seven.

\* \* \*

Khemet slipped from the queen's salon by way of the same secret rushlit passages through which he'd entered, his presence noticed only by a very few of Neferisu's most trusted servants.

Although it had been years since he'd set foot in the palace, his steps neither faltered nor hesitated. How often had he and Mahenef played here as boys? Making up adventures, fighting evil tomb robbers, man-headed scorpions, and other monsters... listening in on mostly-dull discussions between nobles, priests, and scribes...

He stopped, nerves pricking, pulse quickening, sensing someone else nearby.

"So, you finally return to us." A figure emerged from an adjoining doorway, and Khemet stood stunned and blinking for the span of several heartbeats.

"Sia," he said, once he could form words.

"Khemet."

"You have… changed."

"As have you."

He looked her up and down, from the painted toenails of her sandal-clad feet to the jeweled pins holding her intricate black braids in place. His gaze could not help but linger over lithe limbs and firm curves. "I think you have changed… more."

A smile crinkled the corners of her eyes, which were outlined in darkest khol and shadowed with the iridescent indigo dust of powdered scarab shells. "What was it that you said to my mother? Ah yes… I was a child then."

"No longer."

"No longer."

Khemet found himself at a loss for words. The girl he remembered, Mahenef's second sister, had been a reed-thin creature, pretty but shy. This was a woman grown, Bastet incarnate, and however ill-at-ease he'd been in the company of the queen, he felt far more stricken in the company of her daughter.

Then, her words came through to him, and he looked at her again, more sharply. "You heard our conversation?"

"Of course I did," Sia replied, as if he were being foolish. "Tanit and I often played in these passages as well. We knew all the spying-places."

"Then you know what the queen commands."

Her graceful, bare shoulders lifted in an idle shrug, mirroring her mother's. "She wants you to go to Sefut-Aten, to stop Pharaoh from this madness."

"By any means necessary."

"That, indeed, is what she said."

"And you know… about me. What I am. What I've become."

She took a step closer. He both smelled and tasted the sweet fragrances of cosmetics and perfume, and beneath those the even sweeter fragrances all her own.

"I know that after Mahenef died, you joined the Sons of Apophis. Now you are their leader. A warrior of darkness, a serpent-commander in the army of the night."

"We are no army," he said. "There are no chariots for us, no troops of spearmen and archers. My men are soldiers, but trained in the ways of stealth. Stealth, and murder."

Sia nodded.

"Does that not frighten you? Fill you with abhorrence and disgust?"

"Should it?" She took another step.

"Shouldn't it?"

In a slow, deliberate movement, she raised a hand and trailed her fingertips along his jawline from earlobe to chin.

He caught his breath. Warrior of darkness, serpent-commander, Son of Apophis, and her touch made him tremble.

\* \* \*

Six where there should be seven.

One of their number is missing.

They move – with silent swiftness – past more tents and huts and houses.

A fat slave-master stumbles yawning into view and pauses to relieve himself against a mudbrick wall. He does not see or hear his death approaching. He only voids his bladder in a wilder and more vigorous spraying stream as breath is strangled from him. They do not let him fall, but lower him carefully behind the wall, covering him with a loose strew of hay.

Torchlight burns the night. Not solitary sentries but a group of three temple guards, a patrol. Wearing tanned-hide breastplates with yellow sun-disks painted on their chests, carrying round bronze shields, each with a sickle-shaped *khopesh* sword hanging at his hip. The one who holds the torch is young, barely out of boyhood.

Six against three, it would be no contest.

Six against three, in silence?

*The serpent waits to strike.*

In the deepest shadows. Flinty heads lowered, scale-clad bodies powerful and poised.

The guards walk past the wall behind which the slave-master's corpse is hidden. Not entirely oblivious; they notice the drying wetness upon the mudbrick, the puddle soaking into the earth. The boy with the torch raises it. They look around. The tallest leans to peer over the wall.

It must be done.

A signal is given.

Now.

*The serpent sinks its fangs.*

Long and thin, sharp and curved.

Into unprotected backs, piercing linen before penetrating flesh. With unerring accuracy, avoiding ribs and shoulder blades and spine, puncturing the lungs, skewering the heart.

The younger guard, with the torch, is seized around the neck. His head is jerked violently to the side. The crack must seem loud to him, loud as the end of the world, but it is the only sound that's made, and to any other ears would be no more than a snapping twig.

His eyes are wide and still-seeing as he crumples boneless to the ground. Perhaps he watches as the torch is deftly plucked from his hand before it falls into the straw. Perhaps he sees his companions. The taller of them is slumped over the wall, a much thicker flood of wetness running down the mudbrick now to puddle on the earth. The other sprawls facedown, and as the serpent rears up from him, the fangs slide out in twin glistening curves.

And perhaps he sees, by what had been his own torchlight, the looming scaled shapes around him. The slitted eyes glinting from beneath ridges of flint. Then the torch is rudely snuffed, and whatever the young guard may have seen, he now sees nothing more.

The men are dead, their breath stolen, their lives swallowed, but this will be much harder to conceal. Time is of the essence, time and speed.

* * *

From *The Book of Beginnings*:

Then, when the first floodwaters receded, there arose from them a primal mound of rich, red earth. Atop this mound sat a goddess, who soon gave birth to the sun.

This newborn sun blazed so brightly, he blinded his mother with his brilliance. The goddess, unable to see her child, to find and hold and care for him, began to weep. Her tears fell. Sorrow filled her heart and despair filled her throat.

Before she choked, she spat out that black bile of despair. She spat it into the vast waters surrounding her mound of earth. And as she did so, it became an immense snake, with a head of ridged flint and a long, scaly body.

"Why do you weep, oh goddess?" asked the snake.

"The sun," she said, "my child, burns too bright to look upon! His brilliance blinds my eyes! What mother would not weep?"

Meanwhile, the child, who also could not see through his own brightness, cried tears of his own as he wailed for his mother. His golden tears, when they fell onto the earth, would become the seeds from which men and women sprung.

"Ah!" said the snake. "If that is what's the matter, it is easily remedied!"

So saying, the snake unwound his mighty coils to stretch his length up from the sea. Water sheened and glimmered like oil on his scales. Swift and silent, sinuous, he moved toward the young sun.

"What are you doing?" asked the goddess, who was of course still blinded.

But the snake did not answer, for he had gaped wide his jaws, gaped them so wide he closed his mouth around the sun and swallowed him down whole.

Then, the burning brilliance gone – gone down the snake's vast dark gullet – the goddess blinked her eyes and found she again could see. When she realized what had happened, she let out an anguished cry.

"You have devoured my child!"

"Now you are no longer blind," said the snake.

"Give him back to me, you monstrous beast!"

"This is some gratitude to show me; I shall do no such thing!"

As it was, however, the sun yet lived, and went on to fight and force his way through the snake's seething innards – which caused the snake no small amount of discomfort – until he emerged from the other end. Much of his light had been dimmed by the difficult journey, so that his brightness was no longer blinding his mother.

The goddess was overjoyed to be reunited with her child, but the snake warned her he was far from finished with them.

"I will swallow him again!"

"And he will win free again!"

"I will keep swallowing him!"

"He will keep winning free!"

So they said, and so it was, and so has it ever been, and so there are day and night.

\* \* \*

While Bennu consults with the physicians, Sennu gathers the folds of his yellow skirt-robe to his bony knees and makes haste up a sloping corridor.

His sandals slap flat echoes of his footsteps. The walls are tight-fit blocks of stone, covered floor to ceiling with sacred writings from *The Scrolls of the Arisen Sun*. In alcoves spaced at intervals, bronze sun-disk dishes hold burning candles.

He reaches the inner gate, puffing and sweating.

It is night. It is dark. He does not want to go out there, even bearing with him the fire of Ut-Aten in one of the sun-disk candle holders. The blackness looms so large, so ominous and deep.

But, Sennu reminds himself, it will not last for long. Soon, the sun will shine eternal. Soon, the serpent will be banished forever into chaos, and order will rule all.

Comforted by these thoughts, he passes through the gate.

Once, the pillars supporting the roofs of the walkways edging the courtyard were statue-images of the old beast-headed gods; their features have been chipped and chiseled into anonymity, awaiting the sculptors who will remake them in more appropriate design.

As the work continues.

As the money is brought in.

As the fame and power of Sefut-Aten rises, gaining strength.

Everywhere are piles of materials, skeletal cages of scaffolding, stacks of bricks, slabs of stone, beams and winches, casks of oil and lime and river-water, half-hewn obelisks, levers, ladders, tools. A crude and temporary arrangement of slats and rope serves as the outer gate until the massive bronze one can be finished, the massive bronze gate with its sun-disk of gold and rays of precious gems, which will surely dazzle and humble all who come to this place.

Sennu's feet grind and crunch on grit and gravel, pebbles, dust, debris. He crosses the courtyard – it will be a lush garden when all is said and done, perhaps with a menagerie to rival those of the greatest Nubian chiefs – and enters that section of the structure given over to the royal living quarters.

Pharaoh has been calling again for *her*.

His Lily-of-the-Nile, his flower, his golden lotus.

Personally, privately, Sennu considers the woman to be something of a she-jackal: clever, opportunistic and sly. But, even in his priestly celibacy, he cannot deny her striking beauty… and she is a devout worshiper of Ut-Aten, her influence even having helped convert Pharaoh himself to the true faith.

Her chambers are guarded by two of her own hand-picked warriors, who wear leopard-skins, gold pectoral collars set with polished onyx, and very little else. They wield long, thick, stout staves capped with sharp-edged disks of burnished bronze.

The Lily-of-the-Nile claims that they are eunuchs. No one dares suggest otherwise.

They smirk as Sennu scurries past. He wakes a round-faced, round-bodied slavewoman, who goes to fetch her mistress.

Left briefly alone, feeling out of place and out of sorts, he wanders the room. It is opulent. There are palm fronds and feathered fan-plumes, hangings, cushions, decorative chests and coffers. He frowns briefly over a shelf of small jade figurines, but they are merely trinkets.

The sudden creeping sensation of no longer being alone, of being watched, makes him turn. Too fast, the candle jitters in his hand so that its light flickers.

The child stands there. His pudgy body is half-hidden by the shadows of a luxurious reclining-couch, but his wide and wide-spaced eyes catch the candle's flame like yet more polished mirrors. Unlike most boys his age, his head is not shaven into a side-lock; his hair tumbles in sleep-tousled ringlets to his naked, dimpled shoulders.

Sennu twitches. He has never been much at ease in the company of children. This one, least of all. Soft of feature, full of lip, weak of chin, bow-legged, with smooth and chubby little fingers…

They look at each other. Man and boy, priest and prince.

Silence hangs between them, a thick and tangible thing, growing and swelling, the gas-gut bloat of a waterlogged corpse, a hippopotamus left to rot in tepid river shallows.

Where is that wretched slavewoman? What is taking her so long?

He manufactures what is meant to be a reassuring smile, wondering which of them he's trying to reassure.

Those wide and wide-set eyes stare, unblinking, filled with mirrored fire. A fat pink tongue squirms between full lips. One of his chubby fingers pokes into his navel. His other arm, he slowly raises, and extends. Something dangles from the child's hand. A length of cord, a strip of cloth, some sort of toy, Sennu thinks.

As he lifts the candle to shed a better light, he sees it for what it is. Long and limp and slender, a dead snake held by the tail.

Its fine scales are green and black, delicate patterning fading to a paler underbelly. Its head… its head is misshapen, squashed, oozing. Like an overripe date or fig that has been stepped on, or squeezed in a strong fist.

211

Sennu's mouth and throat are dry, desert-dry, sandstorm-dry. He fears his knees will give way.

Then, from behind him, he hears voices and movement. Pharaoh's Lily-of-the-Nile glides in, pinning closed a garment of linen so sheer it makes the gesture of modesty moot. She has taken the time to apply fresh cosmetics. The slavewoman waddles after her, muttering, offering up choices of rings and bangles from a jewelry case.

"He has a snake," Sennu says, pointing. It is not what he'd intended. It is hardly a proper greeting. The words just... fall from him, like a crumbling rill of sand.

Lily-of-the-Nile sways past and bends, reed-supple, over the boy. She somehow gives the impression of stroking his tousled hair without touching him at all.

"Yes," she says, all but crooning. "I have one brought for him every afternoon."

Sennu gapes, incredulous. "But *why*?"

"We kill it at the moment of the sunset, don't we, my shining little god? To show the demons of the night they cannot hope to harm *us*, no, oh no, they cannot."

The child giggles, lifts his arm again – the dead snake trailing – and licks a smear of congealed gore from the back of his hand.

It is all Sennu can do not to shudder.

\* \* \*

"Do you also remember," Sia whispered, settling her palm against Khemet's cheek, "how Mahenef would speak his plans of the future? How he and you would marry Tanit and I, and become true brothers at last?"

"Sia..." he said, resisting the urge to lean into her caress.

"Before she died – it was the bone-weakness, same as our Uncle Thut – she requested her sarcophagus be placed alongside Mahenef's in his tomb. To be united with him in the next world, *ba* and *ka* and soul and body."

"I had heard." His voice was not quite steady. "May they be forever happy in the houses of Osiris."

"While here we two still are, yet among the living."

How beautiful she was, how confident and sure. He had never, until this moment, so regretted his decisions. By Ma'at, by Isis, she was lovely. And to have a woman look at him, touch him without apprehension… he did not like to think how long it had been since that had happened, since he'd enjoyed the pleasures of such company without paying a price… even then usually to be met with stoic endurance …

"The last time we saw each other," she said, "we shared a kiss."

He shut his eyes and did allow his cheek to press against her palm. Her skin was as warm and fine as oasis sand. He savored her scent, yearned to part his lips and taste her unique salt-sweetness upon his tongue.

"It was a clumsy thing, that kiss, and awkward," she went on. "Our noses bumped. I couldn't stop blushing, and you were so anxious we might be seen. Do you remember that, as well?"

"Vividly," he said.

"I wonder." Her murmur, a soft evening breeze rich with promise… the nearness of her… "Would we be better at it now?"

He nearly groaned. "Sia…" he said again, struggling for word, for thought, for action. "I've already given your mother my answer. You do not need to—"

From caress to stinging, ringing slap!

\* \* \*

They find their missing seventh at the end of a long trail of blood. As if having dragged or been dragged through the dirt. Struggling, slithering, a painstaking crawl.

Scales and skin slashed open.

A bronze spearhead lodged deep.

Organs and bone.

The spear-shaft snapped off, broken, trailing.

Nearby is a sentry, his throat a garish red weal, swollen and angry—

*—the serpent strangles, squeezes—*

—but somehow eluding, escaping for a moment. Getting a chance to strike back. Desperation and luck, raw luck. Enough to wound, wound badly, even fatally.

Not, however, enough to save himself.

The sentry is dead. Smothered, suffocated. Face pushed into mud. Held there. Held there as clay clogged his nose, filled his mouth, covered his eyes. The scent of dank silt. The gritty taste, the feel, wet sand in his teeth. The hot, coughing pain of damp earth-clots being sucked into his lungs.

*The serpent steals breath.*

*The serpent swallows life.*

To take his killer with him is the best he has been able to do.

Which is far better than many could say, given the circumstances. Far better than most.

The sentry was also at least unable to raise an alarm. Their seventh has done that much, has kept the swiftness and the silence. Has kept to the purpose, the mission.

Now they know. The question is answered, the mystery solved.

Honoring the loss of one of their own must come later.

This is their time, in the dark hours.

The sacred fire burns bright in its tower. A tiny sun, arrogant, insolent, defiant. A bronze beacon behind the temple-palace walls.

They make for it.

Swift and silent, scaled and sleek, the serpents of the night.

No other unfortunates get in their way. No workers and no witnesses; no whores, drunkards, or slaves.

Fanged and ready. Shadow to shadow.

Toward the temple, the tower. Walls and scaffolding surround palace houses and courtyards. The shoddy wooden temporary gate is guarded, an open-walled hut to each side and four men to each hut. Not sentries here but soldiers, again in tanned-hide breastplates, with shields and curved *khopesh*-blades.

These guards are alert, not dozing, not gambling, not telling jokes and lies about women. Lanterns shed broad circles of light, overlapping on the great flat slab-stones in front of the gate.

*The serpent waits to strike.*

Glances. Gestures. Flinty heads nod understanding.

Two, the stealthiest, move forward. Move to the very fringe-edges of the light. Their fangs have been withdrawn; sometimes the serpent must strike from afar.

With a whisper-soft hiss and snap, no louder than the click-whir of a scarab's wings, each finds its mark. Not stinging vulnerable flesh but snuffing, blink-fast, the lantern-flames from their wicks.

Blackness drops like a weight. The guards gasp in surprise.

It is a last breath to be stolen. There is no time to cry out, no time to draw their weapons. The serpents are already upon them.

* * *

Khemet's eyes flew open at the slap. His nostrils flared and his body tensed.

He caught her by the wrist almost before the sharp crack finished ringing in his ears, the stinging heat still spreading on his face.

Sia did not flinch. Her fierce gaze held and challenged his.

"Is that what you think I'm doing?" she demanded. "Is that what you think of me?"

*The serpent coils, crushes.*

His fingers coiled, poised to crush. To crush her fine and fragile bones. To crack and grind them in his fist.

"You think I would seduce you on my mother's behalf?" she went on.

*The serpent...*

*No.*

*Not here. Not now. This is not the serpent's place.*

"No," he said, aloud, and relaxed his grip. "That is not what I think. Sia, I am sorry."

215

She yanked her arm away. "Though you might be right to think so. Why not whore myself for her purpose, instead of being whored for Pharaoh's?"

Khemet almost asked what she meant by that, but then he understood. He closed his eyes again, exhaling through clenched teeth, letting his shoulders fall.

"I am the eldest surviving daughter." She uttered a bitter laugh. "It would make me queen of all Egypt, the dynasty secure."

"Yes," he said heavily. "Yes, it would."

* * *

Fangs plunge and impale, piercing lungs, piercing hearts. Muscles curl and constrict, tightening, powerful, inexorable.

Windpipes and voice-boxes collapse in muted crunches of cartilage. The guards grope feebly, kick with futile struggles as they strangle. Gristle crackles in their necks. Bodies fall with meaty thumps.

In a nearby hut, a dog whuffs. Once, and twice. A third is interrupted by a man's impatient, drowsy grumble. The dog whines plaintively.

Then all again is silent.

The sacred fire in the tower burns on, unabated. Those who tend it go on doing so, chanting, oblivious to danger.

For now.

To raise the gate would mean risking noise, its wooden creak and rattle, the squeal of pulley and rope. The serpents go up it instead, swarm up it with fluid ease, up and over, dropping soundlessly into the courtyard.

They flow across it like currents of dark water, parting and passing around piles of bricks and cut stone, mounds of dirt and gravel, beams, casks, straw-bales, and the disfigured visages of gods.

Swiftness. Silence.

Dark shapes within the larger darkness of the night.

216

First, they will strike at the barracks. In that long, low-ceilinged room, more guards sleep on woven mats. Unarmed, naked, unprepared, presenting no challenge to the sinking fangs, to the strangling coils. From there, they will go to the tower—

But, before any of that can be done, a moving firelight flicker strengthens brighter in a doorway.

*  *  *

"However..." said Sia, "I am the eldest surviving daughter anyway. No matter who I marry, would I not still be queen?"

Khemet glanced at her, feeling even more uncertain, as if their conversation took place upon some deceptive stretch of quicksand.

He almost, in that instant, yearned for the dark caverns below the desert, carved in sunless secrecy by age-old underground rivers. There, at the hidden stronghold the Sons of Apophis called home... there, where the immense black avatar basked and rested, accepting offerings of flower-garlanded heifers with gilded nubs of horn... there, where he had lived, had trained... where their ways, their rules, were simple and easily understood...

*The serpent...*

The serpent, yes, the Serpent. Apophis, Apep, the Maw of Night, Eternal Devourer of the Sun.

*The serpent swallows life.*

His life as well? Khemet's own? Freely given, offered up like any other sacrifice, offered and accepted?

And why not? He'd had no close family – a soldier father long since dead, a mother who'd put him in the care of an aging aunt when she remarried, a stepfather and various half-siblings he barely knew. The aging aunt, a cosmetician to the ladies of Pharaoh's court, had done her best to raise him, and her favored status afforded him much freedom and indulgence. Even she was gone now, having succumbed to the damp-lung before the war in which Mahenef had died.

217

So, indeed, why should he not have taken on the Scales and Fangs and Coils?

It seemed, at the time, a reasonable decision. One he could anticipate little cause to regret. Although he had learned no other trade but battle, the armies did not want him, believing unluck was his shadow. Likewise, he would have no wife or children to support. And, despite a princely education gained at Mahenef's side, his aunt had left only a scant inheritance once her final arrangements were complete.

Might as well make the most of his solitude and ominous reputation. Might as well pledge himself to the Serpent.

Yet now, here he was… and Sia… if she was suggesting what it seemed she was suggesting…

Their youthful infatuation, her brother's joking plans, and that single fumbling awkward kiss of bumped noses and blushing… those belonged to another time, a gone time, another world. Didn't they?

The way she touched him, though. The way she looked at him and stroked his face. The soft warmth like fine, smooth, heated sand in her caress, her voice, her gaze.

How could she want him, knowing what he was? Knowing what her own mother had commanded him to do?

This business dark and grim, as she had phrased it.

If he did not – if he refused, or failed – then any hope with Sia would be gone. But if he did, if he succeeded…

There was no crime greater than the shedding of royal blood. The bloodline of Pharaoh was the bloodline of the gods.

Ordinary murder was more than wickedness enough.

Her words and his, speaking of Mahenef and Tanit… *united with him in the next world,* ba *and* ka *and soul and body… may they be forever happy in the houses of Osiris.*

And Neferisu's words as well… *he will be waiting for you in the Seven Halls.*

No crime greater than the shedding of royal blood. No crime more certain to weigh a heart heavier than stone in the balance-scales held by Anubis. Instead of the houses of Osiris, it would be the monstrous Ammit. It would be utter obliteration.

Conflicting thoughts and emotions seethed in him, roiled like a pit of snakes, churned like the primal seas of chaos.

With a sudden, violent cry and gesture, he dashed them all from his mind. He stood, jaw clenched, hands raised, fingers stiffly splayed, air hissing harsh and rapid through his teeth.

*The serpent...*

"Khemet?"

She took a step, began to reach for him.

*...coils, crushes.*

He seized her, pulled her to him, coiled his arms around her body, crushed her to his chest—

*...steals breath.*

—and claimed her lips in a fierce kiss.

\* \* \*

The firelight flickers.

Brightening, strengthening.

A false dawn.

Gleaming gold in a doorway, casting a gangly moving shadow against a wall.

A man appears, tall and thin, angular as a heron. Even with a heron's walk, beak-nosed head bobbing with each stilted step.

His robe and sun-disk jewelry proclaim him a priest. He carries a candle in a dish of bronze. It quavers in his grasp, and his eyes dart about like anxious flies.

The swiftest and most silent of them, at the signal, moves to attack.

Fangs emerge whisper-quick. And strike. Piercing just below the collarbones, just above the ribs, to either side of breastbone, plunging hilt-deep into lungs.

A single, startled gasp, barely begun... eyes bulging wet with horror... and it is done. The bronze dish falls from the priest's loosening fingers but is caught before it hits the ground. The candle tumbles from it, rolling across flagstones, flame guttering and sputtering.

Then, it all goes wrong.

Then, somebody screams. A high voice, piping and shrill. In the doorway is a child, a boy, soft and well-fed, his hair a mass of curls. Other voices join in, a clamoring alarm. Two women are there, one short and squat, the other slim and shapely. Several men rush past the women, muscular men in leopard skins and gold pectorals. They carry stout staves topped with rounded, sharp-edged blades.

Coils lash and snap, black in the dim-lit gloom. One twines about a staff and yanks it from the hands of the wielder, sending it to clatter. A second snares the same man by the calf and ankle; a hard pull flips him off his feet. The lengths of other coils entangle wrists, encircle throats.

The closest serpent, the one who struck the priest, darts at the screaming boy. But the boy, surprisingly fast for his soft pudginess, scurries out of the way. He flings something limp and ropelike in the serpent's face – a cold, dead snake. The squat woman seizes him, pulling him back as if to hurry him to safety.

"Murderers!" shrieks the shapelier woman, she of the exquisite beauty garbed in sheer, thin linen. "Murderers and thieves!"

Another coil whips toward her. She dodges with a dancer's grace. It misses wrapping her slender neck; its tip splits the skin of her shoulder. Blood runs down her arm. She shrieks again, as much in outrage at her marred perfection as in pain.

With a lunging leap, the priest-killing serpent is upon the shorter woman. The curved fangs plunge again. Her last act is to shove the boy through the doorway, to almost throw him in a final desperate burst of strength.

From rooms around the courtyard come the sounds of waking query, confusion, concern. On high in the sun-tower, the chanting abruptly stops. Burnished mirrors swivel, casting sunbeams of false day over the commotion. Shadows leap stark and strange against the walls and pillars, against the ruined visages of gods.

The fangs draw blood. The coils constrict.

A staff swings. A serpent twists aside; the rounded blade's bronze edge shears through scales and flesh in a long but shallow cut. It swings again, up-around-down in a whistling arc. Heavy wood cracks on flinty head, on bone. The serpent drops, stunned… or worse.

* * *

Releasing her was as difficult as he'd expected, and he'd expected it to be all but impossible.

Khemet stepped back, every sinew feeling drawn tight as a bowstring, his body surging like the rising Nile floodwaters.

Breathless, yes, she was breathless. The carefully-daubed carmine of her lips had become a rich, red smear.

"You will be queen," he said.

Sia gazed up at him, eyes hazed with desire, heavy-lidded in a slow cat's blink. Her cheeks were flushed, her intricate braids in disarray. The fine-pressed pleats of her linen garment hung rumpled and askew.

The way she had melted against him, molded to him, melded, her own kiss as fervent, her own hunger as intense… in the privacy of that rushlit passage, unseen, unknown, they could have…

"You will be queen," Khemet repeated.

Then he turned, striding perhaps not silent but still swift. He dared not linger, dared not wait for her to speak. Dared not tempt himself further.

In a matter of moments, he had reached a sunlit alcove overlooking a bustling crafter's yard. Potters and painters, weavers and carvers, and others of such normal trade went about their business. The bright air rang with voices – chattering, haggling, laughing. Children ran about, side-locked naked boys just as he and Mahenef had once been, getting into mischief. He smelled pan-bread frying in oil, fish and water-fowl roasting on spits.

Life, this was life, ordinary daily life. And here he was, apart from it. Squinting; his vision, like his spirit, more accustomed to the dark.

With the ease of much practice, he slung a loose fold of his black shoulder-wrap to drape around his head. A lozenge of polished onyx, set with chips of flint and two small green gems, weighted the cloth at his brow.

He made his way through crowded streets and marketplaces, avoiding contact, being avoided in turn. Those who happened by chance to notice him were quick to divert their attention elsewhere.

At the river's edge, a small boat waited, likewise studiously ignored by most along the docks. The serpentine design woven into its reed construction was subtle, as was the stitching in its shade-awning. The men waiting with it wore garments similar to Khemet's, their shaved and oiled heads similarly covered.

They nodded as he approached, picked up their steer-poles as he boarded, and pushed the small craft off into the wide and smoothly rippling waters.

\* \* \*

They are five now.

Five, and more guards are coming.

Charging from the barracks, some with tanned-hide breastplates hastily buckled, having grabbed shields and spears, brandishing *khopesh*-blades. Many priests run into the courtyard as well, priests carrying bronze knives or torches.

And, beyond the wooden gate, others have begun to gather. Workers. Merchants. Sentries. Slaves. The builders and people of Sefut-Aten, calling out to one another, shouting with confused consternation. Most are men, strong men, builders, arming themselves with whatever tools they find most handy.

The last of the leopard skin-clad warriors has fallen. A serpent has snared the beautiful woman in his Coils. Pharaoh's mistress, his favored concubine, his Lily-of-the-Nile. She struggles and spits and scratches like a cat. She curses them with vile language for presuming to lay their hands upon her.

Then the boy, the irksome and obnoxious child who's caused

them all this hardship, comes running back out. Demanding they release his mother, promising them the burning deaths of a thousand angry suns, do they know what they are doing? Do they not know who he is?

He snatches up the dead priest's dropped candle. Before any of the serpents can stop him, he hurls its guttering flame into a broken bale of straw. The dry and brittle stuff ignites with a gusty flare. The boy's next action is to heave all his pudgy weight at an oil-cask, which overturns.

Two serpents seize him by the arms, haul him off his feet, carry him suspended between them. He is visibly shocked by this, astounded, as if he earnestly believed they could not touch him.

But the damage has been done; the spreading spill of oil feeding hungry fire, hastening its appetite for wood and rope and scaffolding.

In a mere span of heartbeats, the entire courtyard is ablaze.

* * *

The sun had set into cooling darkness by the time Khemet and his men emerged from their hidden stronghold in its deep river-carved caverns below the desert.

He chose six to go with him, six of his best, six of his fellow Sons of Apophis.

Instead of their simple tunics and shoulder-capes, they wore the Scales. The close-fitting armor covered their entire bodies, made from supple oiled hide to which small overlapping pieces of stiff black leather and greened copper had been sewn. On their heads were helm-caps covered with angled wedges of flint.

At his waist, each man carried the Fangs, twin knives with narrow, curving blades and needle-sharp points. Around their wrists and forearms were tied the shorter sets of Coils, sturdy lengths of cord suitable for binding or strangling. The longer Coils, loops of limber rope-whips, hung on their backs, snakeskin-wrapped handles within easy reach.

"To betray our king," one said, in a musing, thoughtful tone.

"To save Egypt," another replied.

"By any means necessary," added a third.

"Even the shedding of royal blood?" the fourth asked.

"No crime greater," said the fifth.

"No crime more certain to weigh the heart heavy as stone," the sixth agreed.

"I will not put so great a burden upon you," Khemet said. "No, *that* task I shall take upon myself, and answer for it to Anubis and Ma'at."

They rode for Sefut-Aten on the dark winds of the night.

\* \* \*

"Now you are done for, you wretched crawling snakes!" says Lily-of-the-Nile, as the fire grows and the guards advance. "Pharaoh will flay you alive and leave your corpses for the jackals."

She is terrified, but she is also furious. Her shoulder is a sheet of pain where the whip split her flawless flesh. They've bound her wrists behind her back and hold their knives poised at her throat. Her most faithful slavewoman and half a dozen of her hand-chosen warriors are dead.

And they have her son. Her precious Utatenhotep. The look he gives her is a strange mix of betrayed belligerence and fear. How many times has she told him this would never happen? It must be *her* fault, his sullen pout proclaims. She must have lied to him or failed him; how *could* she, when he has been so good? Her own little shining god, and now she has let the demons get him!

The guards seem cautious, even hesitant. None wish to be the first to charge, whether for their own safety or hers and the child's. The priests also hesitate. She sees Bennu or Sennu among them, whichever of the heron-legged brothers is not splayed in the dirt with holes piercing his lungs.

Rising flames leap and roar, racing up ladders and

scaffolding. At the gate are cries of *Fire!*, cries for water and sand, to quench it before all their work is undone, before Sefut-Aten lies in ashes.

A shape moves in front of her, blotting hot light with his dark shadow. Beneath the flinty edges of his helm-cap, his eyes are not the monstrous slit-pupiled glowing green she has imagined. Ordinary eyes. An ordinary man, after all. Not some creature of Apophis.

"Where is Pharaoh?" this serpent – this *man*! – asks her.

Lily-of-the-Nile spits in his face. The movement earns her a sharp pinprick jab to the neck, but she does not care. It is worth it.

The man, leader of serpents, gestures. The two who hold Utatenhotep between them by the arms drag him forward.

"Where is Pharaoh?" he repeats, placing a scaled hand on the boy's shoulder.

Utatenhotep begins to snivel.

"You dare not harm my son." She lifts a defiant chin. "He is Pharaoh's child, of the royal bloodline of the gods."

The flint-edged head tilts one way, the man's grim mouth tilts the other. "The gods you have forsaken?"

"Not Ut-Aten! My son is Ut-Aten's chosen, Ut-Aten incarnate and reborn! He will rule over all of Egypt—"

"With Pharaoh's daughter as his sister-queen," he finishes.

"Ha!" Lily-of-the-Nile scoffs. "He'll have no need of *her!*"

Even as she says this, she realizes it is somehow a mistake. The man's eyes – which still are not slit-pupiled, still do not glow – narrow and become more dangerous than ever. He moves his scale-covered hand to encircle the boy's throat. Strong fingers press deep indentations into soft and vulnerable flesh.

"Oh, she will be queen," he says. "I have promised her that."

\* \* \*

In the cool, shaded salon, wine sat untouched. No music wafted on the garden-fragrant air; the harpist had been sent elsewhere, as had the maids. Even the tame white monkey nibbled its fruit in some other corner of the palace, though the cats, of course, sleek and pampered, with their collars of gold, continued lounging wherever they pleased.

Neferisu waited, tranquil and elegant as a statue of a goddess. Her serene, noble features displayed no outward sign of impatience.

Sia was another matter.

"You'll wear holes in your sandals," Neferisu said, after a while of her daughter's pacing.

"There should be more news by now."

"We shall hear it when there is."

What little they so far had heard was, as such news tended to be, fragmentary, filled with rumor and exaggeration and contradiction. Sefut-Aten had been destroyed, the entire city swallowed up by the desert just as the Great Devouring Serpent swallowed the sun. Sefut-Aten had not been destroyed, far from it, but would-be murderers of Pharaoh had been captured and burned alive.

Pharaoh *was* murdered. Pharaoh may have been murdered, but rose again from the dead to take his revenge. Black snakes rained from the skies and killed a hundred of Ut-Aten's priests. A thousand bronze fire warriors were marching, would be here with the dawn, and brought with them a mirror so immense it would sear people to cinders and melt the sands to glass.

That famous beauty, Pharaoh's Lily-of-the-Nile, was a witch, a witch dripping her sweetly poisoned nectar into his kingly ear. No, Lily-of-the-Nile had been bestowed to him as a gift to guide him on the path of the new god. No, she was a test, a trick, sent by Isis to determine if he could be so easily swayed.

Her child was Pharaoh's own son, of the royal bloodline. So Lily-of-the-Nile claimed, and no one would publicly dispute her, but hadn't it been years since he fathered any children by any wife or concubine? Why her, why then? The will of Ut-Aten, of course! Though it was hardly as if she lacked for company.

So it went, the news, on and on as the long day passed.

"The sun *is* setting," Sia said.

"You did not truly believe they would banish night forever."

"Of course not. I believed Khemet would do what must be done."

Neferisu smiled gently. "To save Egypt."

"By any means necessary."

"And if he did, if he has, could you still love him?"

"I always have."

"I expect," said Neferisu, her smile widening as she glanced past Sia toward the discreet doorway of the hidden passageway, "he's glad to know it."

Sia whirled, braids flying, crossed hands pressed upon her breast. A cry burst from her lips. She all but sprang across the salon to meet the dark and weary, wounded figure who stepped into view.

He had paused long enough to divest himself of Scales and Fangs and Coils, Neferisu saw, and to rinse away the worst of the travel-dust, blood, and smoke. Wildly improper though it was, and painful though it looked, he caught Sia in his arms. He held her to him, shaking, head down upon her shoulder.

"Well?" Neferisu prompted, after giving them a moment.

Without raising his head, Khemet replied, "It is done. The Fire of Ut-Aten is snuffed out, the priests and their followers slain, the survivors scattered."

"The woman and the boy?"

"*The serpent sinks its fangs*," he said. "*The serpent steals breath.*"

"And Pharaoh?" asked Neferisu. "What of my husband and king?"

At that, he did lift his head to look at her. "As you commanded. We have brought him home."

# SEAL TEAM BLUE
## A New World Novella

John O'Brien

## Prologue

It first made its appearance in Cape Town, South Africa and quickly spread to the rest of the world with a speed seldom before witnessed. Many fell into its grasp, the phone lines into businesses filled with more people calling in sick than with customers. The aged, the young, and the ill succumbed to the virus, numbering in the hundreds of thousands. Services within cities became limited, prompting action by national governments. A coalition of pharmaceutical companies was formed to develop a vaccine, and money flowed from nations to speed up the process. Without the usual testing, the vaccine was released to military forces, followed a day later to the public.

In terror, verging on panic, most of the world's populace was inoculated within a short period of time. Within seventy-two hours most of the world's military lay sick in their beds, feverish and sweating. The vaccine was recalled, but it was too late. Ninety-six hours later, seventy per cent of them were dead. With the exception of a scant one per cent who proved immune or didn't take the virus, the remaining were transformed.

Within those infected, the live virus caused genetic mutations that created elevated hearing, enhanced smell, the ability to see in the dark, and to communicate telepathically through the use of picture messages. The fast-twitch muscles were increased, allowing quicker responses, greater speed, and more agility. Higher brain function and memories were obliterated, leaving only anger and a lust for blood. Skin pigmentation was so altered that sunlight burned instantly, causing great agony and almost immediate death. Those transformed became ferocious creatures of the dark. Now pack animals, they laired during the day in shadowed places. When the sun sank below the horizon, they emerged to hunt the darkened streets, tearing apart any living thing they found. Dubbed the night runners, they ruled the night.

For the one per cent, life became a daily battle. Death was one moment of carelessness away. Outnumbered nearly thirty to one, that ratio increasing with each passing day, the survivors fought back as best as they could. Firepower was the only way to keep the ravenous hordes somewhat at bay.

# SEAL TEAM BLUE

C hief Petty Officer Vance Krandle lies prone along the rubber gunwales of the zodiac combat raiding craft. One hand grips his suppressed M-4 while the other grips the rope handhold. Spray is thrown off to the side as the zodiac bounces through the rough waters, occasionally splashing up and over him. Wiping his goggles clear of salt water, he glances to his rear at the rest of his team.

Speer, currently hunched over and driving the raft, is his point man and resident joker. He grew up hunting in the Ozarks and can track with the best of them, but his attitude and seemingly constant sarcasm grate on Vance at times. However, there isn't a better point man in the business.

Ortiz, lying just behind Krandle, runs slack – second position – and the little Puerto Rican is the picture of fury incarnate under fire. Perhaps it has something to do with his growing up in the East LA area. It has taken Krandle a while to bring that part of him under control.

Blanchard, crouched in the rear, is the designated medic and a skinny, quiet, unassuming kid from South Chicago. That quietness is belied by an internal fortitude. He will, without hesitation, venture into the thickest of combat to help a fellow teammate. Blanchard is also the one mostly on the end of Speer's barbs. The tightness of the team makes these attempts good-natured without creating a fracture within the group.

His XO, Franklin, lies in the rear across the other side of the zodiac. The black petty officer from Atlanta is one sharp tack and will make a fine team leader someday. Well, he would have had events not changed the world.

Miller, lying directly opposite Krandle is a full-blooded Sioux who grew up in South Dakota. He rarely speaks, and even then his replies are limited to only a few words. Krandle is sure there are weeks when Miller's word count never exceeds double digits. But, he is a master at covering their back trail. There were times when they had to backtrack and were unable to do so via any signs of their passage. He is that good.

Together, they make one hell of a fine team. They have fused into a single organism, each knowing the other's thoughts and actions – knowing each other's strengths and weaknesses. If anyone can make it through what they are facing, it's them.

They've been inland once before, finding and rescuing a small band of survivors. Spotting smoke drifting above the wooded coastline of Oregon, Leonard brought the sub closer in and sent the team to investigate. "Remember, chief, you are it for us. No hero stuff. If it looks like too much trouble, withdraw. No matter what you find, be back an hour prior to dark," Leonard had briefed before to sending them ashore.

Another splash coats Krandle's goggles. Wiping them clear, he braces himself for the landing, mentally rehearsing actions as he's done a hundred times before. Riding just in front of the surf, the waves diminish. The shore becomes visible over the tops. The tide is nearly at the high mark. Sand stretches wide, ending at a rocky bluff nearby at one end, and an inlet on the other. Past the waterway, the beach continues for a short distance before meeting a similar rocky cliff. Ahead, the beach terminates at small dunes with strands of grass waving in the wind. Beyond that, beach houses line the edge. In the distance, lines of smoke rise in plumes over the tops of trees.

Nearing the shore, Speer guns the motor and raises it at the last minute, the raft gliding the final few feet. As the raft kisses the sand, Krandle rolls off at the same time as Miller. Together, they fan out and race across the sand, their eyes searching every dune, every corner of the buildings ahead, into every window. In their wake, the remaining four grab the rope handles and pull the raft over the sand.

Krandle's boots dig into the soft sand, creating divots as he powers across. Startled gulls screech as they're driven to flight. Other than that, he only sounds are his boots driving into the beach, his breath forcefully exhaled, the hissing of the raft being dragged over the sand, and the muted roar of the Pacific.

He slides to a stop behind a short dune, its shadow created by the morning sun. Taking out the finely-honed knife strapped to his leg, Krandle cuts the rubber band holding the condom placed over his suppressor. He tosses the rubber into the sand where it potentially joins others used for their original purpose. A gust of wind carries fine grit that makes its way down his collar, and ruffles the pant legs and arms of his fatigues.

*An onshore flow, great. Our scent will precede us. But, it's daylight, so as long as we stay out of the buildings, we'll be fine.*

Krandle looks back to the expanse of the ocean. There's nothing that interrupts the vast expanse of water stretching to the horizon, but Krandle knows the USS *Santa Fe* lies submerged just under the surface.

Inching to the top of the dune, Krandle parts the stiff grasses. Opened doors lead into darkness and curtains dance as drafts blow through broken windows. Nothing moves in and around the cottages. Overhead, gulls glide on the winds. Kneeling behind the dunes, the other team members alertly wait for his call.

Pressing the button on his throat mic, Krandle radios, "Stow the raft between the dunes. We're heading for the light yellow house directly ahead."

Hunched over, Speer leads, focused on the area directly ahead. Several paces behind, Ortiz concentrates his attention to the left quarter. Third in line, Krandle watches to the right front. Following is Blanchard, then Franklin, with Miller bringing up the rear.

Each knows their only worry in the daylight is from their own kind. Once the sun descends below the horizon, the night runners emerge from their lairs to begin their hunt. Their speed, cunning, and numbers make them extremely dangerous. While he and other survivors may own the day, they take a step down the food chain once night falls. Any darkened building is to be avoided, and only entered in the event of dire need.

Climbing a couple of steps, really nothing more than a few railroad ties, the team enters the yard and stacks against one of the corners. Krandle peers into the open back door. Closer to the house, the darkness peels back and the radiant light reveals upended furniture. Other objects lie strewn on a floor covered with a fine layer of sand blown in from the beach. It's as if he's looking upon a snapshot; the moment in time forever frozen with only the house carrying the memory of what happened within.

The hinges of the screen door squeak as a breeze passes through. Pulling his attention away from inside, Krandle makes his way to the corner and crouches just behind Speer. "What do you have?" he asks.

"Nothing. A street running parallel in front with more houses across. Just to the left, there's an intersection with another road heading inland."

A strong gust buffets the team; a screen door to the rear to slams against the door frame. All six jump and turn toward the sound.

"Fuck, I hate that!" Speer sharply whispers. "I think I just peed myself."

"Well, get yourself cleaned up and lead us inland toward those smoke plumes," Krandle says.

"Have I mentioned how much I hate this?" says Speer.

"Too many times. Now, get moving."

As Speer rounds the corner and sidles toward the front, Krandle wonders if he's ready for another day of listening to Speer bitch and moan. However, the sixth sense Speer has makes every complaint worth what he brings to the table. Speer halts near the front corner of the house and looks up and down the street. With a hand signal that it's clear, Ortiz and the rest of them roll around the corner and kneel next to small bushes lining the side of the cottage. In place, they rise as one and dash across the avenue, piling at the corner of the house adjacent the intersection. A startled flock of birds takes flight, squawking their indignation at the intruders.

Krandle moves in front and stares down the road that heads deeper into the coastal community. Trees line the median on both sides of the street, shading overgrown lawns. Once trimmed bushes grow wild, their leaf-covered branches sticking out like morning hair. Along the street, several vehicles are parked against the curb with drifts of sand and debris piled up against their tires. Grit completely covers the pavement in places, the wind having created ripple-like patterns. As each breeze blows through, sand is driven across the surface, making it appear as if the street is in motion.

Shouldering his M-4, Krandle selects the 4x setting on his SpectreDR scope to get a closer look at the houses and surrounding area. At one abode, the tail of a cat quickly vanishes around the corner. In various locations, trails cut through the otherwise pristine layers of sand, possible evidence that night runners prowl these streets.

*Something's made their way through here recently.*

Although he can't see into every window from his vantage point, everything looks clear.

"What do you think?" Krandle directs his question to Speer.

"I think we should turn around and get the fuck out of here. These empty towns give me the fucking creeps."

"And what if those smoke plumes are a sign of people who need help?"

"That's their problem."

"Well, too bad for you this isn't a democracy. That's where we're going. Why do you have to be such a pain in the ass?"

"Someone in this outfit has to be the voice of reason," Speer says.

This is Speer's way of dealing with tension; the man has no intention of turning around, and would complain if Krandle suggested it.

"So, now that you've taken your dick out and waved it around, what do you think?" Krandle asks.

Speer shrugs. "It's clear, but I wouldn't want to be around after dark. There are more than a few night runners who come through here."

Krandle directs Franklin, Blanchard, and Miller across the street, then places a hand on Speer's shoulder. "Lead on."

They head out, inching down opposite sidewalks with Franklin and the other two taking a staggered position behind. They've been through a couple of these abandoned towns before, but he's with Speer on the eeriness. With the warmth, there should be the sound of kids playing, lawns being mowed, cars driving along the streets, and the smell of barbecues wafting on the breeze. There is only the swish of the wind through the trees, the soft crunch of their boots on the sand, and the occasional cry of a gull in the distance.

Only a few of the houses are intact; most have their windows broken and doors ajar. It's quiet enough to hear a sporadic creak or moan of wood expanding in the rising heat. They come across tracks in the sand; trails leading down the street and through lawns. Speer halts and analyzes the impressions of each, coming up with how many night runners passed through and when. Each track is a reminder of what could be hiding within every building.

The team crosses several side streets, empty houses and parked vehicles along each of them. Sand piles against every object – the beach slowly reclaiming the city. There's not a single scream from within any of the buildings, meaning the night runners of the city lair elsewhere. Krandle is well aware of their keen eyesight and ability to pick up the faintest scent. The barest whiff of prey will send them into a frenzy.

Exiting the residential neighborhood, Speer halts at a larger thoroughfare, crouching next to the wall of a building. Traffic lights swing from their wires over the intersection. Along the main avenue, several of the larger paned glass windows of the storefronts are broken, the interiors hidden in darkness.

The worst sign of the carnage that swept through the coastal town are body parts strewn along the street. The shredded remains of a pant leg lies in the middle of the intersection, the white of shin bones protruding from one end and a faded sneaker from the other. In a nearby shop, the rear of a pair of jeans humped over a broken window, the rest of the body hidden beneath a sand drift. Another deep drift invades one of the vehicles, its door open. The skeletal remains of a forearm, the dried remains of tendons still attached, extends from the sand as if attempting to pull the rest of the body clear. The upper torso protrudes from another drift. The skull sprouts a full head of hair with pieces of desiccated flesh dangling from the cheek and jaws. All along the avenue, tattered clothing and bones extend from drift of deep sand.

"Looks like it was some party," Speer mutters.

"That it does," Krandle says.

He knows the horror those lying in street experienced, not able to comprehend what was happening and trying to escape the sudden onslaught. The terror of knowing they weren't going to make it, their last moments filled with the agony of having their flesh ripped from their bones.

A scream rips through the silence, quickly followed by others. The shrieks echo from deep within the darkened buildings, spilling out onto the street. Doves gathered on ledges take flight with a flurry of wings.

"Fuck me!" Speer says. "I think we just rang the dinner bell."

"Yeah. I guess our company knows that we're here," says Krandle.

All six subconsciously edge back a step, weapons trained on the windows and doorways. Even though they know the night runners won't emerge into the sunlight, the sounds reverberating throughout the town chill them to their very marrow.

They have several hours before they have to reverse their steps and begin making their way back to the shore. In the distance, rising above the roofs, the smoke that brought them inland still faintly plumes before being whisked away by the wind.

"What do you think it is?" Krandle motions to the smoke.

"Well, the power is off, so it can't be some appliance that overheated. It's too dark to be trees that caught fire. It's not moving..." Speer trails off.

"So, you're saying that you don't know," Krandle says.

"Pretty much."

"Why didn't you just say that?"

"I did."

"Remember those columns of vehicles that we'd come across in Iraq after A-10s would work them over?" says Ortiz.

"In case you haven't noticed, this isn't Iraq and I don't recall seeing strafing warthogs," Speer says.

Ortiz shrugs.

"Stow it, Speer." Krandle agrees the plumes of smoke do look like the columns they periodically came across in Iraq.

"Which way?" Speer says.

When Krandle spied the smoke through binoculars atop the sub's bridge, he had thought it to be on the far side of the town, but now he isn't so sure. 'Highway 101' runs along town rather than through it. Looking again at the smoke, he opts to follow the highway signs. If they come adjacent to the plumes before reaching the highway, they can circle around.

The drifts stand taller and wider here. In places, the sidewalk is completely covered, forcing the team into the avenue. The bones poking out of the sand and lying in the street have deeply etched bite marks. They step over and around purses, shoes, and other detritus from those that happened to be on the darkened streets when the night runners hit.

As they walk, the sun rises higher, but the swirling winds keep the heat at bay. The screams fade, become background noise.

Reaching the city limits, cars are haphazardly parked in the lots of a gas station to one side and a café to the other. Ahead, the access road leads through a stand of trees and ends at a stop sign bathed in the sun's rays.

*Well, the world is fine. It's humanity that was flushed.*

There's no sign of the smoke above the tall firs, the winds won't allow it, but Krandle knows the source is somewhere ahead and to their left. The smoke has grown fainter – the fire was dying down.

"It looks like whatever is burning is coming from on or near the road," says Speer.

Krandle nods. "I agree. Take us into the trees. We'll approach from there and get eyes on whatever it is."

Six successive metallic clicks sound as each checks for a round in the chamber. A strong gust of wind marks their departure from the city limits. Leaving the fading screams of night runners behind, they angle across the avenue toward the trees.

Moving slowly to minimize sound, Speer leads the team through an outer layer of undergrowth, pausing to move branches out of the way before slithering past. With only an occasional brush of leaves against clothing and packs, they silently vanish, becoming one with the natural landscape.

The terrain under the firs opens up with only a scattering of underbrush. A few rays of sunlight find their way through openings in the boughs, angling amid the tree trunks. Insects dart in and out of the light in a never-ending stage show.

Once inside the woods, the going becomes easier. Taking care where to place his feet, Speer leads them along the edge of the outer-growth. They take their spacing between each other, more out of habit than from any threat. Six pairs of eyes search through the gloom, trying to pierce the shadows as they look for movement or the outline of a body.

Although it's too light for night runners to be out, the danger lies with their own kind. Without the constraints of civilization, there are those who believe the changed reality means they can do as they please. The virus didn't distinguish between bully and saint, making the world a much more dangerous place. Trust regarding strangers has been laid aside in the name of survival and the ones left are just as likely to open fire without question as to invite one into their hearth.

Nearing the highway edge of the woods, they halt. "Speer, Ortiz with me. The rest of you watch our six."

Dropping their packs, Speer finds an opening under the bushes. Side by side, they crawl toward the road. At the edge, Krandle parts the leaves of the last screen of bushes, searching for a sign of anyone in the forest across the highway. Nothing. Inching forward, he looks toward where the smoke should be.

Up the road, a large fir lies across the road, the needle-covered branches obscuring a clear sight beyond. Past the fallen tree, faint plumes of smoke rise, climbing to a level just above the forest tops before being blown away. Near the barrier, the ground is churned up on both sides of the pavement.

"Looks like someone set up an ambush," Speer whispers.

"Sure looks that way," says Ortiz.

Krandle remains silent, turning his gaze down the highway in the opposite direction to where the steel girders of a bridge rise in the distance. Tapping Speer and Ortiz, he nods back toward the others. Easing the branches back into place, they inch back from the highway, covering their tracks as a matter of habit.

"Someone set up an ambush and triggered it. End of story. So, I'm all for calling it a day and heading back to the boat," Speer says.

Krandle glances upward. "We still have a few hours and there may be survivors who need help."

"I was afraid you were going to say that," Speer says despondently.

"If there is anyone left, they're going to have itchy trigger fingers," says Franklin.

"We'll just have to be careful, then," Krandle says.

"Those were tire tracks we saw leaving the road… a few of them. They might still be there," says Speer.

"Possibly," Krandle says. "We'll work our way to where they came in and circle around."

"So, we're going, then?" Speer says.

Krandle looks at each team member. Franklin and Blanchard both nod, Miller shrugs.

"Fuck. You're all going to be the death of me," Speer says.

"We all gotta go sometime," says Ortiz.

Krandle knows that's just the way Speer deals with stuff; he's not truly against going. He'd give you the shirt off his back, but bitch about it the entire time.

They continue near the inner screen of shrubs. Their pace slowed, knowing there is a good chance there's trouble ahead.

Speer advances ten paces, and then holds to watch and listen, measuring his next steps. They watch for a sudden flight of birds, listen for the wildlife to go quiet. The onshore flow continues to sweep through, the gusts beginning to calm. Six men silently creep through the woods, so quiet not even the animals are aware of their presence.

Speer arrives at the vehicle's point of entrance and crouches. Each man lowers in place and scans their sectors, weapons ready to unleash a torrent of fire in a heartbeat.

Speer motions Krandle forward. "Looks like seven or eight quads, but it's hard to tell," says Speer. "They're only a few hours old. It looks like the same thing across the road. Most are obscured, but look at the ones on top. The tread pattern shows them exiting the tree line."

"So, they entered, triggered the ambush, and left?" asks Krandle.

"It would appear so. However, whether all of them left..." Speer ends his comment with a shrug.

"There's no smell of exhaust," Krandle says.

"No. Whatever went through here did so hours ago. And there aren't any quads idling ahead. Even with the wind, we'd hear them from this distance."

"Take us back into the woods and circle us around so that we come in from the side," Krandle says.

"What's our timetable?"

Krandle checks his watch. "We have four hours. So, that or until we finish verifying if anyone needs help."

"Or we're fired on."

"Or that."

Heading deeper into the woods, they resume their slow advance. Fingers stroke trigger guards or selector switches. With each step, small branches have to be moved out of the way, the weight gradually transitioned to avoid the crunch of needles. All their gear had been taped to prevent any metallic ping.

Speer finally calls a halt. "We're past the tree. Do you want to head in from here, or circle around farther behind?"

Krandle looks in the direction of the highway, squinting to see into the shadows.

"There's no one in the trees, and no sign of quads," Speer states, watching Krandle. "But, there are people on the road."

Krandle tries to see what Speer sees.

"No, chief, listen."

Krandle strains to hear, but gives up and shakes his head.

"There are voices coming from the highway. They're faint, but they're there," Speer says.

"How in the fuck can you hear that?"

"Pretty sure my grandpa fucked a dog, or something like that."

"That's messed up, Speer. You're saying your grandma was a dog?"

Speer shrugs. "She was kind of a bitch."

"You're too much."

Krandle thumbs the throat mic. "We're going in from here. Move out on line."

With weapons ready and eyes searching, they work their way toward the highway. After a short distance, Krandle begins hearing the voices Speer mentioned. He looks over at his point man, who gives him another shrug. As they advance, the forest floor gives evidence of recent travel. Halting away from the edge of the tree line, Krandle halts the team and motions for Speer to move up with him.

They both crouch at the edge of the tracks. Beyond the bushes, the murmur of voices with a shout occasionally rising. The smell of burned rubber, oil, and gas permeates the trees. Speer moves up and down the torn forest floor, studying the tracks.

"Whoever it was, they arrived on eight quads, which they parked over there." Speer points. "They set up along the edge of the bushes. I can't say for sure, but it looks like one person per quad, making it eight on this side. Given human nature for keeping things even, I would say seven to nine on the other side as well. It looks like they entered the tree line, did whatever they did, and left. There are indications of drag marks, so I'm guessing they took some non-compliant dinner guests with them."

Speer motions to a woman's shoe lying on the ground. "Of that nature."

It appears raiders ambushed then kidnapped several of them, including at least one woman. Are the voices on the other side of the bushes from the assailants or victims? Did the attackers spring their ambush, take hostages, and leave the rest alive? If you're going to go through all of the work involved, why leave the opening for retribution?

*Perhaps the raiders feel overconfident... the 'do as I please without reprisal kind of attitude.' That's if the ones on the highway aren't those that attacked.*

"Marauders or victims?" Krandle whispers, pointing toward the road.

Speer shrugs.

Krandle is left with the feeling that a band of survivors were waylaid and the women taken. Fading back to the others, he tells them the situation.

"Speer, Ortiz, you're with me. Franklin, Blanchard, Miller, keep our six clear. We're going forward and make contact if the ones ahead are victims. If they're bandits, we'll fade back and plan according to the situation," Krandle says.

Expecting a reaction from Speer, Krandle is surprised when his point man just stares at his carbine, pretending to pick at an imaginary flake of rust. By the way everyone is looking at Speer, they are anticipating the same.

Speer glances up and sees everyone staring at him. "What?"

Shaking his head, Krandle says, "Let's get on with this. Like Franklin said, if we're dealing with victims, they're apt to be trigger happy."

Closer to the tree line, Speer freezes, holding up a fist. He sinks to his knees, his head turning a slow arc to the left. "Two sleepers. Near the split tree," Speer whispers into his mic.

Krandle finds the location and focuses, his vision moving inches at a time, attempting to pick out an outline that doesn't fit.

*There, a pair of legs.* The pant legs and shoes now clearly defined.

"Do you have a clear visual of both?" Krandles asks.

"Yeah. They think they're being sneaky, but not doing a very good job at it."

"Wait one. I'm moving to your location."

Krandle edges forward, carefully setting his foot in order to remain silent. Going to one knee, he gazes to where Speer nods. Two heads peer over a shrub, looking toward the group on the road.

"Bandits or survivors?" Krandle asks.

"Bandits for sure. One lifted a carbine and simulated shooting while the two snickered."

"They must have left these two behind in case they were followed. That implies radios," Krandle says. "Is that all there are?"

"On this side of the road, yeah. Take them out?"

"We can't very well leave them here. If they have radios, we'll do our best to simulate traffic if they're called," Krandle says. "You take left, I have right."

The two SEALs slowly lift their barrels, eyes down the scope. Krandle settles on his target, settling his breathing to keep his sight steady.

"Three… two… one."

Two soft pops bounce off the trees, carrying no further than a few yards. The high-speed projectiles cross the distance nearly instantly, impacting with two almost simultaneous, meaty thunks. The two heads vanish beneath the branches in a mist of red. While the two have their weapons trained, two others from the team edge from the forest to verify the kills.

Kills confirmed, Krandle edges forward, going prone at the edge of the bushes and begins to slither through the undergrowth. Several needles make their way under his shirt and poke into his skin. Ignoring the pricks, he moves twigs out of his way before hauling himself forward a few more inches. Spread out to either side, Speer and Ortiz do the same. Reaching the outer edge, Krandle slowly lowers a branch and peers out into the highway.

Parked a little ways behind the fallen tree is a line of smoldering pickups, SUVs, and a couple of RVs. Just beyond the wreckage, the highway makes a sharp bend. Three small groups of people are gathered amid the wreckage, each cluster kneeling beside a figure lying on the ground. Near the fallen tree, a person stands on either side, looking up the highway toward the bridge. All of those on the road are men and the fact they're all unarmed gives credence that they were the victims of the ambush.

"Move back," Krandle quietly says, keying his throat mic.

Once gathered, Ortiz leans over and whispers to Speer, "Not like Iraq, huh?"

"Shut up, East LA."

"Says the hillbilly."

"Hey, Blanchard. Do you have anything in your bag for an aching prick? I have one sitting beside me," Speer says.

"The only aching prick here is the one between your legs. I warned you about fucking goats," Ortiz returns.

"A goat? I thought that was your mother. Can't tell the two of them apart."

"Both of you stow it," Krandle says. "It looks like we're dealing with victims. There are fourteen unarmed men, counting three injured. Although it looks like the far side is clear, Franklin, take Speer and Ortiz to make sure. The road curves beyond the wreckage, so cross past that point. Be alert for any sleepers on that side. Once we're secure, we'll make contact. There are injured, but we need to see to our own security first."

The three depart, leaving Krandle with Blanchard and Miller, forming a tight perimeter. While keeping an eye through the trees, Krandle looks toward the path they took to get here. There's no sign of their having traversed the forest floor. He wonders if he'll ever get over his amazement at how well Miller can erase signs of their passage.

*I'll have to ask Franklin if he hears soft chanting and spells being cast behind him. One of these days, I'm going to make a thorough mess and see if Miller can cover it up.*

Time passes. The angle of the sun's rays pouring through the trees changes, some vanishing and others appearing. The voices on the road rise and lower. Krandle glances at his watch for the hundredth time, knowing the three making their way to the other side are being cautious in their approach, but it's taking forever.

They don't have long before they have to begin their trek back to the boat. The injured on the road will create a challenge. Even if the bandits leave them alone, without their vehicles and with injured, they won't make it very far. When the sun sets, the night runners will pick up the scent of those in the road, especially with the smell of blood. And, once it begins to cool, the wind will most likely change to an offshore flow, bringing their scent directly into town. Even though the town is small, there will still be thousands of night runners.

Let's say there were six thousand in the town before the gates of hell opened. What did Captain Walker say? That some seventy percent became infected? That leaves, well, a whole hell of a lot. Forty-two hundred? Is that right? We each have thirty mags, including those in our packs. That gives us... fuck I hate math. Thirty times thirty equals... nine hundred, I think. And that times six is... fifty-four hundred, minus the one shell we leave out of the mags. So, barely enough. And if the town held more people...

"Far side is clear." Franklin's voice crackles in Krandle's ear piece, drawing him out of his math class.

"Stay in place, we're moving up to make contact," Krandle replies. Retracing his route, Krandle parts a branch. Keeping a low profile, he calls out, "Ahoy there in the road."

All eyes snap in his direction, the panic visible even from a distance.

"We're friendlies and coming out. Please don't make any sudden movements."

Into his mic, Krandle directs Franklin and the others to hold position on the other side. Those in the road rise, the ones by the tree remain frozen in place, all staring in this direction. Krandle rises and exits the bushes alongside Blanchard and Miller. There's a collective gasp among those on the road as they observe three heavily armed, camouflaged soldiers emerge from the bushes.

"Are you Army?" one man calls out.

"Navy SEALS, sir," Krandle says.

The held gasp is replaced by simultaneous sighs of relief, followed by a chorus of voices; some asking to help the wounded, others trying to explain what happened. Krandle holds a hand up, bringing silence.

"Blanchard, see to the wounded," Krandle says. Into the mic, he continues, "Miller, Franklin, into the trees near the corner. Speer, Ortiz, the woods near the fallen tree."

Blanchard unshoulders his pack and proceeds to triage those lying injured on the ground.

"What happened here?" Krandle asks the man who first called out.

"We were coming out of Portland, picking up others along the way, and came across this tree in the road. We got out to clear it, thinking it had fallen and were attacked from the sides. A couple of us were armed, but they took those away. We didn't really have much of a choice," the man says. "I'm Doug, by the way."

"Chief Petty Officer Krandle. How many were there?" Krandle wonders how anyone could fail to spot such an obvious ambush, but leaves that unsaid.

"I don't know exactly… fifteen? Twenty?" Doug says.

"Go on?"

"Well, they shot Shaun right away. They said it was to show us they were serious. After disarming us, they ordered everyone out and made us gather by the tree. They went through the vehicles, taking what they wanted. Then, they said they were taking 'our women' as they so quaintly put it. They started grabbing them. Mark fought back as they were grabbing his wife, Lindy. They shot him, then one of the assholes asked if there was anyone else who wanted a piece. I've never felt so damn helpless in all my life. I had to watch them drag our wives and daughters away."

"Daughters?" Krandle's anger rises.

"Yeah. They took everyone. Five of our wives and two teenage daughters," the man says, tears forming in his eyes then streaming down his cheeks.

Krandle notes the man's tightly clenched fist. "I know it's difficult, but finish the tale if you can."

"That's it. They took our women and weapons. Oh, and shot Adam as they left, telling us not to follow them, that we should count ourselves as lucky and move on. Lucky? I wish they had killed me."

"How did they leave? Vehicles?"

"A couple of vans drove up on the other side of the tree as they were leaving," says Doug. "They loaded our supplies and threw the women in. I heard motors crank up in the woods and they left."

"Did they take the turn into town?"

"No, they drove up the highway toward the bridge. I lost sight of them after a bit."

"Okay. Do you have food and water?"

"Not anymore."

"We have some. Where were you heading? What was your destination?" Krandle is curious if there was some haven they had in mind.

"Nowhere really. Just south. We planned on driving during the day, stopping where we could to refill our tanks... find what food we could. At night, we'd hole up out of populated areas. We kind of figured a place would just show up and we'd know it when we found it. Now, I'm walking until I find those fuckers and get my wife back."

"Unarmed? Alone?" Krandle raises his eyebrows. He knows the anger and fear the man must be feeling... the hopelessness.

"I'll find something along the way and I'm sure the others will want the same thing."

"Hold that thought," Krandle says.

"Are you going to chase them down? I guess I mean, will you?"

"Just hold that thought."

Krandle removes what water and food he has, handing it to the man. "It's not much, but pass it around to the others." He steps over to Blanchard and crouches. "What do you have?"

"One with a sucking chest wound. Another with a hole in his stomach. The third one looks like he has a cracked femur, but he'll be fine," Blanchard says.

"And the other two?"

Blanchard sighs. "I can't do much for the sucking chest wound. I have it sealed, but it will need constant deflating and he'll need surgery pronto. He's already exhibiting subcutaneous Emphysema, you know, bubbles under the skin. If we had a medevac available, he might have a chance. We don't, so…

"The gut wound is iffy. I'll do what I can, but if he doesn't die from blood loss, there's a good chance Sepsis will finish the job," Blanchard says. "I've given them all morphine, so at least they don't feel it."

"Can they be moved?"

"They probably won't survive the trip to the boat, if that's what you're thinking."

Krandle frowns in thought. "What about to that bridge?"

"I don't know what good that will do, but probably that far and not much more. Honestly, chief, with night coming on, these people will be better off leaving these two and finding somewhere safe. If they leave now, they may be able to put enough distance between them and the town."

"Do what you can," Krandle says, rising and heading toward the now huddled group of survivors.

"Okay folks, here's the deal. And, you may not like it much. I know you've already been through a lot, but I'm going to lay this out bluntly. First off, we can't take you aboard the sub we came in on, there's just not enough room. As you may already know, there's a town on the other side of those woods, along with thousands of night runners. So, staying here is a death sentence," Krandle says.

"So, you're not going to help us? You're going to just leave our wives and daughters in the hands of those assholes," one man says.

"I didn't say that. I'm just laying out the situation for you."

"Let the man speak, Phil," Doug says.

"Thank you. Two of your wounded may not make it... more than likely they won't, and they can't be moved far. With nightfall coming on in a few hours, one choice is to leave them and put as much distance as you can from the town. You'll have to carry the man with the leg wound."

"We can't do that. We can't just leave them to die all alone. That would be akin to murder," another man says.

"I said that's one choice. Another is stay here with them, but you won't make it through the night. That's just a fact and it won't help your loved ones much. I know you're wondering if we can help, both through the night and for your wives and daughters. I and the others will want to stay, but the overall choice isn't mine to make. I know you may not understand, but we're it for a bunch of other folks, too. It's a fucked up world. It sucks, I know, but I just wanted to let you know your options if we can't stay. I'm going to try and convince my boss to remain. I'll leave you to talk things over."

Krandle calls the others in and relates the information he received.

"How could they be so stupid?" Speer asks.

"You know, everything aside, leaving them with wounded to slow them down so they can't follow makes some kind of tactical sense. That shows what we may be up against if we opt for a rescue attempt. Although, they may not have had that in mind and are just assholes," says Franklin.

"Ah, shit. We're staying, aren't we? I know that look in your eye," Speer says.

"Do we really have a choice?" says Krandle.

"No. But, dammit. I don't mind missions and shit, but I miss the downtime in between with beers and women."

"You don't get women, Speer, unless you pay for them. And then, it's still fifty-fifty. Remember Bangkok?" Ortiz says with a grin.

"Shut the fuck up about that. That… never happened. And I get more than Blanchard over there." Speer points toward the medic hovering over the injured.

"You know, I seriously doubt that," Miller says, glancing at Blanchard with a speculative expression. "I bet he gets more than the rest of us combined."

"What the fuck do you know, chief?" Speer says.

Miller shrugs, his words for the week spoken.

"Those guys who ambushed these poor fuckers were on quads, so they can't be that far," Ortiz says.

"Agreed, but we'll deal with that later, unless we come across their tracks. It's a fair bet they'll be far enough away to be out of range of the night runners. Right now, we need to think about getting through the night. The ammo we're carrying might not be enough for the night runners laired in the city," Krandle says.

"More good news," Speer mutters.

"We have claymores and grenades," Franklin says, ignoring Speer.

"That we do. If we're saddled with the wounded, we won't be able to make it far. Blanchard says they'll make it to the bridge south of us. It's the best defensible area in sight, effectively giving us a single front," says Krandle.

"Then the bridge it is. Have you spoken with Leonard? He may order us to return," Franklin says.

Krandle shook his head. "No, not yet. I'm going to give him a call now and I may leave out a detail or two."

"I have my shiny armor all polished if we're going to rescue those damsels in distress come morning. All I need is a white horse," Speer says, looking around for one. "Let's just hope the dragon is asleep."

Krandle steps away and raises the sub on the radio and gives Leonard the situation. He informs him of their desire to stay with the wounded and move them out of harm's way, to watch over them for the night before sending them along on their own. The radio silence that follows is palpable.

"Chief, you realize you're all we have… that you have other responsibilities as well," Leonard finally says.

"Aye, sir."

"I don't like it, but very well. You make it back, and that's an order. We'll be standing by in case." Leonard's frustration with his SEAL team leader is evident.

"Aye, aye, sir. We'll radio our coordinates when we have them."

There isn't a reply and Krandle knows that he's in for an earful once they return. But, that was their bargain for Krandle and his team staying. They had a chance to leave with Captain Walker and his group when they all met at the Bangor Naval Station. Leonard commanded the sub, and in essence, his SEAL team. But, the world had changed and even Leonard eventually came to recognize that. For Krandle and his team staying, an agreement of sorts was made. Krandle could make the final decision whether to go ashore and when to pull back or proceed. Leonard was still in overall command, and could have ordered them back, but gave Krandle the leeway as the on-scene commander.

"What did he say?" Franklin asks upon Krandle's return.

"It's not so much what he said, as what he's going to say when we get back."

"That sounds like it'll be fun," Franklin mutters.

"About as much as a visit to the proctologist. Okay, we're heading to the bridge. I want Speer and Ortiz to scout ahead on the left. Franklin, take Miller with you on the right. I don't have to tell you to keep an eye out for our mysterious guests."

"Copy that," Franklin says.

"We'll get the wounded loaded and follow."

The four scouts fade into the woods on both sides as Krandle returns to those gathered.

"Okay, we're staying. We need to build stretchers for the wounded and move toward the bridge. It's not far and we can expect company this evening, but that's where we're staying," Krandle says.

Fourteen shoulders sag in relief, looking almost like candles melting under high heat.

"Thank you," Doug says.

"I hope you understand it's not like we didn't want to help, it's—"

"We understand," Doug interrupts. "And thank you again."

"Do any of you have any weapons? Those that weren't taken?" Krandle asks.

"Only in that," Doug says, pointing toward the smoldering wreckage of vehicles.

"Fair enough. Your people will carry the wounded. My medic will stay with them and monitor them. I want to be clear, they may not make it very long. You need to be prepared for that."

Doug nods. "And our wives?"

"We'll talk about that in the morning. We have an interesting night to get through first."

Gathering a few thicker branches, they create a couple of makeshift stretchers using ponchos and Para cord. The femur isn't broken, but Blanchard suspects it's fractured. Using a crutch cut from a bough and the help of a shoulder, the man is able to hobble along. Another small dose of morphine helps, but Blanchard is fairly sure they'll have to make a third stretcher before they reach the bridge.

The group manhandles the stretchers past the fallen tree and begins the trudge down the highway toward the distant bridge. Knowing the other four of his team has the front covered, Krandle positions himself at the rear. Gazing up at the afternoon sun, they'll have only a couple of hours of light once they reach the span. Time weighs on his shoulders and he mentally urges the group to move faster, knowing they'll have a lot to do once they arrive.

"We're at the edge of a ravine that the bridge crosses. All clear to this point," Franklin radios.

"Continue across and scout the far side. We don't want any surprises coming from there. We'll be a while yet getting there," Krandle replies.

"Copy that. We're on the move."

As they walk, Krandle observes the group's nervous looks toward the trees, as if expecting the bandits to suddenly materialize. He assures them the others in his team have reached the bridge and reported the way clear. That does little to alleviate the anxious looks. Several times during their trek, Blanchard has them halt and tends to the man with the chest wound.

As they step onto the span, Franklin and the others emerge from the tree line on the other side. "No sign of anyone for at least a mile," Franklin reports.

Krandle nods. "Have the civilians set up on the far end away from town, then grab your packs and meet me at the near end. If night runners show up tonight, it will be from that direction. We need to arrange a welcome."

With the group positioned, the team empties their packs. Krandle looks over the landscape while radioing in their position to the sub. The bridge itself is almost an eighth of a mile across, spanning a fairly deep gorge with a stream running its length. The tree-lined ravine shallows as it nears the shoreline, as does the stream before it empties out onto the sand and the incoming waves.

Ahead, the two-lane highway stretches straight with narrow medians of tall grass to either side. The sward gives way to firs reaching skyward.

*Good line of sight to the front, but if they emerge from the trees nearby, we won't have much reaction time.* Krandle studies the terrain. *They can't move across the ravine, unless they go all of the way to the beach. And, the bandits won't come out once the sun sets, so our rear should be secure.*

Krandle relates his thoughts to the team, "So, we need to focus on the front. If our scent is picked up, we have the potential of thousands heading our way. We'll set our twelve claymores singly. I want one on each of the front girders with another two spaced along the ravine on either side in case we're rushed and need to create a little room. The others staged in the grass along the highway. If they see us, they'll make a beeline toward us… at least initially. Let's not forget they're cagey and have the capability to change strategies."

Turning to Blanchard, he asks, "How are the wounded?"

"The one with the gunshot to the leg will live, although painfully for some time. I had to aspirate the chest wound several times. The one who is gut shot is bleeding out and I've run through all my IVs."

"Is there any chance those two will make it?"

Blanchard shakes his head.

"Then, I guess the only thing to do is make them comfortable," Krandle says.

"Any more morphine will kill them. But, I guess that doesn't really matter," says Blanchard.

"Will you be needed with them tonight?"

"There's not really much I can do. I'll give them a last dose of morphine, but that's about it."

"Okay. I want you up here with us once the sun hits the horizon. We may need every weapon online."

"Aye, chief."

Krandle looks toward the beach and the sun closing in on the horizon. "Speer, how long will it take you and Ortiz to reach the shoreline, get to the raft, drag it near the stream, and make your way back?"

"Are you asking about being stealthy, or going at a flat out run?"

"Somewhere in between," Krandle replies.

"Well, seeing that Ortiz runs as fast as a turtle in mud... two hours... give or take," Speer says.

"Fuck you, Speer. I can outrun your skinny hillbilly ass any day of the week. The only time you may be able to run faster is if your mom caught you with your sister again."

"The only time you can remotely run fast, East LA, is if you hear the words 'freeze'."

"If you two are done making out, you have two hours. That's about all of the time you have unless you want to be supper. If the sun sets, you'll both get a chance to set land speed records. Before you go, leave your claymores and clackers with Franklin."

As Speer and Ortiz disappear into the tree line, Krandle and the others set to laying the claymores and trailing the wires back to the bridge. Finishing, Krandle stands. Just as he feared, a slight breeze flows toward the ocean from the inland side. Staring toward where the others were waylaid, he knows that with the offshore flow, the scent of blood at the scene of the attack will make its way into the town. That will draw the night runners out and possibly to their position. He isn't exactly sure to what extent the night runners have an enhanced sense of smell. It's entirely possible they may investigate the site and not know the group is at the bridge.

*I can only hope we're far enough away.*

Krandle turns toward the beach, seeing Speer and Ortiz manhandle the raft across the stream and store it in the dunes.

"You know that won't hold everyone. Even if they hang onto the sides," Franklin says.

"I know. But, if we get overrun and get scattered, it's there."

"Did you tell them about it?" Franklin asks, motioning to the group of civilians.

"I will if it comes to that point. I don't want them to get antsy if shit hits the fan and for them to make a run for it early. That will leave us stranded," Krandle says.

"Fair enough."

The sun is near the horizon, the western sky a myriad of oranges and reds. The beams of the dying sun ripple across the ocean, an endless dance of light. Speer and Ortiz arrive, pulling spare mags from their packs and storing them in every available space. They replace those that they can't find room for and shoulder their packs. Donning their NVG gear, they take a knee near the front of the bridge.

Krandle would have liked to create a barricade, but there weren't enough materials. It may not have slowed the night runners any, but it would have given a little mental lift knowing there was something between them and the predators of the night. The sun dips below the horizon, light flaring upward, then vanishing. The deep blue sky to the east darkens, turning to black velvet which slowly invades the heavens. Stars stab out from an ebony background, twinkling silver. The sight of something so vast makes him feel small, as if their problem is so minute within the universe as to be non-existent. In the distance, screams echo across the newly darkened night.

Time passes. Behind the NVGs, his eyes feel dry and gritty from lack of sleep. He scans the trees, looking for any sign the night runners are venturing from the city. Even with binoculars, there's no way to tell if they are hovering around the ambush zone. With the drafts of winds swirling around, he knows the night runners had to have caught scent of the spilled blood. It's just a matter of if they pick up on their trail or catch wind of their current location. They haven't seen any to this point.

*So far, so good.* Krandle turns to glance toward the civilians.

There's no sight of them at the far end of the bridge, having been told that it's paramount they remain hidden. Although the night runners are able to see in the dark, again, Krandle isn't sure exactly how well. A slight breeze chills his neck as it flows from behind. The world beyond is bathed in a green glow for as far as he is able to see. The limited area of vision means they won't have a lot of time to react should they be discovered.

"I don't have a good feeling about this. They feel close," Speer whispers in Krandle's ear piece.

A chill runs up Krandle's spine and the hairs on his neck stand on end; this time it's not associated with any breeze. He's learned to listen to Speer's senses. When Speer voices one of his 'feelings', it's damn near a fact in Krandle's book. His finger runs along the trigger guard as he peers into the green-lit night.

"There, to the left... near the road," Speer whispers.

A night runner emerges into view, its pale face almost glowing. It takes a step, face upraised as it sniffs the air. Another step, the head turning left and right as it attempts to pinpoint whatever scent it's tracking. It's too far away to ensure a killing shot. To fire now and only injure it will guarantee discovery. If it draws closer and hasn't alerted any others, they'll take it down before it can draw more into the area.

"Remember gents, semi-auto," Krandle whispers. "If we're

located, wait until they're close. We need to make every shot count."

Another night runner joins the first, then another, all with their noses pointed to the heavens. Krandle's experience tells him they left their lairs, raced to the smell of blood, and have been tracking the source ever since; moving from one side of the road to the other to pick up a trace scent in the swirling breeze, perpetually drawing closer. It's just a matter of time before they're located.

*Just a little closer.* Slowly shouldering his M-4, he hand-signals targets to the others.

His heart thumps solidly against his ribs, and he forces himself to draw in slow, deep breaths to calm his nerves. Each second feels like an hour, that moment in time just before a storm releases its fury… the waiting for it to unleash… hoping it will turn aside at the last instant.

Krandle anxiously watches as the first night runner tenses, its body becoming rigid. In his mind, Krandle hears the rumble of storm clouds. The creature's head snaps toward where the six of them are kneeling and leans forward. Its eyes glow with a silvery light, making the hairs on Krandle's arm stand upright. He knows the night runner is staring directly at him. The two other predators standing in the grass also suddenly turn their heads. Krandle looks out from his NVGs at three pair of liquid silver eyes staring back at him.

"Oh fuck!" Speer whispers.

The night runners lift their heads and shriek, the ear-piercing screams echoing off the trees and along the road.

"It's go time, gents. The dinner bell has been rung and they'll be bringing guests," Krandle says quietly.

The three night runners leap forward, one instant standing still the next, closing the distance at a full sprint.

"Speer, Ortiz, Miller… left, middle, right," Krandle says aloud, the need for quiet past.

In the time it takes to breathe once, the night runners have closed half of the distance. Krandle knew they were fast, but has only encountered them inside of buildings. Those times, they appeared like monkeys with crazy agility. Here, in open terrain, they seem like jaguars streaking toward their prey. Three nearly simultaneous muted shots leave the barrels with accompanying quick flashes of light. The rounds streak out and rapidly close the distance, uncaring of what they hit, only obeying the laws of physics and going where they're pointed. Amid the shrieks, the minute metallic tinkle of expended shells strike the pavement.

Krandle watches as the lead night runner's head as the bullet strikes home under its eye. The projectile hits the solid bone and mushrooms, angling upward through the eye and carving a tunnel through soft gray matter. It slams into the inside of the skull, shattering the bullet. The back of the night runner's head explodes in a spray of bone, blood, and chunks of flesh. The rest of its body, not realizing that it's dead, continues running a step. The creature's feet leave the ground and its back slams onto the highway.

The other two go down in quick fashion, their fallen bodies partially hidden by the taller grass. In the distance, answering screams carry on the night air, growing louder. The faint smell of nitrate drifts quickly away. The shrieks grow in intensity and volume, becoming a din as groups of night runners pour into the field of vision. Krandle radios the sub, letting them know they have company.

"Can you exfil?" Leonard asks.

"No, sir. It's a little late for that and we'd lose the civilians. But, we may need some of your toys if it gets too rough."

"We'll need five minutes to any of the pre-plotted targets, ten if there are any new ones," Leonard says.

"Copy that, sir. The pre-plotted ones will be fine. I'll let you know. Out."

Small groups of night runners stream across the grass and along the road, the screams permeating the area. Gunfire streaks out from the team lined across the bridge, periodic tracers crossing like fiery spears. While others have differing ideas about how they load tracers, Krandle loads his mag with the third to last round going out as a tracer so he knows when he's down to his last shell. In his mind, it makes it a whole hell of a lot faster to reload, getting a visual representation rather than waiting for the slide to lock back.

Krandle adds his fire to the left. Speer and Ortiz are concentrating on the ones near the road, Franklin and Miller to the right. Blanchard, with the clackers arranged at his feet, is directing his fire into the groups racing from the left. The first small groups of night runners are mowed down, each figure going down with splashes of blood spraying into the air. More fill their places, leaping over the bodies of their fallen and charging forward.

Krandle zeroes in on one head, fires, then makes a minute movement to scope in on the next, only marginally aware of the previous one falling. Night runners continue closing in until they fill the area from one tree line to another. Shrieks pierce the night, seeming to vibrate his skull. Calls of "reloading", the screams, the background sound of continuous gunfire, and spent shells hitting the ground combine to create a cacophony of noise. The smell of gunpowder fills Krandle's nose.

Bodies fall one after another, yet the scene is filled with the glowing faces of night runners pushing forward. Dozens go down, dead, dying, or injured, yet the horde draws ever closer. Krandle knows there is a tipping point at which the night runners will surge forward and there's nothing they will be able to do about it.

He grasps Blanchard's shoulder. Above the din, he has to lean over and yell in his ear to be heard. "We need to create gaps. Blow eleven and twelve."

Blanchard grabs two of the clackers, squeezing each repeatedly. On either side of the highway, two large explosions rip through the night in succession. Ball bearings, propelled by C-4, tear through night runners in their path. Those nearest disintegrate into clouds of pink mist, the heavier chunks of flesh and bone hitting the pavement with meaty thunks. Beyond, limbs are separated and bodies ripped open, spilling their contents to the ground. Bodies are lifted into the air and thrown backward.

"Nine and ten," Krandle yells.

Two closer blasts rock the night, sending more night runners sailing. The explosions cause a momentary pause of the night runners in front as they turn to look at what erupted in their midst. The rolling blasts of the claymores fade, ending in a moment of silence.

"Holy shit. Did you see those bodies?" Speer says.

In the immediate silence, Krandle's ears ring. As one, the night runners in front turn toward the bridge and shriek.

*Break's over.* Krandle delivers fire into the midst of night runners again racing forward.

Intent on focusing on one night runner after another, he's taken aback when he looks through his scope to find... nothing. He jerks it back and forth, seeking a new target. There's only a green glow filled with bodies, but none of them upright. Lowering his weapon, he gazes out at the destruction. Figures lie in heaped piles, or singly, some crawling as if to get away from their pain. Finally, he notices the lack of shrieks. There are only the groans and screams of the injured. Beside him, the others of his team stare out at the carnage.

The scent of gunpowder dissipates, bringing the raw iron scent of spilled blood and the stink of torn intestines on the swirling wind. Hundreds of night runners, possibly over a thousand, lie across the chewed-up ground with barely a clear space showing.

"Is that it?" Speer asks.

"I doubt it. There have to be thousands in that town and we've never seen them just give up," Franklin says.

"Ammo check. They'll be back. The claymores made them hesitate. Be ready for a change of tactics," Krandle says.

"Twenty, plus whatever I have left in the current one," Speer says.

The rest of the team reports on their ammo situation; they've used nearly a third of it.

"Figures you'd have the most mags left, pretty boy." Speer directs his remark to Blanchard after an ammo check.

"Had to blow the claymores," Blanchard says with a shrug.

"Test the remaining wires," Krandle tells Blanchard. "We need to know how many are still operational."

Blanchard disconnects the clackers and puts the tester on each one.

"All circuits test out," he says, finishing.

Shrieks, other than those coming from the wounded, grow louder, but also somewhat muted. Krandle looks along the road, but it and the flanks remain clear. He turns his head, attempting to locate the origins. Each time he thinks he has it, it changes.

"They're in the trees," Miller says.

All eyes look to the left and right, trying to peer through the undergrowth. The shrieks grow louder, coming from both directions.

"They're going to try and rush us from both sides," Krandle says. "Speer, you help with the left if they do. Blanchard, you stay right next to me. Franklin, you, Miller and Ortiz have the right."

As if a switch were thrown, the screams go silent. Except for the injured in near the road, a hush falls.

"Well, that's fucking creepy," Speer whispers.

In the distance, near where the four claymores blew holes in their ranks, night runners emerge from the woods, filling the roadway and median. Rank upon rank gather, their eyes flashing silver as the light catches them right. Behind the front ranks, more filter out. Thousands gather, filling the highway beyond sight.

"Fuuuck me!" Speer again whispers.

Krandle's throat tightens and his stomach clenches. He heard stories from Captain Walker about their ability to change tactics, but he never thought them truly capable of something like this. He had thought them animals, perhaps cunning, but mindless nonetheless.

The night runners in the middle jostle, as if something was moving through their midst. The front line parts and a solitary night runner steps forth, coming to halt several paces ahead of the others. The massed night runners and the SEAL Team stare across the open space at each other, neither moving. The lone night runner lifts its head upward, looking from left to right, seeming to gaze at each horizon. Then, lowering its head to look directly at the group holding the bridge, it screams. The horde of night runners surge around him, the night once again filling with shrieks.

Krandle thinks about pulling back to the middle of the bridge to create a chokepoint, but the night runners will climb the girders and be in their midst in no time. He radios the sub.

"We're going to need those toys, and soon. Fire on plots one and two, south to north along the highway."

"Five minutes, chief... ready, ready, hack," he receives.

Krandle hits the button on his watch to start his timer.

"Five minutes, gents. We need to hold the line here. Give them all you have. Blanchard, blow the claymores as the line reaches each one. Save the four near the bridge."

Krandle thumbs his selector switch to auto and, with the others firing, begins sending burst after burst into the charging night runners. The front line goes down as if they hit a tripwire. As the night runners encounter the bodies on the ground, they begin leaping over, making it difficult to get a clear shot. Some jump over bodies, only to fall forward as rounds strike home. The once solid line becomes ragged, but the empty places are filled quickly. There are more bodies racing toward them than outgoing fire and the line draws inexorably closer.

Two explosions tear through the night, momentarily drowning out the screaming horde. The line staggers as ball bearings rip through the ranks. Night runners leap through the dissipating smoke, charging forward. Bullets continue to thin the front ranks, bodies piling up. Two more blasts, but still they come. Glancing at his watch, Krandle is left with the sinking feeling they won't make it the remaining three minutes.

Offshore, the surface of the ocean erupts in a geyser of water as the cruise missile is pushed into the sky. Through the plume of water, the engine ignites in a roar. The missile sails across the open water, tailing a barely visible flame. Five seconds later, a second missile bursts through the surface and is thrust skyward.

Krandle thumbs an empty mag free, jamming another one home and hitting the bolt release. The slide slams forward and he delivers more fire into the closing ranks. One burst, then another, not bothering to take aim other than into the midst of bodies. His bullets will hit something, and that's all they need at the moment – night runners down.

The fire from his team is relentless, the air in front of them thick with outgoing rounds. They slam home into bodies, hitting arms, legs, shoulders, chests, and heads. Skin is torn and bones shattered. Hitting knees, the bullets angle upward, tearing through bowels before exiting the shoulder. The ground around the team is littered with the gleam of spent casings and emptied mags. Still, the night runners inch ever forward in a relentless tide.

*Two minutes.*

The last of the claymores blow, mangling numerous night runners, but the surging point is drawing near – the point at which the SEAL team will only be seconds away from being overrun and annihilated. The line is near and their fire is keeping the monsters at bay.

*This is like fighting a wave of water. Any slack and that wave will crest.*

The bodies stack higher at the front, slowing the efforts of the night runners.

"Trees!" Krandle hears Miller call.

Daring to glance away, Krandle sees night runners pouring out of the nearby tree line.

"How long do you think it will take us to run to the other side?" Krandle yells to Blanchard.

"Eighth of a mile… forty seconds. Thirty with these bastards on my tail."

"Speer?"

"I can fucking teleport there if I need to."

Thoughts race through Krandle's head at light speed. If

the team leaves too early, the night runners will make it to the bridge and be among them. However, they won't be able to keep the new horde of night runners and those on the highway back at the same time.

*Fuck it! We gotta go.*

"Franklin, take the others and set up mid bridge. I'll wait and blow the claymores. Don't fucking shoot me. Now, go!"

The others turn to run. Without the fire holding it back, the wave of night runners crests and surges forward. The ones streaming from the woods are close, some even falling into the ravine from the tight-packed bunch.

Looking down, he sees the four minute mark pass.

*Good enough.*

Krandle rapidly squeezes the clackers, one after the other. The near explosions, coming seconds apart, rock the bridge. A wet mist mixes with the roiling smoke. Without another look, he races to his teammates setting up near the middle of the bridge. He reaches them and turns, each of them delivering a mag into the recovering mass of night runners.

"Time to go," Krandle yells, glancing at his watch.

There's no need to tell the civilians to run; they have already taken to their heels. Well, most of them. Two are assisting the man with the wounded leg – assisting being a matter of perspective. A better definition would be dragging.

Near the end of the bridge, Krandle notes two bodies with the remains of stretchers over them. He has no idea when they died. A roar and tail of flame flashes overhead. He and his team dive into the grass beside the road as they hear several loud 'pops' from behind.

A series of explosions tear through the night, becoming one continuous roar. The team all turn to take care of any night runners on the bridge, but their light filters are overwhelmed by the cluster munitions dropped. Another roar streaks overhead, adding its payload to the thundering explosions.

The echoes die away.

The team rises to their knees, weapons trained on the bridge. Expecting some night runners to remain, Krandle is confused by the empty bridge. His NVGs recover. There is devastation on the other side of the ravine.

The ground is churned beyond recognition. To the sides, the underbrush lining the trees is all but gone, the trees scarred in a hundred different places. Bodies and body parts hang from branches as if from some macabre scene in a movie. The remains of arms and legs poke out from mulches of dirt. Even from this distance, Krandle smells the aroma of torn bowels and blood, mixing with that of gunpowder. Not a single night runner is in sight or can be heard.

"I'm not walking back through that," Speer says, shaking his head.

In all of his years, Krandle has never seen destruction on this scale. He radios the sub and gives an all clear and his thanks, informing them that they'll spend the rest of the night on the bridge. The civilians return, the wounded man looking pale. Little is said throughout the night as each ponders what they went through.

"If they weren't already, I bet those bandits are long gone by now. I know I would be if I heard that shit happening nearby," Speer says.

Krandle shakes his head. Speer says whatever is on his mind at any given moment, not realizing how it may affect others. There's truth in what he said, but that truth means the wives and daughters will be gone as well.

*He just isn't socialized, that's it.*

"I don't know. They may just hunker down for dear life, not wanting to show themselves and risk an accidental meeting. We'll see in the morning."

\* \* \*

The rest of the evening passes without event. Far off screams are heard periodically, but nothing draws close to the killing ground. Even the night runners have apparently had enough. Taking turns on watch, they get what rest they can.

It took Speer and Miller all of about forty minutes after sunrise to find the quad tracks leading up a logging road. A short distance up a hill, nestled within evergreens, Speer found two shipping containers resting on level ground with fourteen bandits scattered around it. The quads and vans were parked to the side. Some of the women had been tied to trees, the others not visible – probably being kept the containers. The tied women and the type of vehicles are all the verification Krandle needs. Leaving the civilians to dig shallow graves for the two who succumbed to their wounds, Krandle and the others join with Speer and Miller.

Speer points out three leaning against trunks farther into the trees, apparently the watch they set. One is positioned just off the road in front of a large fir. The other two are off to the sides, all focused — if focused is the correct word — toward the highway. They have evidently concluded that any threat will come from that direction, that nothing can come at them from within the woods. Considering the sound of gunfire and explosions, Krandle is a little confused by their nonchalance.

*Perhaps that's what comes from thinking the world is yours for the taking.*

"I didn't see any radios on the guards," Speer says.

Krandle momentarily ponders coming at them from their unsecured side, but opts to take the guards out first. *Always better to deal with the perimeter first, then move in.*

Krandle directs Speer and Ortiz to take out the first guard, setting the rest of the team to cover their approach. If the camp becomes alerted, Speer and Ortiz will eliminate the other two guards while Krandle and the rest of the team engage those within the camp. That means a firefight, which is always risky.

"Don't worry about the bullet with your name on it," one of his instructors had said. "It's the ones marked anonymous you have to be concerned with."

If the team can catch them by surprise, they can take the bandits down before they have a chance to fire a shot. If it comes down to a fight, one of the marauders may just shoot the women as a final 'Fuck You'.

Speer snakes his way under the trees, pushing small limbs and needles out of the way prior to setting his foot down. Ortiz follows silently behind. The guard sits on a fallen tree, intently studying his finger nails. Leaning against the bark to the man's side rests an AR-15 style carbine. A short distance behind the man, Speer and Ortiz slowly lay their M-4s on the ground and Speer withdraws a six-inch blade from a sheath.

Approaching from behind, using the trees for cover while keeping the man in sight, the two SEALs inch toward the guard. One step, crouch and wait, another step, crouch and wait. The man is oblivious to the danger edging toward him, that his life is measured in seconds. So silent are the two men, they move to within a few feet directly behind the guard.

The man, apparently finished with whatever manicure he is contemplating, looks up and gazes toward the logging road. With a nod toward Ortiz, Speer rises and takes a step forward. He brings one hand around the man's head, grabbing his face to cover his mouth and pinch his nostrils. Pulling back his head, Speer brings his knife around, plunging it under the bottom ribs and driving it up into heart. Removing the knife, he plunges it in again, this time going for one of the lungs.

Ortiz, upon seeing Speer grab the man's head, steps over the log and takes a firm hold of the man's legs to hold them still. The other guards are close enough that any sound of a scuffle will reach them and may cause them to investigate. Speer feels the body stiffen with his first thrust. Hot blood spurts against his hand covering the mouth and he feels it pour down his knife hand. Withdrawing his blade again, Speer drives into the side of the man's throat.

Speer remembers one of his lessons. "Never stop until your target is down for good. Don't stab and step back to admire your work or wait for a reaction."

Blood gushes from the wound and pours through Speer's fingers to run down the man's cheek. With the head pulled back, Speer stares into his eyes and watches them dull. The body goes limp. Quietly, Ortiz lifts the man's legs over the tree and they lay him out of sight along the fallen tree.

"That shit never gets any easier," Speer whispers, cleaning his blade on the man's jeans.

"No. No, it never does," Ortiz says.

Lifting the carbine, Ortiz ejects the mag. "Kind of them to give us more ammo. Do you want me to get the next one?"

"No, I'll do it. I just don't have to like it."

Retrieving their weapons, they leave the iron smell of blood behind and creep back toward the next guard with the others moving up to provide cover. Ideally, they would have taken all of the guards out at once, but nothing is ever ideal. One by one, they dispose of the remaining guards in much the same fashion.

A scream erupts from the bandit camp a short ways uphill. The team turns as one toward the sound, spreading behind cover, weapons ready. Another woman's scream reverberates through the trees, followed by a couple of loud voices.

"Online and quietly push upward," Krandle radios.

With eyes on the camp, Krandle watches as a woman is dragged across the ground and unceremoniously dumped in the middle of the encampment. Three men kneel beside her, one holding her legs with the other two on either side. The others, with a variety of weapons hanging from their shoulders, stand in a semi-circle, grinning.

"I count fifteen. Does that match what you have, Speer?" Krandle whispers into his throat mic.

"Yep."

"Franklin, Miller, Ortiz, take the three near the woman first. Watch your shots. No use waiting. Let's hit 'em hard," Krandle orders.

As one, the team rises from cover, carbines going to their shoulders in one fluid motion. Together, they flow into the camp like a fast-moving dark mist.

*Pop pop pop.* More follow like a string of firecrackers.

The two men next to the woman collapse to the side, blood misting from where rounds slammed into their skulls near their ears. The man holding the woman's legs falls back on his rear, looking down at the red flowering on his chest. A round strikes his nose, the bullet splitting as it penetrates his nasal cavity. He crumples to the side.

Most of the men drop to the ground as if mowed over with a scythe. Some have a split second longer and attempt to use it to make it to cover. They manage one step before speeding projectiles intercept their path, sending them to fall face first onto the forest floor.

With blood spraying across her, the woman continues her screaming, trying to crawl backward away from the bodies. It's over in seconds. Whitish smoke drifts across the camp, dissipating as it moves. The women stare at the scene in shock. Several of the injured bandits moan and attempt to crawl away. One reaches his arms out in front and pulls his body forward a few inches. Blood seeps into the dirt around him. Settling his red dot on the man's chest, Krandle fires twice. The man's shirt puffs up and the body jumps as each round strikes. With a forced sigh that stirs the dust around his mouth, the figure goes limp. The rest of the team begin delivering rounds into the wounded.

*Whatever world materializes from the ashes of the old one, these kind of people don't need to be inhabitants.*

"Blanchard, see to the woman. The rest of us will form a perimeter. If they're able to move, we'll head back to the others courtesy of these vans," Krandle says.

Blanchard kneels next to the first woman, looking for injuries. As she answers his questions, her expression reflects a measure of fear and shock. She watches his ministrations, her gaze wandering down to the knife secured to his leg. Narrowing her eyes, her frightened look changes to one of anger, with the red glow of hate hiding just behind.

"Is that sharp?" she asks, nodding toward the six-inch blade.

"Uh, yeah," Blanchard says.

"Can I borrow it?"

"Um, what for?"

"For something."

"Chief, she wants to borrow my knife."

Krandle looks over and sees a look of vengeance hidden

deep within. He has an idea of what the hours may have held for the women, and understands what her request will probably entail. Glancing at the bodies, he knows the bandits have long since departed this world and won't feel a thing. He feels torn between desecrating a body and the understanding that the woman needs something to gain a measure of herself back.

"Give it to her," Krandle says.

After a couple of women enact their vengeance upon the bodies, they team helps gather supplies from the bandits' storages, including their weapons. They load them into the vans for the civilians to use on their journey. The bodies are left lying on the forest floor, their blood congealing and soaking into the dirt.

\* \* \*

The thanks are unending as the men and women are reunited. Krandle has never been good at the emotional things, so he just nods and gives the expected responses, wanting nothing more than to leave. The women are physically well for the most part, but he's sure the emotional trauma will haunt them the rest of their lives.

With the sun rising higher in the morning sky, Krandle hands the keys of the vans to the group, giving them directions north to Olympia where Captain Walker is fighting back against the night runners and building a sanctuary for survivors.

They hit the rolling surf, the chaotic water soaking the men aboard before the raft noses up and over. The waves turn into breakers, Speer timing it so they don't roll up on a cresting wave. Powering down the backside, they motor through Pacific swells. Ahead, a dark menacing shape slowly rises from the surface, clearly one of the ocean's predators. Speer drives the zodiac onto the barely awash deck. Stowing their gear into the locker, they make their way below decks. The USS *Santa Fe* submerges as quietly as it surfaced, the ocean once more just an endless series of waves.

# A DEBT REPAID
## A Tales of the Prodigy Story

Tim Marquitz & J. M. Martin

**G**ryl crouched on the roof's ledge, knees long since gone numb. His fingers played at the rope in his hands of their own volition, plucking at the frayed strings as he waited, eyes on the dark alley below. He huddled inside his cloak and bit back a curse. Spring had come to Amberton weeks before, hints of green returning to the woods sitting sentry north of the walls, but winter had yet to surrender. A frigid breeze cut through the narrow streets once the sun retired, stirring the trash into a frenzy and chasing all but the most foolish or entitled of citizens inside.

It was the former that brought Gryl back to the city for the first time since he'd laid Korbitt low in his quest to rescue the Xenious girl, Vai. Memories stirred in the wake of the warlord's name, the sweet tang of his fear, teeth shattering to make way for righteous steel. Gryl had left his mark in both blood and terror, hence his clandestine watch atop the roof. Even with all the time between, the people of Amberton would remember the Avan prodigy who'd left more than a dozen bodies littering the floor of the Broken Lizard.

The town had scrambled in the wake of Korbitt's death, or so Gryl had heard, their illicit leadership so brutally and publicly cut down. The void left behind threw the city into chaos until the empress herself took notice and sent her knights to secure its peace. Their presence was the true reason Gryl was here. In these times of war, all traffic leading to the Southern Reaches, to the heart of Shytan, was routed through Amberton first.

A sudden rush of noise broke the silence – giggles and soft platitudes spilling from an opened door, the clink of well-earned coin – telling him his target had left the lurid embrace of the brothel that stood two buildings down. Boots scraping awkwardly against the weathered cobbles of the nearby street set fire to Gryl's veins. He stretched to chase away the stiffness, reveling in the caterpillar of *pops* that reverberated down his spine, while he tightened his grip upon the rope. The time had come at last.

Even from the roof, Gryl caught whiffs of perfume and musky incense wafting off the man, remnants of his excesses laid bare by the traitorous wind. He appeared around the corner several moments after his scent had marked his approach. Gryl smiled with recognition, the silver he'd paid the local boys to learn the overseer's routine well spent. And as foretold, Jaret Gailbraith, Mayor of Amberton – if only in title since the knights had come to town – stumbled off the walk and, secure in his safety by dint of royal decree, staggered drunkenly down the alleyway without so much as a cautious glance.

Gryl swallowed a chuckle at Gailbraith's misplaced confidence. The prodigy had come to Amberton to tweak the nose of the empress. One more misdeed would hardly tip the scales against him given what he intended. She could only want him *so* dead.

He checked his snare one last time, ensuring it was levered about the nearby chimney, and set his ambush into motion. The rope slithered through his fingers and struck home, the noose cinching tight with a satisfying *hurrrk*. Gryl wasted no time reeling in his squirming catch. Hand over hand, with easy motions to keep from snapping the mayor's neck, he hauled Gailbraith up the wall until the man's purpled face appeared above the ledge, his feet swinging three stories above the alley. The man clasped at the rooftop with desperate hands, fingers digging grooves in the aged mortar between the stones, finally managing to secure a tentative hold with the prodigy's help. Gryl leveraged the rope around his elbow, loosening its hold just enough so Gailbraith could breathe, and leaned in close.

"Scream and I drop you."

The mayor's eyes widened into black pools. Hood peeled back and skullcap set aside, Gryl's scars gleamed in the pale moonlight, his pedigree on full display. Gailbraith offered a shallow nod at seeing them, choking himself with the effort, but he remained silent otherwise.

"Where is he?"

"Wh-who?" the mayor asked, the word little more than a ragged gasp.

Gryl let the rope slide through his fingers a few inches before tightening his grip again. Gailbraith gasped as gravity threatened to pull him down despite his grip on the ledge. The barest scent of urine tainted the air until the breeze swept it away. His frantic heartbeat fluttered at his temple.

"Bal Surathanan, the slaver," Gryl answered. "Don't make me ask again."

"The… the knights have him," Gailbraith offered, only hesitating for an instant. "At the Lizard. One of the rooms above the bar."

Gryl bit back a groan. He'd seen enough of the tavern his last trip through town. "And the woman who was with him?"

The mayor shook his head. "I don't know anything about a woman." Gryl wiggled the rope. "I swear it! There was no one with him save the knights."

No reason not to believe the man, his soiled pants attesting to his honesty, Gryl nodded. He let the rope play out and peeled Gailbraith's fingers from the ledge, the mayor dropping to dangle below the rooftop by his neck. He hissed and clawed at the rope squeezing the life from him. Gryl leaned down and clasped the man's flailing wrist and slipped the other end of the rope into his hand. The mayor seized it out of instinct, his other hand following suit not a second after.

"Hold tight," Gryl told him as he released the rope.

"What are you—?" Gailbraith managed to squeeze out before he was suddenly grappling with his own weight, the noose tightening even further. Veins stood out like serpents against his neck, eyes bulging. His knuckles gleamed white against the tan braids of the rope, a line of crimson snaking its way down the length as he tightened his grip and the rough cord bit into his palm.

"I've no interest in killing you, Mayor, but I have to admit, I've nothing to gain by letting you live either," Gryl said with a shrug. "Therefore, I leave your fate in your hands. Literally."

Gryl turned away without so much as a glance back and headed toward the latticework on the far side of the building. As he slipped over the ledge and started down he heard the *fwip* of the rope coming loose of the chimney and a sullen *thump* a moment later. Gryl sighed. He hadn't wanted the mayor's death on his hands but he couldn't deny it was for the best.

He would let nothing get in the way of his freeing Jacquial.

\* \* \*

Night still clung to Amberton when Gryl reached the Broken Lizard. Much as he wanted to take his time and prepare his assault upon the knights and their charge, the sands were against him. Dawn would find the mayor dead and the city would erupt, every shadow scrutinized, the empress's soldiers closing ranks to deny him. Gryl couldn't let that happen. He had but one chance to prise the location of the lord of the Guild Infernal from the slaver and he damned well intended to take advantage of it.

Grateful it was after hours, the tavern locked up tight, he pried a shuttered window open and slipped inside after making certain there was no one on the street to notice his untoward entry. He eased the shutter closed behind him, his teeth clenched at the muffled *creak* of it, and drifted across the tavern toward the one room he was certain of: the proprietor's.

Gryl circled around the bar, where the room lay, and cracked the door open. He swept inside as soon as he spied the tavern keeper tucked in his cot. A hand over the keeper's mouth and a dagger to his eye is what the man woke to. A moment later Gryl had his answer as to where the knights had settled for the night. Gryl nicked the barkeep's neck and waited until the poison on the blade took full effect. Then Gryl left the room, the proprietor fully aware, but paralyzed in his cot for many long hours to come. He would tell no one of Gryl's visit until long after the prodigy was gone.

The stairs creaked as he made his way upward, each step a spark of flint on steel, threatening to ignite the past, but Gryl would have none of it. He pushed aside the memories of Korbitt standing atop the landing, holding Vai's naked body as a shield like the coward he was, knife to her throat, and focused on the task at hand. Clarity was what Gryl needed, not the fury that rumbled in his belly and made a forge of his ribcage. He'd brought death to the Lizard once more but this time it swept in on a whisper rather than a storm, padded footfalls its only warning.

Gryl took the last step at a leap, loosing a dagger the moment he cleared the baluster. The knight who sat sentry at the end of the hall, red-eyed and blinking away the boredom that no doubt pleaded dereliction of duty, spied the prodigy too late. The blade sunk into the knight's eye and he slumped into his seat with a bubbled sigh. Gryl righted the man before he could topple and pressed his ear to the door. Only snores rumbled beyond.

With the key scavenged from the dead knight, Gryl unlocked the door. He drew a deep breath as he slipped his short sword from its sheath and eased into the room. The first of the knights went silent when Gryl dragged his blade across his neck. The second knight followed an instant after, meeting the same fate. The third, and last, of the empress's men came to at the sound of his companions' feet thrashing under the covers. He bolted upright in his cot as they gurgled their last and met the cold steel of Gryl's blade splitting his ribs and spearing his heart, the point of the sword *thumping* against the wall behind him, pinning his corpse there.

A lantern burst to life and Gryl tugged his sword free, spinning about to level the blade at the man who'd chased the darkness from the room. Their eyes met.

"Oh… shit," the slaver muttered, recognition spreading the sour tinge of disappointment across his features, his thick black mustache twitching at the corners of his mouth.

"Oh shit indeed." Gryl gestured toward the cot with his sword, droplets of blood spattering the covers at the motion. "Have a seat, Surathanan. You and I have much to discuss."

The slaver did as he was told. "And here I thought I'd seen the last of you in Feln, Prodigy." He shook his head, chasing away his malaise and replacing it with a practiced grin. "You do know the empress herself sent for me, do you not? And I'm certain she expects me to arrive whole and hale, all my sundry bits and pieces intact and in their proper place. I imagine she would be quite vexed to learn you'd done me harm."

"You overestimate my concern for the empress's feelings." Gryl answered the slaver's grin with one of his own, pressing the tip of his sword against Surathanan's collarbone. A dot of blood welled beneath it, standing out against the man's tanned flesh before running south to stain his rumpled tunic. "But, if it eases your worries, I don't intend to kill you. At least not as long as you answer me truthfully and keep your glib tongue in your mouth otherwise."

Surathanan chuckled. "And I'm to take you at your word, Avan? Three men are dead, hardly *proof* of your restraint and honor, if we're to be honest." He waved his arms about, gesturing in turn to each of the knights cooling in their cots. "Their only crime was their gods-awful snoring. Annoying, certainly, but not worth being murdered over."

"Five men actually, as there've been a couple on the way here" Gryl told him. "And I can easily make it six if you're so desperate to sail the seas of Avraxas, but we both know you're rather fond of your existence, shallow as it might be. Tell me where she is and I'll leave you to greet the sunrise. If not…"

The slaver raised his hand in surrender. "No need for all

that now. Better you're the empress's problem than mine." He exhaled slowly before continuing. "Your dear Jacquial is being held in a makeshift gaol, built in the cellar of a prominent businessman here in Amberton. Kertol Mallister is his name, if I recall correctly. I hear he's a cousin of Empress Patah Re Shah, or a nephew or some shit. Hard to keep track of who beds who in royal circles these days." He shrugged. "Regardless who spat him out, he is not without influence. He has his own men to guard the property, not to mention the dozen knights tasked to ensure Jacquial reaches the capital without delay. His home's quite the fortress, or so I hear. Haven't been there myself. You're not likely to get anywhere near your precious thief friend before they cut you down." Surathanan grinned. "But, by all means, don't let that discourage you. You're up for a challenge, aye?"

Gryl ignored the jibe. "You can point me to this Mallister's house?"

"I can indeed, especially if it will hurry you on your way." Surathanan glanced about the room, looking from body to body. "Your handiwork is beginning to smell and I'd like to find less… *ripe* accommodations before the empress's men bring word of your death and usher me into her presence."

"Tell me then." The slaver offered the directions without hesitation, going silent as soon as he finished, his last act of smug defiance. The prodigy nodded and took a step toward the door, only to stop and turn back, raising a finger and waggling it at Surathanan. "Oh, one more thing…"

"What is it now? I've told you all I damn well—"

Gryl twisted at the hips and drove his fist into Surathanan's jaw. Bone collided with bone and the slaver went stiff, collapsing on the cot, eyes buried deep in their sockets.

"I haven't forgotten your role in Valtus's disappearance, in case you were wondering," he told the unconscious man. "And while I said I wouldn't kill you, I suspect you'll be sorry I didn't once I turn you over to his father, Delvin. That old priest harbors secrets; dark ones. Ones I suspect are best left hidden, though I imagine he's quite eager to make an exception and cart them out." He chuckled. "I wouldn't want to be you."

Gryl hoisted the slaver over his shoulder and left the dead knights behind, seeking someplace to secure Surathanan until he could return for him. Dawn was fast approaching and Gryl had yet to accomplish his task. If it didn't happen soon, it never would.

\* \* \*

Mallister's manse was just as Surathanan described it. A wall twice Gryl's height encircled the property, and crooked and jagged barbs protruded at all angles from the top, leaving no room for a would-be intruder to avoid losing blood on the way in. The only entrance was barred by a great iron gate and the mechanism to open it was hidden, well out of reach behind the wall's double-hand-span thickness. Three men paced beyond its bars and Gryl was surprised to see their eyes so clear, so aware, at this hour. A fourth and fifth prowled the area outside the wall and made it clear that Mallister had spared no expense when it came to his security. These were no peasant militia men. Still, the empress had Jacquial imprisoned in the house and it would take her entire army to keep him from her.

His first thought was to storm the property, knife the men at the gate, and race for the house, but if Mallister could spare a handful of men for the gate in the middle of the night, Gryl could be certain there would be a dozen more between it and the front door of the manse. Even if he were to win through, it would give the empress's men inside time to mobilize or flee and neither suited his needs. Stealth was the order of the day. He only hoped he had time for such cautiousness.

Gryl circled the property, slithering through the shadows, dodging the guard who patrolled the grounds nearest him, and leapt to the wall as soon as the man was out of sight. Rusted steel points bit into the prodigy's hand as he grasped the lip of the wall, cutting through his glove and slicing flesh. The barbs punctured deep but his Avan masters had long since bled him of pain, leaving him to feel nothing more than a vague pressure at the point of each puncture. Blood oozed from his wounds as he pulled himself up the wall by the one hand, leveraging himself at the top and taking a moment to bend a few of the other barbs flat. Old and weathered, they gave in, one snapping with a brittle *pop* and two more creaking aside so their tips bit into the stone of the wall, their sting muted. Gryl scrambled the rest of the way up, balancing in the narrow space free of metal spikes, and surveyed the property.

A well-manicured garden covered the majority of the yard alongside the house, leaving only a couple horse-lengths of open space on either side of the makeshift wilderness. Walkways of white marble, gleaming in the moonlight, spread serpentine throughout the greenery, seeming to run everywhere and nowhere at the same time, a labyrinth of white amidst the green. Trees and shrubbery cast deep shadows over the remainder of the lawn and, while the garden offered Gryl plenty of cover on his way to the house, it also offered Mallister's men a dozen opportunities for an ambush. Still, outside of skirting half the property to avoid it, risking being seen by roaming sentries, there was no other way to reach the pair of sunken doors he'd spied near the rear of the house. With all the windows barred by iron rods, that seemed the most likely entrance to the cellars.

Gryl cast one last glance in search of hounds and, seeing no sign of any, dropped over the wall. He landed in a crouch and raced for the garden, only drawing breath after he was safe inside its verdant sanctuary. The wind rustled the leaves and set the branches to swaying but he could hear nothing beyond the willowy serenade of the trees; no shuffle of hidden feet, no anxious hands creaking against leathern grips. Still he waited to be certain, counting the moments in his head and cursing each and every one of them before determining he was alone in the garden. The warble of insects returned. Only then did he inch his way forward, following the winding marble pathways in the direction of the manse. To his surprise, he reached the other side without event. He hunkered down to observe the house.

Two more of Mallister's men stood guard within the recessed archway, if their efforts could be seen as such. Unlike those at the gate, these men could just as well have opened the door for Gryl and ushered him inside for all the dedication they showed. They hunched between the twin stone pillars, backs to him, hiding from the chill wind, neither watching anything save for the shuffling of their feet.

"Might well as be waiting for the grass to grow," Gryl heard one say, his voice drifting across the field.

"Better this than what those poor bastards down there are stuck doing," the other man said, gesturing toward the doors as a great puff of gray smoke billowed from his mouth. "Least out here we can sneak a smoke and a nap and don't need to be nowhere near *her*."

"Aye," the first agreed. "You're right about that, Arlen. That twat is right evil. Wonder what she's hiding under all that—"

Gryl darted low across the open field and launched a dagger, their words driving his hand as if it had a will of its own. He wondered of his feelings for Jacquial while the blade sunk into the sentry's neck, steel grating against bone. The man toppled, surprise etched across his features as Gryl took the broad stairs three at a time. He dodged the falling sentry and thrust his sword through the eye of the remaining guard when he turned to watch his companion tumble away. The man grunted and went still and Gryl shook his corpse from his blade, letting it crumple onto the landing. He stared at the bodies and sighed. Myr Eltara had stolen his desires just as she had his agony, his childhood castration assuring that, and yet here he was, carving his way through Amberton for a woman he could never love.

The heat that stung his cheeks spoke otherwise.

Believing it better to act than contemplate such uncertainties, Gryl rifled the bodies and opened one of the doors, peering inside. A short landing met his gaze, another set of steps plunging downward just beyond. Nothing moved in the guttering light of the lanterns hung on the wall on either side of the entryway. Gryl dragged the dead men inside and sealed them in, before plunging down the dark stairwell, blades at the ready.

The air was cool inside the cellar and he could taste moisture with every breath, the harsh winter having settled into the bones of the house. He eased down the last of the steps and pressed his back to the wall. Three passageways jutted three different directions but there was no mistaking the way he was to go, only one path illuminated with more of the lanterns dangling from bronze hooks. He stared down the other two corridors and listened for any signs of activity but heard nothing. For all of Surathanan's bluster regarding the empress's relative, Mallister had made it easy on Gryl.

*Too easy,* he felt.

He drifted down the hall, every muscle tensed, his pace falling in sync with his heartbeat, and still nothing leapt from the darkness to challenge him. That was worse than if something had. His lungs ached, desperate to expel the stale air he held captive as he crept along. Only when he thought his chest might explode did he hear the shuffle of footsteps ahead; slow, scuffing movements speaking of boredom more than a reaction to his presence. Gryl drew closer to the archway at the end of the tunnel and spied a row of gray bars just beyond. Barred windows against the back wall let slivers of moonlight into the chamber, assuring him he'd reached the dungeon at last.

A sharp sniff sounded just inside the archway and Gryl stepped inside, took the barest of an instant to aim, and stabbed the sentry. Blood spewed from the man's neck and spattered Gryl's face with warm dots. A twist of his wrist and a hard yank freed his sword and finished the guard, his head lolling, half-severed. He died without a sound.

"I'd expected someone to attempt a rescue, but I hardly expected *you.*"

Gryl turned to see Jacquial, the lord of the Guild Infernal, lounging atop a wooden stool inside the barren cell. She stared out at him from beneath wild, raven locks. She hardly looked a prisoner, dressed in her customary plain black tunic and loose-fitting pants clasped tight about her ankles, swallowing the soft leather boots beneath. Only the slight gauntness in her cheeks and the sallow pits beneath her emerald eyes spoke of her predicament.

"Toad sent word of your... *predicament*, a regiment of knights having come to collect you and Surathanan in the middle of the night. He thought it best that I tempt the empress's ire rather than the guild. Seemed a reasonable request."

She smiled, chasing the shadows from her features. "My uncle is a fool if he believes the guild won't suffer for this no matter who was sent." Jacquial rose and came to stand at the cell door, shaking her head.

"A well-meaning fool, at least."

"He is that." She rapped her knuckles on the bars. "How about we catch up another time and you get me out of this hole before the empress's dogs realize what you're about."

"Too late for that," a sharp voice said from behind them.

Gryl spun to see a sleek figure in silver blocking the only doorway, a group of knights gathered at her back, the swooping raven sigil of Shytan standing out stark against the black and red of their tabards. Chainmail gleamed in the open spaces beneath, naked steel wavering with impatience.

"By order of the empress, Patah Re Shah, lay down your arms and surrender, Prodigy. You will not be given another opportunity to comply."

Gryl exhaled slowly as realization washed over him. It had been a trap all along, Surathanan offering the guild lord to the empress, certain Gryl would follow, fool that he is. This gleaming knight had been who the guards spoke of outside, not Jacquial.

"Who are you?" he asked the armored woman, playing for time.

"She's one of the empress's Exemplars, her personal guard," Jacquial answered for the warrior, her words heavy with the burden of apprehension. The sound gave Gryl pause. "She is *runesworn*. It is rumored they cannot die."

The woman stepped forward, her slim white blade, mystic sigils woven in gold along its lower half, leading the way. Gryl could feel its essence in the marrow of his bones, his scars throbbing at its closeness. The Exemplar's eyes glistened like stars through her helm. Her armor looked as if it were crafted of cloth, flexing easily with her every movement, yet there was no denying the authenticity of it, the sheen of fine steel reflecting the dim light. Gryl had never seen such exquisite handiwork and he wondered at its resilience.

If only for an instant.

Not one to offer advantage to a foe, or to believe one couldn't be slain, Gryl darted low and went to disembowel the woman. She met his attack and turned it aside with casual ease, countering with a speed that made him feel as if he were clawing through a mire. Her blade etched a long gash down his biceps and sent him stumbling back to avoid a second blow.

"You've made a poor choice, Prodigy," she said, though the excitement in her voice told him this was what she'd wanted all along.

He wasted no breath on words, launching himself at her once more. He feinted high and swung low, slipping a dagger out from the sheath at his back as he did. The exemplar stood stoic, parrying his strike with a flick of her wrist and knocking his dagger aside as he tried to jam it into her armpit. Her forearm collided with his nose, the *crunch* of cartilage reverberating in his skull, only to be followed by a kick to his midsection. Gryl crashed to the stone floor, losing his dagger at the impact. He mouthed a silent prayer to Anklor for allowing him to retain his grip upon his sword. He clambered to his feet as the Exemplar advanced with slow, predatory steps. Even though he couldn't see her face beneath her helmet, he could sense the smile she bore. The malice shined through.

He lashed out again, letting instinct guide his motions, but the woman was simply too fast. Steel met steel and he was thwarted again and once more as he attempted to counter. Her free hand caressed a sigil on the blade as Gryl retreated, and he swore he saw sparks as the sword began to hum, its steel seeming to blur, leaving a gray trail in its wake as she advanced. Gryl whipped his sword up to parry the blow only to realize too late that was what she intended him to do. The weapons clashed once again, only this time there was no resounding *clang*.

Instead, a sharp *crack* filled his ears and Gryl felt his sword break before he saw it. Vibrations shot through his palm and numbed his fingers, sending striations of lightning the length of his arm. His blade, cut clean, left nothing but a useless couple of inches protruding from the hilt. He was drawn to stare at its impotent edge, unable to look away.

Molten fire churned in his gut and Gryl realized his hesitance too late. He twisted and threw himself backward, tearing the Exemplar's sword loose of his flesh. Blood spilled from the wound and he stumbled to a knee. Pain, the likes of which he remembered only in the haze of his nightmares, scalded his nerves and brought tears to his eyes. He gasped, struggling to draw breath.

"Don't kill him!" Jacquial shouted, banging her fists against the bars. "You don't need to kill him."

"But I do." The Exemplar drove a boot into Gryl's chest, knocking him to the ground once more. Only then did he release his hold on his ruined sword and draw another dagger. The silver knight gave him no chance to use it.

She stepped in and cut a crevice across his wrist. His hand spasmed and popped open of its own accord, the dagger falling away from numb fingers. Jacquial screamed but Gryl barely heard her as the knight carved a bloody trough along his chest. He howled only to catch an armored fist in the mouth, burying his voice beneath the *crunch* of broken teeth. Gryl slumped, barely aware he'd fallen to his stomach. Cold stone pressed against his cheek while the Exemplar cut gory pieces from his back. Blood pooled on the floor and every breath gave birth to crimson bubbles as an unfamiliar agony flooded his senses.

Unable to lift his head, his nose and mouth filling with his own blood, he dragged his arm to his face and forced it under his cheek. He moaned as his face slipped inched upward, struggling for breath as warm fluid gushed from his open mouth. It ran across his slashed wrist, the white of his nearly-severed tendons clearly visible in the gash.

"Wait!" he cried out, little more than a whisper, waving his one good limb at the knight behind him.

To his surprise, the Exemplar halted her attack. Still, he could feel her hovering over him.

"Speak your last, Avan, while you still have the breath to do so."

"I would die on my feet," he said, barely able to get his tongue to form the words, "not like this."

He heard Jacquial mutter a curse but the knight drowned her out. "Then stand, Prodigy. Stand and meet your last moment as a warrior. Avraxas will have your soul but, by all means, meet your end on your feet if it eases your passing."

Gryl drew his knees beneath him, his face cradled in the crook of his arm. Out of sight of the Exemplar and her men, Gryl bit down and ripped a chunk of meat from his forearm nearest his wound, sealing it inside his mouth with a sour grimace. When at last he managed to stand, the floor slippery with his claret, he straightened and met the cold gaze of the Exemplar as best he could.

"Any last words?"

Gryl shook his head, wiping the blood from his mouth.

Jacquial loosed a bitter, "Noooooo," and continued her futile efforts to pry the bars from the wall, motes of gray dust her only reward.

The knight stepped forward and aimed her blade at Gryl's heart, cruelty slowing her hand, the need to make him suffer apparent. It was what he'd hoped for.

The prodigy slumped the moment the sword came at him and the thrust that would have ended his life pierced his shoulder instead. He screamed and dug his hand beneath the knight's gorget and clasped the rim of her breastplate, tugging at it with all his might. She cursed and shoved him away, ripping her sword loose and sending him tumbling to his back. He stayed where he fell as the Exemplar examined herself.

The woman chuckled after seeing he'd done nothing more than smear his life's blood down her chest. "Your last act of defiance was to sully my armor?" she asked. "I expected more from you, though I know I shouldn't have. You aren't the first of your kind to die at my hand but I'd hoped for a challenge this time around. The empress believed you were different for some reason, assured me of it, in fact." The Exemplar advanced. "I'm sorry to have to report otherwise."

Gryl grinned and met her stare. "Perhaps you should have listened more closely to your master."

She raised her blade, ready to deliver the final blow, only to have a tremble rattle her frame and stay her hand. Her eyes went wide behind the slits of her helm, her free hand clanging against her breastplate as if hoping to break its shell. "What have you done?"

Gryl said nothing.

A hiss sounded beneath her armor and the exemplar gasped, stumbling and slamming her back into the cell. Wisps of black smoke billowed up through her helmet, spilling from the eye slits. Jacquial pulled the knight's sword arm through the bars and bent it backward, leveraging it against the bars and jerking downward. There was a sharp *snap*, the sound of a tree branch giving way, and the exemplar shrieked while the guild lord pinned her in place on the ground before the cell.

The knights who'd stood at the doorway in arrogant complacence came alive and burst into the dungeon. Gryl, using his blood to grease his passage, slid across the floor and grabbed the dagger the Exemplar had forced from his hand. He clasped trembling fingers about its hilt and batted the woman's flailing arm aside. As quick as he could, he slit the leather clasps on the side of her breastplate and rolled away.

"Lift her," he shouted.

Jacquial did as ordered, not questioning his intentions. She ignored the woman's screams and yanked the knight to her feet by her shattered shoulder. Her blade clattered to the floor. The Exemplar's cuirass fell away as she was pulled upward, exposing the charred cavity of her torso, scored and blackened by the magic of the scars Gryl had slipped beneath her armor. Fire burned in the well of her chest.

The flames, not beholden to the laws of nature, erupted outward as soon as the steel carapace holding it in place was

286

removed, a geyser of fiery energy spewing forth. The knights at the front of the charge caught the burst head on. They were dead before they could even scream. Like candles tossed in a campfire, the men withered and melted, flesh running in steaming rivulets, spreading their remnants over the floor. The tabards of those behind them caught fire, driving the knights back, the men struggling to keep the flames from spreading and taking hold.

Jacquial shoved the scorched remains of the Exemplar after them once they'd retreated, the fire gnawing at her insides and lapping at the floor where she fell.

"Not to sound ungrateful, but you didn't happen to grab the keys off the guard before you set the place alight, did you?" the lord asked.

Gryl glanced to the doorway and groaned at seeing the waxen outline of what had been the sentry guarding the cell. "I... did not." The only entrance to the cellar engulfed in supernatural fire that would burn for days before exhausting itself, he turned to Jacquial and let out a weary sigh. "I *meant* to rescue you, if that counts for anything."

"Definitely the thought that counts," she answered, offering up a weak chuckle. "Still, all said and done, I'd be far more grateful if you actually pulled it off, you know. I'm needy like that."

The heat prickled Gryl's skin, smoke stinging his throat, as he looked for another way out. His gaze fell on the Exemplar's breastplate, his mind churning as to how he could use it.

"The sword!" He spun and pointed at the thin white blade laying inside Jacquial's cell. "Pass it to me."

She scrambled over and grabbed the weapon, handing it to Gryl through the bars. Flames snapping at his back, he ran a hand across the same sigil the knight had when she'd cleaved through his blade and willed it to life. It replied without hesitation, the sword quivering in his grasp.

"Stand back," he said, barely waiting for Jacquial to comply before he struck the bars of her cell. The sword cut through the iron as if it were parchment. Gryl swallowed his thrill at seeing the severed bar and struck again and again and again, cutting a hole in the cell door. He squeezed through to join the lord inside, doing his best to ignore the sharp edges that scraped skin from his wounded body.

"Uh, the idea was for us to escape, not to imprison yourself alongside me."

Gryl chuckled and gestured toward the narrow windows set high on the back wall. The bars gleamed in the moonlight. "I found the key but I think it best you turn the lock. I'm a bit winded." He handed her the blade, still vibrating in his palm.

Jacquial grinned. "Forgot about those."

She snatched the sword and went to work. Once she'd rid the window of its bars, Jacquial climbed through and helped Gryl to follow, pulling him through the slim opening. They crept across the moist grass, staying low to avoid the blackened roil of smoke spilling from the dungeon, the prodigy clutching to her to keep from falling over.

Jacquial stopped after a moment and stared at the red-orange tongues licking at the cell they'd just abandoned. "What is it with you and fire?"

"Not everyone had toys to play with, you know." He chuckled and nudged her toward the wall. "This way. We've a slaver to collect."

Jacquial nodded and handed him the runesworn's blade. "Here. You may need this."

He took it, gazing at the flickering metal. "I think I know just where to put this."

"I thought you might." A flicker of a smile broke through the soot smeared across her lips.

They set off over the wall as Mallister's manse burned behind them, lighting their way.

# GROUND ZERO
## An Alpha Unit Story

### Kirsten Cross

**M**IND THE GAP! MIND THE GAP!"
The perfectly enunciated voice boomed through the station. Authoritative, masculine, and tinged with a fat dollop of 'don't fuck with me' undertones, it had cowed an entire generation of commuters into compliance. You could practically hear it pronounce the exclamation marks. But it was almost drowned out by the teeth-clenching squealing of brakes and the pulse of stale air that always announced the arrival of a tube train at Highgate station. Waiting commuters got shotblasted by a cloud of dust and grit as the train burst out of a pitch-black tunnel and into the fluorescent glare of Platform Two. It sounded like a king-sized tin of thundery whoop-ass had been given a damn good shake and then opened in a confined space, accompanied by all the screaming, tormented souls of Hell.

The train squawked to a halt with all the grace of a car in a crusher, as metal wheels with metal brakes made contact on metal rails. It even threw up a few sparks for effect. Doors hissed open and a high-pitched bleep ticked down the seconds before exiting or entering the carriage would become much more of a challenge than it already was. A surge of humanity broke onto the shoreline of the carriage like well-dressed flotsam and flowed into the garishly bright interior, where the fittest and fastest plonked their arses into still-warm seats.

Alpha Unit moved with the flow of the mob, guiding a

couple of stubborn civvies out of the way through the careful application of subtle but painful pressure to various points on the body, carefully disguised under the cover of a crowd crush. Each team member knew exactly where they needed to be. They'd planned this dekko just as meticulously as if it were a live-rounds assault. This particular theatre, though, was packed full of non-combatants. And that was always a problem.

Subtlety was the name of the game today. Black ops didn't always have to be flash-bang-wallop, gun-toting mayhem. Sometimes, it could be a sneaky-peaky before things got up close and personal with the organophosphor rounds later on. It's all very well kicking in metaphorical doors, but Alpha Team knew it helped to know *which* damn doors to kick before you started lacing up your boots.

They had basic kit with them, stowed in the large holdall Gary Parks carried. They hadn't really come for a fight, but it paid to have at least a little bit of kit with you, just in case. They'd come to find out just how bad the Highgate infestation had become, and how much of a threat this particular nest of Taints were to the local food source. Or 'Northern Line commuters', as the poor, unfortunate bastards were known.

The four-man team positioned themselves strategically throughout the carriage. Gary Parks, in a very real sense of the word, 'occupied' the space next to the far exit. He entertained himself for a few seconds by staring intensely at a scrawny little skinhead sporting a piss-poor home-made 'White Power' tattoo. The skinhead, now nose-to-nose with a huge black man encroaching on his 'personal space', suddenly looked like he felt very alone in the world.

Yolanda Jaeger propped herself in a corner by the central doors. From here she could see both Gary Parks and the other end of the carriage, occupied by Colby Flynn and the interminable Micky Cox – master of electronics and generalised mayhem. The Unit's former SAS and REME make-it-happen guy was currently staring at a smartphone like a good little commuter.

Three of the team blended in relatively seamlessly with the

surrounding hoi polloi. Gary Parks, however, looked like a rhino gatecrashing a tea party.

"For chrissake, Gary, try to look a bit more commuter-y, will you?" Yolanda hissed into a Bluetooth device. The smartphone revolution meant appearing to talk to yourself was now part of digital life, making it almost impossible to tell the nutjobs from a crack team of SF soldiers on a dekko. Of course, there were those who claimed the two were not mutually exclusive.

Gary responded to Yolanda's comment, avoiding any obvious eye contact as per oppo protocol. *"As opposed to what, exactly, boss?"*

"As opposed to a bag of footballs in a suit. Damn it man, I can see the outline of your Glock from here – and no, Micky, before you chip in your five-pennyworth, that is *not* a euphemism! Seriously, Gary, didn't the QM have anything that actually fitted you?"

Colby Flynn's voice crackled over the comms. *"Yol, c'mon, cut him some slack. His tailor sure as hell can't."*

*"Fuck off."* Gary frowned at the skinhead, who assumed the comment was meant for him and did everything he possibly could to comply.

Colby grinned and notched it up a turn. *"Seriously. The poor guy's a medical freak. He gets his underpants from Marquees-R-Us, you know."*

Gary's frown turned into a full-power scowl. *"Come down here and say that to my kneecaps, puny little man."* He forgot ops protocol for a second and glowered up the carriage towards the definitely-not-puny Colby Flynn.

Flynn simply grinned back and flipped Gary the finger. *"Hulk smash!"*

*"Fuck... off!"*

Yolanda stopped the banter in its tracks. "Gentlemen, cease and desist, please. Gary, quit intimidating the racist, would you? There's a good chap. Flynn, eyes on, you reprobate, and stop tormenting the giant man in the bad suit. Micky, are we ready?"

"Ready, boss. I'm plugged into the train's electronic control system. I've by-passed the safety protocols and remotely disengaged the Dead Man's Handle. Should be pretty straightforward to interrupt the power."

"I'm so very, very proud of you, you clever boy. A simple 'yes boss' would have sufficed. Just kill the damn power on my mark." Yolanda pressed closer to the door to try and cancel out the reflection of the carriage interior. She peered out into the darkness as it blurred past the windows. "Three, two, one, mark!"

Micky stabbed at his smartphone and the tube train squealed, slowed, and finally juddered to a halt. A few seconds later a nasally voice mumbled over the tannoy. "*Good morning ladies and gentlemen, this is your driver speaking. We seem to have suffered some kind of electrical malfunction. No need to worry, we should have you moving again in a few minutes. Thank you.*" A rousing chorus of very British tutting clicked through the carriage in response.

Yolanda checked the carriage and then spoke into the Bluetooth again. "Now the lights if you would, please, Mick."

Micky stabbed at the smartphone again, and frowned. The carriage lights stayed resolutely on. Yolanda turned and raised an eyebrow in Micky's direction. "In your own time, Mister Cox."

"*Trying, boss. Let me rotate the frequency, see if I can hit the sweet spot.*"

"Micky, I genuinely don't care what you rotate, just get those bloody lights turned out."

The lights flickered and then went out, and the only illumination in the carriage came from dozens of smartphone screens. London's hardy commuters again clicked and tutted their annoyance like a pod of angry dolphins. In between signal dropouts they relentlessly carried on tweeting, texting and facetiming, unaware they were witnesses to a black op happening right in front of their noses.

"Anything?" Yolanda ignored the winter-wonderland twinkle of smartphone backlights and stared out into the gloom. The tunnel was much wider here, with columns, arches and walkways intersecting the various lines. This was a major junction, and they were also very close to the old abandoned Highgate tunnels.

Perfect Taint territory.

*"We've got movement."* Gary's deep voice came through the comms. *"Yep, they're out there all right. They're taking the bait. Cheeky little fuckers, too. Didn't expect 'em to be this close."*

"Flynn?"

"Nothing this end… wait, nope, scratch that. We've got action here too, Yol. And they're moving in."

"Wait out. Remember this is recon only. We are not to engage, repeat, *not* to engage unless absolutely necessary."

Micky Cox's voice chimed in. *"And by absolutely necessary, boss, you mean…"*

"If they clamber on board and start eating commuters, what the bloody hell do you think I mean, Mick?"

*"Judging by the amount of eyeshine out there, that's a deffo probable in the very near future, Yol. Twelve o'clock. I count at least five, possibly six."* All the earlier brevity had evaporated from Colby's gravely voice, replaced by a much more serious tone.

*"A minimum of six here too, boss."* Gary glared out into the darkness.

Yolanda cursed. "Oh, bollocks! I bloody *knew* this was gonna go sideways. Wait out." She slid her right hand slowly back underneath her jacket, and her fingers curled around the butt of the adapted Glock. The object of this operation was to assess a possible nest and see just how close they were willing to get to the trains as they passed through the tunnel. Okay, it meant using a train full of commuters as bait, but it was a necessary part of the operation.

And now it looked like they had their answer.

Bloody close.

A scrabbling outside the doors made Yolanda tighten her grip on the Glock and flip the safety catch to 'off'.

Okay. Make that *too fucking close.*

A swarm of hungry and emboldened Taints were now just inches away from the commuters, separated from 'lunch' by nothing but a flimsy metal door. The genetically enhanced vampires with a less-than sunny disposition and a voracious appetite were single-minded, relentless and fearless. Their exceptional strength and speed meant the doors on a thirty-year-old tube train would pose no problem for their venom-tipped fingers. If one of them got purchase on a gap and put their shoulder into it, they could have the doors open in a heartbeat.

So effectively, all that stood between biblical carnage and a tube full of commuters was a thin metal shell, four Special Ops soldiers with a very limited supply of ammo, and the good will of the Northern Line gods.

Yolanda prepared to repel borders by shooting an organophosphor round into the face of the first bastard that came through the door. That would definitely catch the commuters' attention, and would instantly turn what was supposed to be a low-key surveillance operation into a Twitterverse 'trending' topic. And that would not please the Colonel. It pretty much defeated the whole 'black ops' ethos if the damn thing immediately got its own hashtag and went viral.

Further up the carriage, Flynn had eyes-on with a Taint of his own. The drooling, snarling mutant was worrying away at the outside of the carriage. The scrabbling of talon against metal caught the attention of a young woman and she looked up from her smartphone. Colby gave her a friendly smile and nodded towards the door. "Rats."

The girl shuddered. "Ugh. I hate rats."

"Don't worry. They can't get in."

"Oh. Good." The girl immediately lost interest in the rat-slash-slavering, ravenous, genetically altered vampire, and went back to playing a game. Micky craned to look at the girl's screen and then shook his head. She was playing 'Vampire Hunter'.

Yolanda had seen enough. "Micky, I think about now would be a good time to restore power and get both us and these nice, vulnerable commuters the hell out of here, don't you?"

"*Copy that.*" Micky stabbed at the screen.

The lights flickered on and off again.

"Um, Micky?"

"*Trying, boss. Bear with me…*" There was a waver of anxiety in Micky's voice.

"*Tell that to Bitey McBiteface out there, Cox. These fuckers are working to their own timetable, fella, and it's deffo on the hurry-up!*" Gary's hand tensed around his own Glock. "*Boss…*"

"I said wait out!"

"*Yol, I've got a damn talon here…*" Colby put the sole of his boot against the needle-sharp talon that protruded through the gap in the door, and crunched down hard. The resulting yelp made the girl look up again, and Colby did a quick impression of a buck-toothed rat, complete with ears and comic-effect "Eek!" for emphasis.

The girl rolled her eyes, muttered a quick "Weirdo!" at Colby, refocused on her screen and updated her status.

Flynn threw a look to the heavens in thanks, and then double-checked the venom-filled talon had withdrawn. He peered into the darkness and watched the Taint scuttle back into the shadows, cradling its hand. They were getting much, *much* too bold. He glanced down the carriage towards Yolanda. She was eyes-on and totally focused, but he could see the tension in her face even at this distance. This was bad. This was very bad. His own spidey-senses screamed blue bloody murder. He reached back to where his adapted Glock sat in its holster and unclipped the retaining catch.

Halfway down the carriage, Yolanda stared out into the tunnel, watching the Taints move into position for a full-on attack. The onslaught was imminent. The muscle in her jaw twitched. "Micky? I hate to rush you, fella, but now would be good. I would be really *very* pleased with *now!*"

"Damn it, boss, I'm trying!"

"Try *harder!*"

"*Wait, wait, yep, okay, I got it!*" Micky stabbed at the screen and the train's lights blazed once again. The carriage jerked forward, accompanied by the traditional 'About bloody time!'

round of tutting from the commuters. Not one of them had any idea they'd been just seconds from the worst start to a Monday anyone could possibly have.

The train finally pulled into Archway station and screeched to a stop. The doors hissed open and the team surfed the wave of humanity out onto the platform. They reconvened in the centre, letting the commuters flow around them.

Yolanda ignored the swirling and buffeting as the whole in/out/shake-it-all-about commuter dance played out once again. The four of them stood just to the side of the entrance to the carriage so they could assess and do a field debrief without interruption. "Well, *that* was a hoot and a half, wasn't it? Right then, opinions and options, please."

"We've definitely got a problem, Yol. And sooner or later someone who isn't us is gonna notice there's something distinctly moody going on down here. Then there's going to be full-on panic. Cop an eyeful." Colby nodded at the side of the carriage. Tramline scrapes were etched deep into the metal around the door, and a streak of black blood where Flynn had given the Taint an impromptu manicure was obvious. Thankfully, to the untrained eye it simply looked like a smear of oil, and none of the commuters were close enough to notice the acrid chemical tang either.

"Bugger. That *was* close." Yolanda pointed her phone at the door and snapped a succession of photographs. The Colonel would need documentary evidence if they were going to risk going into the tunnels for a seek-and-destroy op, but she didn't want to alarm any of the commuters still milling around. Sneaky-peaky. Keep it off the radar and don't alarm the herd. The last thing they wanted was a stampede. "I need to get a swab of that for the forensics team before this train buggers off. Gentlemen, would you mind awfully giving me a bit of cover, so the civvies don't get freaked out by the crazy lady taking DNA swabs off a train carriage door, please? Thank you."

The team moved to shield Yolanda from view as she took a swab of the blackened blood. She stood, dropped the cotton-tipped bud into a plastic tube and snapped on the lid. The tube was deposited into a plastic zip bag and secreted into a jacket pocket with all the dexterity of a street magician pulling a card trick. Not a single 'civvy' noticed.

Taints were continually evolving, and the swab would give the team a chemical blueprint of their current stage of development. It would probably be bad. It usually was with Taints.

"Right then, let's get this back to base." Yolanda nodded towards the exit, and Micky, Colby and Gary set off at a brisk walk towards the stairs, dropping instinctively into the standard staggered two-two formation, even in this supposedly 'safe' environment. It was hard-wired into their DNA through years of training, operations and that overriding instinct to stay the fuck alive. So far, it had worked rather well.

Colby paused and turned, aware that Yolanda had dropped back. She was still standing in the middle of the platform, a puzzled frown creasing her forehead. "Yol?" He walked back towards her and laid a hand on her arm. "You've got that 'look' again. 'Sup?"

Yolanda turned and looked behind her. At the far end of the platform, and right in the CCTV's blind spot stood a massive figure. It ignored the commuters that flowed around it. Unusually for Londoners, they didn't jostle or push past, but gave the looming figure a wide berth, repelled from making actual physical contact with him by some internal survival instinct. Colby snorted a laugh and shook his head. "Damn, that dude's bigger than Gary!" He looked at Yolanda. "Yol? Hey, c'mon, you're starting to freak me out. You okay?"

"Yeah. Big lad, isn't he? Now look closer, Flynn." Yolanda's gaze never left the figure at the end of the platform. "Remind you of anyone?"

Colby looked at the hulking figure and frowned. Then a look of recognition finally spread across his face. "Oh, *hell* no!"

Yolanda nodded. "Yep. And *there* it is…"

Colby reached for his Glock in one smooth, flowing move.

Yolanda grabbed his wrist and shook her head. "Stand down, Flynn." For a split second she battled with him. "I *said*, stand down!"

Colby glared at her. "He's right there, Yol! He's *right fucking there!*"

"And so are god-knows how many civilians! We start shooting now, all hell breaks loose, we are royally burned, and people die. And if two blocks of C4 in Tokat couldn't take the bugger out, do you honestly think a single clip of organo jackets'll do the trick? Now, stand *down!*"

Colby relented, but didn't take his eyes off the figure at the end of the platform. "Okay, but we need to bang out of here sharpish and call in a lock-down team. *Now.*"

"Not until I know that every civvy in here is out safely. We wait."

"Are you actually kidding me? I am *not* just standing here playing platform chicken with that son of a bitch!"

"I said, we *wait!*" Yolanda's gaze never left the brooding figure in front of her. She clicked the Bluetooth. "Micky. Find the station manager. Close the station. *Now.* Then call in containment. I want all trains on this line stopped immediately. Usual 'suspect package' or 'major emergency engineering works' bullshit, you choose. Gary, get your arse back down here. FUBAR. FUBAR like you wouldn't bloody believe. I need you and your bag of tricks here. Move."

Two voices responded in sequence: "*Copy that.*"

Yolanda refocused on the figure in front of them. It wasn't just the size that was so intimidating. It was the way that his mere presence seemed to suck the very light out of the air. And those teeth. Man, those teeth! He smiled slowly, revealing a mouthful of dazzlingly white and needle-sharp dentistry.

Vlad.

In London.

In the middle of the morning rush hour, on platform two of Archway Underground station.

One of the most savage and evil monsters ever to walk the

face of the earth was currently standing casually on a London underground platform as if it were the most natural thing in the world, dressed in normal clothes, and looking every inch like a bog-standard commuter. A hidden horror, right there, in plain sight. And nobody except the two soldiers had the faintest idea what ancient evil had wandered, unseen and unchallenged, slap-bang into the normalcy of everyday London life.

Tinted glasses masked his distinctive golden eyes from the gaze of his human fellow travellers. But nothing could hide who he really was to Colby and Yolanda. And he was about as welcome as finding a scorpion in your boot.

He stood there, a snarling smile taunting the two soldiers.

Then, from the same carriage stepped another figure. Almost as tall as Vlad, he was lithe and wiry, not as muscular but certainly a contender for ugliest Northern Line commuter of the day. He stood slightly behind Vlad, subservient to the monster. Yet there was a quiet, confident menace that permeated from the creature. He had authority. He had standing. He had a connection with Vlad that went beyond that of a mere 'foot soldier'. This was a Taint of some importance.

Colby glanced at Yolanda. "Like father like son?"

Yolanda's eyes didn't leave the two figures. She shook her head. "More likely one of his Lieutenants. Remember, Col, this bastard may be a monster now, but he was a military man once. And a great one at that. He'll have his own chain of command."

Colby scowled. "Great. So we've got a second tango to deal with. This day just keeps getting better and fucking better, doesn't it?"

"Focus on the primary, Col. If the secondary advances, engage and shoot the fucker in the face. And keep shooting until it goes down and *stays* down." Yolanda's hand tightened around the grip of her Glock.

Okay.

So this could go either way…

Vlad glanced sideways as a pretty blonde, wrapped in her own little commuter-world full of bland pop music, LOL texts from

'Angie' and wearing the standard-issue officeware of white blouse, dark pencil skirt and cheap, clattery high heels, tried to squeeze past. He sensed Colby and Yolanda holding their breath as they watched his fingers flex and ripple.

Motionless and still smiling, Vlad gazed at the woman, sensing every fluttering beat of her heart as she manoeuvred past him.

Then her perfume hit him.

Like a storm surge, it sent a wave of ancient memories crashing into his mind, overwhelming him for a second. He didn't care about the insignificant life of this woman. He had taken thousands – hundreds of thousands – of lives over the centuries. One more wouldn't make him any more evil than he already was. Sparing her would not redeem him either.

But that perfume...

It was the scent of lilacs on a soft, summer evening. It was the scent *she* had worn, all those centuries ago.

Brief seconds slowed to the speed of dripping molasses. Vlad watched the girl move past him in slow motion and took in every detail. Her red lips. Her silken blond hair. But above all, that dizzying perfume that had the power to stir such a fire in his blackened heart. She turned and looked at him, and for a split second he could have sworn the girl's face transformed into *her* face. His love. His sweet love.

Taken from him by soldiers.

Soldiers who had wanted to make sure his dark legacy ended at Tokat. There would be no more children. No more sons. They had gutted her like a fish. Soldiers had butchered his love in front of him. Soldiers had tainted the sweet scent of lilacs with the coppery tang of *her* blood.

And now, this vapid... *child*, tottering past him on ridiculous heels, had the audacity to wear the same perfume as *she* did? Vlad's mind reeled and insanity roared inside him. It warped and twisted that brief flutter of clarity – of light, of beauty – and morphed it back into a black, blood-soaked chasm of hatred. How *dare* she walk on this earth, while his love rotted in the ground! How *dare* she!

Vlad's madness, fuelled by the scent of his long-dead love, boiled. For a moment, his focus had shifted away from the soldiers standing just a few feet from him. The girl and her perfume had filled his world.

His lieutenant saw the black madness in his master's eyes and twitched his finger. It was enough to bring Vlad's attention sharply back into focus.

The girl was nothing more than an impostor.

A mere memory of his love.

A haunting reflection, stimulated by the scent of lilacs.

But the soldiers… Ah, now *they* were something else.

They were toys to be played with, before he unleashed his lieutenant and his pack of slathering Taints on them.

But not yet. Not yet…

The grandfather of all vampires studied his opponents, taking in every micro-expression, feeling every hammer-blow of their hearts, and hearing the blood rushing through their bodies. He could almost taste the fear-tinged frustration they felt at being so close yet so far away from protecting an 'innocent'.

It delighted him.

Watching the impotent rage boil and churn in the bellies of his enemies was exquisite. He relished the thought that for the rest of their probably very short lives the two soldiers would have that gut-punch of shame every time they remembered they had had no choice but to simply stand and watch a monster decide the fate of an innocent girl. In the most normal of surroundings. Where the girl was supposed to be safe.

But this was a tactical confrontation, too. A chance to see how his enemy reacted. How they moved. How they prioritised potential collateral damage. Examine their weaknesses.

Vlad chuckled quietly. Time to take things up a level. He nodded to the lieutenant, who bowed slightly and smoothly stepped back on board the train. Inside, a handful of oblivious passengers sat starting at their smartphones, unaware of what stalked their carriage.

The two soldiers instinctively reacted by stepping forward a couple of paces. Vlad held up a finger and wagged it from side to side. They froze again, closer to the door yet not quite close enough to make a difference.

Colby snarled at Vlad, that taunting laugh sending a pulse of fury through him. He hissed. "Fuck. Yol, we need to get that bastard off of that train. *Yol…*"

"I know. I know, damn it." Yolanda ground her teeth in frustration. *Oh, you clever bastard, Vlad. You clever, clever bastard! Split your targets. See how we prioritise. You son of a bitch, you're on as much of a dekko as we are, aren't you, you fucker?*

An ear-splitting beeping warned of the impending departure of the train. The two soldiers knew those passengers were trapped now. Trapped inside a tin can with one of Vlads lieutenants. And there was nothing, *nothing* they could do.

"Fuck! *Fuck!* Yol, we have to stop that train!" Colby's voice cracked with pent-up fury.

"Damn it!" Yolanda watched as the lieutenant sat beside an elderly woman. He glanced back towards Colby and Yolanda and smiled a vicious, spiteful smile, and draped his arm around the back of the seat.

Yolanda glared back at the lieutenant, clicked the Bluetooth and hissed into it. "Micky, get them to stop the train! Stop the *damn train!*"

Static. Fucking static. *Shit!* Those few steps they'd taken towards Vlad and his lieutenant must have put them slap-bang into a dead spot. She knew that if she moved a muscle, she could instigate a reaction from Vlad. And that would be bad for the long-term prospects of blondie in her clattery heels and tight pencil skirt. "Micky! *Micky!*"

Still nothing but the tormenting hiss of dead air. *"Fuck!"*

Back on the platform, Vlad snarled, and reached out. His long, sinewy fingers brushed the woman's hair as she passed by, a caress as gentle as a lover's touch, as delicate as a butterfly – and filled with so much potential for violence. All he had to do was change that caress into a snatch, wind his fingers in the girl's hair and drag her towards him…

The electric motors of the tube train whined into life and the carriages started to move. Out of the corner of her eye Yolanda saw the lieutenant give her a little wave and then lean in towards the old woman. The last thing Yolanda saw as the carriage started to blur past was a sweet little old lady strike up a conversation with a 'nice young man'...

The noise grew into a mechanical roar, and the air pressure increased. Garish fluorescent lights flickered, combining with the flashing tube train to create a violent strobe effect. The air blasted along the platform, turning the girl's blonde hair into dancing strands and tangling them around Vlad's fingers.

"Yol!" Colby couldn't hold back any more.

Screw this.

"Engage!"

Screw the whole 'low-key' bullshit. They couldn't just stand there impotent and motionless any more. They were burned. Might as well make it official, then. Their Glocks flipped out and the business end of two adapted G17s pointed straight towards where Vlad—

—Wasn't.

Colby cursed long, loud and passionately. "Shit! Shit! *Shit!* Oh, you sneaky, mother-fucking, greasy, undead son of a *bitch!*"

Still holding the Glocks out in front of them, Colby and Yolanda moved forward at a rapid scuttle, ready to start blasting at anything that didn't look like a commuter.

The girl stood alone, alive and paralysed with fear as two grim-faced, gun-toting figures moved smoothly towards her. They were using that feline, cross-step gait that always hinted at extreme violence and explosive power bubbling just below the surface. What were they, Special Forces? Police? Security Services? What? Whoever they were they looked like they'd shoot her in a heartbeat. She stood, frozen with fear, hot tears of terror rolling down her cheeks. "Please! Please don't kill me! Please!"

"Get out. Move. *Move!*" Yolanda moved past the girl, reached back with her left hand and shoved her hard in the back, not wasting time with nice reassurances or any of that touchy-feely shit. The girl didn't need telling twice. She staggered under the surprising power from Yolanda's shove, regained her balance and then clattered her way along the platform towards the exit, where she saw another huge man running down the stairs with a menacing look and equally menacing Glock. Her tears started to dissolve the cheap mascara she wore, and it ran down her face in two gritty black streaks. This was *not* a normal workday commute.

The back end of the train disappeared into the far tunnel behind them, and Yolanda stopped at the point where the platform ended and black oblivion began. She lowered the Glock and unleashed a shit-ton of real passion into an uncharacteristic outburst of cursing. "Fuck! *Fuck!*"

Colby jumped down onto the tracks and started to move towards the darkness.

Gary dumped the kit bag on the floor, looked over Yolanda's shoulder and watched his best friend heading purposefully towards the tunnel entrance. "Colby, you daft bastard, stop! There's an entire army of Taints in there, and the next train is about a minute away from turning you into a smear! Colby! *Colby!*" He glowered at his friend's back and muttered. "God *damn it*, you stubborn…" Gary, still questioning Colby's parentage under his breath, turned and took up position behind Yolanda. He kept his back to his team, eyes fixed firmly on the other end of the tunnel, just in case the Taints tried a pincer move on them.

Yolanda raised the gun, targeting the nose of the Glock straight at Colby's back. She scowled down the barrel and her sharp voice echoed through the station like broken glass. "*Mister Flynn!* You will stand down *immediately* or so help me, I *will* shoot you in the back!"

Flynn stopped, and slowly lowered his gun. He glared into the blackness, trying to ignore the itchy sensation between his shoulder blades. He could practically feel the green dot from Yolanda's sighting laser. She probably wouldn't shoot him, he knew that. Well, probably. *Possibly.* Actually? Thinking about it, she might squeeze the bloody trigger just to prove a point, the crazy bint. But that was just Yol's way. And that's why he loved her. It was nothing personal, just Yol trying to save his stupid, hot-headed idiot self from dying a wasteful, pointless death.

She was right, of course.

The Jaeger family had been hunting and killing vampires across Europe for generations. Even the name meant 'Hunter' in German. There was also the small technicality that when they were on duty Yolanda Jaeger was Flynn's CO too.

So he complied. Not doing so would mean the mother of all arse-kickings in the training gym later. The bloody woman fought dirty. But she'd also stayed alive by knowing which battles to pick, and which to walk away from. It was a lesson he was finally starting to understand. And this was definitely one of those 'walk away' times, no matter how much that pinpoint of fury currently burning its way through his chest told him to chase his quarry down and end this once and for all.

Colby stood motionless, staring into the black of beyond. The clustered eyeshine of at least a dozen Taints winked and twinkled back at him, taunting him, daring him to run away from the safety of the bright platform and into their dark, death-ridden world. A pulse of warm air throbbed down the tunnel, indicating that he had about fifteen seconds to get back to the platform before thirty tons of London Underground rolling stock really fucked up his day.

\* \* \*

"*Vlad?*" Colonel North's voice was sharp.

"Yes, sir." Yolanda nodded. She paced the platform with the phone pressed to her ear. Colby sat on the bench, glowering at the darkness. Micky Cox had got a reluctant official to close the station due to a 'suspect package', so the team were currently alone in a deserted tube station. All Northern Line trains were at a standstill. Gary Parks stood sentry at one end of the platform, a fully loaded shotgun pointed at the north tunnel, while Micky patrolled the south end.

"*You're sure?*"

"Yes, sir."

*"In the middle of the bloody day?"*

"Well, technically, it was the morning rush hour, but yes, sir."

*"You're absolutely certain it was him?"*

"Yes, sir. I'd know that bastard anywhere. It was him. And I'm pretty sure he knew who we were too. His lieutenant hopped back onto the train before it left. We couldn't contain both of them. I'm sorry, sir."

*"You did what you could, Captain. This was supposed to be a rekko, not a damn meet and greet. The fault is not yours, Yollie. It's Vlad's. Always remember that."* Colonel North sighed. *"Okay. So what's your appraisal of the situation?"*

Yolanda answered quickly and succinctly. "The tunnel between Highgate and Archway is infested, sir. Looks like it's ground zero for this particular nest. London Underground is uber-pissed about us limiting access to the Northern Line between the two stations, but we've pulled our usual 'national security' number on them, so they've been forced to comply. We've got a lot of angry, inconvenienced commuters, but that's nothing new."

"Good. I'd rather they were annoyed and alive than happy and dead."

"Nobody who travels the Northern Line is happy, sir."

"True. Right then. Solutions?"

"We're already on the ground. The station's closed and we're ready to go in and evict the little buggers with extreme prejudice. If you could have Terry Warner and Bravo Unit suited up for a bug hunt and to us with supplies asap, we can try and do a seek and destroy right now. I'd like to keep Vlad off balance by hitting hard and fast. We may not be able to take Vlad out now, but we can certainly show him we're not just going to roll over..."

Yolanda's report was interrupted by a loud bang. She instinctively flinched then spun to face the southern end of the tunnel, where Micky Cox was pointing the smoking barrel of a 12-bore pump-action shotgun into the darkness. Yolanda rolled her eyes. "Jesus! What the hell, Micky?"

Micky turned, grinned, and re-primed his shotgun, ignoring the screaming, thrashing, heel-drumming Taint behind him. "Sorry, boss. Little bugger got a bit lunge-y at me." There was a *'wuuumph!'* sound and a cloud of ash floated gently down onto Micky's shoulders. He casually brushed it off and shrugged.

Yolanda shook her head. "Eyes on, Mick." She returned her attention to the Colonel. "Sorry about that sir."

*"Everything all right, Captain?"*

"Yes, sir. Just Micky getting trigger happy with a Taint. But that just goes to show how bold they're getting."

*"Hmm. They are getting a bit cheeky, aren't they? Anything else?"*

"Yes, sir. I'd like permission to go after that damn lieutenant of his if possible, too. I don't like the look of that bastard." Yolanda paused. "Sir, we need to move quickly on this if we're going to keep it under the radar. If the press get hold of it we're going to face an epic shitstorm, and right now I'd rather keep this on a need to know basis."

Colonel North responded with a grunt. *"Agreed. I'll have Corporal Warner and Bravo Unit en route to you in fifteen. Good hunting, Yollie."*

"Thank you, sir. I'll keep you updated." Yolanda ended the call and put the phone in her pocket. She glanced up. "Upstairs, chaps. We're meeting Terry and Bravo team in the ticket area." A nasty smile crept over her face. "We've got ourselves a bug hunt, lads."

Micky and Gary grinned back. Colby merely stared into the blackness of the tunnel and glowered at the blinking, winking eyeshine.

He wanted that lieutenant. He wanted him *bad*.

There was something about that nasty little bastard that made Colby's skin prickle…

\* \* \*

Outside the tube station's locked metal gates a throng of commuters milled about. A single London Underground employee, resplendent in a hi-viz jacket and with absolutely no clue as to what was really happening, tried to shepherd the muttering masses towards the nearest bus stop. A scribbled note stuck to a sandwich board apologised for the inconvenience, while the hi-viz employee reassured passengers that yes, the station would probably reopen shortly. Even *he* didn't believe that bullshit line.

Terry Warner walked up to the guy and flashed an ID. "Clean up crew. Open up."

The man – currently engaged in telling an officious, besuited commuter that no, he didn't have any further information and no, he didn't know or in fact *care* who the man was, he'd have to wait like everyone else – flickered his attention towards the ID. He puffed up his chest and looked as 'official' as he could. "Suspicious package. Security alert. Nobody gets in."

Terry carefully pulled his boilersuit open so hi-viz guy could just see the butt of a Glock 17 tucked under his armpit. He made damn sure the stroppy commuter couldn't see anything. His blue eyes hardened and he stared intently at hi-viz guy. "Listen, fella. I have neither the time nor the crayons to explain this to you in any detail. I *said*, clean… up… crew. Translation, open the *damn* gate. *Now.*"

Hi-viz guy, now completely ignoring the still-stroppy commuter, focused on the 'clean up team' and, in particular, the tall, fierce-looking man carrying the Glock 17. They were the most evil-looking bunch of 'cleaners' he'd ever seen. They were all powerfully built, probably heavily armed too, and scanning the crowd like a bunch of SAS soldiers on an operat… oh. *Shit…*

Realisation kicked in and hi-viz guy gulped. He quickly decided pursuing any kind of argument he might have about who was allowed where and when was probably trumped by the sheer amount of ordnance this 'clean up crew' were packing. He fumbled with a key and unlocked the gate, opening it just wide enough for the team to squeeze through.

As Danny Smith walked past the man he stopped for a moment. He kept his voice low, so as not to alarm the civvies.

"Listen, fella. Things are going to get a little bit *urgent* in a while. So when you hear screaming and a shit-load of people stampeding up the stairs, you open this damn gate and you let them out. Got it?" He gave hi-viz guy what he thought was a reassuring smile.

"I… I… I…"

"I *said*, got it?" Danny's smile melted away.

"Y-yes. Yeah. I got it. Sure. Why the hell not?" Hi-viz guy nodded. He really regretted not calling in sick this morning.

"Adda boy." Danny patted the man on the shoulder just a tiny bit harder than he needed to, and followed his team into the bowels of the station and out of sight of the crowds outside.

Inside, a lone London Underground official stood shaking in a corner. Watching the team pull balaclavas over their faces, wrapping throat comms around their necks, and opening up bags filled with automatic weapons did nothing to rebalance his peace of mind. He let out a little yelp.

A pair of hard, steely eyes immediately connected with his own. He could tell the face was scowling underneath the black fabric. Terry barked out two words. "Which platform?"

The official pointed a shaking finger towards the escalator. "P-p-platform two…"

Terry gave a curt nod. "Thank you. Now fuck off."

The man fucked off at a rapid scuttle, and Terry motioned to Bravo Unit. "Move out." Time to tie up with the boss…

\* \* \*

"You're late."

"You're welcome!"

Terry gave Micky the finger and threw a kit bag at him. Micky Cox caught it with all the grace and dexterity of a one-armed blind man in a dark room. Terry chuckled. "Careful, fella. That's the bag with the UV flash bangs."

Micky plonked the bag down and crouched next to it. He unzipped the bag and pulled it open. "Okay. Wadda we got, then? Big, honking great bullet chuckers?"

"Check."

"Spare organo FMJs?"

"Check."

"Sneaking-around black ninja outfits with anti-Taint kevlar weave?"

Gary Parks glanced over and primed his Remington 870 shotgun as an underline, before attaching it to a lanyard and picking up a C8. "Micky, we are not doing sneaking-around ninja shit. We're going in dressed as a team of London Underground Northern Line fluffers who've had all the love, hope and faith in humanity sucked out of them through years of working in one of the city's shittiest hellholes. So it's regulation boilersuits, boots and beanies. No ninja shit."

Micky looked puzzled and glanced over at Yolanda, who was busy checking the recoil on her Glock. "Um, boss? Question?"

Without even looking at him, Yolanda immediately responded. "Fluffers are teams who clean the underground tracks."

"Oh, so they're not…"

"No, Micky. No. They're really not. You bloody pervert."

Gary laughed. "Mate, you watch far too much porn, you know that?"

"Yeah. Porn with your mama in it."

Gary gave Micky a blank look. "Seriously? Did you actually just throw down with a 'yo mama' joke at me?"

Terry Warner turned to Colby. "Are they always like this?"

Colby grinned. "These two? Fella, this is a good day. They're usually going at each other like an old married couple." Colby dropped the magazine out of the C8, tapped it, checked and re-inserted it with a snap. He primed and checked the primary holographic sighting, making absolutely sure that he hadn't accidentally knocked the switch from 'Safe' to 'Rapid' – or 'NoKill' to 'Parp', as Micky liked to call it. The team were using the more compact 10-inch barrel version. The 16-inch barrel might be more accurate, but when you were going in up-close-and-personal with a grabby Taint full of bad intentions, then the longer barrel tended to snag and get in the way. There was no point attaching the standard bayonet either. That would just tangle you up even more, and if you were using a bayonet against a Taint then you were probably *way* too up-close-and-personal already.

A clatter of heavy boots announced the arrival of a worried-looking Danny Smith. He was carrying a tablet in one hand and a C8 in the other. "Boss, you better see this." He spoke rapidly. "Came in via our covert channels about three minutes ago. It was addressed to the team." He glanced at Colby. "Personally."

The team gathered around the tablet and studied the flickering, jerky picture. Yolanda squinted at the screen. "That picture is piss-poor, fella. What are we looking at?"

"Hang on…" Danny pointed at the screen. "There."

Gary groaned. "Oh, now, *this* isn't good." On the screen was a figure that, while the face may have been blurry and grainy, there was no question as to whom it was.

Vlad's lieutenant sat among a train full of oblivious commuters and stared up at the CCTV, a smirk tugging at the corner of his mouth. Next to him, the old lady had her head down on her chest, looking for all the world like she was simply having a quick nana-nap in-between stops. The team, however, knew immediately that she wasn't asleep. They could all see a dark mark on the side of her neck; a small wound with the tiniest trickle of blood running from it. That was one 'nana-nap' the old girl wouldn't be waking up from, bless her heart…

Gary glared at the screen. "Mother*fucker!*"

Yolanda stared at the screen. "Is he sending us this via live feed?"

Danny nodded. "Yes, boss. The train's been held in the tunnel next to Tufnell Park on an emergency 'suspect package' order. The entire Northern Line this side of the water is at a standstill. The commuters are getting majorly angsty, and I'm guessing Vlad's lieutenant is just a finger-snap away from unleashing that pack of Taints you saw and turning that train into an all-you-can-eat buffet." Danny paused. "Boss, there're a lot of people on that train. A lot. And we've basically put them slap-bang in the middle of a potential feeding frenzy."

Yolanda nodded. She pushed the Glock back into her leg holster. "Get the train moved back here and hold it. Doors shut. We move. Now." The steel in her voice told the team it wasn't a suggestion. It was an order.

They grabbed their kit. The time for a bit of pre-op, barrack-room banter was well and truly over.

\* \* \*

The team had picked a quiet spot well away from prying eyes and in the station's CCTV dead spot. Nobody needed to know what was going on down here, least of all some jobsworth security 'spotter' in a grey room somewhere. They were here to clear the nest, get the civilians to safety with minimum collateral, and take out the lieutenant at the very least. Not provide some bored security guard with an impromptu reality show.

Yolanda sniffed sharply, and looked straight at Colby. "Right then. What's his end game here, Col?"

"Fuck knows."

Colby was concentrating on balling that churning knot of fury he had twisting his insides up into a focused and precise pinpoint. Random, uncontrolled rage was useless. It would probably get you killed. Focus and you released the true killer inside. It was a side of his personality Colby didn't particularly like, but it had kept him alive up to now, so he had learned to embrace it and use it when necessary.

Combat wasn't just about training. It was about unleashing the monster within that everyone has but nobody wants to acknowledge. And doing it in such a way that allowed you to achieve your objective without thinking about the blood and carnage you were inflicting. You needed to disassociate yourself from that side of combat. Otherwise you'd freeze. And if you froze, you died. Really quickly.

Combat was a means to an end. It was about protecting your

team. Protecting yourself. And protecting those who couldn't defend themselves.

And it was about royally fucking up enemy combatants with pointy teeth and centuries of hatred twisting up their intestines.

But now wasn't the time for navel-gazing or introspection on the Art of War. Yolanda studied her oppo and brought him back to the here and now with a bump. "Fuck knows isn't an answer, Flynn."

Colby looked up and shook his head. "Yol, you know more about vampires than any of us. Just because I got up close and personal with Vlad in Tokat doesn't mean I've got an inside on his chain of command or their reasoning."

Yolanda scowled. "Bullshit. You're our strategist and battlefield tactician. That's what you do. And you're damn good at it. So start bloody strategizing! I need to know what his game play is, and what we have to do to make whatever he wants to happen *not* happen." She ignored the slightly puzzled look from Terry Warner. "From my perspective, Old World vamps want one thing. Power. I'll put a week's pay on Vlad not showing his face openly to us again. One exposure was a meet-n-greet. Two would be pushing it and he's not stupid enough to expose himself to any potential risk if he thinks we're ready for him. So I'll guess we'll be going up against that lieutenant and his squad, not Vlad."

Colby nodded. "Agreed. Which at least means we should get a kill out of this shitstorm at the least."

Gary chipped in. "Would Vlad risk one of his top people against us? I mean, like you said, he's a general. He values good lieutenants."

"Not enough to avoid sending them up against us, Gary," said Yolanda. "Nah. As important as this bugger might be to Vlad, he's not irreplaceable. He'll be a tough bastard, so expect a fight. But he can be killed. Remember that, no matter how ugly it gets."

Colby nodded. "Yol's right. This is a game of chess to him. He's a strategist, and a damn good one, too. Don't ever,

*ever* underestimate this guy. Look, if you're planning any kind of whacko world domination shit, you take out your enemy's strongest keystone first, right? As far as Vlad's concerned, the primary threat is us. So he's gonna throw one of his lieutenants at us and see how we do. If we lose, he's golden. If we win then okay, Vlad's lost a link in his armour, but it's not as if he can't get a replacement." Colby sniffed. "It also helps if you spread a bit of panic among the general populous at the same time, too. Makes it harder for the military to contain the situation and mount a counter-offensive. Hearts and minds can be used in a negative context too, you know."

Micky scowled. "So, okay, what is it then, Col? Whacko world domination shit? Revenge for Tokat? Sheer bloody mindedness? Indigestion?"

"Honestly, who the fuck actually cares right now? We've got a train full of commuters that matey's got lined up as today's chef's special, and no plan other than going in and giving him the biggest beasting we can while minimising collateral." Colby looked at Yolanda. "Back-up?"

"If you're asking if there's a plan B, that would be a no. Like you said, we've barely got a plan A. Back-up is at least another fifteen minutes out." She shook her head. "We're on our own with this one."

"Perfect. So Vlad's Rupert, plus guests, plus a shit-load of panicked collateral in the way, in a confined space, and a team of eight with limited ammo. Oh, happy fucking days." Terry shook his head. "Ah well, more to go around, I guess."

"Yeah. The one with the least number of kills buys the pizza." Gary primed his C8 carbine...

\* \* \*

They stopped on the last broad landing before the steps reached the platform. Crouching on either side with their backs to the wall, they were all ready and waiting for the go from Yolanda. She nodded. "Right then. We all know what we're doing. Watch your backs. Objectives. One, get the civvies out and clear. Two, eliminate the nest. Three, take out that lieutenant with extreme prejudice. Four, bang out sharpish and let the cleaners in to bag and tag. No collateral, and I mean *none*. Everyone gets out. Except that arrogant little fucker. Are we clear?"

The entire team answered as one. "Crystal!"

Yolanda glanced at her watch. "Right then, gentlemen. We're on the clock here. Let's go to work, shall we?" She gave them a dark little smile.

They all knew what that meant.

Bug hunt time…

Alpha and Bravo Unit moved silently down the stairs towards platform two. Everyone knew their role. Staggered two-two formation. Two teams of four. Minimum comms. Chain of command was Yolanda as primary point of contact, Colby leading Alpha team, and Terry Warner leading Bravo.

They'd practised this a thousand times in the old Charing Cross tube station on the Jubilee line, selected as a kill house because it was the most recently abandoned station and had the most up-to-date layout. Now they had to put that training into real-time action, but with both warm bodies and a shit-ton of civilians adding an unknown element into the mix.

The plan, if there was such a thing, was simple. Kill the lights. Bravo team led by Terry Warner would hit the tunnel end and take out any close proximity Taints. Alpha team would take the platform to lay down cover if needed while Colby and Danny dropped down and used Primacord blasting cord to daisychain a series of detonations on the train doors. Create a series of small, contained explosions that would be enough to blow the doors open, cause maximum diversion and allow the passengers to get the hell out of Dodge on the hurry-up. Bravo team would get the civvies out. Alpha team would breach and attempt to take out the tango with extreme prejudice. As fast as Vlad's lieutenant was, even he wouldn't be able to contain an entire tube carriage of stampeding London commuters *and* take on a determined and highly-trained Special Ops team at the same time. Plan A just might work.

315

Well, that was the theory, anyway.

The teams stopped at the bottom of the stairs, just out of sight of the stationary tube train. The darkened platform wasn't entirely pitch black, but there was more than enough deep shadow to mask their movements. Yolanda turned to Danny and Flynn, keeping the commands to a minimum, delivered in a sharp whisper. "Doors. Go." She turned to Terry and the rest of Bravo team. "Tunnel. Go." Finally, she glanced to her left. "Micky. Exit point. Go."

Danny and Colby hunched up and scuttled along the length of the train, staying tight against the metal skin and expertly positioning a series of Primacord strips on each set of doors. As they placed each strip, they cautiously checked for commuters standing too close to the doors, and waved them back. The orange Primacord2 had a central core of 2.1 grams of PETN explosive per meter of cord, which shouldn't be enough to actually kill anyone, even close up. But an injured commuter could slow the extraction process. This needed to be fast, furious and with minimum casualties. And the entire team knew that 'minimum' in Yolanda's book meant no fucking casualties at all.

A link cord connected the blasting caps on each strip, and led back to the detonation button cradled in Yolanda's gloved hand. She was conscious to keep her finger well away from the button at this point. It might not be enough to kill, but the Primacord could certainly take a hand off at the wrist.

Danny and Colby took up position at the far end and gave the 'Ready' signal. Yolanda nodded and glanced back towards the tunnel, where Terry nodded and gave another 'Ready' signal. Micky nodded and made it three-for-three. The whole thing had taken less than a minute.

She held up three fingers, ensuring all the teams could see.

Stand by.

Three... two... one...

Yolanda flipped up the cover switch and pressed the detonator.

The teams recoiled from the daisychain of blasts that ripped through the station. The tube train doors tore open, accompanied by screams and shrieks from dozens of terrified commuters.

In the tunnel, Terry and Bravo team unleashed an organophosphor shit-storm towards the glistening eyeshine. The waiting pack of Taints were mowed down in a heel-drumming firework display. The organophosphor payloads sent their bodies into overdrive, coursing through their veins like lava and igniting into an explosion of guts and body parts. An intense fire consumed every last one of the bastards, sending clouds of hot ash cascading and tumbling into eddies and whirls, which pulsed down the tunnels and sent the ex-Taints spiralling into oblivion.

A series of double taps took out the last stragglers, including one that lunged towards Terry's face, slashing at him with a freshly mutilated hand. Terry calmly grouped two FMJs in the centre of the bastard's chest, and watched the creature thrash on the floor. This must've been the one Colby stomped on earlier. "Manicure *that*, motherfucker!" Without even a hint of a reflexive flinch, he grinned as the Taint exploded. Terry shouldered the C8 carbine and did a quick double check. "Tunnel clear."

*"Get the civvies out."* Yolanda kept her instructions minimal and crystal clear. She trusted every one of her team to do their job. They didn't need babysitting.

Terry responded. "Copy that," and motioned to Bravo team. He stabbed a finger towards the train. "Civvies! Out!" The team sprinted back up the tracks and up onto the platform, each taking a carriage and shouting at the terrified passengers to *"MOVE!"* First one and then a flood of commuters poured out of the carriages. They were shoved unceremoniously towards the exit by Bravo Team. Micky Cox stood on the stairs, ushering the flow of terrified humanity up the stairs and to safety.

From the end carriage a screaming, rolling roar of fury echoed around the platform, amplified by the station's acoustics. It stopped everyone dead in their tracks – civilian and squaddie alike. Something deep inside every man, woman and child's soul sat up and screamed in terror.

It was a primeval sensation that stripped away the cosy blanket of safety from an ultra-modern world, like the growl of a wolf next to your ear, or the brush of talons on the back of your neck. It spoke of vast, dark forests and starlit, shadow-filled nights, the sharp tin tang of snow in the air and the metallic taste of your own blood bubbling up in your throat.

It promised nothing but death.

And it was pissed. *Man*, it was *pissed...*

Yolanda barked commands, breaking the stunned silence. "Danny! Colby! Fall back! *Now!*" She threw a quick glance towards Terry and Mick. "Get those bloody civilians out of here! Move!"

Danny and Colby moved carefully backwards towards Yolanda, their C8s trained in front of them, waiting for the sinewy shape of the lieutenant to emerge from the end carriage. Colby's sighting laser didn't waver, and Danny targeted his own so the two grouped tightly together. "Don't cross the streams," Danny muttered, prompting a snort from Colby.

"That would be bad. That would be very bad."

They cross-stepped their way back towards the exit point. "Where the fuck is he? Where is he, Col?"

"Focus, Dan. He'll pop up any second now. We've pissed him off. He might not engage this time, but he's sure as hell gonna show himself, you can bet on it."

The Taint didn't disappoint. Right on cue, he emerged from the end carriage, dominating the platform. He turned and faced his challengers, a vicious snarl curling his lips back from those teeth. He held up his right hand.

Danny squinted towards the monster. "What the hell is that motherfucker holding, Col?"

Colby peered through the darkness, and nearly threw up on the spot.

Dangling from its bloody fingers was a severed head that had quite clearly been forcibly torn from its body. Blood pooled at the vampire's feet, dripping like a broken tap and bouncing off the tiled floor. The grey curls were tangled in his fingers, and the head swung gently in the hot breeze that wafted through the tunnel. Tendons and nerves dangled from the shredded neck, and two streaks of black and red ran down the cheeks, a combination of cheap, gritty mascara and blood.

The Taint threw his head back and laughed – a cruel, dangerous sound that spoke of violence yet to come. He tossed the head casually down the platform like a bowler aiming for a ten-pin strike. It rolled and bounced, coming to a stop at Colby's feet.

Colby looked down at the once-gentle face and then back at the vampire. Sheer rage overtook him. He aimed the green laser at the thing's chest and roared. "FIRE!"

Danny and Colby unleashed a swarm of organophosphor FMJs straight at the Taint.

He didn't explode. He didn't twitch and writhe as fire consumed his body. He didn't scream and drop to the floor, heels drumming and body twisting. He merely threw his arms wide open as if welcoming the bullets into his loving embrace. His body took impact after impact.

Nothing.

The bastard didn't even bleed.

"CEASE FIRE! CEASE FIRE, DAMN IT!" Yolanda's voice cut through the cacophony of noise and gunfire. The last shot echoed around the tunnel and finally, silence fell.

Danny and Colby stood motionless, their fingers still on the triggers of the C8s. There was no point wasting any more ammo on this son of a bitch.

"Fall back!" Yolanda, Terry and Micky gave cover as the two men slowly moved back.

The team regrouped by the stairwell, a veritable clusterfuck of ordnance pointing straight at the lieutenant. Yolanda barked an order. "Danny? If you wouldn't mind?"

Danny grinned, stepped forward and hoisted an AT4 Anti-tank weapon onto his shoulder. Designed specifically for confined spaces and urban warfare, it fired an 84mm round of death and destruction at anything you pointed the bastard at.

Gary turned to Colby and grinned. "Man, you gotta love those Swedes. They might be neutral, but they make seriously funky ATWs!"

Colby grinned back. "Yeah. Let's see the bastard catch this and still smile." He glanced up at Danny. "Fuck his day up, mate!"

"Boss?"

"Fire at will, Dan. Like Col said. Fuck his day up, there's a good chap." Yolanda glared at the smirking lieutenant, and suddenly gave him a bright smile and a wink. "Hey! Toothy! Catch!"

Danny took aim, and squeezed the trigger. The projectile exploded from the smooth-bore barrel and fizzed like a firework along the length of the platform.

Too late, the lieutenant realised the missile was considerably bigger than the FMJs he'd batted away like bees. His mouth formed an 'O' as the missile hit him directly in the chest.

The entire team flinched back from the blast. Even though the AT4 was designed for use in close quarters, the blast was still a little *too* close for comfort this time.

As the smoke and dust cleared, the all looked towards where Vlad's lieutenant had stood. All that was left was a dark, sooty mark on the floor and a pile of ashes that danced and whirled in the backdraft from the tunnel entrance.

There was no heel drumming.

No thrashing.

No fireworks.

The fucker simply vaporised on impact. As did a bench, three advertising hoardings, a 'NO ENTRY' sign and every single tile on the end of the platform wall.

Danny lowered the AT4 and sniffed. "I ain't payin' for the damage, boss. Not on my wages."

Yolanda stood and walked towards the end of the platform. She stopped and crouched where the old lady's head lay, discarded and bloody. She unzipped her jacket and took it off, carefully covering the old woman's remains.

She looked up and into the darkness of the tunnel, and quietly spoke.

"I'm coming for you, Vlad. I'm *coming for you…*"

# DEEPEST, DARKEST

## Hank Schwaeble

The most disturbing thought that crossed Hatcher's mind as he scanned the team members lining the interior of the fuselage wasn't that this may have been the first time an audit letter from the IRS was a pretext to coerce participation in a covert op, but rather that it likely wasn't.

The C130 landed on a dirt strip in Malawi, seven miles from the Zambian border. The plane slowed to a bumpy roll, almost coming to a stop, and the pilot turned a tight radius using the right engines and left brakes. She goosed the engines and taxied the big bird back toward the other end.

Hatcher unbuckled from the nylon webbing of the jump seat and stood, hooking a hand on a support along the fuselage wall. A pale glow was spilling in from the front of the plane through the cockpit. The pilot eased the big transport into another turn, then began shutting down the engines, moving sets of controls protruding from a center console. Hatcher stepped toward the cockpit and leaned in.

"How long?"

The pilot tugged her headset down from her ears, let it hang around her neck. "Ten nautical miles out a minute ago. ETA in about five."

Hatcher nodded. The inbound chopper would take them into Zambia just as the sun was breaking the horizon. It was a short hop to the LZ.

"You know him? The pilot, I mean."

She gave him an enigmatic look, like she had to think about the phrasing of her answer. "Not really. He's Army."

Hatcher glanced at the co-pilot, who looked like he was about to graduate junior high. The kid smiled and shook his head.

"He sure seems interested in knowing *her*," he said. "Or knowing her better. He's been coming up with excuses to check in with her all day." He pointed to a display on the console where there were two sets of numbers. He was indicating the second set. Five digits, the last one separated by a decimal point. Vacant frequency, Hatcher guessed.

"That's quite enough, Lieutenant," the captain said.

"How long are you in-country?"

"Twenty-four hours," she said. "We're flying back to Lilongwe, spending the night there. We're supposed to wait for orders. I suppose those will be to pick you up?"

"Let's hope." He looked at the numbers on the radio again, thinking of the COMSEC limitations his team would be operating under. Zero Airwave Presence.

The whine of mechanisms grew slower and lower, whirring sounds, pinging sounds, ticking sounds. Hatcher stepped back into the main body of the transport and looked over his team, strung together some words in his head. He gave a nod to the one named Woodley, who gave one back. Woodley was some sort of contractor, had done this kind of thing before. Why that guy wasn't team leader, Hatcher still couldn't figure. He hated being in command.

"All right," Hatcher said, projecting his voice. "You all know the mission and the plan. Time to suit up and go Tom Clancy. If you have any questions, they better be good ones, because the time to ask them was during the six hours of briefing, not now. Otherwise, get your weapon and lock and load."

"I got one." It was Garza. Sniper. Ex-Marine. Short and top heavy. Scar deforming the side of his upper lip. "Why aren't we doing this under dark cover?"

It was a good question. One he'd asked himself, when the operational parameters had been explained to him. He was told not to volunteer the answer if it came up, to give some lame rationale about airspace and international treaties and technical distinctions between hostile incursions and minor violations. But he wasn't going to keep anything from the team.

"The people we're working with on the ground, including our contacts, are superstitious. I'm not sure how else to put it. They believe there are threats in the darkness, risks they aren't willing to take. They insisted on daylight. That's why we're being dropped at the crack of dawn."

Hatcher knew the locals were right. There were threats in the darkness. But he doubted what they were afraid of had anything to do with the kinds of things he knew to be true, the kinds of things he knew to be lurking in the dark. And he seriously doubted there was anything to the particular superstitions that caused many in the region to participate in a robust black market for albino body parts, prizing them for some sort of mystical qualities it was believed they possessed – a practice that apparently motivated the woman Hatcher and his team were tasked with rescuing to do volunteer work in dangerous territory, angering dangerous people—other than maybe the power that comes from a long history of folklore. Still, the thought bothered him.

The loadmaster was a small NCO. He stood near the rear and began a roll call of assigned numbers. The first guy to grab his M4 from the man chuckled. His name was Ivy, ex-SEAL. He tapped the magazine against his helmet. Ivy was medium height, medium build. Well proportioned. Very dark skin with high cheek bones.

"Superstitious," Ivy said, chin swaying. "Never known a brother who wasn't."

Some laughs from the group. Zorn, an athletic looking guy with sandy brown hair in a neat flat top sat up stiff, making a show of concern. "Hold it, now, I was told *you* were the only black guy I'd have to put up with. And they promised you weren't allowed to speak. They ain't paying me enough."

A few more laughs. Ivy made a comment about Zorn's mama having plenty of quarters to spread around, last he'd heard, and

Hatcher stepped in to shut everyone up. This, he figured, was why they didn't want that kind of thing talked about. An off-color joke, a poorly-phrased comment – the slightest wrong note at a fragile moment could spell trouble. Cooperation could be cut-off instantly, especially when you were dealing with people who had it rough, people who had little else but their pride.

"Not a word of it. Not to our hosts, not to anyone from this point on. You all have the Ugly-American angle covered well enough with your looks." He stared each of them down, one by one, before catching Woodley's eye. "When the bird lands, you and I are out first. Ivy, Zorn, you're next, but on signal. Garza, you follow them. And watch it with the jokes. Save 'em for the flight back. Game-face time."

Hatcher gestured Woodley near. He was the first in the group Hatcher'd been introduced to in that basement dungeon of offices, during the carrot portion of the pitch, right after the stick. Tall, athletic in a lean way. Smiled way too much, kept patting Hatcher on the back and talking about how glad he was Hatcher was on board. Hatcher had taken an instant dislike to him. The gung-ho attitude and Aryan features screamed poster-boy for the Hitler Youth. "You understand why we're first, right?"

Woodley chewed on it, but not for long. He registered his comprehension with a pop of the eyebrows. "Got it."

The muted rhythm of helicopter blades thumped against the aluminum skin of the plane. The rear cargo hatch lowered like a drawbridge. The loadmaster called out the remaining numbers, handing each man his rifle and five magazines. Hatcher went last. After the weapons and ammunition were distributed, the loadmaster unlocked a separate container and handed Woodley a silver metallic briefcase. The men exited single file, headed straight toward the chopper. Hatcher waited for everyone else to board, scanning the tree lines, before climbing on.

There was no preflight briefing. There were headsets, but none of the team reached for one and Hatcher decided not to, either. The right-seat pilot shut the sliding passenger door and climbed back in. The engine grew louder a moment later and the craft shifted, a sliding feeling, then it rose. The nose dipped before it got twenty feet off the ground and then they were accelerating forward.

The ride was smooth. It was Hatcher's first time in a Lakota. Much nicer than the Hueys and Chinooks he was used to, but he reminded himself that had been over a decade ago. He watched the terrain roll by below, green concentrations of heavy vegetation, beige-yellow plains. They were barely ten minutes into the flight when the pilot gestured back, then pointed. The helicopter descended into a clearing.

Hatcher slid a hand to the small of his back, feigned like he was scratching. He touched the tiny metal cylinder tucked behind his belt, a tool he'd taken to carrying everywhere, ever since his last run-in with the police. Why the feel of it at a time like this gave him comfort, when he was armed to the teeth, he wasn't sure. Maybe because he felt trapped, roped into an operation against his will, and the reason he always carried it was to make traps seem less hopeless. The idea made him feel silly.

Two automobiles emerged from beyond the tree line, approaching. One was an olive-green Land Rover with an open rear and a large metal frame instead of a roof, what looked like a podium extending over the hood surrounded by a railing. Safari observation platform, Hatcher supposed. The other was a bleached-out tan Humvee. Both were beat up, with numerous dents and bond-o blotches and mud-caked rugged tires that were worn long past their replacement date. The Land Rover had a driver but no one else in it. The Hummer had a driver and a passenger.

Woodley opened the door and glanced at Hatcher. The others were all in various states of lean, ready to go, but Hatcher held up a fist. He picked a headset off a hook, made sure it was plugged in, and spoke into the mouthpiece.

"There's always a chance they may pull weapons. At the first sign of anything that I or the team member with me can't handle, you get these men out of here and abort."

The pilot nodded. Per the mission rules, there would be no radio traffic. Extraction was set by time and coordinates, with a contingency meeting point set two hours later. There was no host government involvement, so risk of a communication capture was to be avoided with extreme priority. While nobody liked those kinds of orders, Hatcher grudgingly understood. The entire mission was a gross violation of national sovereignty. The ramifications could be far reaching and threaten myriad pacts and alliances, formal and informal. There was no escaping politics.

Woodley hopped out and Hatcher followed. They double-timed it in a slight crouch until they reached the Hummer.

The driver opened the door and put one foot on the ground, standing, but didn't get all the way out. He was wearing mirrored sunglasses that reflected the glowing sky to the east. A khaki shirt, pockets but no sleeves. To Hatcher's surprise, he didn't appear to be armed.

The man slapped the outside of the open door – *pop pop* – then held out his hand at an expectant angle. His dark skin was wrapped tight around a lean, corded arm, a bump for a bicep, a knob for an elbow. He snapped his fingers, fanned his hand toward his body.

Hatcher shifted his eyes to Woodley and gestured with his chin. Woodley stepped forward with the briefcase. The man grabbed the handle and tossed the case into the jeep behind him without so much as a pause to glance at it.

Woodley stepped back. The man leaned on the vehicle door, hiding behind his mirrored lenses. He seemed to be waiting for something else.

"You got your money," Hatcher said. "Now, where are we heading? Distance and direction."

The man stared at Hatcher. His upper lip and the side of his mouth curled enough to show teeth, but he said nothing.

"You're either the leader of whatever gang or outfit or tribal clan you belong to, or the guy sent by the leader. That means you speak English."

Woodley started to say something, but Hatcher threw up a palm without looking at him.

"Well?"

"I am thinking," the man said. He took a long minute eyeing Hatcher, head tilting up and down. "About what I am being paid to do. It is not easy to betray someone."

The whine of the helicopter hummed in their ears. Hatcher felt Woodley tense, sensed him shifting his weight forward. He stuck out his arm like a road block.

He didn't like any of this. Didn't want to be there, didn't like being in charge, and sure as hell didn't like having been blackmailed into the whole thing. But even if he'd signed up willingly, he would have hated this plan. This was supposed to be a hostage rescue, but they were paying for the location. Half rescue, half ransom. That meant dealing with shifting allegiances and incomplete information of unknown reliability. His objections had been overruled. The plan was put in place at too high a level to change it, he'd been told. And that plan was to pay the money, get the location, and extract the young doctor with the powerful parent back home who'd made the possibly fatal mistake of doing her volunteer work in the wrong country at the wrong time.

"Then don't," Hatcher said. "Stick with the deal as planned. The one you made with the people who sent us. What you're doing will free an innocent woman. That's not a betrayal. That's doing the right thing. No need to complicate things." A moment later, he added, "any more than they already are."

The man ran his long fingers down the side of his face. His knuckles were cracked and chalky from callouses and scabbing.

"That is a good way to think of it. I will take heed of your words." The man seemed to shift his attention to Woodley for a moment, then back to Hatcher. It was hard for Hatcher to tell with those glasses. "The camp is nine kilometers northwest. We will take you and your men to a location a little less than one kilometer from it. From there, I will escort you and one other to the perimeter. Exactly as agreed. Then, my men and I will take our leave."

Hatcher nodded once. He turned to the helicopter and held up an arm, pointed his index finger to the sky and swirled it. His team egressed one at a time, moving swiftly, heads low, weapons in a ready position across their chests.

Leaning in toward Woodley, Hatcher said, "Keep your eye on him." He gestured with his eyes back to the driver. "He's hiding something."

Woodley swallowed. The exchange had clearly rattled him; a greasy film of sweat slicked his forehead.

"Why do you say that?" he asked.

Hatcher'd openly wondered at the first briefing why they hadn't just put Woodley in charge, since he seemed to be the only one in the group with current military ties – though his actual status had been vaguely referenced as classified – and knew more about the situation than any of them. One reason had become obvious. He was jittery, uncertain. Maybe the powers-that-be weren't as oblivious as Hatcher had assumed.

"Well, aside from the fact I can tell… the only people who don't count money from strangers are ones who are doing it for something other than the cash. And I don't know what that something is. Do you?"

Another swallow, followed by a deep breath. Woodley looked over his shoulder at the driver, thoughts swimming behind his eyes. He dropped his gaze to the ground, his body stiffening, as if gathering resolve.

"I don't know why anyone does anything, anymore," he said. "So I sure as hell don't know what motivates these guys."

The drive through the jungle was only about five miles, but the indirect route carved out of the terrain made it seem closer to twenty. The road was more of a trail, the destination a location chosen for its remoteness and lack of accessibility. Branches and fronds draped themselves over the path, rubbery, leafy shapes swatting off the windscreen of the lead vehicle, the wilds of an untamed land trying to reclaim its own.

Far from the chopper, the sound of the vehicles was not enough to drown out the fluty call of birds, the piercing ululations of... what? Monkeys? Hatcher couldn't be sure. He just knew that at each tight curve, as the engines slowed to idle, the hue of wildlife was like a background track. Whistles and whoops and trills.

The lead vehicle pulled to a stop where the path took a sharp turn. The other vehicle stopped behind it.

"This is as far as I can take everyone but two of you. I will show you the camp. But your men will have to stay back. I do not want to get caught in the middle of a firefight."

"I didn't catch your name."

"Mbuyi."

"No offense, Mbuyi, but this sounds an awful lot like a trap."

The man shrugged. "One of me, two of you. I will take you to where I can show you the path to the camp. But no farther. I have one pistol. You have automatic weapons." He shifted his gaze to Woodley, looking him up and down with what seemed to Hatcher like a palpable disdain. He wondered if it was the blond hair. "I am in no position to control what happens after that. I will do exactly as was agreed."

"How far is it?" Hatcher asked.

"Half a kilometer, perhaps."

Woodley looked at Hatcher. "Your call. We can tell the rest of the team to be ready for a rapid response."

Nothing to like about it, but they needed eyes on the camp to decide the specifics. That was always the weakest part of the plan, which was saying a lot. But they hadn't given him much of a say in the matter. They hadn't given him much of a say in anything.

"Do it. But get us back here in thirty."

Woodley signaled to the others to stand ready in place, threw up three fingers then a circled palm, fingertip touching thumb. This had been part of the brief. If they weren't back at thirty-one minutes, the team was to treat every non-team member as a hostile.

Mbuyi tossed a wave over his head to his associates and started driving again. The path was narrower now, used infrequently, barely two ruts through the trees, whose branches clawed at the windshield and scraped the metal above their heads.

After maybe three or four hundred yards, Mbuyi braked and put the vehicle into park. He stepped out and gestured to Woodley, pointing into the back. Woodley looked down, then handed him a machete that was on the floor. Mbuyi dipped his head toward the heavy brush past him.

"This way. One hundred meters or thereabouts. There is a clearing."

The machete hissed and thwacked its way through branches and stems and vines, fans of green, nets of hairy ropes. The route Mbuyi forged had been cut before and the jungle had all but reclaimed it, leaving Hatcher to wonder if that sort of reclaiming had taken weeks, or only days. The going was slow but steady, within a few minutes, the growth became less dense. An area opened; a small spread of field. It was littered with the skeletal remains of animals. At least, Hatcher hoped they were all animals. Ribs and spines and giant drumsticks. Straight ones, curved ones, broken ones; jagged and smooth and bleached and yellowing. Large and small.

A light breeze puffed their faces. The stench it carried was unbearable.

"This place is called the Garden of Bones. You will find such gardens throughout the nearby valley. And the areas that surround it."

Hatcher glanced at Woodley, tightened his grip on his M4, raising it slightly. Woodley wrinkled his nose and hitched a shoulder, frowning with one side of his mouth.

"Why are we in the 'Garden of Bones,' Mbuyi? Where's the camp?"

"I'm afraid you will find out soon enough."

Movement along the far treeline. Hatcher dropped to one knee and raised his rifle to a ready-fire position.

"Hostiles. Woodley, cover left."

"Unfortunately," Woodley said. "I'm too busy covering you."

Hatcher turned his head. The barrel of Woodley's rifle was pointed straight at him. Its bearer was staring down the sight, weapon securely in firing position.

Six men emerged from the brush. Most had AKs. One had an Uzi. All were pointed with varying degrees of apparent know-how in his direction. No uniforms, just jeans and sweats and t-shirts and a few caps. A woman was with them. Her wrists were pulled behind her and a dirty pillow case covered her head. Her bare arms were pale beneath smears of grime.

Hatcher eased the grip on his rifle, letting it sag in his arms. "I don't even have any live rounds, do I?"

Woodley gave his head a shake. "Dummies. Had to make sure the weight and balance was just right. Knew you'd check."

The approaching men drew closer, their steps slow and cautious. Hatcher set his rifle down and stood.

"So, what's the play? Me for the girl?"

"That's the general idea."

Hatcher looked at Mbuyi, then back to Woodley. "What could possibly make me so valuable?"

"You'll have to ask them," Woodley said. "I'm sorry about this, Hatcher. I really am."

"I bet."

"Believe what you want, but it's true. They had me by the short hairs. Worse than you, a lot worse. I'm just following orders. Nothing personal, man. It's all part of the plan. Remember how you kept saying, trust in the plan?"

Hatcher never remembered saying any such thing, but saw no use in arguing. One of the men eyed Hatcher as he addressed Mbuyi. Whatever he said was in a tongue Hatcher couldn't identify, let alone understand.

"He says he thought you would be bigger."

"I've never had any complaints."

Mbuyi paused, considering the words. Then his mouth spread into a toothy grin. He said something to the other man, who laughed. The man gestured in the direction of the woman, and one of the others grabbed her above the elbow and led her to

Woodley. She stumbled along, almost losing her footing as her head darted. Hatcher guessed her mouth had a gag in it and her ears were plugged, since she seemed to have no idea what was going on around her.

Woodley took the woman's arm, a bit more gently than the guy handing her off, and started to lead her back in the direction they'd come. He stopped after a few steps, guiding her past him, and looked back at Hatcher.

"For what it's worth, they would have killed her. Doing it this way not only saved her, but prevented any other potential casualties on the team. Like I said, all part of the plan. And it sort of makes you a hero."

"In that case," Hatcher said as two of the men neared, weapons raised and shoving toward him while another produced a pair of handcuffs. "What does that make you?"

Woodley raised his brows high, gave a tilt of his head. "Underestimated."

He winked before taking a step back.

One of the men took Hatcher's helmet while another patted him down and removed the tactical knife from its sheath. Woodley took the helmet and yanked the microphone off. He pulled out some of the internal wiring near the earpiece and threw it into the nearby brush, then tossed the helmet back near Woodley's feet. The woman flinched when he took her by the arm again.

Mbuyi started to follow Woodley and the woman, then stopped to look at Hatcher. Woodley paused at the mouth of the trail, an impatient set to his stance.

"It is not betrayal if you free an innocent woman. I was having second thoughts until you told me that."

Hatcher held the man's gaze. "In that case, just make sure she actually gets out."

The words seemed to catch him off guard. The man pinched his lips tight and dipped his head. "The joy of life is to be continually surprised. That is also its burden."

The muzzle of a rifle poked Hatcher in the rib, hard enough to make him wince. The leader made a gesture, and his captors started moving. One of them shoved him hard enough to make him stumble.

Mbuyi remained where he was, watching. Hatcher looked back over his shoulder as he crossed through the array of bones, the serpentine weave of vertebrates, the curled fingers of ribs. Mbuyi nodded to Hatcher one final time, then turned and walked away. Woodley guided the woman between the trees, Mbuyi a few steps behind. Within seconds, the jungle had swallowed all three of them.

\* \* \*

The camp was a collection of huts. Some thatch weaves over cobbled scrap wood, some sheets of corrugated tin nailed to trees. In the middle of the camp was a shot-up armored vehicle without any wheels, collapsed on one side, like it had been driven across an IED and then abandoned where it lay.

They sat Hatcher on a stump at the mangled rear end of the vehicle and ran a dense chain between his arms behind his back, over the links between his wrists, and passed the shackle of a heavy duty padlock through both ends where they sandwiched a large metal loop. The loop was connected to the frame of the vehicle, welded solid.

One of the men tugged on the chain, testing it. Two others stood nearby and nodded their approval.

"Do any of you speak English?"

The three men stared at him, glancing occasionally at each other.

"I speak English."

The voice came from behind one of the men, who stepped aside and looked back. The man it belonged to was seated in front of one of the huts, fashioning something out of a piece of wood with a small knife.

"Mind telling me what you guys want with me?"

"We do not want anything with you."

"Then why am I here?"

"Kongamoto."

The men near Hatcher seemed to grow uneasy at the sound of the word. Their eyes darted, casting nervous glances from one to the other.

"What the hell is a Kongamoto?"

The man in the knit cap who had seemed to be their leader when talking to Mbuyi – Hatcher hadn't caught his name – barked out a few angry words, slashing a hand through the air for emphasis. The man with the knife sat up straight and kept his eyes down, returning his attention to whittling. The other two hurried away in opposite directions, chastened.

Knit Cap stopped in front of Hatcher, ran his eyes in an arc from one end of his body to the other and back. He was wearing an open military-style green blouse with the sleeves cut off over a faded yellow t-shirt with a worn out soft drink logo on it. His rifle was slung over his shoulder and he was holding a walkie-talkie in one hand. He raised it to his mouth and spoke words Hatcher couldn't understand. It squawked, a crackly voice responding in ways equally unintelligible. Then he walked away.

Hatcher kept his eyes on the whittling guy. The man seemed to be forcing himself not to look, which was good. Slowly, Hatcher worked his fingers into the waistband of his trousers at the small of his back. He scissored his index and middle finger around a three-inch rod, fishing it out. It was titanium, with a tooth on one end and the other, sheathed end sharpened to an edge you could shave with. *Slow, slow, slow.* Careful not to move his upper arm or shoulder, working entirely with his forearm, fingers and wrist. The small tube slid up and over the lip of his belt and dropped, landing in the curl of his fingers.

He squeezed his fingers closed as he heard the sound of a car or truck, something with a big engine, rumbling closer until it stopped somewhere to his rear. The motor cut off, a door opened and shut. Voices. Footfalls.

Knit Cap strode into view, rifle across his chest, stock cradled in the crook of his arm. Another person joined him. A woman.

She was tall, as tall as her escort. Her skin was dark and

smooth, a sheen to it that gave it an onyx glow. Her lips were full and pouty. Her kinky hair was teased out and pulled back on each side with a clip, a frizzy puff in the back. She wore an unbuttoned tan shirt over a stretchy white tank top, with khaki safari pants.

Even if she hadn't been physically attractive to the point of it seeming absurd, Hatcher would have known by the way her presence made him anxious, that tingly, aroused feeling that her scent caused. She was a Carnate. No doubt about it. A physically perfect half-human, half-demon woman with sexual charms that were all but irresistible. They lived for seven generations and never seemed to age. All they lacked were souls.

"Jake Hatcher," the woman said.

"Small world," Hatcher said. "That's my name, too."

"That famous wit. I am Aleena. You know, some of my sisters in America have talked so much about you, I feel like I've known you for years."

She spoke with a lilt, her voice polished and smooth. There was an accent, but he had no idea what kind.

"In that case, how about you let me go. Just this once. For old time's sake."

"Alas, that I cannot do. My most sincere apologies. I went through a lot of trouble to get you here."

"And why would you go and do a thing like that?"

"I'm afraid that is a bit too complicated to explain at the moment. My friends here have been vexed by an entity you are well acquainted with. Or shall we say, is well acquainted with you. They have been desperately seeking a way to, shall we say, get him off their backs and to stop interfering with their lucrative business interests. They have sought out the aid of every sorcerer within a thousand miles, created a demand for the body parts of people unfortunate enough to have been born albino in a part of the world where such a condition is believed to carry mystical properties."

"And how do I fit in to all this?"

"Oh, don't you worry, Mr Hatcher. You will find out soon enough. Tonight, in fact."

Hatcher shook his head, frowning. "Ooh, tonight... you know, that just doesn't work for me. Maybe we can reschedule?"

"I have heard the stories, been told how charming others have found you. Your manly directness, your facetious banter in the face of perils sure to break the composure of those with lesser mettle. Mostly, they seem amused by your belief you can talk your way out of things, when we both know that has never happened."

"There's always a first time."

"Yes. This will be one of those. Just not for that."

She dipped her head to Knit Cap guy, then turned to walk away.

"What happens tonight?" Hatcher called after her. "So I know what to wear, what to bring. Not going to make me buy two bottles of wine, just to be safe, are you?"

Aleena pivoted on the heel of her boot, turning herself just enough to look back at him. Her lips spread to show a set of perfect white teeth.

"Red, Mr Hatcher. The color for tonight is most definitely red."

\* \* \*

Hatcher spent the next few hours evaluating his situation. He could unlock his cuffs – courtesy not only of the escape rod resting in the fold of his curled fingers, but also the failure of his captors in not turning his hands palms out before cuffing him. But what good would that do? It was broad daylight, miles into jungle terrain, which was the worst of all worlds. His absence would draw immediate attention, which told him these guys were smart for putting him in the middle of the camp instead of stuffing him into some hut. And even if he found an opportunity, some distraction or diversion, he'd need a firearm. Accomplishing that would draw its own attention. If they had any lying around, waiting to be grabbed, he hadn't noticed.

So he waited.

At least one question had been answered. This was the real point of the whole production all along, not that garbage they'd BSed him with. Get him to the federal building under the guise of an audit, have him met by Secret Service agents who led him to a sub-basement more secure than a Bond villain's lair, then acquaint him with the velvet hammer. A guy named Keegan, someone high up in the Administration, but exactly how high, or exactly who he was, was never made clear. What *was* made clear was the offer. He could either cooperate, or face all manner of trumped-up tax problems, including civil forfeiture of every dime he had. Criminal prosecution was all but promised, and more than a few not-so-subtle hints were dropped that certain matters involving dead cops may be looked into again with a good deal more scrutiny. Or… he could take what's behind door number two. Help rescue a young doctor doing volunteer work helping to stop the mutilation and occasional slaughter of albinos whose body parts were believed to be powerful objects for magic. A young woman who just happened to warrant all this attention because she was the Vice-President's secret and illegitimate daughter, that last bit being more implied than stated, neither confirmed nor denied.

The more he thought about it, the stupider he felt. Why hadn't he just told them to go fuck themselves, like his gut wanted him to? It wasn't a real question, because he knew the answer, and had from the beginning. Amy. The threats weren't just to him. They were more than willing to go after her, just to prove a point. And they'd clearly done enough homework for the threat to be credible.

Less than four days later, here he was.

Heat flowed through the camp like a current, like something that could be touched and scooped and bottled. Perspiration soaked through Hatcher's clothes, drenching him with a salty, stinging slickness.

Men moved about slowly, finding shade, playing cards, cleaning their weapons. Hatcher could sense some tension, the buzz of anticipation, but the heat seemed to keep everyone subdued. He could tell they wanted to move, wanted to pace and burn off nervous energy, but they were forced to fidget instead, trying to keep cool.

People came and went. Everyone seemed to stop and look at him more than once. Some of the men from the Garden of Bones, some who were at the camp when he got there, others who arrived later. Most would stand directly in front of him with appraising eyes, some made comments to others Hatcher couldn't understand, some tilted their heads one way or the other, quietly assessing him. A handful smiled. Most didn't.

Around two in the afternoon, there was activity. A vehicle arrived, followed shortly by another. Knit Cap walked up, grunted some words to a few others. Two rushed over to Hatcher and unlocked the chain. One clamped a hand on his elbow and half pushed, half dragged him toward an old extended cab pickup truck. There was some sort of mechanical device in the back, taking up most of the bed. Hatcher couldn't quite tell what it was for, but it had the familiar shape of a weapon and what looked like a grappling hook on the end, pointed like an arrowhead.

People were climbing into vehicles. One opened a rear door to the truck and Hatcher was shoved toward it, then prodded in with the barrel of an AK. The whittling guy slid in next to him and another jumped in the passenger seat up front. Knit Cap behind the wheel.

Hatcher was in the second vehicle in a four-car caravan. They drove through tapestries of tangled wilderness and stretches of simmering plains. They crossed a narrow river over white water rocks. They passed through a small village of tiny buildings with women in colorful garb and children practically naked. A few minutes later, they were in forest again. Jungle. Vegetation so dense it was like a wild wall, a collective beast that would swallow you whole. Leaving only a Garden of Bones.

"What is that contraption?" Hatcher said, gesturing to the rear with a twitch of his head. He figured asking where they were heading would be pointless.

"That is Chigi's invention." The man jutted a chin toward the driver, whose eyes caught Hatcher's in the rearview mirror. "His father drowned when his truck was swept away crossing a river."

Hatcher turned to look at it. Calling it an invention was a stretch, but it was definitely homemade. He could now tell it was a catapult. Crossbow design, compound, augmented with what looked like axle springs. He tried to imagine ways it could come in handy. Other than during a flashflood, or while teetering on a cliff, he couldn't think of any.

"What's Kongamoto?"

Whittling guy opened his mouth to speak, but then the brush thinned and Hatcher saw the first vehicle start to brake and finally stop. They were near the steep embankment of a sizable hill, visible beyond a layer of forest.

The guy in the passenger seat got out and opened Hatcher's door. He tugged Hatcher's arm, pulling him out and shoving him through a narrow gap in the growth toward the hill. Whittling guy followed, pointing his rifle, a contrite smile on his face.

The side of the hill was rocky, almost a cliff. Vines weaved down its face, fingers and hairs spreading out from ropey trunks to cling, finding purchase in cracks and protrusions. Hatcher expected to see a cave or tunnel entrance, something that would signal why he was being led this way, but the jagged wall of earth and stone looked solid.

He stopped a few feet from the hillside and turned to face the men behind him. Five rifles, all pointed at him, varying states of readiness. He scanned their faces. It seemed like a long way to drive just to have a firing squad.

Two of the men stepped aside to let Knit Cap walk through.

The man stopped a few feet away. His face was grim despite a grin that displayed a good amount of teeth. His rifle hung from a frayed sling around his neck and over one shoulder, the opposite arm holding it steady across his body. He raised the other hand and pointed toward the escarpment. When he spoke, Hatcher had no idea what he was saying.

Two impatient snaps of his fingers, and Whittling Guy hustled forward, followed by another in the group. Skinny, face slick with sweat. The other guy slung his AK over his shoulder and hurried to the wall, the two of them working together, pushing aside some of the vines, grabbing others. Whittling Guy yanked and ripped until he was able to separate the ones he wanted from some overgrowth. Hatcher saw that the vines he'd pulled free had been tied together to form a rope ladder, rungs fashioned out of cable and wire, scavenged material, secured by a variety of screws and nails and even twine, here and there.

More words Hatcher didn't understand. Apparently sensing this, Knit Cap paused. He pointed a finger at Hatcher, then raised it toward the top of the precipice.

"Up."

*They expect me to climb.* He looked at the one holding the vines. The guy gestured back and another joined him as he took hold of one of the makeshift rungs above his head, tugging it. Looked to Hatcher like someone about to start pulling himself up. Hatcher took a quiet breath, let it out halfway. There were two ways to play this. One was to keep going along. A climb meant parsing out their numbers, and that meant at the top he'd have an opportunity to improve his odds. The problem was, if they expected him to scale a steep wall, they were going to uncuff him. That meant however they handled it, however many they sent with him, before or after, they'd be more attentive, more cautious. Probably have rifles from the ground trained on him the whole way up. He'd lose most, if not all, of the element of surprise.

That left the other way.

Hatcher nodded, lowered his head. He had already positioned the escape key in his fingertips. He slipped it into the left cuff and gave it twist. The teeth disengaged and he felt the strand practically drop open, careful to keep his hand pressed against his back so the metal didn't make any noise.

Knit Cap reached into a lower front pocket of his Army-surplus blouse and retrieved a key. He held it up and Hatcher worried for a moment he was going to keep his distance and toss it toward him, make Hatcher kneel down and fumble to pick it up off the ground to open the cuffs himself, which would have been the smart thing to do, but instead he took a step forward. That was all it took.

Hatcher took a step himself, a much quicker one, slamming full frontal into the man, wedging the AK between them. He threw one arm around the man's neck, clenching him tight, hooking his chin from behind and giving it a hard yank. He swung his hand up to grab the stock of the AK between them at the same time, clamping a hold of it to keep it steady, and braced for the sting.

The rifle erupted in a rapid tattoo of shots, *bap-bap-bap-bap-bap-bap-bap*. The sound jackhammered his ears, more distinct and a bit louder than an AR. The barrel swept in a tight arc as Hatcher spun the man by his jaw, the burst of rounds taking out the four men in front of them before they could return fire, their boss being in the way causing all kinds of confusion. A stream of scalding brass bounced off his chest, a few singeing his neck and face.

The firing stopped. No surprise there. Full auto only lasts a few seconds

Other than the guy he had wrapped up, there were two left, the ones prepping to climb the vines. Hatcher gave another violent torque to the man's neck. The guy was trying to resist, most of his efforts directed at regaining his balance, but the laws of kinesiology were governing him for the moment. Where the head went, the body had to follow.

A complete circle, the man stumbling around Hatcher's radial until Hatcher stuck a leg out and threw himself backwards, dropping the man on top of him as he let go of the rifle and stabbed a hand at the man's sidearm. He jerked it free of its holster, aimed at the one of the remaining two who had gotten his weapon the highest, and squeezed the trigger.

The hammer pulled back on the double action, then punched forward with a click. *Son of a bitch.* Hatcher bit his lip in disgust, but didn't have time to curse his luck. Rather than relinquish his grip on his shield's neck, which would have taken more time anyway, he rotated the pistol sideways and slammed it against the man's head, digging the rear sight into his temple as hard and as deep as he could, and in one continuous motion shoved the handle forward. The man screamed as Hatcher racked a round into the chamber.

One of the gunmen let off three rounds, apparently writing his boss off for dead. Two of them hit the man, jolting his body, the other sizzling past Hatcher's skull. Hatcher fired one shot at center of mass that knocked the shooter back just as another round, this one from Whittling Guy, took a chunk of Knit Cap's head and splattered blood across Hatcher's face. Hatcher fired another shot, this one missing, but far worse than that was the sight of the slide open, stuck halfway back, the end of a protruding shell visible in the ejection port. A jam. Hatcher knew before he'd even glanced at it, knew without even thinking about it. Cheap loads, limp wrist. To clear it, he'd have to slap his palm against the bottom of the magazine and rack the slide again. But that would mean tossing off his shield. And there wasn't enough skull left on the body lying on top of him, now dead weight, for him to try another forced rack. He looked to be out of options. To make matters worse, the first gunman he'd shot wasn't even down, he was pressing his hand against a wound in his abdomen, intent on rejoining the fray, a bit hunched over, but looking directly at Hatcher and managing to point his rifle using his other arm. The second one, Whittling Guy, seeing the malfunction, stepped forward, focused on not wasting any more rounds, the set of his jaw dead serious, moving in for the kill shot.

He'd have to risk it. The chances of him not taking hits seemed about zero, but there really wasn't any choice.

Hatcher rocked to the side, ready to throw the body off him, hopefully have enough momentum to roll over it, pop onto a knee on the other side, tap-rack-fire. The closest rifleman snapped his AK higher, sighting it in, just as Hatcher flung the body over.

The eruption of rifle fire hammered his ears. His back seemed to be exposed for dozens of bursts. He braced himself for the burn, tensing in anticipation, figuring at least the pain would let him know he was alive.

He bounced up, one knee down, just as planned. He was already slapping his hand against the bottom of the pistol, jacking the slide back, thrusting the barrel out.

No one was there. No one standing.

Whittling Guy was on his back, body arched and slowly sagging to ground as his neck went limp. The other rifleman was facedown, several wounds in the top of skull leaking thick streams of blood.

A voice projected from the jungle a few yards away.

"Hold fire!"

Hatcher remained still for a moment, then lowered his weapon. Woodley emerged, gesturing above his head. Others appeared from different points, rifles trained on the bodies, barrels snapping from one to another to another. No one appeared to be taking any chances. Only Woodley seemed confident the threat had been neutralized.

Half of Woodley's face tightened into a smirk. "Didn't really think we were going to leave you in the hands of a bunch of guerrillas, did you?"

Hatcher narrowed his eyes at the man before bouncing glances at the others. They were too engrossed in the task at hand, checking the bodies, alert for undetected hostiles, to make eye contact. He let himself exhale fully for what felt like the first time in minutes. His body suddenly felt heavy, his limbs weighted down. He stared at the ground and gathered enough strength to push to his feet.

"Why?" Hatcher said, running his gaze over the bodies.

"I know you've got lots of questions. First, let Ivy take a look at you, make sure you're not carrying any unwanted metal or losing any tomato juice anywhere."

"*Why,*" he repeated, less a question this time than a command.

"You're angry. I get it. I would be, too. But you know how it works. Orders."

"Bullshit. That doesn't answer the question, and it sure as hell doesn't let you off the hook."

"Whoa, now. I'm the guy who just saved your ass, remember? Yes, it was a shitty thing to do. The world's a shitty place."

"I'm only going to ask one more time. Why?"

"I can only tell you what I know, which is what they told me. The PMU that had her, that was their price. They asked for you – demanded you – by name. A swap."

Hatcher straightened up. "They asked for me, by name."

"That's what I was told. My orders were to accomplish the exchange, clear the hostage, then track and retrieve you." Woodley took his eyes off Hatcher, snapped his fingers. "Ivy, check him out, will you?"

Ivy slung his rifle behind his back and approached Hatcher, removing a pack from his belt.

Hatcher barely glanced at the man, keeping his eyes on Woodley. "You have no fucking idea what you've done."

"Hey, it's not like I was the one who came up with the plan, or even had a vote. And, in case you're wondering, the others didn't know. Ivy here didn't know. I briefed them once we were clear."

Hatcher flinched as Ivy reached toward his face with a swab.

"There's a lot of blood." The man's expression was apologetic. His lips were pulled tight in a flat smile that was more of a sympathetic frown. "Just let me clean it off and make sure none of it's yours."

The swab felt cool, even as it stung. The smell of alcohol scraped his nostrils. It perked him up a bit. A slant of sunlight stabbed through a net of leaves and fronds, flashing in his eyes. It was almost dusk.

Almost dusk meant almost dark.

There was too much information to process and not enough information to process it with.

"That looks better. Lemme give you a quick exam and we can get out of here."

Hatcher locked his eyes on Ivy's, then fixed his attention back on Woodley. One piece clunked into place.

"That's not the plan, though, is it?"

Woodley said nothing.

Ivy paused. "What do you mean?"

"Tell him the truth, Woodley. Tell them all what we're really here for. Because I'd like to hear it myself."

"Hold on, now. I haven't lied. I told them after we rescued you, Phase One of the mission would be complete. That's the truth."

"But you didn't tell them extraction wasn't until Phase Three, did you?"

"No," Ivy said. "He didn't."

"He sure as hell didn't," Garza said. "Next thing up was supposed to be evacuation."

"Guys, I'm just following instructions, same as you."

"That's a load of horseshit and you know it. You may be an ass, but you're not a dumb one. If the mission was to rescue a captive, trading me, you could have staged an assault right after the exchange. You could have attacked the camp. You could have done it a dozen different ways that would make a hell of a lot more sense than this. And you would have told them that, so Keegan or whoever was calling the shots had to give you more."

Woodley tilted his head to the side and rolled his eyes. But his embarrassed smirk gave it away.

Another piece clicked into place. "You put a tracker on me. Where? My boot?"

"Yes." Woodley nodded, letting out a weary sigh. "Good call. In the heel."

"And you couldn't let me in on it because they knew I'd refuse, because the plan was stupid and risky and unnecessary. And because I would know if they asked for me by name, there were factors in play that make this whole operation a very, very bad idea. And you couldn't tell the others because they would also point out there was no need to delay the rescue and would have to be let in on the real mission."

Ivy turned his head back and forth between the two men a few times. "What's the real mission?"

"They needed the people who took me to lead them to something," Hatcher said. "Isn't that right?"

"Well, golly gee fucking willickers, Hatcher..." Woodley tossed a hand up and let it drop, slapping his thigh. "You might as well give the whole briefing, if you know so much."

"No, that's about all I got. I have no idea what they were wanting these guys to lead them to. But I can tell you that whatever it is, we don't want to be anywhere near it."

Garza stepped closer. "It was bad enough we find out about Hatcher after the fact, Woodley. You didn't tell us about any other mission, you son of a bitch."

"Yeah," Zorn said. He was the biggest of the group, with pale skin and a corn-fed look that at the moment was turning a shade of red beneath his crew cut. "Why don't you fill us in before you're grabbing your ankles and yelling BOHICA?"

"Everybody just calm the fuck down, okay? Jesus. Now that we've liberated our asset, the next phase is supposed to be the easy part. All we have to do is kill some animal. A big dumb thing the locals are afraid of."

Hatcher took a breath. "Animal. What kind of animal?"

"Natives call it Kongamoto. Some sort of giant bird. They're very superstitious about it, scares them to death. They practically worship it, like some demon god or something. If things are still going according to plan – and there is no reason to think they aren't – they've led us to where it nests. All we do now is perforate it with a few hundred rounds and we can get the hell out of Dodge."

"You've got to be kidding me."

"Scout's honor. Look, as much as it pisses you off to hear it, I really am just following orders. We're supposed to kill the bird and get our asses out."

"Why?"

"What do you mean?"

"I mean, *why*? For fuck's sake, Woodley, the 'why' is always what matters. So, why the hell does the US government, or even just some rogue bureaucrat, want us to kill this thing?"

"What can I say? It's all political. You know, do a favor for this leader, have a chit to call in later... Who knows? I'm just a worker bee, here."

"Political? That's—" A piercing screech ripped through the air before Hatcher could finish. The trees shuddered silently as every other sound seemed to disappear. The echo throbbed several times before fading away.

The ensuing silence was finally broken by Garza. "What in the name of Jesus tap-dancing Christ was that?"

"I'm going to go out on a limb and say it was Kongamoto, whatever the hell that is." Hatcher turned to Woodley. "We need to get these men outta here. Right now, like this damn minute."

"Let's just get a grip, okay? Whatever it is, I doubt it's fucking bullet-proof. I mean, show some sack, all of you. We've got enough firepower to cause an extinction event. What the hell do we have to be afraid of?"

"What did they tell you?"

"About this thing? It's supposed to fly. Maybe like a pterodactyl or something similar. Possibly related to a bat. But it should be an easy target. It's big. Should be hard to miss."

"How big?"

"They weren't sure. Size of a small plane, they guessed."

"A plane?" Garza threw his head back and did a half-pirouette. "You're talking about a dinosaur, for Christ sake!"

"They assured me it's just an animal," Woodley said, snapping the words. "All we have to do is put some rounds in it. What the hell, people? Going up against armed militia, you don't bat an eye, but shooting some animal that can't fire back makes you piss your pants?"

Hatcher looked through the trees, eyed the dappled golden glow starting to recede. "Woodley, I'm not going to say it again. We need to get everyone out of here. Now."

"In case you hadn't guessed by now, you aren't actually in command here, Hatcher. I know you're pissed, but everything really is going according to plan. Except that, maybe, you forced our hand a bit earlier than I'd have liked."

Hatcher struggled to control his anger, most of it at himself. Of course, he hadn't actually been in command. But they needed him to think he was, so that he wouldn't have the luxury of sitting back and analyzing Woodley for tells, so that he'd be too wrapped up in the feeling of responsibility for the team to look for the indicators he'd otherwise so easily have spotted.

"*Now*, Woodley. It's getting dark. I don't have time to argue with you about it."

"Darkness is what we're supposed to be counting on. The thing won't show itself in full daylight. We have state-of-the-art NVDs and FLIR. It should be like shooting ducks at a carnival."

"Listen to me. You don't understand *dick* about what's going on. If they wanted me, and specifically me, this isn't just some animal we're dealing with. This has nothing to do with being gutless. This is about being an idiot. A soon-to-be dead idiot, at that, if you don't shake the shit out of your head and start listening."

Woodley held Hatcher's gaze for a long moment. There was a cloud of doubt in those eyes. Hatcher could see the man thinking, weighing his options, working through how it would play out. Wondering if maybe he'd misread the situation.

He started to speak, but before a complete word escaped his mouth, another screech erupted.

This one was much closer. It stabbed Hatcher's ears, caused him to flinch. He looked up just in time to see a creature diving straight down, ballistic, traveling at something close to terminal velocity.

Garza raised his head just as the thing smashed into him, the sound of bones snapping and crunching clearly audible even in Hatcher's ringing ears. The man's body compressed into a misshapen sack, numerous splintered pieces held together by skin and cloth.

The thing screeched again, a full-throated scream. It was a shimmering shade of black, almost glossy. It stood over Garza's mangled body, stomping a taloned foot onto his chest and spreading its wings. The first thing that struck Hatcher was its size. Enormous, at least eight-feet tall, a wingspan that had to be more than twice that. It had an elongated head, something almost bat-like, but round and protruding downward, shaped like a mule's. Its wings were leathery and it had four clawed fingers curving out at the apex of each. It looked straight at Hatcher, eyes ablaze with a crimson glow.

Zorn had been the closest. The creature's dive had caught him by surprise and he dove to the side, rolling a few times to gain distance, and was now popping off rounds. Ivy was doing the same, having dropped his first-aid kit and swung his weapon off his shoulder.

The thing hissed and raised its wing, using the upper part as a shield, then seemed to collapse into itself, forming a tight ball over Garza's body. Hatcher could almost feel it coming, sense the tension coiling, ready to explode.

"Get down!"

Hatcher dove at Ivy, tackling him just as the creature spun out of its curl, the thing spiraling so fast it was barely more than a blur. Garza's skull rocketed past, smashing Woodley in the shoulder and knocking him to the ground.

The creature dropped back onto its feet, grabbed what remained of Garza's corpse in its talons, and leaped into the air. Hatcher felt two powerful flaps of its wings, the gusts forcing him to blink, and when he looked it had cleared the trees and soared into open sky.

Hatcher pulled himself off of Ivy. The man sat up, peered up into the gloaming and dusted himself off.

"Ho. Lee. Shit."

Pushing himself to his feet, Hatcher looked back at Woodley. The man was holding his shoulder, rolling his arm forward and back. He shook his head and waved Hatcher off. Garza's head lay wedged against a clump of grass a few feet away, mouth open, eyes dead slits.

"Little help!"

Zorn was cradling his abdomen. Hatcher glanced at Ivy, who nodded and picked up his first aid kit. He was a few steps behind when Hatcher reached the man.

"Wouldn't you know it," Zorn said, coughing. He pulled his arm away from his stomach. "Boned by a teammate."

Ivy sucked in a loud breath through his teeth. Hatcher felt himself wince.

Three bones, what looked like ribs, protruded from Zorn's midsection. Flesh and muscle and connective tissue still hung in clumps from each. They seemed joined at a piece of breast bone.

"Can you remove them?"

"Not without a risk of him bleeding out."

Zorn coughed again. "Right here, guys."

Ivy turned to set down the first-aid kit and retrieve dressing material from it. Under his breath he said, "He needs an OR, Hatcher."

Hatcher gave a curt nod. "Want to prove what a tough son of a bitch you are, soldier?"

"Not especially," Zorn said, his voice rough, rasping. "Is there a pussy option?"

"We need to get you out of here. Not to mention, us. Think you can move without slicing any vital organs?"

"Maybe. If you got some good junk for me to shoot up. Hurts like a bitch, man."

Hatcher glanced at Ivy. "What about it?"

"I might be able to dose him enough to help without knocking him out."

Hatcher tipped his head back, searching the sky. Then he cut his gaze to Woodley.

"How far's the extraction point?"

"Thirty clicks or so west. But not for another twelve hours."

"Failsafe?"

"No. Complete disavowal, remember? No radio contact, no homing. We show up. Or not. Failing that, same as you were told. The embassy."

"Yeah, in Zambia. How far is that? Fifty miles? A hundred?"

"What do you want me to say? I'm in the same boat you are. Our only known contact was Mbuyi. And he took off to drive the hostage across the border. We just have to make it through the night."

"Yeah, but in order to do that, we have to get as far away from here as possible. So, we need to get to the vehicles and not waste any more time arguing about it."

"Look, Hatcher, I know you're pissed. I don't blame you. Really, I don't. But don't you think our best bet is to do what we came here to do and kill that thing?"

"You mean, what *you* came here to do. I came here to rescue a hostage, remember?"

"Still, it caught us by surprise, that's all. We have RPGs in the floor of the Hummer, for crying out loud. If we just prepared —"

"The answer is no. We have one KIA – our sniper, at that – and another down in need of urgent medical attention. And I have no doubt whatever it was could have taken us all out right then if it had really wanted to."

Woodley gave him a skeptical look, brows cinched. "Then why didn't it?"

Hatcher didn't respond. He looked down at Zorn, who gave him a weak thumbs up as Ivy administered a syringe, slowly depressing the plunger.

"What do we have for transportation? Same as before?"

"Yes. Plus what they brought you in."

The words seemed to echo in Hatcher's head for a moment. Something shifted in his head, revealing a new question.

"You never answered my question. Why?"

Woodley shook his head, frowning. "I told you. The brass figured they'd take you to where it nests or hangs out or whatever."

"No, I mean, why do they want us to kill this thing? Please don't expect me to believe they care about the plight of some third-world poverty hole, because they don't."

"What can I say?" Woodley said, shrugging. "Above my pay grade."

"You're lying. I can see it in the direction your eyes moved before you answered, in the timing of the shrug as you spoke, in the way your lids hooded as the words passed your lips, and in the way you curled those same lips back over your teeth, as if to bite them closed and stop more lies from coming out."

352

Woodley shook his head, grunting an exasperated puff of air as he tossed his arms up.

"And despite being a fucking idiot, you're not stupid. You would have asked these same questions, demanded answers. And you did. So quit holding back and tell me everything."

The man sucked in a deep breath, held it as he searched the ground, then let it out, his body deflating some.

"Cliché as it sounds, it's classified."

"Is it vital enough to national security that you're willing to endure broken arms and missing teeth? Because I wouldn't bank on me being above all that if I were you."

Ivy stood, took a step closer. "Answer the damn question, Woodley."

Seconds passed as the man's gaze volleyed back and forth, Hatcher to Ivy to Hatcher. His eyes lingered on Hatcher for a long moment, then he lowered them, thinking.

"Helium," he said.

Zorn let out a laugh, a rummy, drug-induced chuckle.

"What does that even mean?" Hatcher said.

"Apparently, the world only has a finite supply. Who fucking knew, right? All kinds of high-tech shit uses tons of the stuff. But it doesn't exist everywhere, and supplies have been starting to run low, low enough some places have banned party balloons and that kind of crap. Then they recently found a huge cache of it in Tanzania, enough to supply everyone for a few more years. But not forever. The shortage got a lot of people spooked."

"Keep going."

"Seems there's another valley like it, same rock formations and satellite indicators or whatever it is, and they suspect this field is even bigger. Maybe two or three times as big. Enough of the stuff to last twenty years. Only when they've tried to drill core samples..."

Hatcher glanced around the jungle, then tilted his head to search the sky. "Their engineers have disappeared."

"Something like that."

"That's just great."

353

"Hey, it wasn't my goddamn idea. The way they explained it, this was important stuff. Medical devices, lab equipment, all kinds of crap that requires it to function. The world needs an ample supply. Without one, people all over the globe will be fucked."

"By 'they', you mean, Keegan. And you believed him. *Still* believe him."

"Why wouldn't I?"

"How about because if this were actually about saving the world, you think he'd send a team of five contractors? Guys he had to blackmail? For Christ's sake, wake the hell up. Did he ever show you credentials? I never saw any. Nothing with his name on it. Nothing with anyone's name on it. Just clandestine meetings in government basements. Off the books. No paper trail. Jesus, Woodley, this is the same asshole who made up some BS story about the vice-president's daughter to explain all the secrecy, why it all had to be off the books, untraceable, when you have to know by now it was just some poor aid worker in the wrong place at the wrong time. Just some good woman trying to help albinos, or whatever. But who do you think orchestrated that? Hell, who do you think arranged for her to be taken in the first place? This was planned from the beginning, right down to the tiniest detail. It had to look real. Real people, real news stories."

"I don't understand..." Woodley blinked. "You're saying there's no helium?"

"No, I'm sure there is. I'm sure there are a gazillion metric shit-tons of the stuff, or however they measure it, just like he said. And I'm also sure the rights to it are worth a few metric shit-tons of money."

"Money? Wait, you're telling me..."

"Yes. That guy cut a deal. Whoever the hell he is. A big, fat gild-your-toilet deal that will make him millions. Maybe hundreds of millions. No wonder he told me he was retiring, that this was his last gig. Jesus."

"But, he must have thought we could do it, then, right?"

"No. He probably thought all of you would die." *All except me*, Hatcher thought. *Me, he needed to keep alive.* He didn't know how he knew, just that he did. "Open your eyes, Woodley. Why the hell do you think they asked for *me... by name*?"

"He said there was a vendetta of some sort. Didn't get into the details. All I was told was, they'd take you somewhere, and we were supposed to retrieve you and terminate the target."

"There's a vendetta, all right. But not with some guerrilla clan." Hatcher turned to look at Zorn. "Think he can move now?"

Ivy hitched a shoulder. "I guess we're gonna find out."

The two of them helped Zorn to his feet. His eyes were glazed, lids half closed. He had a dreamy smile on his face, even as he winced a few times.

"Keep your eyes on the sky," Hatcher said, looking at Woodley. "You have those NVDs?"

Woodley nodded, reaching into a pack.

"You see it, let us know. If it sees *us*, open fire on it. Three round bursts. How're you set on ammo?"

He detached the curved magazine from his rifle and replaced it. "Four mags. A couple dozen more in the Hummer."

Zorn had a few magazines of the same caliber, so did Ivy. But it didn't matter. If they needed more cover than that to make it to the vehicles, they never were going to reach them, anyway.

"It'll have to do. Let's move." Hatcher picked up Zorn's rifle and replaced the magazine before shouldering it. He looked through the trees. Little diamond-shaped sparkles between the leaves. "The sun will be completely gone in a few minutes."

He let Ivy point the way, each of them with one of Zorn's arms around their necks and over their shoulders. Zorn, for his part, helped more than Hatcher expected, so it wasn't quite dead weight. He alternated between laughing and grunting. Like he could feel the pain, but would have a hard time caring less.

"How is it looking back there, Woodley?"

"Nothing, and lots of it."

The jungle was thick. The path they were following was recently slashed, broken stems of rubbery plants dangled in places on each side, partially sliced, other parts lay flat from being pressed with boots, various leafy shapes of deep green and purplish red padded the ground underfoot. An occasional caw from what Hatcher supposed was a bird, the call of what may have been a monkey. The trill of insects rose and fell in waves.

To Hatcher's left, those jeweled twinkles of light flashed and then disappeared. Hatcher looked up. Darkness was creeping across the twilight like a weeping wound.

Hatcher tapped Ivy and stopped. "Now might be a good time to break out those NVDs."

Ivy nodded. Hatcher took Zorn's weight and pivoted to look at Woodley, who was a few yards behind. Woodley's rifle dropped from its sling as he got the message and fit the goggles over his head. He made some adjustments along the sides, staring first at the ground, then the sky, then leveling his gaze at Hatcher.

Something wasn't right.

"*Listen*," Ivy said, pausing, goggles near his face, ready to be slipped over his head gear. "You hear that?"

Woodley shrugged his rifle higher and leaned his head back, scanning the heavens. "I don't hear anything. Don't see anything, either."

"That's what he means," Hatcher said. "Everything's gone quiet."

Darkness seemed to fall like a blanket. The surrounding jungle became a jumble of strange shadows with shapes suddenly both closer and farther than before. Woodley was still visible, but hard to see. It was gray beyond him, a dark background populated by deep shadows. Something even darker moved. Fast.

"Look out!"

Woodley started to turn, but there was no time to act. Hatcher felt a buffet of air against his face as he raised his weapon, could make out the ink-black shape as it swooped through. The slashing sound of movement whipping through the air, a wet, popping crunch. Something loose bounced off Hatcher's M4 a split second before a large curve of hair and skin and bone slapped his abdomen. In the dying light, he could make out a nose and eyeless lid as the piece of skull slid like a broken saucer off his boot. By the time he raised his eyes, he couldn't make out anything else but shades of ebony beneath a slate sky.

Ivy scrambled to take aim. The air swirled and something cut and fanned just feet above them.

"Jesus, Mary and Joseph," Ivy said. "It's like, it's like... Hatcher! You gotta see this thing! Oh my *God!*"

Hatcher wasn't sure what the man could be seeing that they hadn't already got an eyeful of, but he didn't have time to ponder it. He could make out Woodley's NVDs on the ground in front of him from the glow and picked them up. A dull, greenish light shone in the view side of the lens. He pulled them over his head, groping the sides with his fingers and fiddling with the sliding controls until the area around him seemed in focus. These were high quality. Not the best he'd ever tried, but good enough.

He panned the sky, then swept his head around. Nothing.

"Gone," Ivy said. "It just pointed itself up and shot like a missile! Never seen anything like it. I mean, damn."

Hatcher looked at Woodley's body. He lowered his head to see the piece of Woodley's face on the ground.

"How far to the vehicles from here?"

"Click, click and a half. We were just behind your convoy. This should take us right to them, more or less."

"Not us. I'm going to draw it away," Hatcher said, heading to where Woodley lay.

"What? No. We should stick together. I can't handle him myself."

Zorn laughed, then gagged for a few seconds. "Too much man for you," he mumbled.

"You can if you're not being attacked. Look, I think it's me it wants. I also think it's going to pick everyone else off one at a time until it gets me. Unless I can draw it away and it thinks I'm alone."

"How do you know that?"

"I don't. Don't ask me to explain. There's no time, and I really don't have much of an explanation to offer. I want you take him back to where you found me. Just stay there. Hunker down for about an hour. And do what you can to keep him alive in the process. If I'm the only one headed for the vehicles, it may think I'm trying to escape and come after me."

"What if it doesn't follow you?"

Hatcher inhaled deeply, surveyed the sky for a moment. "If I'm wrong, we're probably all dead anyway. That thing can pick us off whenever it wants. But I'm pretty sure I'm the one it's really after."

"And if you're right? What are you supposed to do if it does come after you? If you don't make it to the Hummer?"

"What I was brought here to do, whatever that is. Don't try to understand, just go."

Ivy shook his head, then nodded. He hooked Zorn's arm over his neck and started to move back the way they'd come, sidestepping past Woodley's corpse. Hatcher watched for a moment, then checked Woodley's pocket's for magazines. He rolled the body over and could see Woodley's face in the greenish monochrome, part of it missing, the face of someone unmasked while straining an organ in the catacombs of an opera house.

A quick calculation of rounds told him he had a hundred and twenty. But part of him was certain for any of them to do any good, he'd have to be up close, practically shoving the barrel in the thing's mouth. It had already absorbed a couple of dozen hits, at least. Its leathery hide must have been as thick as an elephant's. There wasn't much doubt its wings were strong enough to handle high velocity rounds. It left him wondering if there was anything they *couldn't* handle.

He stared down the makeshift trail until Ivy and Zorn were out of sight.

"All right," he said, his voice loud but not overly so. Anything louder than necessary would come across as baiting. At least, that was what his gut told him. "Here's your chance."

He let out a breath and broke into a run. The NVDs kept the terrain visible, and he was able to move at a double-time pace.

He kept his rifle up, stopping every few dozen yards to sweep the sky to his rear with the barrel, controlling his breathing, listening, watching, watching, listening.

Minutes passed. He had to have traveled over a kilometer. Run stop sweep, run stop sweep. Nothing but eerie glowing jungle with a pitch background to all sides. No choice but to keep moving.

A break in the foliage seemed to jump in front of him. Dirt road. Nothing visible in either direction. He headed to the right, more of a sprint now. Nothing. He was about to turn around when something came into view, a bright monochromatic outline around a curve.

The back of a truck. He recognized it as he drew closer. The one he'd arrived in, with the grappling hook launcher in the rear. He should have turned left. He'd practically come full circle.

He stopped and scanned the sky, swept the dense cluster of forest to each side. His thoughts turned to Ivy, Zorn. For all he knew, they were already dead, or in the process of being dismembered. There was no way to be sure.

But he didn't believe it. He had to be the target.

He jumped in the truck, placing the rifle across his lap. Keys were in the ignition. He closed his eyes and breathed a grateful sigh.

*What if you're wrong?*

No. He shook the thought from his head. He'd been through too much, seen too much, not to know. He was the one it wanted. It wouldn't just let him go.

*But what if you're wrong?*

The truck started on the third try. He pulled off his NVDs and turned on the headlights. He shifted into reverse, then drive, then reverse, using all of a seven-point turn to get it aimed in the opposite direction. He maneuvered past the other vehicles, then gunned the engine and bounced down the dirt road.

*What if you're wrong?*

He made it a couple of hundred yards before the headlights reflected off more vehicles. The team's, he realized. A Hummer and a safari truck. They were pulled slightly to the left, probably to hug the tree line. He could tell they had stopped here to follow him on foot, laying back far enough not to be noticed.

Hatcher slowed the truck, squeezed it by the two vehicles. The road was narrower at this spot. Branches drummed and scraped on the passenger side, a shriek of metal on metal erupted on the right as it side swiped the Hummer.

He was just past the second vehicle and starting to accelerate when something slammed into the roof of the truck, caving it halfway in. The truck swerved. He was barely able to correct it before there was a second hit, this one smashing the windshield and causing him to veer off into the bush. One wheel of the truck jumped a felled trunk and popped it onto its side.

Seconds passed. He braced himself for another impact. Nothing.

*Goggles, weapon.*

He turned off the headlights, then climbed out through the driver's side window, jumping to the ground. He adjusted his NVDs, tilted and swiveled his head in every direction.

There it was. Circling overhead. It started to form a tighter and tighter gyre, centered on Hatcher, spiraling downward.

*Holy shit.*

Through the night vision, he could see what Ivy was talking about. The creature didn't look like some giant bat anymore, not exactly. It seemed to have the same form at its core, but its skull was long and hooked, with enormous horns curving into sharp points. Surrounding its body was a burst of snake-like appendages, tentacling outwards and writhing like antennae.

*We even have RPGs in floor of the Hummer.*

Hatcher launched himself into a low sprint. He looked up as his fingers hooked the latch on the Hummer's door to see the creature in a dive bomb, wings swept back, rocketing toward him. Before he could get the door open, it flared, slamming its feet into the vehicle, talons digging into the roof. Hatcher felt the latch rip from his hand as the Hummer jumped into the air. With two slaps of its wings the thing lifted the entire carriage off the ground, a feat Hatcher could barely believe he was witnessing. Another flap, then another, until the wheels were fifteen feet over Hatcher's head.

Hatcher snapped the M4 up, let out three bursts, followed by three more. Aiming was difficult, but he tried, picking areas to target rather than spots. The creature let go and Hatcher flung himself out of the way as the vehicle slammed onto the patch of road, part of it crunching the back of the safari truck, causing the front wheels to pop up and jounce back down.

The thing soared higher, then started to spiral into a dive.

*The wings. It didn't like getting hit in the wings.*

In the UV glow of NVDs, Hatcher could see a difference between the upper wings, which seemed to be stiff, flattened arms with joints, and the lower parts, which were flexible, like leather sails. He pictured the way it had curled itself into a ball, using its arms as shields. It wasn't just protecting its body, it was protecting the soft parts of its wings.

He looked over to the pickup truck, still laying on its side. *Maybe.*

The thing was swooping toward him again. He fired two more bursts, held his ground until it seemed he could reach out and grab it, then dropped to his back and fired two more. It shot past him and rounded up, banking into a tight turn. Hatcher flipped onto his feet and bolted for the truck, making a show of ditching his rifle.

*This better work.*

He dove into the bed, felt the creature's talons rake his back, claws ripping through his shirt and gashing his flesh but unable to grasp. Those feet punched against the cab of the truck, talons smashing the rear glass and puncturing the roof as it clamped down.

Bursts of wind on his back. He felt the truck shift, sensed it break loose from its traction on the ground. The rear of the bed started to hang.

He slid over to the grappling catapult, spinning it around and wedging himself between it and the tailgate. The truck swung beneath him and he felt gravity go negative for an instant, sensed everything below falling away, then the truck swung back and his own weight pressed him down, trying to pin him.

Struggling against the schizophrenic g-forces, he leveled the sight of the catapult at the creature. The thing's wings would not stay in one place, whipping back and forth, presenting a broad side for just a flash, then disappearing. There would be no perfect shot; at best, it was a Hail Mary. He pulled back the heavy spring on the charge bolt, and tugged the enormous trigger.

The mechanism snapped and the umbrella of hooks shot like a spear. Cable spun out behind it, the reel whirring. The tip tore through the lower part of the left wing, barely.

Barely was good enough.

The creature let out a high-pitched shriek. The sound cut through the ringing in Hatcher's ears, stabbed at his brain. A second later, the thing dropped the truck. Hatcher tried to brace himself, his body light and swimming. He tucked his head, wrapping it with his arms, and forced all the breath out of his lungs. The truck crashed into the ground.

His next conscious thought was that he was still alive. He could tell by the competing pain, his hip screaming to be heard over the shouting of his ribs, his wrist hollering even louder when he went to move.

He was on the ground. Breathing was a challenge, as every expansion of his ribcage sent shockwaves through his torso. He managed to sit up. The night-vision goggles were askew on his head and he fought through the pain in his wrist to adjust them back over his eyes. The scene tumbled back into perspective when he saw the truck on exploded tires a few feet away. Through the buzzing in his ears he became aware of the whirring of the reel, the cable still letting out.

Then there was a clank, the groan of metal, followed by a vibrating *twang*, and the truck started to move. Across the ground in fits and starts at first, surging up and crunching down, until soon it wasn't touching the road anymore, just swinging forward, rising into the night. Dipping, jerking up, dipping, jerking up, penduluming forward, then back.

There wasn't much time to decide. There were only two choices; go back for Ivy and Zorn, or go after the creature. That thing was too smart, too strong, not to figure out a way to free itself. And if it managed to do that before they could all get to safety, it wouldn't end well, he was certain of it. There was too much night left.

He scrambled to retrieve the M4. No choice. He had to go after the thing, find a way to kill it. He hurried back to the safari truck, checked the ignition, the visor, the seat, found the keys hanging from the rear-view mirror on a lanyard.

The vehicle started right away, sputtering until he revved it. The transmission clunked into drive and the truck lurched forward and was moving again, doffing the NVDs and using the headlights, and tried to keep the truck from fishtailing as he sped down the road at a far higher speed than he knew was wise.

Over a mile had passed before the truck came into view. Still following the road, still swinging in spasms. Never getting higher than fifteen or twenty feet. He closed the distance, studying the tree shadows of the jungle surrounding him.

*It can't clear the treeline. Or it's scared to try. It wants an open path.*

Hatcher gunned the engine. It whined and he saw the tachometer was practically redlined, but he only needed it to last a few more minutes. Seconds, if he caught a break.

There it was. Up ahead, a curve in the road. He held the accelerator down until the hood of the truck was almost touching the dangling end of the pickup. The front end of the pickup swayed over the hood then down over the road. Hatcher bumped it a few times as he tried to keep pace.

A blink before the turn in the curve Hatcher stomped on the gas, pressing the pedal to the floor as hard as he could. The truck slammed into the pickup. The safari railing smashed through the windshield, stabbing into the upholstery, hooking itself over the dashboard and steering column. Hatcher held the wheel straight, the pain in his wrist howling curses that burned their way up his arm. He felt the front wheels lift even as he held the accelerator down until he threw himself out the door the moment before the truck impacted a tree.

He separated his shoulder on impact and tumbled almost twenty feet over the rocky dirt road. He thought he could hear the cracking of several ribs, but whether he actually did or not didn't matter, as he knew several were fractured whether he heard them crack or not. He had a hard time finding a part of his body that wasn't on fire in some way.

No time for a survey of injuries. He struggled to his feet, favoring his left arm. A few of the lights from the safari truck were still on, visible a few yards into the jungle. He took a step and noticed a glint on the ground. The M4. He hefted it, gingerly minimizing the use of his left arm, felt its balance, reseated the magazine and racked another round into the chamber, just to be sure.

The walk to the truck was excruciating, each step a mix of sizzles and stabs. When he reached it, he saw it was still entangled with the pickup, both of them enmeshed in the foliage. He managed to reach through a broken window and retrieve the goggles. Only one lens still worked. It was cracked, but he was able to see through it after a few adjustments.

He followed the cable from the pickup, fighting his way through the webbed reach of plants and limbs. A couple of hundred feet later, he saw the creature. It was impaled in several spots. It had taken a long, thick bone through the stomach on its way down, and one wing was completely broken. Several other long shards of skeleton – ribs, from the look of them – had pierced it in various places. Hatcher could picture the fall, an accelerated arc swinging it down like a huge sledge hammer, pounding it through the growth. Down into a Garden of Bones.

Through the functioning NVD lens, Hatcher could see the parts of it up close, parts invisible to the naked eye. Tentacled appendages wriggling; a skull overlay that looked like a cadaverous vulture; a serpentine tail.

To his surprise, it moved, not without difficulty, but enough to cause Hatcher to take a step back. The thing looked at him with eyes that burned a strange shade in the monochrome. It opened its beak-like jaws and made a grating, squawking roar, like the death rattle of a thousand souls. Maybe more.

Hatcher leveled the M4 and squeezed the trigger.

No three-round bursts this time. He unloaded the magazine in barely a second, retrieved another, then unloaded that. He seated his final magazine and moved closer. The thing was no longer trying to move, but a series of hisses and snarls were still coming out of it. He positioned himself as close as he could, held his ground as a tentacle rose like it was going to strike, and shoved the barrel into the thing's mouth.

The sound it made drowned out the shots. Hatcher's head felt like it was collapsing in on itself. He managed to look through the NVD as he dropped to his knees, saw a glowing phantasm tear itself from the body and rear back, a shape of flame surrounding a creature even larger than the one it had occupied, an enormous crocodilian skull sandwiched between twin spirals of horns. Just as the thing seemed to be reaching for Hatcher, ready to consume him in some horrific embrace, it flashed out of existence, leaving swirls of tiny wisps flickering like embers before they, too, vanished completely.

He lay on the ground for the better part of an hour, drifting in and out of consciousness, not fighting it either way, finally pushing himself to his feet in response to some mental clock going off like an alarm. He winced at the aches and the burns and the stiffness setting in and forced himself to start walking. He followed the dirt road back toward where the encounter had started, walking for around fifteen minutes, every other step forcing him to bite his lip, suck in a shallow breath.

Headlights. One was a high beam, mismatched. He was too exhausted to worry about whose they were. He stood in the middle of the road, let the beams wash over him, barely able to raise an arm to shield his eyes.

The vehicle slowed to a stop, audibly shifted into park. A door opened.

"Hatcher?" Ivy's voice came from behind the lights. Then his figure cut a shadow. Before Hatcher realized he was that close, he felt a firm but gentle hand take hold of his arm. "Jesus, you look like... what the hell happened?"

The feel of support abruptly caused his legs to give. Ivy helped him to the jeep. He vaguely recognized it as having been part of the caravan parked along the road.

With Ivy's help, he eased himself into the passenger seat. Zorn was in the back, presumably asleep. Hatcher could make out ragged breathing.

"You're still kicking, at least," Ivy said, settling behind the wheel. "Does that mean that thing isn't going to be a problem?"

"Not for us," Hatcher said. He tried to adjust himself to find an elusive position of relative comfort. Wasn't going to happen. "Not tonight."

"I can't wait to hear all about it."

Hatcher wondered how much he could explain, how much he even understood himself. Whether he even dare try to tell Ivy about the Carnates, about demons, about his tainted soul, his battles with the ruling elite of Hell and the civil war that seemed to be raging below. Or whether any of it would make sense if he did. Whether he was even able to understand himself why he was growing increasingly certain this whole thing was part of an even more elaborate plan, a plan within a plan, designed to occupy him, to get him as far away from the States as possible. A giant distraction from something he had no conception of, for reasons he couldn't begin to imagine.

"In the meantime," Ivy continued, "I need to get us to the LZ. Extraction is supposed to be at dawn."

"Don't bother. There won't be any."

"You serious?"

Hatcher leaned back in the seat, closed his eyes. "As a heart attack. The only thing likely to be waiting for us at the extraction point is another group of paramilitary types, all promised a bounty for each kill."

"So, what, then? Embassy?"

"Not if we can avoid it." Hatcher opened his eyes, looked around the interior, grimacing with each twist. "There a radio in this thing?"

"Not that I've seen."

"Well, then, that's our mission, for the moment. Just drive. I think there was a radio in one of the trucks. Two clicks or so ahead."

Ivy shifted into drive, eased the jeep forward. "Who you gonna radio?"

Hatcher felt the breeze flow over his cheeks and scalp. It stung a bit, and he realized what a mess his face must be, but it was the closest thing to a pleasurable sensation he'd had in a while.

"I know a gal," he said, inhaling as deeply as his ribs would allow. "Who maybe knows a guy."

"Then what," Ivy said.

"Then, we go home. And I track down a certain Fed who thinks he's about to retire a wealthy man and put him through an interrogation he'll wake up in cold sweats remembering decades from now. You're welcome to join me, if you like. But you'd probably be wise to stay out of it and hope they leave you alone."

Ivy shook his head. "You kidding? I wouldn't miss it for the world."

"Good man," Hatcher said, feeling himself slip into a light doze. "Good man."

# RAID ON WEWELSBERG
## – A Valducan Story –

Seth Skorkowsky

*31 March, 1945*

**B**ombs erupted in the distance, crackling like popcorn in a kettle. I lifted my gaze, searching for any signs of aircraft moving across the stars. Thousands of silver contrails striped the blackened skies to the north, heading east.

"They gettin' closer?" Dennis Buckland asked beside me. The huge man nervously fingered the flanged, iron mace, *Velnepo*, at his hip.

I shook my head. "They're keeping their distance. Which means the Americans might be closer than we anticipated." I scanned the horizon, unable to see the castle beyond the treetops. Despite the futility of the endeavor, I searched the shadows across the road for Audrey to no avail. *Good.*

Dennis peered back across the empty field beside us as if expecting the approaching army. "Shouldn' we move?"

Peter Brown sucked a palmed cigarette, its orange glow welling beneath his closed fingers. He leaned against the car, his calm a complete opposite of Dennis' unease. The black SS uniform fit the American well. The only part of his ensemble that appeared out of place was the sacred axe, *Glisuan*, tucked at the back of his belt. His chiseled cheekbones, strong jaw, and pale eyes made him look every bit the part of Himmler's elite, although I doubted he would want to hear such a compliment. His brother had died fighting the Nazis in Italy. "I told you we should have setup closer to the castle."

"We keep to the plan," I said, ignoring Peter's remark.

We waited in silence. The bombs slowed and finally ceased, leaving only the sounds of crickets, breeze-rustled leaves, and the occasional artillery shell thundering in the distance.

Footsteps hurried up the road toward us. "Lady Meadows," Richard Simon said, his wool coat flapping behind him. "They're coming."

I straightened at once. "Everyone in position." My hand moved to *Feuertod* at my hip, squeezing the grip to calm my worn nerves. If our plan didn't succeed, the holy weapons stolen by the Third Reich might be lost forever. They were mankind's only defense against the demonic forces bent to destroy us all. While the sacred rapier could not speak, I felt his soothing comfort nonetheless. Like the war at large, only one outcome was acceptable here. Victory. Doubt was a luxury I could not afford.

Richard slowed as he neared. His bronze, Celtic sword, *Saighnean*, hung from his shoulder like a slung rifle. His beakish nose and small chin made him appear almost child-like beneath the flared black helmet. Appearances aside, he was one of the most capable Valducan knights I'd ever known.

Peter pulled one final draw from his cigarette before dropping and grinding it out beneath his boot. He clicked on a torch and shined it under the car's open bonnet, muttering angry curses as if the vehicle were truly broken and our approaching audience could actually see him.

The tell-tale growl of a motorcycle rumbled ahead, growing louder. It rounded the bend, its single lamp masked beneath a hood, allowing only a sliver of white light. A blocky sidecar bounced at its right like an ill-sized dance partner, its mounted machinegun reminiscent of a knight's lance. A moment later, a large truck followed, its own lights darkened.

*On with the show.* I stepped forward, a leather attaché clutched to my chest.

The motorcycle slowed as we came into view, our car blocking the road. The soldier in the sidecar swiveled the machinegun us at us.

"Don't shoot!" Dennis shouted, raising one hand to block the light from his eyes.

Richard stepped up beside him, palms open.

The truck's brakes whined to a halt behind the motorcycle and its lamps flipped on, bathing us in light. The machine gunner appeared to relax his grip as he noticed our black SS uniforms.

A head clad in a peaked cap leaned out the truck's passenger window. His harsh voice shouted, "Identify yourselves!"

I pushed my way to the front. "We were sent to speak with Major Heinz Macher. And turn off your lights you fools – the invaders are near."

The lights flipped off.

"Who are you?" the man demanded, his voice still edged with suspicion.

"Elfriede Gar," I lied, holding the leather case out like a talisman. "We've come from Bremen with artifacts and records."

"He is not here."

I swallowed. *Hell's bells!* "Do you know where I might find him? It's very important."

The man sat silent for a moment, then waved us forward.

I hurried to the idling truck, Dennis behind me. I climbed up to the driver's side window as Dennis approached the side where the speaker sat. "Have you seen Major Macher?"

The officer in the peaked cap frowned, his thick monobrow creasing in the middle. "He's still at the castle."

"Are you transporting the relics?" I asked, a bit more desperation in my voice than I had intended.

"What do you want?"

"We have more artifacts for him. Himmler himself ordered us to bring them personally." I pushed the leather attaché in through the window, forcing the confused driver to remove his hand from the wheel to accept it. "Our auto broke down. Can you take us to him?"

The lieutenant accepted the case from the driver and fumbled with the clasp. "No. We will not turn around."

"But, the Major must have these," I urged. "Look." I drew Feuertod from his scabbard and held the ornate swept hilt up for him to see.

The man gave a frustrated huff. He glanced over the stack of papers inside the case. I knew he couldn't read them in the scant light, which was fine. They were a meaningless distraction. "I cannot take you. The castle is three kilometers back. You can make it, but must hurry."

"Thank you." I lowered my rapier below the window and pressed its point against the truck's door. Every sacred weapon possesses a unique gift, a power beyond any mortal creation. Feuertod's blessing manifests as an astonishingly strong and keen blade. The sheet metal door screeched as I drove the sword through with no more effort than if it were stout cardboard. The slender blade pierced the driver's side, through his ribs, and emerged below his right armpit. The man gave a terrible wheeze as the blade skewered both of his lungs. His reflexive jerk at the violation only served to worsen the injury, the razor edge slicing his flesh like pudding. The truck lurched and stalled as his foot came off the brake.

The Nazi officer shrieked. Papers spilled across his lap as he fumbled for his gun. Dennis sprang up, reached through the window, and rammed a trench knife up and under the bastard's jaw. Blood poured from the SS man's mouth.

The men in the motorcycle cried in alarm. The gunner's hand moved for his weapon.

Audrey Turgen appeared beside them, emerging from a curtain of shadow. She hacked her sword, *Rowlind*, into the machine gunner's neck. Without slowing, she drove her boot into the driver's ribs.

The man cried out in surprise and pain as he fell. He scrambled for his sidearm but she was already up and over the motorcycle, the sword tip pressed against his chest.

"Don't move," she commanded.

The motorcycle driver froze, his wide eyes fixed on the bloodied blade as the machine gunner gurgled and died behind her.

Simon and Peter raced toward us.

Three dead and one prisoner without a single shot. With a satisfied smile, I pulled my rapier back out of the truck's door."Good show."

After disarming Audrey's captive and leaving her to guard, we circled around to the rear of the paneled truck. Something heavy shifted inside. Obviously they were transporting *something* from the fortress. If not the plundered holy weapons, then possibly some of the many rare tomes, sacred relics, paintings, or other treasures Himmler's cult had amassed. Whatever it was, our duty was to make sure neither they, nor the closing Allies, got them. There was no telling how many SS guards were inside, all wondering why exactly they'd stopped moving.

We formed a semicircle before the double doors. Peter stood to my right, his MP40 submachine gun ready. There was no need for the ruse any longer. To my left, Richard drew his bronze sword. Feuertod in one hand, I unholstered my Walther with the other and nodded to Dennis.

The big man slid the mace from his belt and approached the doors. He banged the weapon's pommel against the wood. *Boom. Boom. Boom.* "We're opening the door. Weapons down. Hands above your head." Velnepo ready, he popped the sturdy latch open.

The door burst wide, knocking Dennis to the ground. With a screaming roar, two giant creatures charged from the darkened truck. Thick muscles bulged beneath their hairless, pale skin. Their snarling mouths protruded past the upper rims of their oversized German helmets.

The first one leaped to the ground, landing on all fours and lunged toward me.

Peter's machinegun erupted, spewing flashes of fire. Bullets stitched across the monster's chest.

It stumbled back, but the bloody holes mended in a heartbeat.

The beast roared again, rising to its full seven-foot height. It swiped one of its long arms at Peter. Hooked claws capped each of its fingers. The knight hopped back, replying in kind with another burst into the creature's face.

The howling beast shook its head, flinging blood from its mangled sockets.

Seizing the opening as its eyes reformed, I lunged and drove my rapier straight into the monster's chest.

The beast stiffened. I withdrew the blade, pulling it to the side, and cut a wide gash.

The monster crumpled. Its cloven ribcage cracked wide, spilling its contents onto the rutted dirt road.

The second creature dove toward Dennis, still on the ground. He scrambled backwards on all fours. He'd dropped his mace when the door had slammed into him.

Richard ran forward, twirling Saighnean in figure eights. The weapon's gift was that the blade continued gaining momentum as long as he kept it moving. By the time he had crossed the three paces, the Celtic sword whistled through the air faster than any propeller blade.

The creature ducked and sprang back from the blurring blade. Richard moved in, but a rifle flash erupted from the back of the truck. Richard's helmet pinged with the bullet's impact and he stumbled.

The soldier in the truck worked his rifle's bolt. I raised my pistol and fired three rapid shots. Two hit, and the soldier fell behind a makeshift cover of stacked boxes.

Without Richard's imposing blade, the monster moved toward him.

"No!" I cried, racing to intercept it, but Dennis scooped Velnepo off the ground and dove at the monster's back.

The iron mace struck the creature's side. Bones cracked and the beast folded around the impact like a rag doll struck with a cricket bat. The inhuman force from the blessed mace sent the monster's mangled body fifteen feet through the air before it hit the ground with a meaty thump.

Grabbing the edge of the truck, Peter swung inside, his machinegun ready. He stepped around the wall of boxes and aimed it down to where the shooter had fallen. "He's still alive."

"Make sure he doesn't have any more surprises," I said. "Richard, are you all right?"

He nodded. "Really rang my bell there, didn't it?" Richard removed the German SS helmet and checked the finger-length dent from where the bullet had struck. "I suppose I shouldn't have argued about wearing this." He chuckled nervously.

Satisfied he was only shaken, I was about to return my attention to the truck when something caught my attention. "Richard, let me see that helmet."

"Of course." He offered it out, a little grin at the corner of his mouth. "I assume you'll be wanting one too, now that I've tested it."

Accepting the steel hat, I gave it a closer inspection. White metal, gleaming in the moonlight against the black helm, ran the length of the dent. *Curious.* Why would it do that? "Sir Buckland."

"Aye?" Dennis replied.

"Would you check that soldier's rifle? I would like to see the bullets." I handed the helmet back to Richard, who now studied the dent with closer scrutiny.

"Aye. One thing you might want to see first, Lady Meadows." Dennis motioned to the two dead monsters. "Why aren't they burnin'?"

My eyes widened as I looked again at the crumpled, inhuman forms. When killed with a holy weapon, a demon's essence burns with a phantasmal fire as it leaves the host body. But these did not. In the excitement I'd completely overlooked the phenomenon. My gaze moved to Feuertod's blade, still stained with the monster's dark, and most definitely unburning blood. *Most curious.*

Dennis hurried back into the truck as I examined the corpse of the beast I'd killed. Even now, the huge muscles and elongated bones shriveled back to those of its human host. Angular brands, like runes, scarred its chest.

Richard stepped beside me and stooped, rolling the monster's left arm over. He grunted and I spied the ring on the creature's hand. Similar symbols decorated the silver band while a skull and crossbones adorned the top.

My lip curled into a sneer. A Totenfomphring – the honour ring for Himmler's most loyal. It appeared the demon's human vessel had been SS. *Burn in Hell, you bastard.* I was about to compliment Richard on noticing it when I realized his attention was not on the grotesque jewelry, but at a strip of numbers crudely tattooed on the pale forearm.

"What is this?" he growled, his voice low.

I blinked. *Concentration camp? Why would he be wearing a Totenfomphring?*

"Lady Helen," Dennis said, climbing back out from the truck. "Look here." He held out a single rifle round.

"Silver," I said, looking it over.

He nodded. "Got boxes of 'em."

"That's useful for us," I said, "But why would the Nazis need them?"

He shrugged.

With a final glance at the beastly corpses, I looked at the soldier still under Audrey's guard. "Then let us ask our new friends."

* * *

"Well, what do you know." Peter shone his torch into one of the wooden boxes.

Turning my attention from the crate of books, I peered over the raised lid. Thousands of silver rings filled the inside, each with the familiar skull and crossbones. Upon the bearer's death, each ring was sent to Wewelsburg Castle. Evidently the SS found it important to recover them before the Americans arrived.

Peter let out a low whistle. "That's a lot of dead krauts." He turned to me. "What do we do with them?"

"Load them in the car." I gestured to the books I was scouring.

"This crate as well. Fit as much as you can. We'll burn the rest."
The words stung. As a Librarian, destroying books was among
the highest of sins. But we hadn't room for them all, and from
what my brief inspection had gleaned, whatever foul knowledge
the Nazis had amassed was nothing either side should have. It
was far too dangerous.

I climbed down from the truck, passed the two corpses of
what had once been monsters, now emaciated men with shaven
heads and tattooed arms, and stopped where Audrey and Richard
were guarding our two prisoners. The man I'd shot lay on his
back, his waxy skin glistening in the scant light. He clutched
a red-soaked rag against his side. The other, the motorcyclist,
watched me with cautious, hateful eyes.

"Have they talked yet?" I asked.

Audrey shook her head. "Not a peep." Unlike the rest of us
in our confiscated uniforms, Lady Turgen wore a charcoal gray
poncho, striped in black, and her dark hair was tied in a tight
bun. Her delicate features and cupid bow lips made her appear
more suited for fancy dress than warfare. But as any Valducan
knows all too well, a gentle facade often masks lethality.

"I'll only ask this once," I said to the prisoners, my voice even
and cold, "where are the weapons?"

"Safe from you," the wounded one spat.

"Allow me to be clear. We are not the British or the Americans.
We are not bound by the Articles of the Geneva Convention.
What were those creatures? And where were you taking them?"

"Fuck you, British whore. I—"

His words ended as Audrey ran Rowlind straight into the
man's chest. He gave a wet moan and fell silent.

I turned to the motorcyclist, his wide eyes fixed on his dead
companion. "I will only ask you this once—"

"Augsburg," he blurted. "We were heading to Augsburg."

"And the weapons?"

"Major Macher is escorting those and the cauldron
personally."

"Cauldron?" I asked.

He nodded. "The Life Vessel."

I glanced to Audrey and Richard. They both shrugged. "And what were those creatures?"

"*Die Kesselgeburten,*" he said. "The undying warriors."

I pursed my lips. *Cauldron-born?* "What of the rings?"

The prisoner's hand tightened, his fingers concealing the silver band I'd already seen. "Those who die for the Reich will live forever."

"Through the rings?" Richard asked.

The prisoner gave a reluctant nod.

"What about those men?" Richard's voice grew uncharacteristically sharp. "Prisoners? What happened to them?"

The man didn't answer.

"What did you do to them?" Richard shouted.

I held up a hand. We were losing sight of the immediate goal. "Are the weapons and the cauldron still at the castle?"

"They were when we left," the prisoner said. "Major Macher was to take the other route."

"So they might have already left." I turned to see Peter and Dennis loading the crates into the car. "We must hurry. Richard, do what you must."

I'd made it three steps toward the vehicle when the man cried out behind me. While Richard Simon was a gentleman in every sense of the word, he was also a Jew. Peter had referred to him as my puppy behind my back. But Richard's hatred of Germans surpassed even my own. He was quick with the prisoner, but not merciful. No one objected to the treatment.

I thought of my late husband, eighteen and cut down in the final days of the First Great War. Despite my distaste for the race, Feuertod was technically German. But that was fitting. Germans excelled at killing, and killing was Feuertod's specialty.

"Are we done?" I asked as Dennis heaved a wooden box into the back. He carried one of the newly confiscated rifles with silver ammunition over one shoulder.

"Aye. That's all she'll hold."

"Very well. Peter, can you operate that?" I asked, pointing to the sidecar-mounted machine gun.

He shrugged. "Shouldn't be too hard."

"Then get in."

Peter and Dennis exchanged a look. "Why not Dennis?" he asked. "He's Arms Master."

While a capable knight, his American enthusiasm had caused more than its fair share of tensions between us. Truth be told, I didn't like him out of my sight. His vocal opinions might be contagious. I gave him a flat look. "Because I told *you*."

Peter blew a breath, wiping sweat from his face. "I'd love to give it a whirl."

"Good." I turned as Richard moved up behind me, wiping the blood from his sword. "You drive the auto. Try to keep up."

I removed the riding goggles from the dead driver, happily noting that either Richard or Audrey had taken the silver rings from the bodies. Pulling the goggles on, I straddled the bike. Blood spattered the sidecar from its former occupant, but Peter crawled inside without complaint, sliding his newly plundered rifle between his legs.

"Hold on." I kick-started the engine, unleashing a loud roar. I maneuvered the bike around, a task made much harder with the sidecar, and started up the road.

Audrey hurried from the back of the truck and dove into the car. It started after me and moments later fire exploded from the truck, sending a ball of smoke into the sky.

Wind whipped at my cheeks and jacket. It had been over three years since I'd last ridden, and the rumble of the engine brought that familiar, exhilarating calm. My mind focused. The weapons were still our highest priority. The Nazis had stolen at least three of them in their conquests. Each one housed an angel, and only those the angel found worthy could wield their divine gifts. A Valducan knight is bound to their weapon. It is the single greatest honour to feel an angel's love. Not only had the Nazis stolen and hoarded their ill-gotten gains, they'd murdered the owners. And while I'd never met most of them, or even known their names, they were weapon-bound. That made them family. I gunned the engine and sped toward Wewelsburg Castle.

We passed through a tiny village, the lights out and windows shuttered. Either the occupants were still hiding from the distant bombings or had fled the approaching army. A few automobiles and carts, lashed with trunks and furniture, told that more would be leaving soon. The winding road turned and I could see the great black form of the fortress atop the hill, barely discernible against the night sky.

I slowed as we followed the steep, narrow road. Our disguises might work in staying the trigger fingers of any SS lurking in the trees, but not if we were driving as if on the attack.

The fortress itself was quite simple – two narrow, domed towers and a large, flat-topped one, the walls between them forming a triangle. But it was also the black heart of the SS, and the crown jewel of Hitler's mad vision. God only knew what horrors had transpired within those three stone walls. I'd never wanted to see such an evil place as this.

Reaching the hilltop, I steered us into a darkened car park. It was empty save for two vehicles – a civilian sedan and a blocky army wagon that appeared to have seen its share of combat. Bullet holes riddled the side and back, and a rear wheel was missing.

*Damn*, I thought. *They've already left*. They couldn't have made it far, and we knew they were headed to Augsburg. I rolled the motorcycle deeper into the car park, praying there might be a further portion that I'd missed. A cluster of buildings stood along one side. Barracks or offices, I guessed.

A single motorcycle rested in the shadow of the larger building. The car with the other knights rolled into the lot behind us. Its hooded lights provided meager help in seeing the castle grounds.

"What are you doing here?" a voice shouted.

I lifted my goggles to see a plain-clothed man racing from the barrack house.

He waved his hands above his head. "Go! Get out of here!"

He was almost upon us when Peter raised his StG 44 and leveled it on him.

"What are you doing, idiot?" the stranger shouted. "We need to…" His voice trailed off as he looked at me, seeming to really notice me for the first time. A woman in uniform was rare, but one driving a motorcycle was unheard of. "Who are you?"

"Keep your hands where I can see them," I ordered. "What are you doing here?"

"I… The castle," he stammered. "I'd heard it was abandoned."

I narrowed my eyes. The man could have been a villager. The Nazis had been known to tell the locals to loot as they retreated. It destroyed evidence before the Allies might seize it. But his mannerisms, shoulders back, and straight posture said *soldier*. "When did they leave?"

"A few hours ago."

The car's tires ground over the pavement and Dennis slowed to a stop behind us. I didn't move my eyes from the stranger.

"What's he saying," Peter hissed. He was the only member of our team that couldn't speak German. But his other skills, most especially Glisuan, had warranted his inclusion.

"He said we missed them by hours."

"We know that's bullshit."

"Don't shoot," I warned, sensing his intentions.

The man shifted nervously. Barely turning his head, he glanced behind him.

"Is there anyone else?" I demanded.

"No," the man said. "It's just me."

"Right hand," Peter said. "Ring."

The man must have understood some English because his straight fingers relaxed, curling and concealing the glint of silver on his right hand.

*They're dressed as civilians. Those cars we passed might have been theirs. Damn it!* "When did they leave?" I demanded. "Where's Macher?"

"They—"

The barracks behind him exploded with a terrible roar. Glass, splintered shutters, and flaming debris blasted from the windows. Without the sidecar, the concussion might have toppled my bike. Stunned, my ears wailing in a high-pitched buzz, I looked around. Fire consumed the building, illuminating the lot and the castle beside us. Oily smoke plumed into the sky.

The blast had knocked the Nazi to the ground. He scrambled up and started away toward his now fallen motorcycle, but Peter's gun barked two loud pops and the man staggered and fell. He rolled on the ground, clutching his hip.

The American turned to me, his goggled eyes wide. "Are you okay?" I could barely hear him.

"Yes," I forced myself to say. I gave a quick inspection that nothing was hurt or on fire. "I'm all right. You?"

"Good." He crawled out from the sidecar and started toward the injured man, his rifle trained.

A second explosion erupted to our left. Flames burst from one of the smaller castle towers. Bits of rock and wood rained down like hail stones. A section of wall lurched and fell away. Fiery smoke poured from the opening.

Choking on dust, I turned around, twisting in my saddle. They'd wired the building to blow. We needed to get out of here. The car's windscreen had shattered. "Is everyone all right?" I coughed.

Shielding his eyes from the flickering light, Richard pointed behind me. "Look!"

Whirling, I searched the smoke and shadows and gasped. Enormous, hunched figures poured out from the castle like rats fleeing a sinking ship. They ran from the smoking hole and clambered out the windows, scuttling up the walls.

A pair of beasts burst through the castle's double doors. They charged across the short, stone bridge toward us, running on all fours like albino, hairless gorillas. Snarling, the lead monster pounded toward the injured Nazi.

"I'm one of you!" the man shouted, holding up his bloodied hands.

The creatures slowed, their eyes locked on the silver ring.

"They are enemies of the Reich!" The man gestured our direction. "Kill them!"

To my amazement, the monsters followed his orders, aiming their charge toward us. Any assumptions I'd had that these were mere demons were instantly dashed. I ripped Feuertod from his sheath, ready to take them on.

Shots erupted to my right. Rifle at his shoulder, Peter fired at the creatures with rapid bursts. The lead one stumbled and the second one trampled over it. Bloody plumes exploded across its chest. The silver bullets definitely hurt them, but not enough to ensure a quick kill.

Staggering, the creature bellowed, spraying bloody froth. It swiped its claws at me, but I sidestepped the clumsy attack and slashed my rapier across its side. Split ribs peeled apart and the monster screamed. I moved to finish it off, but was forced back as a third beast leaped toward me. It swung its enormous arm, claws splayed. I raised Feuertod into the attack, bracing the sword with both hands. The blessed blade met the beast's forearm, slicing through the muscle and bone. Blood sprayed and the severed claw flew past my shoulder.

The monster fell without a sound and began shriveling back to its once human form. *The ring*, I thought. *Remove the rings and they die.*

More machinegun fire thundered. Someone screamed.

Creatures continued fleeing the castle, most heading our way. The other knights were out of the car. Richard twirled Saighnean in tight, elaborate circles around himself, the blade accelerating to a metallic blur. Dennis stood behind him, his arm cocked and mace ready. Peter fired the last of his magazine at a charging beast and dropped his rifle. I didn't see Audrey at all.

"What's the order?" Peter asked, drawing Glisuan from his belt as he hurried toward us.

Dennis' response echoed my sentiments. "Kill the fuckin' bastards."

"Do it," I ordered.

Setting his jaw, Peter faced the oncoming hoard and swung the Norse axe as if throwing it. A brilliant purple-white lightning bolt shot from the head with a deafening crackle. It arced and jumped between two of the monsters. Electricity skittered between the fangs on their open mouths and danced across their bodies. Fire spewed from their blackening skin and exploded from their eyes. The monsters fell, smoldering.

More of them poured down the castle's walls and clambered up the low trench, separating it from the car park. A wave of snarling beasts charged toward us.

"Circle up!" I ordered.

Another brilliant stroke of lightning lanced up the castle, knocking one from the roof and setting it ablaze. The bolt's jagged image lingered in my vision even after I blinked. Dennis fired a luger in his off-hand, wounding two with silver slugs before the gun clicked empty. We formed a rough circle with Richard to my left, facing the oncoming hoard.

A closing beast leaped and came down at Richard, claws out. They met the whirring haze of his moving sword and were unmade as the blade shredded them. Blood and bits of fingers and bone sprayed everywhere –a truly spectacular sight had I not been in the red mist's range. The offending ring, destroyed or severed from the host, and the monster crumpled without a sound.

"Helen, I'm opposite you," Audrey's voice called from the shadows. "Don't fire."

Bypassing Richard's field of death, one of the monsters moved toward me. Gripping my rapier tight, I crouched, readying for the attack. The giant beast approached cautiously, black eyes locked on my blade. These things were tough. I needed to kill it or remove the ringed finger in one strike or else it would tear me apart. Moving the blade to the side, I began a feint when Audrey melted out from the space behind it, the shadows peeling from her like smoke.

She slashed Rowlind along the backs of its legs, hamstringing it. Bellowing, the maimed creature lurched backwards. It stepped to catch itself, but its injured leg folded beneath it.

Audrey had already melted back into the shadows before the beast hit the ground. She reappeared two yards away, crippling another as she ran.

I sprang at the fallen monster, and drove Feuertod up under its ribs. Pulling the sword to the side, it sliced a devastating wound.

Glisuan's lightning crackled again. The sharp stink of ozone tinged the smoky air.

Another beast stepped over its fallen brethren and lunged toward me. Stepping into the attack, I ducked the blurred arc of its claws and slashed my sword deep across its belly before moving to the side. Blood and entrails spilled from the wound but the creature refused to fall. Screaming, it took a lumbering step and raised its claw. I rammed Feuertod through its open mouth, sending six inches of steel out the back of its skull. The monster fell so suddenly that it almost wrenched the impaling sword from my grip.

A roar bellowed beside me as a creature fell to its knees, another victim of Audrey's blade. Dennis slammed his mace into its side, launching the corpse ten feet where it crashed into another.

The flames had spread through the castle and completely consumed the barrack house. Audrey's translucent form solidified as the welling orange light flickered across the lot.

A ring of mutilated and burning bodies surrounded us, most dead but a few still messily expiring. The near-forgotten Nazi was crawling to the edge of the car park, trailing blood. Peter launched another stroke of lightning, picking off one of the stragglers loping our direction.

The brief flash illuminated a half dozen more of the monsters racing away down the bare hill below the castle. *Damn.*

"They're going for the village!" I shouted. "Dennis, get in the sidecar. The rest of you finish these off." I stabbed my sword in the crawling man's direction. "And someone stop him!"

Hurrying between fallen corpses, I climbed onto the motorcycle.

Dennis awkwardly folded his enormous frame into the tiny cab.

"Hold on," I said and gunned the engine.

Tires squealed as we took off, the jolt knocking him the rest of the way into the seat. I steered the bike around and started down the walled road. Lightning flashed behind us. The slitted beam from the head lamp cut through the smoky haze. We rounded a turn, a maneuver made slow from the heavy sidecar, and we were now facing the sloping hill.

The great fires above lit the scene before us. Dark silhouettes moved in the distance on all fours headed toward the village. Light peeked through open windows as citizens watched the fortress burn.

We had to stop them. None of the villagers or approaching American army had any defense against the Nazis' abominations.

"There!" Dennis shouted, his words drowned under the engine's roar. Leaning into the mounted gun, he squeezed the trigger, unleashing a gout of stuttering fire. Tiny pink comets of tracer rounds, mixed with the silver ammunition, flew across the open spans. A second barrage peppered one of the beasts and it fell, tumbling down the slope.

The other monsters charged toward us, keeping low as more bullets sailed wildly above them.

A beast leaped as it reached the stone embankment, claws splayed as it flew toward us. Dennis swiveled the gun and unleashed a stream of fire, nearly sawing it in half. The corpse landed in the road just before us. I jerked the motorbike to the side, almost tipping it. The wheels struck the beasts leg, launching us momentarily airborne before the bike thudded down. Amazingly, we didn't crash. Aside from weapons, I must confess that Germans do make a fine vehicle.

We hit a straightaway and I gunned the engine. Wind whipped my face as we shot down the hill. Reaching the curve at the bottom, I slowed and turned, giving Dennis' gun full view of the hill.

The MG34 roared. Pink comets shot up the slope, their ricochets bouncing off rocks like errant fireworks. Two more of the creatures fell. Another stumbled as bullets struck its thick thigh, but the gun fell silent before finishing it off.

"Out!" Dennis shouted.

Dismounting the vehicle, we marched up the slope. I dispatched the final monster with a quick thrust of my sword.

I surveyed my surroundings but couldn't find any more of the creatures. A few silhouettes still watched us from the village's windows. Tomorrow they'd share stories about how the Nazis had burned the castle and in dawn's light see the executed prisoners that had tried to flee. I amputated the corpse's ringed finger and wrenched the silver band free. "Collect the rings. Then let's get back and see what our prisoner can tell us about where the weapons are."


*2 May, 1945*


"They're loading the boats," I said, peering through the field glasses. I lay in the hollow of a bomb crater, with a commanding view of the small encampment. SS soldiers, many of them so young I doubted they could even remember a time before Hitler's reign, patrolled the convoy of trucks parked alongside a lake. Pale moonlight reflected across the still, black waters.

For a full month we'd pursued our quarry. By the time we'd made it to Augsburg, Macher had already delivered the stolen artifacts. A special SS division called the *Nibelungen* had taken the treasures east, destined for Czechoslovakia.

With the countryside swarming with Nazis either preparing for a glorious last stand or deserters desperate to flee their inevitable destruction by the Allies, we had to move slow. Spending our days hiding in barns and bombed ruins, we followed them past Munich, were nearly struck by an air raid outside of Freising, and had nearly caught up at Landshut. However with the bridges out and the Allies drawing near, the Nibelungen turned south. Now, on the shore of Chiemsee, a Bavarian lake, they'd halted again. This time we'd caught them.

"What's the plan?" Richard asked.

I offered him the binoculars. "Appears to be just troops and weapons right now. They probably want to set up on the far side before transporting the artifacts."

"Less for us to deal with," Peter whispered.

I nodded. "Agreed. The weapons and the cauldron are most likely in the truck parked closest to the centre."

"Look to have a nest setup in that old house to the west," Richard said. "Someone there just lit a match."

"We should expect another one on the eastern side as well," I said. "I'll have Audrey take a look."

"I'll see what they have," came a voice to my left.

I spun, my hand instinctively moving to my pistol before I recognized Audrey's voice. Heart thumping, I released a breath. The shadows beside me appeared to pool somewhat, as if cast by some non-existent tree. Squinting, I could just make out the knight's translucent, crouched form.

"Jesus Christ," Peter growled. "You scared the hell out of me."

"You should be used to it by now," she said unsympathetically. "I found a soldier patrolling our way. With luck, they won't realize he's gone until it's too late."

"Good work," I said. Previous attempts at interrogation had proven useless. Himmler had fashioned the SS into a zealot cult – a perverse Teutonic Order. As the mythological beings they'd been named after, the Nibelungen protected a great treasure. They'd happily die before betraying the cause.

"I'll scout around and find the best point of attack," Audrey said. "How long do I have?"

"Make it fast."

She was gone without a word. The faint crunching of boots on grass was the only sign of her passing.

"I can't believe we've almost got them," Richard said.

Peter grunted. "Don't count your chickens. Any sign of those kesselgeburten bastards?"

I shook my head. "Two of the trucks are reinforced. Possibly those. I doubt the Nazis trust them enough to simply let them wander around."

Countless hours hiding and waiting for nightfall had afforded us ample time to read the captured documents. The cauldron was the first half of the Nazis' hideous plan to create an immortal army. Crafted from ten kilos of solid gold, and inscribed with Celtic spells, it served as some blasphemous Holy Grail. The silver skull rings of the Reich's chosen warriors served as the second half. Upon the wearer's death, they trapped the life essence. The ceremony for the resurrection had been incinerated when we'd burned the truck, and I didn't mourn its loss. The Nazis had used the rings to resurrect their fallen by drowning prisoners in the cauldron filled with human blood. Evidently they hadn't expected them to transform into monsters.

Savage and incapable of speech, the creatures served the Nazis, as they were the only ones who could make more of them. Even then, the beasts were prone to violent outbursts and had killed several of their makers. Afraid of their new super-army, the Nazis armed themselves with silver weapons. Silver being the element of their binding, it could also bring their death. Upon learning the true nature of the nine thousand Totenfomphrings, we'd promptly cut each of them in half, rendering them useless.

Our mission objectives had changed. In addition to retrieving the plundered holy weapons, we had to either capture or destroy that golden abomination.

\* \* \*

"Everyone, take one of these." Dennis held out a pair of potato masher grenades, their heads wrapped in gauze.

"What is this?" I squeezed the end, feeling metal shifting beneath the tight binding.

"Little somethin' I made up while waitin' for you to get back from scoutin'. Took some of those cut rings and wrapped 'em up. Recon if more of those big bastards come out, silver shrapnel might ruin their evenin'."

My brow rose. "Very clever."

He timidly shrugged his massive shoulders. "Well, let's hope they work."

"Let's hope we won't need them," Audrey said, tucking one into her belt. She wore two more grenades of the regular variety.

"Are we clear on the plan?" I asked.

"I still say I should take the nest," Peter grumbled.

"Non-negotiable," I said, keeping my voice even.

Richard's eyes dropped away. At least he knew better than to argue.

Peter gave a curt nod. "Understood."

"Good," I said. "Let's have at it. We haven't much time."

Audrey turned and hurried away. She drew Rowlind and ribbons of night wrapped around her. Staying low, the rest of us circled around, exiting the grove of trees and making our way through the cratered field.

Artillery thundered off in the distance. The Americans were close and the Nazis would be alert. Taking point, I crawled to the edge of a grassy berm and lifted my binoculars.

The dome tops of helmets peeked above the low, makeshift wall of a machine gun nest. Scanning further up the line, I let out a curse. A pair of giant, forms moved along the shore, loading boxes into a boat. Checking the truck, I saw that more crates were still being unloaded. There was no way to determine from here which one might contain the weapons.

*Make it fast, Audrey.*

A single soldier stood in the shadows outside one of the trucks, fidgeting with something in his hands. Audrey appeared behind him and hacked his neck. The man crumpled without a sound and she was again gone. A second sentry, further down the line, fell shortly after.

Minutes crawled. The distant shells thundered faster, the raging battle still miles away but creeping ever closer, unstoppable like a glacier. Three more boxes were loaded. The bright lanterns and beams of headlights meant Audrey couldn't enter the area without notice. The nests had to be eliminated first. I focused my attention to the darkened house on the far side.

Finally, I breathed a relieved sigh as a match lit in one of the windows and moved left to right before extinguishing.

"It's done," I hissed, motioning my arm. "Move!"

Peter hurried up beside me as Richard and Dennis quickly

crawled across the open road separating us from the rear of the gun nest.

Giving Peter a silent nod, we moved in a crouch toward the wall of parked trucks.

A loud voice shouted, "*Zwei weitere kisten. Schnell!*"

We reached the first truck. The sharp stink of urine rose from between the mud-caked tires. It appeared I'd found the latrine. Wrinkling my nose, I braved a peek back toward the nest to see Richard and Dennis slip inside, weapons out. Ten seconds later a helmeted shape rose and moved the MG42 around.

"They're in position." I drew my sword and moved around to the rear of the vehicle. I glanced inside the canopied back, verifying it was empty before creeping between it and the neighboring truck. As I'd thought, half the company had already relocated across the lake, leaving thirty or so men. Four of the giant monsters lumbered through the ranks, towering above young soldiers. I motioned to Peter to move forward when shouting erupted somewhere behind us.

"*Eindringlinge! Eindringlinge!*"

*Bloody hell!* Someone had found one of Audrey's victims.

Seizing the moment of surprise, Richard opened fire. The machinegun roared like a buzz saw, tearing through the ranks. Soldiers dove for cover, scrambling behind anything they could find. Their backs now exposed to the darkened house, Audrey opened fire from a second floor window, tracers streaking down.

Roaring, one of the beasts hurled a wooden box at Richard and Dennis' nest. The crate shattered beside the foxhole and a stream of machinegun fire tore into the creature. The non-silver rounds only seemed to slow its charge. A grenade landed in its path. The explosion sent the creature tumbling. Dennis' silver-loaded rifle flashed beside the machinegun's blazing flare.

Tearing my eyes from the chaos, I dove into the first truck and began searching. Peter raced off to check the vehicles on the far side, leaving me alone. Inspection done, I dropped a grenade into the cab and hurried away. Come Hell or high water, the Nazis weren't escaping this time.

The easy targets gone, Richard focused his gun at the lights, shattering them with short bursts. Peter hurled a grenade at a pair of soldiers maneuvering toward the house. Audrey's shooting had already ceased, her job to fire the gun dry and then move once the lights were mostly gone.

One by one I scoured the outer trucks, slashing open bags and flipping back lids, praying to find the weapons. A soldier rounded the corner as I exited a vehicle and I plunged two feet of blessed steel through his chest.

Twin blasts exploded inside the house. I only prayed Audrey was clear of them.

Howls bellowed as three more monsters smashed from the side of a locked truck. Purple lightning crackled and two beasts died before they'd made it fifteen feet.

I'd almost completed checking the trucks when a boat engine roared to life. I rushed out to see it starting across the water. Firelight glinted off an enormous gold bowl at the bow.

Richard swiveled the gun toward the vessel but a barrage of German fire forced him down. A potato masher twirled through the air, landing in his foxhole. My stomach lurched, but the bomb flipped back out before exploding, sending gravel and flames into the air.

Crouching behind a car, one of the hulking beasts charged, pushing the vehicle across the beach toward the foxhole. Richard opened fire, as did Dennis with his rifle, but the bullets only pummeled the sliding shield. More suppressive fire forced them down as the car charged their position like a train engine.

I leveled my gun at a pair of the shooters, killing one and forcing the other to scramble away. I stopped firing as Audrey appeared and slashed him open before vanishing into the shadows.

"The boat!" I screamed, firing ineffectually at it.

More grenades exploded, drowning my words. With a howl, the monster pushed the mangled vehicle up the low wall and down into the foxhole with a crash. Trusting the knights made it out in time, I charged the shore, firing at the fleeing boat.

Lighting flashed, momentarily blinding me. Breaking his cover, Peter raced across the open beach, Glisuan in hand. He launched another bolt out across the water. Electricity danced along the surface. Orange flares of gunfire flashed from the boat.

"Peter, get down!" I shouted.

Bullets whizzed around him. Peter stumbled, but continued on, heedless of the danger.

I returned fire, but through the choking smoke and darkness I couldn't see where I was hitting. *Stubborn bastard.*

With a defiant scream, Peter hurled another bolt across the water. A fuel tank exploded, launching flames into the sky. A burning man tumbled over the side. Clutching his stomach, Peter turned toward me, a triumphant smile on the American's face. Machinegun fire tore through his chest, sending him down in a spray of blood.

"Peter!" I screamed. I spun to see a young soldier, no more than sixteen leaning out from behind a boulder, rifle in hand.

I fired.

My shots struck the rock, sending him back for cover. Anger boiling, I ran for a better position. Reaching the central truck, I spied the killer's leg peeking from behind the large stone. I crouched to take aim, but leaped back as a crate flew out from the vehicle, missing me by inches. It smashed on the ground, spilling clinking sacks. I whirled as one of the great pale beasts dove toward me. SS runes adorned its thick breastplate and armored shoulders.

Slashing my rapier, I spun and leaped aside. The monster growled, white froth dripping from the corners of its mouth. It swiped its huge arms at me, its hooked claws a blur. I hopped back and then lunged. The indirect blow glanced off its armor, leaving a deep scratch.

The beast charged for me, claws arcing toward my face. Ducking and springing away, I slashed the monster's calf as it passed. The creature bellowed in pain as it fell to its knee. Twisting its body, it swiped again and I whipped the rapier around, lopping off its claw at the wrist. Blood splattered my cheek and the beast fell.

Turning back to the hidden soldier, I saw Audrey standing above him, bloodied sword in her hand. In an instant, she was gone. Dozens of dead and dying littered the rocky beach and smoke choked the air. Another grenade exploded, igniting one of the trucks. Dennis popped up from behind a dead beast and shot a charging soldier. He ducked as return fire pulped the grotesque corpse.

I dove into the open truck beside me. It reeked like a pig sty. Five crates rested against the back, the SS rune stenciled across their sides. Strange books, and what appeared to be Egyptian figurines, filled the first one. Pushing it aside, I opened the next. I recoiled at the rows of embalmed human hands, tattooed and packed like sardines. I shoved the box away, spilling them across the floor.

A burst of gunfire barked outside.

*Please be here*, I prayed throwing back the next lid. A golden scepter rested inside, an outstretched eagle as its head. Ignoring the fortune, I hurled the box off the stack and opened the next.

Two swords, an iron spear head, and an elaborate war pick rested inside, cradled in straw and cut-out supports. I blew a relieved sigh, my fingers touching *Lukrasus*, the sword plundered during the Polish blitz. The sacred weapons were all that stood between humanity and annihilation. They were safe.

A man's choked scream sounded outside.

*Not safe yet.* I closed the hinged lid and heaved the heavy box out, holding it by the rope-loop handles. Outside was eerily still. I peered around, seeing no one. A smattering of burning debris floated atop the water – all that remained of the sunken boat.

"Did you find them?" Audrey appeared from the shadows.

"Here."

She hurried toward me.

Peter's axe hung from her belt. There was no need to ask his condition. "Richard and Dennis?"

Audrey took the other side of the box and I hopped down. She nodded toward the line of trucks, most of them on fire. The huge knight hobbled through the smoke, practically carrying

Richard with one arm. The smaller knight's face was scrunched in pain.

*No!* I cursed myself for even bringing him on this mission.

"He took a bad cut to the abdomen," she said as we hurried toward them. "I'll patch them up once we're out."

Trying not to think of his injury or of our fallen knight, I focused only on escape. We made our way the half mile to where our automobile was hidden in the shell of a stable.

Richard's face was ashen as we loaded him inside. "Really... gave 'em Hell... didn't we?" He smiled weakly.

"That we did." I brushed the grit from face to hide my concern. We still needed to slip past the American line, change vehicles, and get back to France.

Audrey climbed in beside him, clutching an olive-coloured med kit.

"The cauldron?" Richard asked.

I glanced in the direction of Chiemsee Lake. "It's gone. No one will ever see that abomination again."

He nodded, seeming satisfied. "Then it was worth it."

Smiling to him, I shut the door. I only wished I could believe my own assurances.

*– Field Report from Lady Helen Meadows, 1945*


UPDATE:

A pair of divers have discovered the cauldron in Chiemsee. It is intact. Recovery or destruction of it are considered Top Priority.

*– Master Alex Turgen, 2001*

# GOD-KILLERS IN OUR MIDST

James Lovegrove and N.X. Sharps

When men come face to face with their gods, it generally means they've died.

In my case, it means I'm going to die.

Probably horribly.

I'm brought to Kha'cheldaa in chains, ascending to heaven in a fiery chariot – or, if you prefer, a fusion-powered reusable shuttle craft. But most people'd call it a fiery chariot. Because most people are dumb.

The journey into near orbit is smooth; the squad of Templars escorting me are rough. For example, as we disembark at Kha'cheldaa's docking bay, the captain of these goons thinks it'd be funny to stick out a leg and trip me up. With my hands manacled behind my back the only thing I have to break my fall with is my face.

Then, for good measure, as I try to get up the same guy clubs me on the back on the head with the pommel of his sword. Could have used the butt of his sidearm, but this way is more ceremonial, I guess.

Still: fucking *ouch*.

"Not such a free thinker now, eh?" the captain jeers. "Not with a bump like that on your noggin."

His subordinates roar with laughter. It's pure comedic gold. No way are they being sycophantic minions or anything.

After that hilarity I'm force-marched along a broad tubular

corridor, one of the many spoke-like arms that radiate in all directions from the hub of Kha'cheldaa. Viewports show us planet Earth in all its glory. The terminator between day and night is crawling across its surface, but few lights twinkle on the black landmasses below. Cities no longer blaze with neon after sunset like they used to. I can just about remember a time when they did, but that's a couple decades back, long gone.

It's a benighted age, a dark age, this new age, this age of the Savior Gods.

Gravity in Kha'cheldaa is weird. Feels like there's no real up or down, although me and the Templars stick to the floor normally enough. The air smells metallic, slightly burnt. Our footfalls have blunted echoes. I'm taking in these sensory impressions because it's all I can do. I can't have many minutes of life left. Might as well clutch and savor each precious remaining second of it.

A couple of antechambers, more Templars, some scurrying servants. The Savior Gods like to have mortals guarding them and waiting on them hand and foot – gives them a warm, fuzzy glow inside – and these people have been led to believe it's an honor to have been chosen for the roles. To live in Kha'cheldaa and be of use to our deities is a privilege, the kind you'd sell your very soul for. Right?

Maybe it's just me, but I can't help feeling some of them are at least wondering what they've gotten themselves into. There's furtiveness in their body language, a secret fear in their eyes. The gods aren't known for their restraint and good behavior. Word is, things can get pretty rowdy up here. There are rumors: abuses, humiliations, rapes, random killings – things to make even Marquis de Sade blush. Omnipotence – it can go to a god's head, you know.

Finally the core chamber, Kha'cheldaa's heart, the huge sphere that is the throne room of the gods.

And lo and behold, they're all waiting for me. The full complement. The Big Twelve. Some sit, some stand. There's food on the tables, drink in tankards, and the light here is coruscating and dazzling, a million hazy rainbows criss-crossing, and I think I hear music, like choirs and orchestras, distant halleluiahs crescendoing and falling. Meanwhile Dominions, tucked away in recesses set high up in the chamber walls, maintain sentinel over their lords and ladies, poised to descend on any aggressor with wings of steel and flame.

I'm supposed to be impressed.

Secretly, I am.

But fuck if I'm going to show it.

The Templars drag me forward. Make me kneel by not so gently booting the backs of my knees. The captain shoves my head down with a gauntleted hand.

"Bow, humanist dog!" he orders.

He actually says that. *Humanist dog*. Like he means it. Like it isn't just what he thinks the Savior Gods would expect him to say.

Trakiin waves an imperious hand. The Templars are dismissed.

Trakiin, god of all gods. Trakiin the Father. Heavyset, grey-eyed, all-wise. He's stationed in a chair that's about five times the size it needs to be. Its back looms sheer, chalk-cliff white, arched and spired like some cathedral tower. He doesn't so much sit in it as occupy it, like an invading army. His robes hang in iridescent folds off his massive shoulders. His hair and beard are grey as thunderclouds.

Got to admit, I never thought I'd feel genuine awe in his presence. I know what this dirtbag really is. I know him for a lying, cheating charlatan, organiser of the greatest con ever perpetrated in history.

But still, he has a… *majesty* is the word. It's there. It's undeniable. He looks every inch a deity, even though he's anything but. If I weren't on my knees already, it'd have been hard to resist the urge to genuflect before him.

"So," he says, in a voice like tectonic plates grinding.

The word resonates around the throne room. It's just one empty syllable but it sounds like it encompasses universes.

"This is he," Trakiin goes on. "The leader of the expedition.

The mortal who dared venture where it is forbidden to go. Who sought 'proof' that we are not who we say we are."

I'm going to reply when Xorin steps forward.

I hate this guy. He's such an asshole. Xorin, God of War, son of Trakiin. You'll never find a stupider god, or a bigger bully. He's like every low-IQ, over-muscled jock you ever knew in high school, mashed into one.

"Let me have my way with him, father," he implores. He's got a fist clenched, poised. It's nearly as big as my head. His *chin* is nearly as big as my head. "Let me show him how disobeying your will is a bad idea."

"No, my son. Not yet. Answers first. Then you may have your fun."

But Xorin has little self-control, so he whacks me in the face, taking a down-payment on the violence he's going to unleash later.

For a moment all I can see is whiteness, all I can hear is a ringing in my ears.

I spit out a tooth and some blood, then raise my head.

"Someone open a window," I say. "I think a butterfly just brushed past me."

This enrages Xorin, as I expected it would, and he draws his fist back for another punch.

Trakiin stops him, as I knew he would. Or at any rate hoped.

"Xorin, stand aside," he booms. "Now!"

Reluctantly Xorin moves off, muttering, pouting. He goes to the side of his mother, Hlaarina, who puts an arm round him and pats him and comforts him like the overgrown baby he is. Hlaarina is, of course, Trakiin's twin sister as well as his wife. Who knew gods and hillbillies had so much in common?

Trakiin rises, saunters over to me, hands clasped behind his back.

"Name," he says eventually.

"You're the god," I reply. "Shouldn't you know it already?"

"I do, Ethan Nash. I know all there is to know about you."

"Oh goody. So we can do away with the whole interrogation bit then."

"This isn't an interrogation," says Trakiin.

"It isn't?"

"This is a trial. We are sitting in judgment of you. We wish to hear your perspective."

"So I can argue my case? Maybe get the chance to win my liberty, like in a proper trial? Do I have the right to an attorney?"

Trakiin leans close. "No, Ethan Nash. That is not how it works. You are going to die here today. Foster no illusion as to that. But what kind of gods would we be if we didn't at least offer you a fair hearing?"

"Strange definition of 'fair'," I say. There's still the taste of copper in my mouth and a huge-seeming hole in my gum where a tooth should be. "I do not think it means what you think it means."

"'Fair' is whatever I say it is," Trakiin declares. "If you don't like it, we can end this now. I can have Xorin set to work on you straight away, beat you until everything is broken and you're no more than a bag of shattered bones and ruptured organs. Or perhaps I will ask Jhan S'reen over there to weave her dark magic and suck the life out of you in slow, agonising increments."

He gestures at the Goddess of Death, plump, pale-skinned and buxom, dressed in a combination of frilly white lace and glossy jet-black leather like she's on her way from a wedding to a fetish party. Her eyes are eightballs – white iris, black sclera – and her fingernails are so long and curved they might as well be talons. They say she feeds on souls. I say she could stand to go on a diet and lose a few pounds, maybe cut back on the number of victims she drains for sustenance.

But I don't voice the thought.

Because something in her eerie eightball eyes, her sickle smile, her curvaceous mama-does-kinky body, scares the shit out of me.

"Thought as much," says Trakiin, off my silence. "So we shall do this my way. I ask, you speak."

"Okay," I say, nodding. If it'll postpone my death for just a few minutes…

"First of all, tell me of the forbidden zone. The location of your petty Luminous raid. Tell me about the mission from the outset."

* * *

The mission was supposed to be a straightforward infil/exfil. Isn't it always? The objective was to scrounge up evidence. Clues, if there were any. Stuff we could show the world. Something to demonstrate conclusively that the Savior Gods were the frauds we at Luminous knew them to be.

It wasn't enough simply to say they were bogus. We had spent years doing just that to little effect as their noose continued to tighten around our collective neck. We had to back up our claims with cold hard data and we believed the ruins of Kennedy Space Center held just the clue we'd been searching for.

The team was five-strong. There was me, of course, the fearless leader and local asset, first-class lady killer and seasoned field agent. There was the decorated sharpshooter Carrie Lind, heavy muscle on loan from the European branch of Luminous. Tales of her exploits were so legendary they pervaded the guerrilla network here in the States. According to scuttlebutt Lind counted multiple Dominions among her hit-tally – and with that composite bow of hers no less. I intended to ask Lind about that dubious claim prior to her arrival but it turned out she wasn't big on kill and tell.

Accompanying her from across the Atlantic was Ben Jorgensen, also ex-military, Lind's full-time spotter and part-time lover. Affable and unaccustomed to the heat, Jorgensen adopted billowy Aloha shirts and cargo shorts as his undercover attire. Nothing screams conspicuous like a 6'5" Scandinavian dressed like a Margaritaville outcast but I wasn't going to argue fashion with the Benny the Friendly Viking.

Ashton Roth, our science guy and allegedly one of Luminous's brightest minds, had journeyed from Mexico to join our crusade. Roth was as tan as Jorgensen was pale. While he wasn't an experienced operator like the sniper or her spotter, Roth roamed the world unimpeded by the Templars and their draconian travel restrictions. He knew all the wrinkles. He could be a ghost when required, slipping under every radar.

And then we had the inscrutable John-Patrick McCreedy, former Catholic priest, faith expert. McCreedy came highly recommended from a persuasive senior officer, though I couldn't fathom what purpose a 'faith expert' might serve during this specific op. He was the nearest by when the call went out, and the two of us spent the better part of a month together waiting for the others to arrive. Three and a half weeks together and I couldn't tell you the first thing about McCreedy save he always seemed to be sucking on a peppermint.

I was basking in the sun at the bar on the patio of Nelson's Folly in Miami when I received the go-ahead to proceed with Operation Iconoclast. Four days in a row I'd visited the establishment, hoping to get lucky and instead slinking back to the safe house with blue balls – metaphorically speaking of course. I nursed a Cuba Libre while leafing through the final issue of *Samson*, a comicbook circulated by an underground press. I found the religious-themed narrative nonsensical and the quality of the print lacking, but I couldn't deny I enjoyed the stylistic depictions of violence.

"Do you often go to the bar to be antisocial?"

I glanced up from a two-page spread of the titular Samson tearing down the pillars of the Temple of Dagon. A young woman with tawny skin and a pearlescent smile sidled up to me at the bar and ordered a mojito. I didn't recognize her but that didn't mean anything – Luminous cells were highly compartmentalized in order to prevent entire sections from being wiped out if one cell got busted.

"Excuse me?"

"You're reading in public," she said. "Makes conversation with other human beings a little difficult."

"You know, once upon a time everyone carried around portable electronic devices with them. They had access to the news, weather, music, books, games all in the palm of their hand. Had their eyes constantly glued to the things. Sometimes even on dates. It made conversation *very* difficult," I said.

She laughed, pretend-incredulous.

"I've given away my age haven't I?"

She nodded, laughed again and sat down at the open seat next to me. I set *Samson* down and she appraised the bombastic cover.

"That looks like something the censors would classify seditious material. Couldn't you get in trouble for reading that?" she asked.

"The authorities are too busy cracking down on those pesky secular humanists to bother with a harmless cartoon strip," I replied, and it was true. I indulged in small sins in order to mask my more egregious transgressions. After all, there's nothing more suspicious than a saint. Tradecraft 101.

"You still haven't answered my first question," she said.

"Hmmm?"

"Do you regularly go out to *not* interact with people?"

"I'm actually waiting on someone," I said.

"Woman?" she probed. "Man?"

"Oh, I figure I'll know 'em when I see 'em," I said and winked.

The bartender returned with her mojito. She thanked him and paid.

"Well, if they fail to materialize and you're in the neighborhood, some friends of mine are having a party tonight. You're welcome to join us." She pulled a pen from her purse and started writing on a bar napkin. "I'll warn you, though. It's going to get wild."

She kissed the napkin, handed it to me, and left, cocktail in hand. I looked down at the scribbled message. Anyone else who read it would see the time and address of the aforementioned party, with an inviting lipstick mark for good measure. To a Luminous operative capable of decoding it, however, it was the confirmation we'd been waiting for. I polished off the rest of my Cuba Libre and shoved the napkin in my pocket.

"Can I get you another round?" asked the bartender.

"Nah, I'll settle up. It looks like I got a shindig to get ready for," I said with a grin and paid my tab.

"Hlaarina's blessing be upon you brother," he said.

"And also upon you," I replied.

I left Nelson's Folly with a little extra pep in my step. It was a possibility I would die in a few short hours. The greater tragedy was that it seemed even less likely the beautiful young woman I'd just met would survive the diversion her cell had planned for us. But the wait was finally over and the excitement of it suffused every inch of my body. The time to act was now.

Per standard operating procedure I took a Surveillance Detection Route – or SDR – on my way back to the safe house. I cut through the crowd to cross the street and headed for the park.

A priest blared the horn from behind the wheel of an electric car, the mass of pedestrians refusing to part. The only motor vehicles on the road these days belonged to the Savior Gods' clergy and enforcers, and as a result people weren't certain how to react. The priest's Templar escort climbed out the passenger-side door and began clubbing the nearest civilians with a baton. The club smashed into an older woman's face and she dropped, nose erupting with blood. The throng quickly got the message and parted to allow the car through.

I clenched my jaw and kept walking until I arrived at the park entrance, good mood forgotten. The public area was relatively empty that time of day and the absence of foot traffic would make it easier to spot hostile surveillance. I used the layout of the walking paths to my advantage, ambling along without any apparent direction. Seemingly at random I sped up and slowed my pace, took abrupt turns and doubled back around a time or two. I passed several other people during my stroll but none struck me as undercover Templars.

I took a detour to make an offering on my way out of the park, as was customary. A statue of Fhariyya, Goddess of Hunts and Wilderness, posed proudly in polished granite, surrounded by hand-carved wildlife native to the area. Or at least she would have posed proudly had some brave soul not spray painted a dick and balls on her in vivid lime green. I stifled a laugh and flicked a dodecagonal coin stamped with Trakiin's face on one side and an image of Kha'cheldaa on the other into the pool at the sculpture's feet.

A beleaguered-looking groundskeeper approached with a bucket of sudsy water and a brush and set to scrubbing the graffiti as though his life depended on it. It very well might have. I made one final circuit of the park and, satisfied I wasn't being followed, went back to home base to tell everyone the good news.

"Luuuucy, I'm hoooome!" I said stepping in the front door of my apartment.

Lind sat on the floor waxing her bowstring. She glanced at me before returning her attention to proper bow maintenance. Roth waved dismissively from the cot where he lay reading some banned science textbook. McCreedy too sat on the floor, fieldstripping and cleaning a Sig Sauer P225. He ignored me entirely.

Jorgensen was considerably more welcoming, wrapping me in his rib-crushing embrace. Did I forget to mention that Benny was a hugger?

"Good to see you too, now would'ya mind letting me go?" I asked.

"Sorry, sorry. I'm getting a little stir crazy is all," he said, admonished. I couldn't fault him. Our crew may have consisted of consummate professionals but they weren't exactly what anyone would consider companionable. Spending days sequestered in a one-bedroom apartment wasn't doing anything to improve their attitudes either.

"I've got good news," I said patting Jorgensen on the shoulder. That seemed to grab Lind and Roth's attention. McCreedy disregarded the announcement as if I hadn't said anything at all, intent on the disassembled parts of his weapon.

"Hey Padre," I said, addressing McCreedy with the sarcastic title I'd bestowed upon him after weeks of trying to crack his prickly shell. His stayed on task but his eyes locked on my own. I suppressed a shiver as my Lizard Brain recoiled from McCreedy's scrutiny. *He's just the retired practitioner of a dead religion*, I tried to remind myself.

Watching how naturally his fingers navigated the handgun made me think otherwise.

"We got the green light. Iconoclast is a go."

\* \* \*

"Yes, yes," says Trakiin. "Fascinating stuff. Your disapproval of us and our methods is duly noted, Mr Nash."

"Disapproval?" huffs Xorin. "Outright blasphemy!"

Trakiin shoots him a look that's equal parts fatherly reproof and kingly contempt. Xorin bristles, but decides he's better off not taking the argument any further. Meanwhile the Dominions, in their recess perches, stir. Wings twitch and flare, and steel-jacketed hands grasp blast-lances that little more tightly. They're attuned to the mood in the chamber, sensitive to the tides of emotion ebbing and flowing, the raising of voices, heart rate acceleration, adrenaline spikes. Their hardwired programming compels them to defend the Savior Gods from any perceived threat, however great or small, with overwhelming lethal force.

My skin prickles as I think about them, about what they could do to me. In many ways I'm more scared of the Dominions than I am of Trakiin or Xorin or even Jhan S'reen. Android angels can't be reasoned with or pleaded with.

*Just stay calm*, I tell myself. *Keep the fear in check. Keep talking*.

But that's easier said than done. I've seen Dominions in action several times, but most memorably at a protest rally in New York. It was during the early days of the Savior Gods' reign. We'd already lost the Forty-eight Hour War but people still thought we had some choice in the matter, still thought that by getting together in public and expressing our feelings we might somehow persuade them our modern society had no need of gods and convince them to leave us alone. I was there, on a hot summer's afternoon in Central Park, waving my placard and chanting the slogans. Mostly I'd gone because my college girlfriend, Claire, wanted to be there and I was too hornily in love with her to say I wouldn't come. I was still at the stage of needing to impress her.

The crowd numbered – best guess – a couple hundred thousand. It was before the Savior Gods shut down all mass communication and texts and social media had spread the word and generated a real grass-roots movement. It seemed to us the gods surely couldn't ignore so much concentrated anger, such a critical mass of opposition. They'd have to pay attention.

And we were right, but in the wrong way. The Order of Templars hadn't been formed yet, but the Savior Gods had an already established means of crushing resistance. Dominions descended from out of the blazing blue sky above the park, dozens of them, firing plasma bolts from their blast-lances indiscriminately into the crowd. Protest turned to panic. As many were killed in the stampede as were incinerated by the Dominions' strafing.

Claire and I were running for our lives, like everyone else. I was holding Claire's hand. We'd nearly made it to the edge of the park, onto Fifth Avenue, and I was thinking we could take shelter inside the MOMA, hole up there until the chaos was over. Then a shimmer of wings, a wave of searing heat, and I was still holding Claire's hand. But only that. Sheared off at the wrist, the stump neatly cauterized. Of Claire herself, nothing else was left. She'd been vaporised in an instant.

And the gods had made themselves a lifelong enemy that day.

Not just because of Claire, although that was traumatizing enough. Because of the sheer senseless slaughter. Fully half the people who attended the rally died that day. Wiped off the face of the planet. Senior citizens among them. Mothers. Doctors. Firefighters. Kindergarten teachers. Kids. All for daring to defy false gods. The massacre proved quite the recruitment drive for Luminous.

"We should expect nothing more, or less, from Mr Nash," Trakiin says. "A Luminous operative is by definition a blasphemer, and one moreover who is so immersed in his heresy that he sees it as a virtue rather than a deadly sin. Luminous exists to defy our rule. They will stop at nothing, and stoop to anything, to rid the world of us."

You have to hand it to old Trakiin: he's a damn good speechifier. Him make talk sound pretty.

"It's at the very least ingratitude," he continues. "Have we gods not created peace? Where there was once discord, we have brought harmony. Where there was once inequality, we have brought fairness. Where there was once despair, we have brought hope. The human race was hell-bent on its own destruction before we arrived. In fifty years, maybe less, it would have rendered its environment uninhabitable and annihilated itself squabbling over the few precious resources remaining. Now it can look forward to a better, simpler, cleaner future, one less reliant on technology, less rapacious, less internecine. Mankind, united by the one true faith."

Ooh, *internecine*. Fancy.

Trakiin stares pointedly at me, as though he can hear my snarky thoughts. "Such salvation is something people like you, Mr Nash, seem determined to reject. Why is that?"

"That a rhetorical question, or are you actually asking me? It's sometimes hard to tell."

"Perhaps you'd care to enlighten me, Luminous."

"Well, on balance, I'd say I prefer to be a free man than a slave to space Nazis. Just my opinion, mind you. Your mileage may vary."

Trakiin's lip curls, amusement crossbred with a pitbull snarl.

"Plus," I add, "it isn't 'peace' if it needs to be maintained with an iron fist. The one kinda contradicts the other."

"Ha ha." He says this more than laughs it. "A paradox, if valid."

Then he strokes my chest, gently, almost like a caress.

And five minutes later I'm still writhing on the floor,

wracked in agony from head to toe, every muscle spasming and clenching. It feels like my heart is trying to hammer its way out of my chest cavity. My lungs are burning, my guts cramping, and I can hear myself making pathetic little mewling, choking noises, like a kitten being strangled. A damp crotch tells me I've pissed myself. I think I know now how a convict must feel in the electric chair. Only difference is, I get to live to tell the tale and the convict gets the sweet release of death.

A lovely, maternal face looms over me, blurred in my tear-clogged vision. Hlaarina. With a brush of her fingertips she takes the pain away, all of it, just like that. Suddenly I feel better than I have in years. A new man.

I straighten up. Stand up. Ignoring the wetness that pastes the fabric of my pants to my thighs, I hold myself tall. Or at least as tall as one can stand in front of gods. I'm compelled to hurl myself flat at Hlaarina's feet and worship her for relieving me of the pain. It takes everything I have to resist.

"So," I say, "would you like to hear some more? I mean, as the condemned man on the stand, I'm allowed to make my statement in full, yeah?"

"I prefer to regard it as a confession," Trakiin says, "but by all means continue. We're all ears."

\* \* \*

The diversion went down in Orlando. Luminous operatives – and I'd guess the woman I met at Nelson's Folly was among them, if not the actual ringleader – set off a series of bombs at Redemptionland, the theme park formerly known as Disney's Magic Kingdom. The explosions were carefully orchestrated so that not one innocent bystander was hurt. The damage was done to infrastructure alone: the exhibits, the chapels, the rides. The Holy History Tour in particular took a pounding, with almost every waxwork tableau getting at least partially blown up. So for a while to come, until it's all fixed, nobody will have the pleasure of viewing, say, *Trakiin's Singlehanded Conquest of Moscow during the Forty-eight Hour War* or *The Friendly Rivalry Between Xorin and His Brother Q'lun* and endure the bullshit recorded narration accompanying these scenes.

Naturally, Templars flocked to the site and, like the good little jackbooted thugs they are, started making arrests and breaking heads. Redemptionland had been busy that day, full of eager sheep, sorry, *tourists* who'd made the pilgrimage to the place from as far afield as California and Canada. Some of these folks would have spent several months' wages for the privilege, the cost including travel permits, tickets for long journeys by solar-powered locomotive or electric bus, and of course the Faith Tithe that funds the Templars and keeps the clergy and theocrats in the luxury they so richly deserve. They weren't expecting to have their day ruined by a series of noisy detonations and the less-than-discriminate attentions of divinely appointed rent-a-cops who uphold the law with batons, swords, and coilguns. Must've come as quite a shock.

Not sure if the Luminous cell got away unscathed or fell foul of the Templars but I'd put money on the latter. If any survived long enough to be captured they'll be in holding cells at the Orlando Temple of Correction, getting their fingernails pliered out and their kneecaps pulverised. I've heard Templar inquisitors are especially fond of holy-waterboarding. You can take the interrogator out of the CIA...

At any rate, Orlando's Templars were busy. Hell, most of Florida's Templars were busy. Nothing kicks the hornets' nest like a good 'terrorist atrocity'. Suddenly the buggers were buzzing everywhere, swarms of them, angry and vengeful and above all undisciplined. Disorganized. Lashing out. Looking every which way but where they *should* be looking.

Which was over on the eastern flank of Florida, on Merritt Island, just north-northwest of Cape Canaveral, in the swampy forbidden zone that had once been the Launchpad and development hub for America's space program.

Because that was where the five of us – me, Lind, Jorgensen, Roth and Padre McCreedy – were getting to work.

We inserted at 9pm, shortly after nightfall. We'd spent the best part of the day hauling our asses from Miami, a couple of hundred miles up the coast by motor launch, hugging the shoreline. Finding a small seaworthy craft with a working outboard had been a challenge, to say the least. Thank fuck there was a thriving black market in the rental of such things, and a very nice guy called Felipe was only too happy to take a thousand cash to let us borrow the boat. Gas was extra, and even more expensive. He might as well have been selling us jerrycans of pure myrrh, the amount he charged. But at least it was all on a no-questions-asked basis, and Felipe looked as though he knew how to keep a secret, judging by the Blessed Virgin Mary tattoo I saw peeping out from under the sleeve of his T-shirt. Like McCreedy he was a covert Catholic, no doubt with a neighborhood church in someone's garage or basement where he'd meet on Sundays with likeminded individuals and share the Sacrament with them and pray they wouldn't get caught.

We chuntered northward, slowing if we passed anything that even smelled like a Templar coastal patrol craft. We made landfall in a creek so overgrown with mangrove and saw palmetto it was little more than a narrow stream in places. We hitched up the boat and waded inland through some of the most inhospitable terrain I'd ever encountered. If the stagnant swamp water sucking at our boots wasn't enough, there were the hummingbird-sized mosquitos sucking at our blood. An alligator as big as a fucking Buick swam past, only its eyes and snout above the surface, giving us a hard reptilian glare as though sizing us up, trying to figure which of us would be the tastiest snack. Lind kept her rifle trained on it the whole time – a British Army SA80-L85 she'd 'liberated' from her barracks arsenal the same day she went permanently AWOL and joined the Luminous cause – until we could safely say, "See ya later, alligator." Even then her forefinger never strayed far from the trigger, and I for one would not have been sad to see a 5.56x45mm bullet turn the creature's brain to so much mush. The dinosaur wouldn't have shown *us* any mercy if it had come back for dinner.

Same goes for the panther that stalked us for a couple miles. That feline sonofabitch was so assured of its status as apex land predator in the area, it barely made any attempt at stealth. It just prowled alongside us at a distance of no more than a dozen yards, sometimes lurking in thickets of bald cypress but mostly giving us a clear, unimpeded view of its tawny pelt and loping strides, as though saying, *Screw you, humans. You're on my turf. Deal.*

Then we came to the perimeter fence.

Or what was left of the perimeter fence.

Chain-link mesh tangled in weeds and thick vines, it was more like a sagging wall of greenery. Plenty of handholds and toeholds. We climbed over it as easily as if it were a child's jungle gym, and paid no mind whatsoever to the sign posted on top which read:

## FORBIDDEN ZONE
## ENTRY STRICTLY PROHIBITED
## ON PAIN OF DEATH

## BY DIVINE DECREE

Because, well, that was kind of the whole point of being there, wasn't it? To enter this STRICTLY PROHIBITED location? With the degree of heat we were packing we were already in violation of so many divine decrees that traipsing around in the forbidden zone would be the least of the Templars' concerns should we be caught.

Once we were safely the other side of the fence, McCreedy crossed himself. *Spectacles, testicles, wallet, watch,* as the old joke goes. But he did it with the Sig in his hand, the fat suppressor threaded on the end of the barrel tapping the four points on his body. I guess, just in case his capital-G God was otherwise engaged, the semiauto offered an extra layer of reassurance. When prayer doesn't work, a 10mm subsonic round can often fill the gap.

Ahead, beyond an undulating landscape of grass and wild shrubbery, the buildings of the old Kennedy Space Center loomed.

"Our intel's good, isn't it?" Jorgensen piped up. "Just asking."

"Bit late for that," said Lind. "We're already committed."

"But if we've gone to all this trouble and we get to those buildings and it turns out there's nothing inside worth risking our necks for…"

"The intel's good," I said, with perhaps more confidence than I felt. Luminous shared information across its various networks as best it could, but communications were never straightforward and messages could be intercepted, corrupted, falsified. You couldn't completely rely on what anyone said. "Now's as good a time as any to tell you that this mission isn't only about looking for proof about the Savior Gods," said Roth.

I arched an eyebrow. "It isn't?"

"No. That's a secondary objective. They're aliens. That's pretty much taken as read. It's the only possible explanation for their enhanced abilities and their apparent immortality. We believe they fled from a world far in advance of ours, technologically speaking. They're not messiahs, just intergalactic scammers – a bunch of chancers who spied an opportunity to lord over a stunted, backwards civilisation and seized it with both hands. And if we can find anything to confirm that, great. Cool. High-fives all round."

"But…?" Lind prompted.

"But… after the Savior Gods arrived and began throwing their weight around, NASA began working on methods of negating their powers, levelling the playing field for us mere mortals. The eggheads examined whatever of their tech they could scavenge from the Forty-eight Hour War and took it to pieces trying to find out what made it tick. There were even attempts to reverse-engineer Dominions' blast-lances and flight capability. The goal was a weapon that could bring down gods."

Jorgensen let out a low whistle.

"For the longest time we were under the impression they didn't get very far, though," Roth went on. "The Big Twelve caught wind of what was up and flew in to personally Sodom and Gomorrah'd the shit out of the place. Scorched earth, motherfucker. The NASA guys never stood a chance. That day, religion disproved science."

"But doesn't that imply there's nothing here now?" I said. "The Twelve would have been thorough cleaning the place out surely."

"New intel suggests it's possible something survived. Sources claim the rocket scientists were in fact closer to their goal than anyone realised. They may even have achieved it." Roth paused. "Somewhere on the premises there may well be something that can kill a god."

McCreedy broke the silence that followed. "'May' being the operative word. What are the odds?"

"No idea," Roth admitted, "but whatever they are, I'm willing to take the gamble. We should all be. The potential reward is just too damn valuable."

Lind and McCreedy both looked skeptical, whereas Jorgensen was nodding avidly.

"So," I said, "we continue to treat this as a regular op, only with possible fringe benefits. Huge ones."

"I had a girlfriend like that once," Jorgensen said, clutching two handfuls of empty air at chest height. "Huge benefits."

"Oh, shut up," Lind said, thwacking his meaty biceps with a fist.

Jorgensen grinned impishly through his thick, Scandinavian-pale beard. "Better equipped than you in that respect, darling. But she couldn't shoot the wings off a gnat like you can."

"And the balls off a Norwegian, too, if necessary."

"I love it when you try to emasculate me."

"You won't love it when I actually do."

"Enough foreplay you two," I said. "We've tyrants to dethrone."

The brief moment of levity over, Lind transitioned back into default ice-cold operator mode. Jorgensen gave me an appreciative wink, and as a group we closed in on the Space Center. We moved slow through the waist-high grass, keeping a low profile and taking advantage of the concealment provided by unkempt foliage. Despite his size, Jorgensen proved to be quite stealthy. Lind moved effortlessly, gliding through the grass like a snake, but to my utter amazement Padre McCreedy gave her a run for her money. Roth tried his damnedest to keep up but I couldn't help but cringe, expecting a barrage of bullets to blast us apart with every clumsy, squelching footstep he took.

Mercifully the Templars had ceased patrolling that far out from the facilities years ago, and with the distraction at Redemptionland there was only a skeleton crew on station. As we drew closer, I recognized the charred carcass of the Vehicle Assembly Building and had an urge to do my best Charlton Heston impression circa '68 – *You maniacs! You blew it up! Ah, damn you! God damn you all to hell!* – but refrained. I'd estimate only a third of the buildings remained standing, and even those Mother Nature was fighting for sovereignty over. If the weeds sprouting up through crumbling asphalt and the kudzu blanketing walls and abandoned vehicles were any indication, the Templars were losing that particular war.

We stopped to allow Roth to get his bearings in the alien landscape. He removed a battered old map and a penlight from his kit. We surrounded him, blocking the light from line-of-sight with our bodies while he worked. We heard the Templar well before we spotted him – stomping around through the undergrowth and whistling a melody from an early 2000s pop song. He stepped out from behind a collapsed structure fifty meters ahead and moved toward us, the torch mounted on his coilgun sweeping lazily back and forth; the product of lax discipline and long hours at an uneventful post.

Padre McCreedy raised his Sig and I aimed down the holographic sight of my MP7A2, but Jorgensen signalled for us to lower our weapons and we complied. Suppressed though they might have been, neither the Sig nor my Heckler and Koch personal defence weapon was silent. Lind slung the SA80 assault rifle and took out her composite bow, nocking a broadhead-tipped arrow from her quiver. She took aim as the Templar closed in on our position, the beam of his torch creeping too close for comfort. With a *thwish* the arrow launched, travelling the short distance between Lind and the Templar, piercing his neck and severing his spine.

The Templar's rifle fell and his body wasn't far behind. Jorgensen rushed and caught him, lowering him gently to minimize sound. He checked to confirm the Templar was dead and incapable of calling for support. Jorgensen turned off the rifle-mounted torch and dragged the weapon and body into a dense thicket off the road. I got the impression from the speed and efficiency of the whole process that it was well practiced and frequently implemented by Lind and Jorgensen.

I'd be lying if I said it didn't turn me on just a bit.

"Are we good to go?" I whispered to Roth.

He bobbed his head and placed the map and penlight back in his kit. Roth indicated the direction we needed to go and we crept that way at a glacial pace. Jorgensen ranged ahead and Padre McCreedy brought up the rear. I covered Roth, and Lind stayed with us, bow held at the ready.

Forty-five minutes of creeping along abandoned streets and dodging patrols later, and Roth gestured toward a relatively intact building. There was nothing to distinguish it from any of the other relatively intact buildings apart from a pair of guards standing by a hole in the wall vaguely shaped like it was made by a linebacker on super-steroids.

*Xorin was here*, I told myself.

These Templars appeared significantly more alert than the one dispatched by Lind earlier. Even more inconveniently, they remained firmly rooted at their station and were encased in complete sets of armor – helmets and all. We watched from a distance for a while but they stood at attention the entire time, not even shifting slightly to prevent cramp. Could've earned themselves a penny or two as human statues on Venice Beach.

Jorgensen cased the joint and found two locked doors in back and around the side and some busted windows too small for any of us to fit through. Every minute we wasted increased the risk of the dead Templar's disappearance being noted.

We needed to act.

Padre McCreedy and I were the only ones with suppressed firearms. Guns are rare enough in the age of the Savior Gods but suppressors are almost impossible to find. I knew my 4.6x30mm rounds could defeat Templar body armor but I wasn't sure if McCreedy's Sig would do the trick, let alone if he could hit the target from that distance with a pistol.

"Got anything capable of penetrating ballistic plate tucked away up your sleeve?" I murmured to Lind, half serious.

She selected an arrow with red fletching from her quiver and showed me the nasty-looking bodkin tip affixed to the carbon shaft.

"Will that do the trick?"

"Hasn't failed me yet," she remarked.

"Fair enough," I conceded.

"You take the goon on the left, I got the one on the right. You shoot first and I'll follow your lead."

I shouldered my MP7 and acquired the guard to the left of the god-shaped cavity. I took deep controlled breaths, in through the nose and out through the mouth. The holographic reticle hovered on the dodecagonal badge of the Savior Gods emblazoned on the Templar's gleaming breastplate. I breathed out one final time, pause, and my finger stroked the trigger.

*Snap. Snap. Snap.*

The guard convulsed and collapsed as three tungsten carbide penetrators bypassed his armor in quick succession and shredded his heart. Beside him the second Templar fumbled with an arrow that had sprouted unexpectedly from his gorget. Before he could cause too much of a racket Jorgensen was there, knife in hand, to deliver the *coup de grâce*. Jorgensen ducked his head inside Xorin's improvised entrance and signalled to us the coast was clear.

We hustled down the street and dragged the dead guards inside behind us and out of immediate visibility.

"Lind, Jorgensen, patrol the perimeter. I want to know if anyone comes within two blocks. Padre, mind our egress point. I don't want any surprises if a Templar manages to slip their net." At this, Lind huffed. "Roth you're with me. Find us that silver bullet."

Whatever purpose the premises once served was no longer identifiable. The God of War had redecorated the interior with the subtle eye for design of an artillery shell. Splintered desks and shattered monitors served as tombstones for skeletons bearing the evidence of excessive trauma. Yet more weeds sprouted from craters stamped into the flooring tiles by massive footprints. Pens and various other office paraphernalia crunched under the tread of my boots as Roth and I delved deeper into the facility.

Roth picked his way through the wreckage, examining each long-dead tablet and opening every desk drawer. I was starting to doubt he would find anything of value to the cause. If there was even anything of value to find. Would the Savior Gods really leave any stone unturned if they believed a threat to their reign existed? It would have been deliciously appropriate to punish such hubris in the manner of the pagan gods of ancient Greece but the longer Roth spent scouring the debris the less plausible it seemed.

"Do you even know what you're looking for?" I asked.

"Have some faith, Ethan," Roth chided. I snorted to hear that coming from a fellow Luminous operative but he failed to register my amusement.

"My life's work has consisted of collecting accounts of the research these brave men and women were conducting here." Roth gestured to a pulverised skull. "Exclusively from secondary sources, mind you. Trakiin and his cronies aren't invulnerable, you know. They're too reliant on the Dominions for that to be the case."

Roth approached a safe embedded in the wall. Or partially embedded anyway. In the process of forcing the fortified door Xorin had wrenched the safe loose.

"Some even theorize the Dominions are intended to protect the Savior Gods from each other as much as from us," he said.

He turned on his penlight and probed inside the gaping hollow. The narrow beam darted around, illuminating naught but bare metal surfaces.

"Nothing," he said.

"Xorin wasn't going to come all this way from orbit, slaughter a bunch of nerds, nearly rip a safe out of the wall in the process of trying to open it, only to leave behind whatever he found inside it," I said.

"Unless he didn't know where to look," said Roth. He stuck the penlight between his teeth and began feeling around the empty box with both hands. The whole mission objective was beginning to seem absurd. I needed to weigh the odds of success against the lives of the men and women under my command. I mentally agreed to indulge him for another minute when I heard a *click* followed by a triumphant "Aha!"

"And this is why you don't send the God of War to recover sensitive materials," said Roth as he removed a steel plate from the safe and placed it on the floor. "False bottom. Classic misdirection. That big meathead would have snatched whatever was in the primary safe and never given it a second thought."

"Well? What's in the box?"

He rummaged around inside the recess and retrieved what looked to be an autoinjector and a sheaf of papers. He flipped through the papers and a smile spread across his face, gleaming white in the dark.

"Salvation," he said.

"Oh."

I hadn't imagined a fully functional blast-lance could fit inside the strongbox but I was hoping for something slightly more impressive than a spring-loaded syringe and an instruction manual. It certainly didn't resemble salvation to me.

"I'm up-to-date on all my vaccines, doc."

"This is no vaccine. This is a virus, a techno-virus to be precise, and it is imperative we deliver this to a Luminous lab to be analysed, reproduced, and tested. If this is what I believe it to be, it could very well end the war."

I was about to ask Roth what the hell a techno-virus was and how it could end a decades long conflict – and that, naturally, was the moment everything went to shit. The only warning given was the sudden widening of Roth's eyes. I ducked, pivoted, and drew my weapon in a single motion, startling the Templars who were breaching the building through our egress point. I hosed them with rounds as they discharged their own weapons in a strobe of electromagnetically propelled ball bearings.

"Side door!" I shouted at Roth over the high-pitched whine of the Templars' coilguns, hoping he was still alive to hear me.

The nearest Templar staggered and sank to one knee, blood pumping from the wide-spaced holes punched into his plate. Those filing in behind him dove for whatever cover the debris provided and I used the lull in combat to scoot on out of there, but not before lobbing a homemade explosive in their general direction to keep them occupied. I reunited with a remarkably intact Roth at the side door and kicked it open, dragging him into the alley with me.

We took off at a sprint, stumbling as the IED detonated with an impressive *crump*. One of my hand's clutched Roth at all times while the other maintained a grip on the MP7. We navigated the ruins of Kennedy Space Center at breakneck speed. The streets crawled with Templar patrols, and after a few more frenzied shootouts I found myself running low on both bullets and bombs. Just as Roth was about to collapse from exhaustion I found a secluded corner to catch our breath. I took a slug of my canteen and passed it over to him.

"What do we do now?" asked Roth between alternating gulps of air and water.

"You and I exfil to the boat and bug-out."

"What about the others?"

The cacophony of gunfire persisted even when I wasn't forced to engage the Templars – primarily the distinctive sound of gauss weapons but punctuated by the bark of more traditional chemical-propellant guns. I'd swear that once in flight from a squad of goons I'd glimpsed a couple pin-cushioned with arrows as if Lind was providing cover for us, but in the chaos and terror I didn't halt to check. At least one member of our team was still alive out there, possibly more, and they were in the thick of it but we couldn't jeopardize the mission.

"What about them? You said it yourself; this techno-virus could end the war. That's bigger than any one of us," I said.

Roth looked like he wanted to argue but rationality prevailed. He was a man of science after all. Roth passed the canteen back, I took another swig and fastened it to my webbing. I loaded my last remaining magazine into the MP7 and we left without a further word. Back past the shells of buildings gone back to nature at the skirts of the Space Center. Back through the long grass and tangling shrubbery that clung to our heels like a one-night stand hinting at going steady. Back over the drooping perimeter fence with its strongly-worded sign ineffectually declaring, *You shall not pass.* Back into that Trakiin-damned swamp and its nose-assaulting bouquet of decaying plant and animal matter.

With guilt weighing heavy on my shoulders the trudge back to the boat was substantially more taxing than the infiltration had been. The farther we got from the Space Center the quieter it got, the silence smothering me like an accusation.

"We made it," I said as we arrived at the location of our lent watercraft, "and someone beat us here." McCreedy stood by the dinghy, Sig drawn and levelled at us as we emerged from the thicket.

"You can lower that heater, Padre, we come in peace," I called to him.

The gun in his hand didn't waver.

*Ahhh, shit.*

"It's us," Roth added, "Ashton and Ethan. What happened back there? We got mobbed by Templars."

"Where are Lind and Jorgensen?" asked McCreedy.

*Shit, shit, shit.*

"We hoped to regroup with them here but we couldn't risk waiting," Roth replied.

"You found it then?" asked McCreedy. "Mission accomplished?"

*Shit, shit, fuck, shit.* My grip tightened on the MP7.

"Yeah, I got it right here," Roth answered.

The night gave birth to stars around us and a barrage of amplified voices commanded *"Drop your fucking weapons"* and *"Get the fuck down"* and *"Hands behind your fucking heads."* The chirp of primed coilguns added authority to the directives.

Shock and awe.

I complied, tossing aside my gun, lacing my fingers behind my head, and lowering myself kneeling in the mud too overwhelmed to even consider resisting. As two VTOL-capable 'chariots' bathed the clearing with the brilliance of their searchlights, I saw the squads of Templars surrounding us.

"Why?" I asked as a Templar stepped up to frisk and disarm me while his comrades trained enough firepower on me to render me a sizzling meat pudding.

"I know what you Luminous heathens did to my God," Padre McCreedy replied, "so I found a replacement."

Mr Handsy finished divesting me of anything even suggestively lethal and secured my hands in manacles behind my back.

"Be gentle with that one, he's carrying precious cargo," instructed McCreedy of Mr Handsy who had moved on to cavity search Roth.

*Bang, bang!*

One aerial searchlight winked out of existence.

*Bang, bang!*

The other searchlight sparked and died. From a separate location another shooter opened fire, wielding one of the Templars' own coilguns against them to fabulous result. Jorgensen and Lind took turns shooting and repositioning. The Templars all reacted with varying degrees of discipline, some going so far as to shoot into the woods at random in all directions. I body-checked Mr Handsy and yelled for Roth to run.

He only managed a few strides before his legs gave out beneath him. At first I thought he'd tripped on his own feet until I saw McCreedy advancing on us, Sig outstretched. I scuttled to shield Roth's body with my own. McCreedy stood poised to kill me when a hyper-accelerated projectile introduced the Padre to his deceased deity. Whether the shot came courtesy of Jorgensen and his pilfered coilgun or from a panicked Templar I'm unsure. I'll never get the opportunity to ask Jorgensen either.

The chariot pilots recovered from the loss of their searchlights quickly enough. They activated whatever enhanced optics those cockpits offer, pinpointed where the incoming gunfire was originating, and rained down hell on our sniper and spotter. I gotta give Lind credit, she still managed to down one of those bastards, but there was no surviving the volume of ordnance those chariots brought to bear.

I knelt over the dying Roth while the napalm-fuelled conflagration blazed around us, a proper Viking funeral that would have made Jorgensen proud. Roth whispered to me his final words and passed away.

\* \* \*

I finish my story. "I mustn't have even made it a mile before your surviving thugs got their shit together, consolidated and captured me. You decreed that the Templar captain deliver me to Kha'cheldaa for questioning, and here I am, awaiting your most merciful, erm… mercy?"

"What a remarkably comprehensive and thoroughly damning account," says Trakiin. Seated back on his throne now, he straightens his posture, jaw coming off fist, no longer imitating *Le Penseur*.

"What I fail to comprehend is the *why* of it all," he goes on. "Why were you willing to endure such hardship, willing to sacrifice yourselves for such petty defiance? Why is Luminous so determined to depose us? How can you be so certain we are not your gods?"

"Who cares, Father?" Xorin bellow. "They piss on the gifts we've bestowed upon them. They spit in our faces. End this farce of a trial and let me execute him!"

"'Bestowed' and 'execute' eh? Don't overexert yourself there, big guy," I say.

The God of War surges toward me only to be restrained by the two nearest Savior Gods, his brother Q'lun and sister Fhariyya. They harbor no love for me but they do fear the displeasure of their father. I sneak a glance. Overhead the Dominions twitch and tense, provoked by the outburst of near violence.

Their movements, though, display a trace of uncertainty. Hesitance, almost.

As though something's up with their programming. As though a ghost has somehow entered the machine.

I stifle a tiny grin.

"Show a modicum of self-control, Xorin," admonishes Trakiin. "Once I have my answer you may do with him as you wish. Now, Mr Nash, before I cede your life to my eager boy, would you kindly answer my previous question?"

"It would be my honor, your most beneficent majesty," I say, "though I'll confess I'm beginning to have some misgivings as to your omnipotence."

Trakiin motions for me to get on with it, clearly arriving at the end of his patience. The time has come. With luck, I've stalled long enough. I think I may have pulled off what I intended to. I *think*.

"How did we peg you for the charlatans you are?" I say. "Simple, really. We killed all our gods long before you arrived in orbit."

"Excuse me?"

"Our gods – Apollo, Loki, Enlil, Anubis, Kali, Ryūjin, Yahweh – all those 'mythological' deities whose archetypes you shamelessly counterfeited for your own personas, they were real. And we killed them all." I state this matter-of-factly. Matter-of-factly because every word of it is gospel truth. "Luminous, the Illuminati, has existed in one form or another since the dawn of history, fighting from the shadows to free mankind from the shackles of oppression. We've slain every Supreme Being who sought to lord it over us, and we'll sure as shit do the same to you."

"Silence!" Trakiin snaps.

"You're frauds, nothing more than cheap imitations of the real gods, and *they* couldn't even subjugate us for long. So what chance do you think you have?"

"I SAID SILENCE!" roars Trakiin.

"And to top it all off, your genealogy is seriously fucked up. It's no wonder Xorin was born effectively brain dead. That's what happens when you keep it in the family."

That does it, as far as Xorin is concerned. He breaks free from his siblings, throwing them to the floor, and hurtles toward me. Time seems to slow to a crawl while he barrels ahead like a sentient wrecking ball, eyes bulging, teeth bared, spittle flying.

Then a thrust from a blast-lance punctures his back. The weapon's pointed rear tip skewers his heart and erupts out through his left pectoral. Confusion scrunches his thick brow as though he were trying to add two to two and getting five. Xorin takes another step forward, and the Dominion levitating behind him withdraws the blast-lance, swings it around so that the business end is against the back of his skull, and releases a plasma bolt that flash-fries his cranium.

Around the chamber the Savior Gods balk at this audacious display of mutiny from one of their trusted protectors. Q'lun is the first to react, leaping to avenge his fallen brother. He smacks aside the blast-lance before it can get another shot off and he hammers a fist into the android angel's abdomen that cracks its carapace, but before he can deliver a second blow another Dominion swoops down and stoves his head in with a mighty airborne roundhouse kick.

Yet more Dominions descend from on high, and the chamber degenerates into total anarchy.

Most of the Savior Gods attempt to fight. Those more inclined to self-preservation make for the exits in hopes of escape. I watch Jhan S'reen, Goddess of Death, hold her own against three Dominions. She weaves between blast-lance thrusts and plasma bolts, her agility contradicting her ample girth. Her touch corrodes the Dominions' reinforced shells and her talons shear through the weakened material with ease. She plucks the wings off one of her attackers but it latches on to her and creates an opening for the other two to finish her. She perishes with a moan of ecstasy.

Hlaarina's dies attempting to resuscitate her daughter Yuu'oria, the Goddess of Love. A series of plasma bolts splatters the two of them across the floor. While their family is being butchered around them, Bræsheen, the Goddess of Agriculture and Harvest, and Kloxiin, the God of Mischief and Partying, cower under the walnut banquet table until the Dominions drag them out by the ankles and transform them into postmodern art.

One by one they all fall until only two of the Savior Gods remain – the King of the Gods and the Goddess of Hunts and Wilderness. Trakiin and Fhariyya stand back to back, armed with the blast-lances of their vanquished foes. They strike and defend like they've performed this dance before, father and daughter leveraging each other's strengths and guarding each other's weaknesses. Demolished Dominions pile up before them, and it's looking as if they might win through when Fhariyya slips and a blast-lance spears into her stomach, exit nozzle first. She tries to pull herself off the lance but the Dominion ignites a plasma bolt and cooks her from the inside out.

Trakiin lets out an animal cry and flies into a rage, obliterating her assassin and the nearest assailants. Blood sheets down his face from a laceration on his forehead. His chest heaves like a set of bellows and his muscles bunch grotesquely under his tattered robes. He spots me through the red haze and takes the shot. The blast-lance rockets through the air – a javelin aimed right at my heart.

A guardian angel dives to intercept the missile, trading its cybernetic life for my own.

The Dominions encompassing Trakiin close ranks and he vanishes from sight. Blast-lances piston in and out, arising bloodier each time, and through gaps in the androids' formation I watch him sink to floor. I approach and the Dominions part to allow me through. Before me Trakiin lies incapacitated, wrestling to find his breath.

"How?" he croaks.

"The techno-virus," I tell him. "NASA discovered a back door in the Dominion programming and developed a virus that would cause them to obey and defend whoever is the virus's host. Roth injected me with it before he died, thinking I could hide the virus in my blood and escape to pass it on."

I turn to one of the pair of Dominions who are now flanking me, blast-lances at port arms, like an honor guard. "Do you mind?" I present it the manacles binding my hands behind my back. The android angel breaks the chains and for the first time in hours I can stretch my arms above my head and roll my shoulders to unkink them.

"I never expected to wind up on Kha'cheldaa," I say, "let alone be invited into your private chamber. And then you permitted me to monologue long enough for the virus to replicate and work its black magic. So, thank you for that. Thank you and fuck you."

I gesture like a Roman emperor at the Circus Maximus pronouncing death for a defeated gladiator. The Dominions – *my* Dominions – oblige. Trakiin lets out a last defiant, desperate scream, a guttural yell of furious disbelief that is brutally cut short.

I climb over his body, the giant somehow diminished in death, and cross the chamber to that chalk-white throne. It was too large for Trakiin, and it's wayyy too large for me. I clamber onto it, have myself a seat, and survey the carnage I've wrought. The victorious Dominions kneel in a semicircle before me, setting down their blast-lances and bowing their heads.

Bowing to me.

My laughter echoes through the corridors of Kha'cheldaa.

# EXTINCTION LOST
## An Extinction Cycle Novella

Nicholas Sansbury Smith

-1-

A dense snow fell on the team crossing the tarmac toward the Sikorsky UH-60 Black Hawk chopper. Crew Chief Hector Webb zipped his parka up to his chin in an effort to keep out the chill. He hated the cold, especially in a place that kept getting colder. But unless the European Unified Forces – EUF – decided to nuke Greenland it was only going to get worse. Thankfully the trip to the island was a short one. The mission that had rerouted the USS *Forest Sherman* from the main European front would only take a couple of days.

Rubbing his gloved hands together, Webb watched Team Ghost moving as one across the deck of the destroyer. It was 0900 hours, but the sun was hiding in the blurry sky. The wind had picked up, sending walls of snow gusting across their path and covering their white fatigues in a blanket of white. The irony was striking, for a moment Team Ghost appeared as apparitions moving through the storm.

The leader, Master Sergeant Joe Fitzpatrick led the group with his German Shepherd trotting along at his side. Webb had heard the stories about the man and his dog single handily fighting thousands of Variants in New York City before Operation Extinction. There were countless tales of the two taking on formidable odds, but Webb's favorite was the one where Fitz had killed the Bone Collector Alpha with his bare hands. Apollo was said to have eaten the monster's heart.

Webb had his doubts, but if he was ever going to have a chance to ask, it would be on this flight. Perhaps he would even throw in a question about the legendary Captain Reed Beckham sending the dog to Europe with Fitzpatrick.

"Welcome aboard, Master Sergeant," Webb said.

Fitz nodded and climbed into the troop hold with his M4 and MK11. The gum-chewing female member of Team Ghost blew a bubble as she jumped inside. Rico tucked a frosted strand of pink hair under her stocking cap and helmet. Sergeant Hugh Stevenson climbed in next, a skull bandana around his throat – he cradled his M249 SAW. Staff Sergeant Blake Tanaka was the next one in. Webb checked the Katana long blade and the companion Wakizashi short blade strapped to Tanaka's back.

*Damn, they are real.*

He'd heard Tanaka had killed over a hundred Variants with them.

The others all carried silenced M4s, including Specialist Yas Dohi, who spat a licorice root out into the snow then pulled himself inside.

None of them said a word as they sat. Team Ghost was a diverse crew that was for sure; from their weapons to their nationalities.

Webb closed the door to seal out the cold then strapped in. He still couldn't believe he was about to embark on a mission with Team Ghost. Just seeing them here gave him chills. Tanaka, the short Japanese-American soldier with tree trunk legs and a shaved head twisted to adjust the strap of his blades. Dohi reached for another piece of licorice from his vest, and Rico pulled out a journal.

"You ready to rock it, Ghost?" asked the pilot, Ted 'Tito' Bones. He turned from the cockpit, scratching at his chinstrap beard with a grin.

Fitz gave a sluggish thumbs up and winced. That's when Webb noticed the bloodstain on the man's left shoulder. He wasn't the only injured one. Dohi, the Navajo tracker with jet-black hair and a silver goatee had a special chest brace.

Webb studied the other members of Ghost. Stevenson, the muscular African American man dipped his freshly-shaved face and closed his eyes. Rico wrote in her journal quietly. Tanaka put his ear buds in and drew in a breath. Dohi began tracing a finger around the bone handle of his knife.

They all looked exhausted.

"How long you been back from France?" Webb asked.

Fitz swiped a strand of red hair under his helmet. "Twenty hours."

Webb nodded because he didn't know what else to say. He had heard they'd hardly made it back from a mission to gather intel in France – intel that was vital to the next stage of the war – Operation Reach. Now Colonel Bradley was sending Ghost on another mission into enemy territory.

Several heads turned to the windows. Outside, a team of Marines boarded an adjacent Black Hawk. Another squad climbed into a third chopper. They were heading to Greenland with Team Ghost, but Webb wasn't sure exactly where the target was. His job was simply to man the door gun and assist with the flight, and he was glad for that, not just because of the cold, but because of the rumors about what dwelled on the world's largest island.

"ETA to target is about two hours," Tito said. "Depending on the storm. Sit tight, Ghost."

The rotors fired and made their first pass above, and Webb held his questions for later. He glanced out the window as the bird pulled into the sky. It only took a few minutes for the USS *Forest Sherman* to vanish on the horizon.

"All right, listen up everyone," Fitz said.

Tanaka pulled out his earbuds and Rico closed her journal.

"There's a reason Colonel Bradley sent us six hundred miles west of the European front, and that reason is Greenland…" Fitz hesitated as the chopper hit a stream of turbulence. The bulkheads rattled and he waited for it to pass.

"Got us some mean looking skies," Tito said. "Better hold on to your breakfast."

The bird vibrated, jerked, and then steadied out. Webb eyed the fort of clouds they were headed for. The other two Black Hawks were about to enter the storm. One by one, the wall swallowed the choppers.

Fitz waited another second before continuing.

"Here's a timeline of events. VX9H9 was deployed over Greenland not long after the outbreak so about six or seven months ago. Kryptonite was deployed two months ago. The surviving government and military reached out to General Nixon about a week ago stating the weapons have worked well in most areas…"

"Except the one we are going to," Stevenson said, shaking his head.

"Correct…" Fitz pulled out a laminated map and held it up for his team to see. "But our mission isn't to determine why." He paused again and scratched at the stubble on his jaw like he didn't want to say what came next.

"Anyone ever heard of the German fortress Hitler was supposed to escape to in Antarctica?" he finally asked.

Rico chuckled. "Sure. The US supposedly launched Operation Highjump there. Story goes they sent ground and air forces to fight the Nazis at their base in the Queen Maud Land of Antarctica. The Germans were said to have UFOs and all sorts of—"

"That shit wasn't real, Rico," Stevenson interrupted.

Fitz directed his gaze at Rico and then Stevenson, silencing them quickly.

"Stevenson is right about Antarctica, but what I was getting to is that there *was* a Nazi base in Greenland not far from this Inuit fishing village," Fitz said. He pointed at the map and Rico sheepishly raised her hand.

Fitz dipped his chin at her.

"Sir, I thought the Nazis only had a weather station in Greenland."

430

"That's what everyone thought, until now."

Dohi pulled his knife and twirled it nimbly despite the rattle of turbulence. If anyone else was doing it, Webb might have told them to stop.

"Nazis? UFOs? What the hell are you guys talking about?" Stevenson asked. "I mean, seriously, what the fuck?"

Rico ignored him and directed her attention to the leader of Team Ghost. "Do you think that base has something to do with Kryptonite not working on the Variants there?"

Fitz folded the map in half, and then into a quarter to examine it closely. "That's what we're going to find out," he said. "The government retrofitted the base into a lab and were working on a bioweapon of their own to kill the juveniles."

"I don't suppose these 'rebels' are going to help us, either, are they?" Tanaka said. "Not that I'm complaining. Just saying. The EUF wasn't there for Operation Beachhead either."

Fitz gave a reply with a quick shake of his head.

"What about the locals?" Rico asked. "Are there any still alive? Perhaps they could give us some intel if there are any out there."

"Maybe if any of them are still alive," Fitz replied. He went back to studying the map as turbulence rattled the chopper. Webb used the time to check the sky. He still couldn't see the other Black Hawks.

"Our orders are to find and infiltrate the facility and destroy whatever weapon they were working on," Fitz continued. "When we're finished, we're ordered to destroy the old Nazi facility."

"And I don't suppose you know what this weapon does, do you?" Dohi asked.

Fitz pulled a small handheld recorder from his rucksack and held it up. "This tape is the only real intel I have. It came from a joint mission between the Greenland military and the EUF. Most of it's in English."

Every member of Team Ghost moved closer to Fitz, even Apollo, who sat on his haunches. Webb unclipped his harness so he could hear.

Fitz clicked the play button.

Background noise, hardly audible over the whoosh of the helicopter blades, broke from the tiny speakers. A voice cracked through a moment later.

"Command, we have found the tunnel to the facility, permission to enter."

"Copy that, Eagle 1, green light."

A few seconds of static passed, followed by a panicked voice. "We're entering the labs. Something happened here... something awful. There are bones and some sort of..."

More static, then the same frightened voice.

"There's something here, Command."

There was gunfire from multiple rifles.

"Lee is gone!" someone else said. "Shit they got Galan, too!"

Webb shuddered at the piercing hiss and shriek that followed.

"Eagle 1, do you copy?"

"Wolf 1, do you copy?"

"Snake 1, do you copy?"

"Command, Snake 1, we're cut off from the other teams... we have multiple contacts... What the hell is that thing!"

"Take it down, Bray!" someone shouted.

Another flurry of gunshots sounded. What came next made Webb swallow hard. The high-pitched shriek almost sounded human.

The tape cut off, and silence filled the troop hold.

Fitz lowered the recorder and scanned his team. Their faces were stone cold, but Webb could feel his own eyes widen from shock.

"That was the last anyone heard from the strike teams," Fitz said.

"How many were there?" Stevenson asked.

"Three teams. About thirty men. Not a single one made it out."

Stevenson made a low whistle.

"Damn," Tanaka added. "So that's it? They didn't send in any more teams to figure out what the hell is down there?"

"They don't have any to spare," Fitz replied.

Stevenson shook his head. "Of course not. Just like the EUF couldn't spare anyone to help the 24th MEU during Operation Beachhead. Why the fuck don't they just bomb the site?"

The chopper hit another pocket of turbulence. Webb grabbed a handhold and looked out the window at fluffy white clouds and snowflakes pelting the window. He searched for the other Black Hawks while Fitz continued his briefing.

"Nixon wants that weapon destroyed internally. We can't risk it getting out. Bombs could bury it, but…"

Webb focused on a flash of motion through the clouds to the east.

"Three American fire-teams against a Nazi base full of God knows what…" Stevenson started to say.

"I'll take those odds any day," Rico said.

Dohi agreed with a grunt. "Me too."

The underbelly of the bird seemed to answer with a groan as they passed through another stronghold of air.

"Jesus," Rico said. She grabbed her stomach. "This is one hell of a rough flight."

Webb glimpsed another flash of movement in the sea of white. He leaned in closer for a better view at a gap in the clouds. Every helmet in the troop hold looked in his direction at the sudden distant crack of gunfire.

"Ghost, we got Reavers!" Tito immediately said over the comms. "Badger 1 is under attack!"

Fitz hurried over to Webb. They opened the door and a blast of cold air swirled into the troop hold.

"You got eyes?" Fitz asked.

Webb shook his head, and then froze. Through the thinning clouds he saw something that seized the air from his chest.

A dozen massive bird-like Variants swooped around Badger 1. The Marine on the M240 blasted away at the monsters while his comrades open fired with their M4s. Badger 2 was to the east, flying adjacent, and holding their fire.

Webb tried to move, but the sight of the Reavers had him

paralyzed with fear. He had never seen one in real life. Their armored bodies and fleshy wings flapped through the sky, surrounding Badger 1 like Turkey Vultures waiting to feed.

A round punched through the bulkhead behind Webb, snapping him from his trance. He ducked with the rest of Team Ghost.

"Holy shit! They aren't watching their fire zones!" Rico shouted.

"Tito, get us clear!" Fitz ordered.

Webb turned for the M240, but Dohi was already manning the gun. He raked the muzzle back and forth for a clear shot.

One of the Variants plucked a Marine from the open doorway of Badger 1 and tossed him into the clouds. Three of the creatures dropped into a nosedive after the man while one of the smaller beasts flapped into the troop hold. It knocked three of the Marines out the other side like bowling pins.

Webb felt his heart rising in his throat as the remaining Marine fired at the Reaver that had climbed inside the craft. The beast retracted its wings so it could fit then slashed the man with a pair of talons, slicing him across the neck. He dropped his weapon and grabbed at the wound, stumbling backward.

Screaming filled the open channel as the pilots tried to keep the bird in the air. They pulled up hard and a body fell from the chopper, vanishing into the clouds. In a matter of minutes, the beasts had killed every Marine in the troop hold, leaving the pilots on their own.

The Reaver got on all fours and crawled up to the cockpit. It retracted a spiked tail, and then impaled one of the pilots like a scorpion hitting prey with its stinger. The other pilot turned from the cyclic stick and fired an M9.

A loud crack sounded to Webb's left. He cupped a hand over his ears and watched the head of the Reaver explode inside the Black Hawk. Ears ringing, he turned to see the smoking barrel of Fitz's MK11 sniper rifle.

When Webb looked back to Badger 1, it was gone, hidden by the cloud cover. Dohi remained calm and steady on the big gun, scanning for a target.

Snow tore into the side of the troop hold, and the cold bit through Webb's layers. He let out a breath in a puff. The blades thumped above them, and for a moment it seemed like everything had slowed to a stop.

When the clouds finally cleared Webb searched for Badger 1, but where there should have been a Black Hawk, there was only open sky.

Stevenson broke the silence. "Odds just got worse, Rico."

Apollo let out a whine as Fitz lowered his rifle. "Keep your eyes peeled," he said. "Those things are still out there."

Webb tried to nod, but he just stood there shivering, and not from the cold. Team Ghost had already lost a fire team, and they weren't even at the target yet.

-2-

Master Sergeant Joe Fitzpatrick had planned on taking a nap on the helicopter ride, but instead he spent the trip watching the sky for Reavers with the rest of his team.

Badger 1 was gone... lost in an attack by monsters that should never have been out this far. Webb, the Crew Chief, had said they were migrating to find food. On top of the attack, Fitz had other worries on his troubled mind. Rumors had reached the European front that something was happening back in the States – rumors of a coup, and attacks on Safe Zone Territories.

Fitz winced as he twisted in his seat toward the cockpit. He had to keep frosty. Worrying about his friends back home wasn't going to do any good when he was all the way out here and couldn't do anything to help them.

"Tito, how far?" he asked.

"We're five minutes from the target, sir."

Jagged mountains rose along the coast in the distance. Below, icebergs floated through the blue water like ice cubes. A wall of mist covered a harbor full of fishing boats and drifted up toward the rocky shoreline.

Fitz strained for a better look for the small fishing village. Most of the residents were Inuit, but there were several locals living here that had worked for the government and in the top-secret lab.

Badger 2 pulled alongside and together, the two choppers flew inland. They passed over rocky beaches and turned toward a road that curved along the shore. On the top of a hill overlooking the harbor, the first houses finally came into view. Wood structures with peeling red and blue paint lined the elevated terrain like colorful gravestones.

Tito and his co-pilot circled along with Badger 2. The main city was just three blocks of aging structures. From above, Fitz couldn't see much. Snow covered the terrain and most of the road.

Dohi looked back from the door gun.

"No sign of tracks down there, sir," he said. "Variant or human. But the snow could have hidden any recent activity."

Fitz nodded back. They were about to drop into a ghost town and he had no doubt the monsters were hiding somewhere down there. He just hoped they weren't going to run into anything like the abominations in France. Black Beetles, Pinchers, Wormers, or God only knew what else was out there. Part of him was glad to have a break from Europe.

He stood and looked for a spot to land. A red church with a short steeple sat on a cliff overlooking the harbor. There was plenty of room for a landing zone there.

"Tito, take us down by that church."

"You got it."

Fitz reached down to check Apollo's vest. The dog had suffered another injury at the Basilica of St Thérèse in Lisieux, France, but hadn't required stitches like Fitz's shoulder.

Apollo licked Fitz's hand and rubbed his wet muzzle against his arm.

"Hold still, boy," Fitz said. He grabbed dog boots from his pack and then slipped them over the Shepherd's paws one at a time.

Apollo didn't like that. He swiped at the ground, trying to remove them, but instantly stopped when Fitz shook his head.

Glancing up with sad, amber eyes, the dog obeyed his handler.

Wind from the rotors whipped up the snow covering the LZ, forming a circular mound several feet deep. Tito and his co-pilot hovered over the church and waited for Fitz's orders.

"All right, Ghost. Lock and load."

Webb stepped up to the open door and glanced down.

"Look's clear, Tito," he said.

Tito slowly lowered the chopper as Team Ghost slapped magazines in their weapons and applied final layers of clothing. Fitz pulled the laughing joker bandana he'd inherited from Staff Sergeant Alex Riley, around his face. He closed his eyes and exhaled in an effort to keep the painful memories from muddling his thoughts.

*All it takes is all you got, Marine.*

He slung his MK11 over his back and pulled his suppressed M4. After palming in a magazine, Fitz stepped to the open door. Wind gusted below from the rotors, stirring up more of the white grit.

He eyed the landscape one more time for contacts. The church, terrain, and road beyond were clear.

"Take us down!" Fitz yelled over the noise.

Tito lowered them a few feet from the ground without touching down.

"Go, go, go!" Fitz yelled. He put a hand on Rico's back and patted her. She jumped out after Dohi and Stevenson. Fitz waited for Tanaka and then grabbed Apollo under the belly.

"Good luck, sir!" Webb shouted. "I look forward to hearing of your victory!"

Fitz looked at the middle-aged crew chief. He had the timid stare of a man that had never seen combat. But that wasn't the only reason Fitz knew he had never fought a Variant. No one that had fought the monsters would look forward to hearing a story like that.

"Good luck, brother," Tito said over the comms.

Fitz nodded and jumped out. His blades sank into the powder and he ducked and ran toward the church. Badger 2 came in next, disgorging the six Marines of Fox Team. Like Ghost, the men were all dressed in white camouflage. They shouldered their M4s and swept the muzzles across the terrain.

Surrounded by his men, Sergeant Jackson Mapes jogged over to Fitz carrying a Benelli M4 tactical shotgun. He was one of the shortest Marines Fitz had ever met, but what Mapes lacked in height, he made up for in muscle and speed. At forty-five, he was still one of the fastest Marines in the 24th MEU.

"Form a perimeter," Mapes said to his men. They fanned out, and took knees with their rifles pointed in all directions. The exposed faces Fitz could see all looked young, far too young to be out here. But that was partly due to a new rule. The military now allowed anyone over the age of sixteen to join.

"Dohi, you and Tanaka do some quick recon. Don't go out too far," Fitz said.

The men were running before Fitz had finished his sentence. He watched the choppers traverse the skyline as Stevenson and Rico took up position with the members of Team Fox.

Tito and the other pilots were headed to a small rebel-run outpost forty minutes away. Forty minutes was a hell of a long time if Ghost and Fox ran into trouble. But it beat having to wait if the choppers went all the way back to the USS *Forest Sherman*.

Fitz drew in a breath of icy air through his bandana.

"Master Sergeant, this sure as hell doesn't look like the foothills to me. I don't reckon you know where the hell we are, do ya?" Mapes asked. A thin layer of snow stuck to the man's graying five o'clock shadow. His breath reeked of cigarettes, and his crooked teeth reflected years of coffee drinking.

"We're approximately three miles from the target," Fitz said. "Figured it would be safer to hike in and clear the town of any hostiles first."

Mapes raised a bushy eyebrow. "A three mile hike in this weather could take us a while, especially if we have problems along the way."

"I'm not waltzing into the facility without knowing what we're up against. The evidence is in this village. If someone is still alive here then maybe we can figure out what happened," Fitz said firmly. He pulled his map out again and gestured for Rico and Mape to crowd around.

"You think someone could have survived in this shit hole of a village?" Mapes asked.

"We're going to find out," Fitz replied. "There are a dozen houses and other buildings between here and the target. I'm recommending we split up to search some of them."

Mapes picked at a gap between his yellow teeth, a nervous tick. It was his way of saying he didn't agree. Fitz noted it with a grain of salt.

"Sergeant, you take Fox this route." Fitz traced a line northwest through the village toward the foothills. "I'll take Ghost to search this route and we rally here, at the target."

"And if it's not there?" Mapes asked.

"Then we search until we find it."

"Weather is getting worse," Rico said.

The light snowfall had turned into flurries. Fitz squinted at the sheets of snow in the distance. He could hardly see the house at the top of the hill.

"We rally in two hours," Fitz said. "If you find anything, you radio it in, but otherwise, radio silence."

Mapes dipped his helmet, slightly. Another tell.

"You got it, Sergeant?" Fitz asked.

"Yes, sir."

Fitz directed his gaze at Rico. "You and Stevenson clear the church before we head out."

"Sir."

The voice pulled Fitz to his left. Dohi was there, his eyes sharp and intense. His tan skin was red from the cold, but he had insisted on not wearing any facial protection. Fitz was afraid to ask what had the big man spooked.

"Sir, Tanaka and I found something…" Dohi said. "You better come take a look."

* * *

Flurries fell to the ground, adding a fresh layer of powder that crunched under Fitz's blades. He followed Dohi and Tanaka around the back of the church with Apollo trotting behind him. The rest of Ghost and Fox held the perimeter.

Fitz raised his rifle to scan the gray sky and the harbor over the cliffs. The slight movement prompted a jolt of pain across his raw injury. The stitches tightened every single time. It was a small price to pay. He had walked away from the battle at the Basilica St Thérèse with his life, something countless innocents couldn't say. Memories of Michel, the other children that had died there with their brave caretaker, Mira, were tattooed on his mind.

*All it takes is all you got Marine.*

He blinked away the memory and kept moving.

Ahead, Dohi pointed at a wood shed with double doors. The one on the right was frozen shut, but the left door was slightly ajar.

Using his fingers, Dohi told the story. No contacts, but there was something inside. Fitz lowered his rifle as he walked the five steps to the open door. He took in a breath to test for the rotting, sour-fruit smell of the monsters. There was a trace of sweat and saliva on his bandana, but nothing to indicate Variants.

Dohi flipped on a light and directed it inside. "Take a look, sir."

Fitz followed Dohi and Tanaka through the opening expecting to find a stack of frozen bodies like Team Ghost had discovered in Building 8 over seven months ago. But this was not a meat locker.

They had stepped into a single tomb.

"What the fuck?" cracked a voice.

Sergeant Mapes stood behind them, staring at the same narrow, seven-foot wood cross Dohi had discovered. Instead of a crucified model of Jesus hanging on the cross there was a juvenile Variant.

Or at least Fitz thought it was. Where there should have been armor plates covering its extremities there were ribbons of exposed muscle, stretched and purple from the cold. Icicles hung from the sucker-mouth on the beast's face. Ribs were cracked and flayed open like a grenade had exploded inside its chest. The organs, stomach, and intestines were all missing.

Fitz recalled the tape they had heard on the flight in.

*There are bones and some sort of…*

Had the military stumbled across something similar inside the lab?

"What the hell happened to this thing?" Tanaka said. He pulled his Katana and used the tip of the blade to raise the beast's chin for a better look.

"Jesus," Fitz whispered.

Empty sockets greeted them, only strings of muscle where the eyes had once been. Fitz couldn't pull his gaze from the anatomy. He had never seen the inside of a juvenile before. What little left there was to see…

Tanaka sheathed his sword and stepped back. "This is some truly evil shit. What do you make of it, sir?"

"I've never seen anything like it… I mean, I have, but not from juveniles. Variants do this to one another, and to humans, but I've never witnessed this behavior from the offspring."

Fitz studied Dohi for a reaction, but the man simply stroked the ice out of his silver goatee.

"We should get moving," Mapes said. "We're wasting time in here."

Fitz glanced at the monster one last time, his guts twisting. Something was very off in this fishing village, and he had a feeling it all had to do with the buried Nazi facility they were supposed to find and destroy.

They returned to the church where the other team members were waiting. Stevenson and Rico stood on the front steps, weapons cradled and relaxed.

"You find anything?" Fitz asked.

"Nothing alive," Stevenson said. "What about you?"

"Nothing alive," Fitz replied.

Stevenson smirked and Fitz walked up the steps to peer into the church. Snow swirled inside from the gust behind him, a mini tornado whipping the grit down a row of pews and up into the rafters. A Christian cross with a model of Jesus hung above an altar at the other end of the room.

The sight made Fitz shudder. He performed the sign of the cross and closed the doors to seal the room. The other soldiers continued raking their muzzles across the terrain around the church.

"All right Ghost and Fox, we're moving out," Fitz said. "Good luck, Sergeant."

Mapes simply nodded and waved Fox away from the church. His men fanned across the snowy terrain and moved northwest. Within moments the wall of flurries had swallowed them.

Fitz didn't like splitting up, especially after what they had discovered in the shed, but one thing he had learned over the past seven months was that you never put all your eggs in one basket. It had almost destroyed the American military during Operation Liberty. They were already down a fire team, and someone had to complete this mission.

"Combat intervals, Ghost," Fitz said. "Dohi, you got point. Stevenson, you're on rear guard. Rico and Tanaka you stay close to me and Apollo. High and low, watch the rooftops and sky for Reavers."

"I can't even see the sky," Stevenson said.

"Do your best," Rico said.

As Dohi raised his gun and walked past, Fitz reached out to stop him. "You all right, brother? I can put someone else on point."

"I'm fine, sir," Dohi replied confidently. He spat a chunk of licorice root into the snow and jogged ahead. He was definitely moving slower than normal, and Fitz could tell the man's ribs and his head were bothering him, but Dohi was the last one to ever complain. When he did talk, it wasn't about himself.

Team Ghost set off to the northeast, following Dohi up a

curving road that was hardly visible under the drifting white. There were still no signs of tracks. Even the tire marks were buried.

The whistling wind echoed as they began their hike. It rose and fell like waves slapping then receding at the beach. Fitz kept to the road where his blades sank through only several inches, crunching the gravel beneath.

Apollo trotted ahead, sniffing the snow every few feet. Team Ghost watched their zones of fire with muzzles sweeping for hostiles, moving with calculated precision. Fitz pushed his scope to his snow goggles to scan the sky again. If the Reavers were out there, he wouldn't have much warning. The road, framed on both sides by mounds of snow and red wood houses, provided little cover. They were sitting ducks out here for the winged abominations and whatever else prowled in the quaint fishing village.

A voice over the wind snapped him from his thoughts.

"What did you see back there, Fitzie?"

He lowered his scope to see Rico walking to his left. The frosted pink tips of her hair protruded from her stocking cap and helmet. Her dimples widened as she chewed on a stick of bubble gum.

"Juvenile corpse…" He didn't want to spook her, but she had a right to know. "Flung up on display like a macabre shrine."

Rico stopped dead in her tracks. "What... What do you mean?"

"Some sort of science experiment. Hell if I know. I don't know what it means, or who did it."

Rico gave him a meaningful look before she shouldered her rifle. "I don't like this, Fitzie. I don't like this one damn bit."

The howling wind seemed to answer her.

Fitz pushed on, his blades crushing the compact powder into the gravel. The cold was slowly working into his layers and his fingers were icing inside of his gloves. He moved them to keep the blood flowing. They had hiked for ten minutes, and he was already cold.

A sensation of being watched stopped him mid-stride.

"What is it?" Rico asked, slowly turning with her rifle.

"Something's out there... watching us from afar. Studying... scrutinizing us."

"You're freaking me out."

"Sorry. Just keep your eyes peeled." He slowly scanned the terrain and the sky. The creatures had evolved to see in the dark, but could they see through the dense sheets of snow?

Fitz continued toward the hilltop. According to the map, the village was on the other side. Dohi stopped near the top, crouched, and balled his hand into a fist. Then he got onto his stomach and scoped the village below. A wave of snow glided over his body as he lay there, still like a fox waiting out prey.

Fitz hung back with Rico and the others. He pulled his bandana down and wiped his fogged snow goggles while they waited. Dohi had the best eyes, ears, and nose in the team. He was a full-blooded Navajo tracker, and Fitz was glad to have him. If anyone could sense the monsters coming, it was Dohi and Apollo.

A flash of motion came from the hill as the drifting snow cleared. Dohi stood and gave the all clear to advance. He continued over the other side with Tanaka running to catch up. Blasts of wind tore into Fitz as he followed. He pulled his bandana back up, tucked his helmet down, and fought the current of air.

*Better get used to Command sending Team Ghost into a shit storm.* Just like in France, Ghost was getting the hard assignments – the missions no one else could complete. Fitz was starting to wonder if he was ever going to make it back to Plum Island to see his friends. As soon as this mission was over he was going to figure out exactly what the hell was going on back in the States. Someone had to know...

When he reached the crest of the hill he stopped to get his bearings. Apollo was just ahead, and Rico was still by his side. He used a sleeve to brush away the ice clinging to his eyebrows.

The road dipped into a valley protected from the wind. White rooftops dotted the landscape. He counted thirteen structures, all of them spread out along three main streets. Several vehicles caked in snow sat idly on the road. Dohi and Tanaka were already making their way toward a truck.

Fitz stood there for another second, staring at the snowy structures of a village that seemed frozen in time. From his vantage, it looked like the inside of a snow globe.

"You coming?" Rico asked.

Fitz nodded and ran down the slope toward the vehicles. By the time they caught up with Dohi and Tanaka they had already cleared the truck. Like the church, it was empty. He was starting to get the feeling they weren't going to find anyone alive here.

Stevenson pulled his skull bandana down and spat in the snow.

"Where the fuck are all the bodies?" he asked. "Even the Variants leave behind skeletons."

Apollo's tail was still up, which was the only good sign Fitz had seen yet. The dog didn't sense any monsters in the vicinity.

"Come on, we need to keep moving," Fitz said.

Team Ghost continued down the road that led to the central part of the village. The first block was comprised of businesses – a hardware shop, café, and a police station. The other signs were too covered in snow to make out. More houses lined the second and third blocks. Abandoned cars sat in the streets, doors frozen shut.

Fitz motioned for the team to spread out down the first block. There was no way they were going to clear each structure, but they had to figure out what the hell happened to these people. It might be the only way to understand what had happened inside the lab.

Fitz flashed signals, splitting the team up. Dohi and Tanaka took off across the street to clear the hardware store. He directed Stevenson to hold security in the street while Rico and Apollo followed Fitz toward a café.

He raised his silenced M4 toward a shattered front door. Shards of glass framed the wood, but a mound of snow had formed on the other side. He reached for the handle to pull it open, but it wouldn't budge.

Rico was already looking for an alternate route in. She walked along a still-intact rectangular window. Drawings of steaming coffee mugs and plates of fish marked the icy glass.

Fitz and Apollo followed her to the corner to a small alley that separated the building from the adjacent structure. Snow swirled into the narrow passage, masking his view momentarily. When it cleared he saw a back door to the café. From the sidewalk, he checked the rest of his team before entering.

Stevenson crouched on the sidewalk and nodded to Fitz.

Across the street, Dohi and Tanaka had already entered the hardware store.

With a breath, Fitz followed Rico into the alley. She stopped at the door, grabbed the handle, and put her shoulder into it after Fitz gave her the okay. Ice fell away from the frame and it creaked open.

Rico stepped back and shouldered her rifle.

Apollo stood next to Fitz, waiting for orders.

"Execute," Fitz said.

Rico kicked the door, and Fitz strode inside, sweeping his rifle back and forth over an empty kitchen.

Pots, pans, and glasses littered the floor.

Apollo sniffed the ground, wagged his tail, and sat on his haunches.

"Clear," Fitz said. He exchanged a glance with Rico. Side by side, they pointed their muzzles toward an open door that led to the main dining area. They slowly walked into the room furnished with booths and tables, clearing opposite sides.

Fitz lowered his rifle and let out an icy plume of breath that quickly faded away. The surface of every table and chair was covered in a layer of snow.

"Not even a single body," Rico said.

She stepped over to a booth and wiped off the snow with her glove, revealing dinner plates and mugs. A bowl of frozen soup sat in the center of the table.

"It's like they got up and left in the middle of dinner," Fitz whispered. He scanned the room, then jerked his chin toward the exit.

They returned to the sidewalk just as Dohi and Tanaka exited the building across the street.

Both men shook their head.

Fitz mimicked their action and turned to wave Stevenson over, but the big man was gone.

Fitz whirled to his left, then his right.

"Stevenson?" Fitz said. "Yo, Stevenson." He kept his voice low, trying not to draw attention, but the only answer was the whistling wind.

Dohi and Tanaka crossed the street, battling gusts of snow and grit.

"Where the fuck did Stevenson go?" Rico asked.

Fitz ran to the position he had last seen the man. He slowed as he spotted a wad of black material resting in the fresh powder. Stevenson's crumpled skull mask bandana.

-3-

Sergeant Mapes couldn't believe his luck. Just when things were rolling forward with Operation Reach in Europe, he was sent to Greenland. Fucking Greenland. What the hell did the United States care about Greenland? He shook his head and continued the march through the western edge of a fishing village with a name he couldn't even pronounce.

The worst part wasn't getting shipped off to this oversized hunk of ice though. It was not knowing if he could trust the new members of his team. He had lost four on the landing in France. Four new faces, four new names, and four new Marines he had to babysit surrounded him in the flurries. The only Marine he trusted was Corporal Mark Carol.

Mapes tucked the butt of his M4 tactical shotgun in the sweet spot in his armpit and continued walking. Carol was on point with his SAW slowly moving back and forth for contacts.

Lance Corporal Dixon and Lance Corporal Preston were working the road to the right. Both men were young, just seventeen and eighteen years old. A little younger than Mapes had been when he joined the Corps. It seemed like a hell of a long time ago in some ways, but in others he could still remember the first time he got an ass whooping for failing to polish his boots properly.

*Oorah.*

The good old days when they were fighting men, not monsters.

He looked to the other two members of his team, Private First Class Johns and Lance Corporal… Shit, Mapes had forgotten the name of the other man. His last name was a big city. He could remember that much.

*Boston. You idiot.*

Lance Corporal Boston and PFC Johns owned the road to the left. They were young bloods as well. Mapes hadn't had the chance to get to know any of the new men, and he was still grieving the loss of those that had come before them. But this was war, and he knew by the time it was over there would be more fresh faces on Fox Team. One of them might end up replacing his own.

He continued through the snowstorm toward a cluster of shacks. Lumpy, white foothills rose like toes on a frozen foot in the distance. The road curved through the small fishing community nestled at the edge. Lines hung from poles in the yards where the owners had thrown up fresh catches to dry out. This was where the locals had lived, in poverty, without any form of electricity from what Mapes could tell.

He sniffled and swallowed a hunk of mucus. It caught in his throat, and he hocked it up, and spat it into the snow. On top of everything, he was catching a damn cold. He hated the fucking cold, hated the cold more than anything. If he ever did make it out of this mess and had the luxury of retiring he was going to do it somewhere warm, like Florida, or perhaps Mexico.

*Damn you, Master Sergeant Fitz.*

Mapes didn't care how many Alphas and Variants Fitz had brought down. Trekking through the village was stupid and a waste of time. They should have dropped in outside the target and infiltrated the facility right away.

Carol balled his hand into a fist as he reached the first house. Then he directed his SAW at a single-room structure to his left.

Mapes jogged to catch up.

"What you got, Carol?"

He pointed toward a mound of white fur sticking out behind the right side of the house. It was the first sign of anything, alive or dead, that Mapes had seen since they began the trek thirty minutes ago.

He motioned for Dixon and Preston to clear the adjacent house. The men dipped their helmets and took off through the snow. Mapes left Johns and Boston to hold security on the side of the road, then jerked his chin for Carol to follow.

Together, the veteran Marines slowly approached what looked like a wolf pelt. Mapes had heard of the furry Variants discovered in climates just like this. The thought sent a shiver up his back. He had killed all sorts of monsters in the past seven months, but there was no denying an abominable snowman Variant with sucker lips was at the top of his list for the most horrifying things he could meet.

*Jesus Christ. Is this real life?*

Mapes knew Jesus wasn't going to save him from anything. He flicked the safety off his shotgun. The only thing that had his back was the 12-gauge he was holding.

The wind howled in the distance. A gust scraped a chunk of snow off the shack's roof, and it punched through the fresh powder. He eyed the foot-long icicles hanging from the awning as he hugged the wall. The last way he wanted to die in the apocalypse was from a spear of ice driven through his skull.

Mapes could already hear what they would say about him back on the European front lines.

*You hear what happened to Mapes? The dummy got hit in the dome by a spear of ice.*

He shook his head and focused on the white fur that was ruffling in the wind. With his left side close to the shack, he inched forward, Carol on his right flank.

They exchanged a nod, and Carol burst around the corner with his SAW at eye level. Mapes moved his finger from the trigger guard to the trigger. Static crackled in his ear as he directed his shotgun on a corpse partially buried by a snowdrift. The white fur wasn't the hide of some animal, it sprouted from the hide of a creature that had once been human.

*They do exist. The furry fucking Variants are real.*

"Fox 1, Ghost 1, do you copy, over?"

Mapes ignored the transmission and crouched to check the body. Master Sergeant Fitzpatrick would have to wait.

Carol held his SAW at the ready while Mapes used a shaking hand to brush off a layer of snow from the cold flesh of a beast he had only heard stories about. The fur was long and tangled from the back to the head like a mane on a lion.

*Was this one of the Inuit locals?*

Mapes pulled his hand away and used the muzzle of his shotgun to roll the corpse over for a better look. As soon as he poked the flesh, a scream rose over the whistling wind.

Twisting, he watched Johns stumbling in the middle of the street with something sticking out of his stomach.

"Johns!" Carol yelled.

Another scream. This time it was Boston, but Mapes couldn't see the young Marine.

PFC Johns staggered another foot, turned, and fell to his knees, a spear through his midsection.

Mapes pulled his shotgun away from the corpse and stood, his mind trying to grasp what he was seeing.

Carol was already running back to the street, and Dixon and Preston had stepped out of the other building.

"On me!" Mapes yelled. He moved to join them but something caught his leg. He looked back down at the corpse. This person wasn't dead after all.

Time slowed as his view shifted to a woman with wild white fur stared up at him with two different colored eyes. The left was the yellow slotted iris of a Variant, but the other was brown like his own. Her lips curled into a snarl. They were not the bulging sucker lips of a monster, but jagged, yellow teeth that clanked together from her bloodied gums.

She was some sort of Variant, but human at the same time – a hybrid.

He snapped alert as she swiped at him with a knife. The blade slashed through his left calf before he could move. He stumbled back a few feet and swung his shotgun around, but her knife was already on its way. This time he moved quickly enough to avoid the blade, and it sailed over his shoulder.

A screech. Then a choking sound.

Mapes didn't have a chance to turn to see what the hell was making it.

"You piece of —" He took aim but the woman dashed behind the wall of the shack.

*Jesus, she's fast.*

Mapes gritted his teeth from the pain racing up his leg, and the anger from the ambush. Adrenaline emptied into his system, prompting a wave of energy.

When he turned to find a target, Carol was on the ground gripping his neck. Blood oozed from between his gloved fingers. The knife the hybrid woman had thrown had hit him right in the jugular.

Mapes knew there wasn't anything he could do for Carol. Johns was dying too, his body jerking in the snow in the center of the street.

Boston was gone.

Dixon and Preston were chasing something to the north toward the foothills.

"Get back here!" Mapes yelled.

They vanished over a hill.

Cursing, Mapes checked for targets again, and then took a knee next to Carol. The corporal was choking on his own blood. The awful gurgling sound made Mapes cringe.

"It's okay, man. You're going to be okay," he lied. It wasn't the first time he had said that to a dying brother.

Carol's eyes widened behind his goggles and flitted from Mapes to the sky.

In a swift motion, Mapes twisted with his shotgun and blasted a figure that was leaping off the roof of the shack.

A body slammed into the snow to Carol's right, face down, arms and legs spread wide, and a gaping hole in the middle of their back.

Mapes stood and swept his gun from left to right and then back again. There was no sign of Boston, and Johns was as still as a board now. Preston and Dixon were gone.

By the time Mapes looked back down at Carol, the man was dead. His hands fell limply from his neck, revealing the blade that had torn through his flesh.

Mapes scanned for hostiles in the storm. Snow fluttered from the sky, caking his visor with flakes. He wiped them away and then reached down to close Carol's eyes. No one deserved to die in this icy hell. Cold and alone.

"I'm sorry, brother," he whispered.

Down two men, and separated from the other two, Sergeant Jackson Mapes limped away. For the second time in as many days, he had lost half his team.

\* \* \*

"It had to be had to be a Reaver," Dohi said. "That's why I can't find tracks. It must have swooped down and grabbed Stevenson when we were inside searching."

Team Ghost had sought shelter from the storm under the awning of a house on the edge of town. The village was empty. Completely empty. Not a single body, nor any evidence of what happened to these people. No blood. No tracks. Not even a skeleton. The entire village gave him the creeps and with Stevenson missing, Fitz was losing his cool.

"Did you hear that?" Rico asked.

"What?" Fitz asked. He stepped out into the flurry of snow and looked northwest. Over the growl of the wind came the unmistakable crack of a shotgun.

"Gunfire," Rico said.

Fitz glared at the frosted foothills. Waves of snow poured from the sky. Visibility was getting worse, but his ears told him what his eyes could not.

Fox Team was in trouble.

The shotgun blast had come from that direction. He stepped back to the protection of the building, pulled his bandana down, and pushed the mic back to his lips while Tanaka, Rico, and Dohi stared at him.

"Mapes," Fitz snapped. "Mapes, do you fucking copy?"

For the second time there was no response.

Fitz cursed again.

*All it takes is all you got, Marine.* Fitz repeated the motto three times before he started to feel better.

"Is that Fox Team?" Tanaka said. "It's got to be, right?"

"What are you orders, sir?" Rico asked.

Her firm and formal question got Fitz's attention. They had seen a lot in the past week, but there was nothing like losing a teammate. He knew he had to make a decision, and make one quick. But first, he needed to get a read on Dohi.

The man was crouched and calm in the snow, staring at the storm with his M4 cradled across his chest.

"You can't find a single trace of Stevenson?"

Dohi shook his head. "He's gone, sir."

"But why didn't we hear a gunshot, or a scream? And where the hell is everyone else?" Rico asked. She chomped on her gum, her big eyes widening.

Apollo's tail was still up, but for the first time, Fitz didn't trust the dog's senses. Maybe it was the cold, or perhaps it was something else, but Apollo hadn't been able to detect a single Variant.

Fitz pulled his bandana back up. "We have to keep moving. Stevenson is gone. We have to accept that and focus on the mission—"

"Ghost 1, Ghost 1…." Crackle. "Fox 1, do you…"

Fitz reached up to cup his hand over his helmet.

"Roger, Fox 1… Mapes, what the hell is going on out there?"

"They got my team." Static broke the next transmission.

Rico caught Fitz's gaze.

"Come again, Fox 1."

"Carol and Johns are dead. Boston's gone. Fuck. I can't find Preston or Dixon."

"Calm down," Fitz said. "Calm down and tell me what happened."

There was another flurry of static, and then, "The locals, man. I think it's the locals that took 'em."

Dohi stood, narrowed brows painted white with snow.

"Where are you, Mapes?" Fitz asked. "Tell me where you are, and *stay put*."

"I'm heading for the rally point."

Fitz shook his head. "Mapes, listen to me. You need to hunker down and wait for us. You're not going to make it to the rally point."

Another flurry of static broke over the line.

Fitz nearly ripped his earpiece from his ear. He took in a breath, exhaled, and focused. Team Ghost was down a man, and now, apparently both of the other fire-teams were KIA.

Tanaka, Rico, Dohi, and Apollo waited for orders as the wind swirled snow around the shack. Fitz hated leaving the village without Stevenson, but they had no choice.

Flashing a hand motion, Fitz ordered Team Ghost toward the foothills. It was the first time he had left a man behind since taking command, and he had a feeling it wouldn't be the last. The burden ate at his marrow, but like Captain Reed Beckham had taught him, Fitz pushed on for the sake of his entire team.

-4-

Preston and Dixon were gone, and Mapes hadn't found a single piece of them. He blinked away the stars before his vision and stopped to look at his leg. Blood oozed from the makeshift tourniquet and dotted the snow. He was leaving a trail of red, but for some reason the beasts that had picked off Fox Team back in the village hadn't attacked him.

He raised his gun and continued his trek north toward the foothills. His boots sank ankle-deep into the snow drifts. The fresh powder was coming down fierce, stinging his exposed face, and working through his layers. He could hardly make out the outline of the trees in the surrounding forest. Skeletal branches groaned under the weight of the snow.

The deeper he ventured into the woods the harder it was to see. A crack, and then a snap like the pop of joints sounded to his right. He whirled with his shotgun toward the sound just as a branch snapped and crashed to the ground. Another crack came from his left, and he swung his gun toward another canopy strained by the weight of the snow.

"Preston, Dixon, do you copy?" he muttered into his headset, although he knew it wouldn't do any good.

Static and the whistle of the wind was the only reply.

His team was gone.

Wiped out in minutes.

Mapes couldn't believe his fucking luck. He had survived the apocalypse back home only to have Europe and now Greenland, shit on him.

He took another step, his boots sinking. The pain in his leg was getting worse, and the cold was numbing his senses.

Another step.

A voice came over the comm line and froze him mid-step.

"Sergeant Mapes... Do you... Help!"

Over the wind, Mapes thought he heard a scream that sounded like Preston. The voice seemed to blend with the wind making the storm sound alive.

"Preston, goddammit, report your location," Mapes said into his mic. "Where the hell are you?"

This time only the screech of wind replied.

His heart caught in his throat when he saw a cloak of white dart between the bases of two trees. Mapes raised his gun and moved his finger from the outside to the inside of the trigger guard.

"Come on, you bastards... show yourselves..."

He jerked the muzzle to the west, then the east. Over the wind came a guttural, animalistic panting and the creaking of joints. There were at least two of them out there, hunting him. Whatever these things were – hybrid, monster, or human – they didn't care if he heard them.

They were taunting him.

He tracked another flash of white to the east and pulled the trigger. The shotgun blast spread out and punched into the base of a tree behind the camouflaged creature. The shot echoed through the forest, and when it was gone, the sounds of the beasts had faded as well. He knew they were still out there, but he'd bought himself some time.

He limped ahead, the blood loss starting to make him light headed.

*Stay with it you old bastard. You are not dying on this turd of ice.*

He blinked again and again until his vision cleared enough to make out the fort of trees lining the bottom of the foothills. He was almost to the target.

Mapes waited a few minutes to make sure he was alone and then walked to the safety of a massive tree. Another gust of wind slammed through the woods. Limbs caked with snow swung and creaked above him.

He raked his gun over the terrain just to make sure it wasn't one of the creatures sneaking up with him. After a second pass, he crouched uncomfortably and pulled his map and compass.

The village was a half-mile behind him now and he was a quarter mile to the base of the facility. He double-checked his math, and then tucked both items back in his vest.

"Preston, Dixon, do you copy?" The wasted words trailed off to static. He checked his leg again and then reloaded his shotgun.

*Almost there... Just keep moving.*

A chill shot up his back as he stood. In his peripheral, a figure to the north. Something was watching him. He slowly turned and raised his gun at a naked man standing between two trees. Shoulder-length black hair hung over his face; gray fur slid over his shoulders, and blue veins webbed across exposed skin the color of snow.

The man rolled his head back and flexed lean muscles across his furry frame as he let out a guttural roar. Mapes centered his shotgun on the man's chest, but before he could pull the trigger, dozens of figures leapt from piles of snow in the forest. Male, female, some clothed, some naked, all came running.

The sight of so many creatures sucked the freezing air from Mapes's lungs. He fired off a blast that hit the black-haired man in the chest. Fresh blood coated the white like a bucket of paint had been kicked over.

Mapes snapped into survival mode. Firing to his left then his right, he back peddled through the powder. Spent shells ejected as he fired. The hybrid beasts were fast. Several dropped to all fours and galloped toward him while others leapt to the trees. More came from the direction of the Nazi facility that Mapes was starting to think he was never going to see.

"Fox 1… Can you hear me? This is Ghost 1. Do you copy?"

"I'm under attack!" Mapes yelled back.

"Where?" Fitz replied. "Where the fuck are you?"

"In the forest! Not far from the target!"

Mapes ignored the next transmission, squeezing off another shot that took the top off the head of a thick male with a mane of black hair. The monster dropped to his knees, brain sloshing out his broken head.

"Fox 1, what the hell is going on out there?"

Mapes didn't have time to reply. He continued firing, hitting a female in the stomach. Her guts splattered on the snow. Mapes wondered if part of Fox Team was inside the steaming pile.

The crack of his shotgun echoed through the forest with screech of the monsters. They fanned out in all directions, making it nearly impossible to kill them. He counted fourteen, but more seemed to be emerging from the sheets of snow in the distance.

"Come on!" Mapes yelled. He jerked the gun up to fire on a smaller beast that had climbed a tree behind him. The blast hit the creature in the side, blowing out a hunk of flesh and exposing the ribcage.

Mapes whirled to shoot a female on all fours skittering over the powder with a knife gripped beneath her yellow teeth.

What the hell were these things?

He centered his muzzle on the beast as she leapt to two feet, knife now in hand.

*Click. Click.*

Mapes cursed, dropped the shotgun, and went to pull his M9 as the creature tossed the blade at him him. He flinched to the left at the last second. The knife was meant for his neck, but sheared off a piece of his trap muscle instead. Warm blood trickled through his layers.

The beast squawked in anger as Mapes screamed in pain. It dropped back to all fours and barreled toward him. He pulled his M9 from the cold holster and fired three shots that punched through her throat, chest, and stomach. He side-stepped out of the way and she somersaulted and came to a rest in the snow. Blood gushed from the wounds as she bled out next to him.

She sucked in frozen breaths and stared up at him, one of her hands twitching as if she was trying to raise it. He walked past her, saving his bullets for the dozen other creatures prowling and forming a circle around him. Several of them stood on all fours and peaked out from behind the safety of the trees to growl at him.

These were not adult Variants, and they weren't human. He had never seen any of the monsters carry weapons. Why would they need them? They were weapons in themselves, and yet two of the females he had killed carried knives.

Mapes raked his M9 from target to target but held his fire. They shied from the gun now like they understood it could kill them. Variants didn't usually do that. These things had more reasoning, like the Juveniles.

He plucked a grenade from his vest in case they decided to rush him. Blowing himself up sounded better than getting torn to shreds.

The grenade seemed to scare the monsters even more. Several of them darted into the curtain of snow and back into the forest, vanishing into the mist of white.

"You want some?" he said, pointing the gun and grenade at a half naked male that remained. It snarled back then ducked behind a tree.

"How about you?" He directed the weapons at a smaller creature with a carpet of hair sprouting from its back. It was crouched in a cat-like hunch, waiting to strike. As soon as he moved his trigger finger from the M9 to the pin on the grenade it backed away.

One by one, the beasts slowly retreated back into the storm.

Mapes kept his finger wrapped around the pin and scanned the terrain, struggling to catch his breath. Blood leaked down his chest, but he didn't dare take his eyes off the forest.

He had found the missing villagers, and if he was going to die he was going to bring them with him. If he pulled the pin it would blow him to pieces and detonate the C4 in his rucksack. There was enough in there to blow up half the forest.

"Yeah, that's fucking right. Run. Run or take you all with me!"

He glimpsed a flash of motion that came so fast he couldn't react. His yell was followed by a guttural *oompf!* A tree branch hit him in the dead center of his chest with such force it lifted him into the air. He was thrown backward several feet; his arms and legs spread-eagled as he sailed through the air and hit something that felt like a wall. The most intense pain he had ever experienced shot through his entire body. Stars broke before his eyes, and then, darkness.

Mapes blinked, struggling to stay conscious. Through tunnel vision, a new figure lumbered through the gusting wind on two feet. Unlike the other beasts, this one was far larger with barreled chest muscles and bulging biceps. Its flesh was covered in tangled, gray fur. Instead of clothes, it wore ridged armor plates on its arms, legs, and chest. Now Mapes knew what had killed the juvenile back in the shed at the church near their LZ.

"What the fuck," Mapes choked. He could hardly speak. Hell, he couldn't even move. It took every inch of energy to even crane his head.

The creature strode forward, stopping when it was ten feet away to tilt a head that looked oddly human aside from the overgrown fur on its face. Something hung from its beard...

Mapes squinted at the dried body parts; a shriveled eye tied to the hair, an ear, and...

The creature's yellow-slotted eye on the left and blue eye on the right focused on Mapes. He squirmed and tried to raise his M9, but he couldn't move anything below his neck. He dropped his head and saw the gun was gone. That's when he realized the tree limb that had hit him was not a limb at all.

The long handle of a spear protruded from his chest. The blade had pinned him and his rucksack full of C4 to the tree like a thumbtack pinning a butterfly to a wall. If he had to guess, the tip had sheared his spine below his ribcage.

Mapes choked on blood and coughed. The pain was gone now, replaced by something he hadn't felt in a long time.

Fear was an odd thing. It could be more paralyzing than any other emotion. But Mapes wasn't afraid of dying. He was afraid of being left out here in this godforsaken ice jungle.

The beast crouched to study him, sniffing the air. Its bi-colored eyes flitted from him to the ground near his boots. He followed its gaze to the grenade in the snow.

In a swift motion, the beast turned and darted away, leaving Mapes to die, alone, and paralyzed in the frozen forest.

\* \* \*

Fitz led Team Ghost toward a fence of trees. The shotgun blasts had come from somewhere inside over thirty minutes ago. He stopped to listen, but heard nothing over the screaming wind.

Sheets of thick snowflakes fell from the sky, air-brushing everything with white. The soft powder stuck to Fitz's carbon fiber blades. A hundred things were running through his mind and none of them were good. But there was a mission to complete and he still held onto a seed of hope that Stevenson was alive.

If he was, he was somewhere through the forest ahead. Fitz had a feeling they would find Stevenson eventually, perhaps in the lab facility.

Fitz directed Dohi to take point and then gestured for Apollo to go with him. Together, the two trackers set off into the forest. Fitz led Rico and Tanaka after them.

The tips of the trees rose toward the sky of white, branches swaying and shifting. Cracks and groans came from all directions like they were on a wood boat in violent seas.

They were moving quickly, as one, keeping close instead of combat intervals. Whatever was out here was cunning enough to fool both Dohi and Apollo, and they had already slaughtered Fox Team. Judging by the lack of gunshots, Mapes was dead now too.

Fitz focused on Dohi's outline through the snow. Apollo trotted alongside, sniffing, wagging his tail, then sniffing some more. For a moment, the sight reminded Fitz of Beckham. Fitz loved the dog, and the Shepherd loved him, but Apollo was Beckham's dog, and Fitz felt guilty for bringing him all this way.

*Just make sure you bring him home in one piece*, Beckham had said.

Fitz exhaled and whispered, "I'll bring him home, brother. Soon."

The thought of seeing his friends again gave Fitz the boost of energy he needed. He walked a bit faster, knowing they were closing in on the target. Get in, find the weapon, blow the place up, and get out. That was all they had to do now. Well that, and survive. And find Stevenson.

Fitz worked his fingers in his gloves to keep the blood flowing. He needed to be ready to fire at a second's notice, and the cold had already penetrated every layer. He raised his M4 when Dohi froze ahead. The tracker balled his hand and crouched next to Apollo. The dog trotted a few feet forward, his muzzle going to work before stopping at a mound that looked like a red snow cone.

Flashing a hand signal, Fitz ordered his team to toward the gore. As he approached he prepared himself to find a body, but instead, there was only a flattened area covered in fresh blood.

Dohi plucked something out of the snow and held it up. He tossed away a shotgun shell and looked up when Fitz arrived.

"Looks like a battlefield," Dohi whispered. He stood and jerked his chin toward the north where bloodstains littered the snow.

Fitz wiped the snow from his goggles.

"But where are all the bodies?" Rico asked.

"On me," Fitz said. He led the team through the site of a battle, searching for evidence of whatever had happened. Every few feet he spotted a shotgun shell and blood, but there was no sign of a corpse.

Fitz stopped mid-stride when he felt eyes on him. Dohi had already stopped.

"What?" Rico whispered. "Why are we stopped?"

Another voice came in the respite of the whistling wind. It was faint, and sounded strangled. Fitz followed Dohi's gaze to the northeast. Through the gusting snow, he saw a figure against a tree.

Fitz flashed a set of motions for Ghost to spread out. With their weapons shouldered, they slowly approached the contact.

Squinting to see the man's face, Fitz hoped to God it wasn't Stevenson, The man's head was slumped against his chest, and a wood pole had him pinned to the tree. Blood blossomed around his white uniform and vest, leaking down his stomach and legs. As Fitz approached he saw exposed, pale skin.

It was one of Fox Team, but there was no way the man could still be alive.

Fitz directed Rico and Tanaka to watch their six and then approached the tree with Dohi and Apollo. They stopped a few feet away, and Fitz reached out to lift the man's head to see Sergeant Mapes. His lips were blue, and ice hung from his nose.

"Damn," Fitz whispered. He slowly pulled his fingers from Mapes's chin to set his head back on his chest and looked to Dohi.

"Help…"

Fitz's heart leapt and he redirected his gaze toward Mapes.

"He's alive," Dohi whispered.

Purple, lips trembling, Mapes tried to talk.

"Water," he mumbled. "Need. Water."

Dohi pulled his water bottle, and Mapes craned his neck, wincing in pain, and tonguing the water

"Hypothermia. Makes the body hot," Dohi whispered. "We got to get him down from the tree."

Fitz nodded, but Mapes shook his head and coughed.

"No," he said. "I can't move anything below my neck. Do me a solid, Master Sergeant. Put one in my head."

Dohi and Fitz exchanged a look.

Fitz had killed out of mercy before, but shooting out here would tell whatever was out there where they were. They would have to knife him instead, but Fitz wasn't sure he could do that.

"Tell us what you saw. Tell us what did this," Dohi said.

Mapes swallowed. "Some sort of…" He coughed and his eyes rolled up into his head.

Fitz grabbed Mapes's cheeks in his gloves and said, "Tell us what you saw, Mapes. We have to know."

Redirecting his eyes, Mapes focused on Fitz.

A branch snapped in the distance, and a pile of snow fell to the ground.

Mapes choked again. "I saw demons. Not Variant. Not human. Something in between."

Fitz glanced down at the spear shaft protruding from Mapes's chest. Whatever had thrown it had done so with such force that it had torn through flesh, bone, and a rucksack. He slowly let go of Mapes's face and took a step back.

"After you complete your mission, come back for my body. Don't leave me out here," Mapes mumbled. "Promise me, Fitz."

Fitz turned toward another snapping tree branch that brought a mound of snow down. When he looked back at Mapes, the man was gone. His head slumped against his chest.

"I promise, brother."

-5-

The lab entrance was easier to find than Fitz had thought. All he had to do was find the poles with Variant and human corpses flung up on display outside a bluff covered in snow and trees.

He pulled his bandana and scarf up over his nose to keep out the stench. It didn't matter that these bodies were frozen; they still reeked of rot and sour fruit.

The sheets of snow had lessened, providing a view of the entire graveyard. There were dozens of the monsters hanging from crucifixes, plus the soldiers from the tape recording Team Ghost had listened to on the flight in. The human bodies were torn apart, their faces unrecognizable from deep gashes and swollen flesh, now frozen. Behind the bodies was the tunnel leading into the hills.

"It's a warning," Dohi said. "My grandfather told me stories about something like this when I was a boy."

Fitz remembered a book in high school about medieval armies posting their enemies on pikes. Dohi was right, this was a warning, but it was also a psychological game designed to scare the enemy.

Team Ghost would not be deterred.

The mission would continue, but at what cost?

Fitz was down a man, and the other two fire teams were wiped out. At least he knew what monsters were out there. According to Mapes, the creatures that had done this were the locals – some sort of hybrid beast. From what Fitz had seen, they could use weapons and set traps. Not the type of traps or ambushes Alpha Variants or Juveniles were known for. These things were experts at hiding. Even Dohi couldn't find them. And apparently they saw any outsider as a threat – human or monster.

"Sir," Rico said. "What should—"

"Watch for bobby traps and keep your eyes on those trees," Fitz said. "We're proceeding with the mission."

Rico hesitated, but didn't protest. She continued with the

rest of the team. They spread out through the maze of corpses. Fitz knew each and every member of Ghost was on edge, but they were prepared for this, and he was proud to have them by his side. Most men and women wouldn't dare follow him and Ghost into the fray.

He walked up to the corpse of a Juvenile hanging on a cross a few feet away. Every single plate of armor was gone, leaving exposed flesh and stringy muscle.

Fitz continued on with his gun shouldered. A bird pecked at the face of a human soldier near the entrance to the lab facility. It continued stripping away ribbons of flesh with its black beady eyes on Team Ghost.

Above the bird, the concrete lip of the tunnel had been etched into a bluff topped with a forest. Fitz couldn't read the sign, but he had a feeling it said, *No Trespassing*. An iron-rod gate was left ajar in front of the tunnel and a pickup truck covered in snow was parked outside.

Fitz continued through the macabre display of corpses, sweeping the area with his M4. A mini-forest covered much of the foothills in this area, leaving multiple blind zones. His first scan revealed nothing but branches and frosted trees, but he could feel something watching him – something was out there, waiting to strike.

Dohi and Apollo stopped when they got to the pickup. Rico and Tanaka took up position behind the vehicle and Fitz approached the door. He glanced down at Apollo, his heart leaping when he saw the dog's tail. It was down. For the first time today, Apollo could sense the monsters.

"Something's watching us," Dohi said. "In the woods."

Fitz raised his rifle toward the tree line. He swept the crosshairs across the base of trees and the branches, but nothing moved in the winter wasteland.

Lowering his rifle, Fitz considered past missions. Back then he was just a Marine following Beckham. Now he was in Beckham's role. What would Captain Beckham do? He had to have known when he infiltrated Building 8 seven months ago that there was something inside. But he proceeded anyway. That's what soldiers did.

Every member of Team Ghost looked to Fitz for orders, and he felt the burn of the heavy burden all leaders carried when they led men and women into battle.

There was only one thing to say. "Stay frosty, and stay sharp."

Fitz jerked his chin around the side of the pickup toward the tunnel entrance, trying his best to manage his heart rate and breathing with positive thoughts.

Dohi was first past the gate. He squeezed through the opening and walked into a long tunnel that stretched deep into the hills.

Fitz and Apollo went next and then Rico and Tanaka. The concrete ceiling was low, maybe ten feet, but the walls were wide enough for vehicles to pass through. Snow covered the ground through most of the tunnel. Fitz searched for tracks, but saw none.

"Dohi, you think there is another entrance to the lab?" Fitz asked.

"I'm sure of it," Dohi said. "My guess is those things have a back door."

Rico stopped and studied the wall to their right. "Where are all the bullet holes?"

Dohi spat on the ground and adjusted his rifle. "I'm sure we'll find some soon."

Fitz nodded. "Keep moving. We should be coming up on the main entrance."

They walked for several minutes, the light and the screeching wind dwindling behind them. It felt good to be out of the cold, but Fitz had a feeling he was trading the freezing temperatures for something much worse.

He turned to check his six and pulled up his goggles just as a curtain of flesh darted on the other side of the fence. It was gone in a blink of an eye.

"What?" Rico asked. "Why are you stopping?"

"Thought I saw something."

Dohi halted at the corner ahead where the passage narrowed. He balled his hand into a fist and waited.

Fitz glanced back at the gate once more and then motioned his team to continue around the bend. Side by side they approached a blast door that was wide open. Apollo sat on his hind legs a few feet from the steel and stared into a hallway that led inside the facility.

"What do you make of it, sir?" Dohi asked.

"I was about to ask you the same thing," Fitz said.

Rico dipped her head from side to side. "I really don't like this."

"Why would they just keep the door open?" Tanaka said.

"We're going to find out. Shoot anything that moves like a Variant. " Fitz put a hand out and touched Rico's sleeve. "Stay close to me."

She pulled the gum from her mouth and stuck it to her helmet. "You stay close to me, sir."

Fitz almost grinned. Instead, he flicked the tactical light on his M4 and nodded at Dohi. One by one, beams shot out and angled into the hallway. The tile floor was covered in snowy footprints. There were boot and shoe marks as well, but the majority seemed to be bare feet.

Dohi bent to examine one, then glanced back up at Fitz. "Looks like Variant to me, sir. Nothing human could walk around barefoot out there for long."

"On me," Fitz said. He had a rule: never let someone do something he could do himself. If they were walking into a trap, he was going to be the first one in.

The team entered the hallway single file, lights dancing across the ceiling and the glass windows framing the sides of the passage. Fitz had no idea what the layout of the lab was, or where the weapon they were looking for might be, but this didn't look like any BSL4 lab he had seen.

They passed windows overlooking offices furnished with leather chairs and metal desks. The walls were white, but there was no lab equipment, and there was no entrance to the offices from the hallway. The odd architecture gave Fitz the chills. *What kind of lab is this?*

"Start setting the C4," he said.

Dohi and Tanaka placed the charges on the outside of the walls and then gathered back behind Fitz.

The hallway ended at another door. He shone his beam at the steel frame and the white bars lining a glass panel window. Approaching slowly, Fitz examined the exterior. The paint had been peeled away, revealing a Swastika. Another chill raced through his body.

He stood, grabbed the handle and jerked his helmet at Rico. She took up position behind him with Apollo next to her. Tanaka and Dohi hung back, watching their rear guard.

Fitz twisted the knob. It clicked. *Unlocked.* He opened the door for Rico. She moved into another hallway, Fitz and Apollo right behind her.

Team Ghost slowly worked the passage with peeling paint and concrete walls. The Nazis had built this place to withstand a bombing run by the Allied Forces that never happened. It had survived all these years, buried and unknown to most of the world.

Fitz made it a quarter way down before he stopped to take a closer look through more glass windows. He directed his light inside the one on his left – a small room furnished with a metal bench, toilet, and sink. Metal bars served as a barrier between the cell and the windows. But where was the entrance?

He flicked his light toward the ceiling where a trap door was sealed shut. *What in the hell?*

Fitz continued to the next window. The next two rooms were the same holding cells with ceiling entrances.

Rico checked the windows across the hall and then looked back at Fitz, her eyes wide. She didn't need to say anything. Fitz could see she was spooked.

They pressed on, nearing the halfway mark of the passage where the first sign of a battle emerged. Bullet holes dotted the ceiling and walls. Carmine stains caked the walls where the soldiers from Greenland and the EUF had perished.

"I thought this was a lab," Rico whispered. "Looks more like an insane asylum."

"Makes you wonder what type of weapon they were working on to kill the Juveniles," Tanaka said. He placed more C4 charges on the walls and the windows.

At the end of the hallway lay another open door. Fitz had a feeling they were about to find the answer to Tanaka's question. He gripped his M4 tighter, and gestured for Apollo to get behind him.

With the wave of his hand, Fitz ordered Team Ghost forward into a large space the size of a gymnasium. At the center of the room was a pit that could have been a very deep swimming pool drained of water. A metal fence with razor wire surrounded the opening. Thirty feet above, a metal platform with a balcony overlooked the room. There were several steel doors on the wall, all sealed shut. It was some sort of observation post, but to observe what?

Fitz strode into the room, sweeping his rifle back and forth. Nothing stirred in the massive place.

"Clear," he said. He motioned for his team to spread out. Apollo suddenly stopped and growled at the fence. Fitz moved his finger from the outside of his trigger guard to the trigger and focused his light on the thick chain-link fence. As he approached, a drop of liquid plummeted in front of his weapon and plopped to the ground in front of his blades.

Fitz slowly tilted his head toward the domed ceiling and angled his light. Three human bodies were suspended by their feet.

"Stevenson," Rico said.

Fitz raked his light over the bodies. His heart hammered in his chest when he saw she was right. Stevenson dangled from the middle of the ceiling like a chandelier, a cord wrapped around his feet. The other two men were from Fox Team. From his vantage, Fitz couldn't tell if they were alive. He put his finger to his lips to keep Rico quiet, but she didn't get the message.

"We have to cut them down."

Fitz cursed under his breath, glared at her, and then flashed hand signals to Dohi and Tanaka. They were already looking for a way up.

Apollo stalked toward the fence surrounding the pit, continuing his low growl. Fitz approached cautiously and peered through the chain links into a pit thirty feet deep. Metal spikes the size of buck knives lined the walls like barbed cobwebs.

He directed his light toward the bottom. On the floor next to a metal bench rested a bowl and a bucket. He glanced back up at Stevenson and the other two soldiers hanging from the ceiling. Why not keep them in one of the rooms or even the pit if they were prisoners? Why hang them up there?

Nothing made sense, why would... Fitz shook the questions away as Tanaka climbed a ladder to the balcony. Dohi had frozen on the floor beneath the balcony.

"Back!" he shouted just as the doors on the top level swung open. They disgorged furry figures onto the platform; joints popping like the branches back in the frozen woods.

A thud behind him made Fitz's heart leap again. The exit to the room had been slammed shut. He twisted and yelled, "Ghost, on me!"

They came together in the center of the room as the platform filled with the creatures that had killed every soldier that had set foot in this cursed place.

Fitz focused on the silhouette of a thick man that stood in front of Team Ghost's exit door. In his right hand he held a long spear, and in his left he gripped a shield made from a Juvenile torso. More of the rigged armor lined his extremities, chest, and genitals.

"I killed you..." Fitz whispered, a memory of the Bone Collector Alpha rising in his mind. "I blew your fucking head off."

The creature strode into the light of Rico's rifle giving Fitz his first glance at the monster. This beast was not the Bone Collector – this was something far worse. Body parts hung from a tangled beard. It flexed barreled chest muscles and snorted at Fitz as it studied him with a yellow slotted eye and one blue one.

This *wasn't* a lab. This was a prison where the scientists had used some sort of weapon to infect the local Inuits, turning them into monsters that hunted Juveniles and, apparently, humans.

But for some reason they weren't attacking. The dozen creatures on the balcony remained in the shadows, staring down and holding weapons: knives, spears, even a bow and arrow. All of the blades were angled at Team Ghost.

"Hold your fire," Fitz ordered his team.

"What?" Rico muttered. "You crazy, sir?"

"We're surrounded," Fitz said. "There's no fighting out of this one. Maybe we can reason with these things."

"That sounds like a bad idea, sir. Variants, don't reason." Rico stepped in front of Fitz, but he pulled her back. Tanaka and Dohi flanked them as the Alpha lumbered forward, snorting again and scanning Fitz and his men. It pounded its chest and raised the spear, but didn't throw it.

"Finally," the beast said with a snort. His voice was almost human, but the voice box seemed atrophied, like the man had smoked cigars his entire life.

"I've been watching you. Watching you all."

Fitz swallowed hard, and said, "What do you want?"

The beast pointed the spear at Fitz and grinned with yellow, jagged teeth.

"Finally I have a worthy opponent. Even if you are just half a man."

Fitz almost raised his rifle to shoot the beast, but gritted his teeth instead.

"Sir, I highly recommend…" Rico began to say, but Fitz raised his hand to silence her and took a step forward. Apollo barred his teeth, snarling at the creature, but Fitz would not be deterred.

"You win, and you get to leave with your friends," the creature said. "I win, and… we eat you."

Fitz glanced up at the balcony. More of the hybrid monsters

had emerged. They weren't just hunters looking for prey. They were cannibals, too.

"Let us fight," Dohi whispered.

"We can take 'em, sir," Tanaka added.

"I agree," Rico said.

"No," Fitz said. Team Ghost had enough firepower to get out of here, but not without taking casualties. It would require trusting the beast. If he fought it and won, then they would all get out of here alive. If he didn't accept the challenge, and fought with his team, then several members of Ghost would die. He couldn't let that happen.

"If I go down, you fight," Fitz whispered. He reached out toward Tanaka. "Give me your Katana."

"Sir..."

"That's an order," Fitz said as he set his rifles on the ground.

Tanaka unsheathed the blade and reluctantly handed it to Fitz.

The beast's grin widened, and it twirled the spear and took a step backward. It motioned for the creatures on the balcony to lower their weapons, and Fitz nodded at his team to do the same.

Taking another step, Fitz gripped the Katana in both hands. It felt light, but he knew the blade could cut through Juvenile armor. He had seen Tanaka do it back in France.

"Be careful, Fitzie," Rico whispered.

"Good luck, sir," Tanaka said.

Dohi let out a grunt and then said, "Kill this bastard."

Fitz took a deep breath, doing his best to suppress his fear. He was used to fighting with his rifle, not a sword, but with the lives of his team on the line, he had no other choice.

*All it takes is all you got!*

With the blade out in front, Fitz lunged at the beast. The creature parried the attack with its shield, deflecting the sword. Then it swung the spear at Fitz, the shaft smacking him in the shoulder before he could duck. He screamed out in pain, the stiches in his shoulder tearing.

Stumbling backward, Fitz regained his balance and then swung the blade wide. This time the tip sliced the creature in the leg. It roared in pain, and went down on one knee. Fitz raised the blade above his head, bringing it down as hard as he could like a hammer.

The creature lifted the shield and once again deflected the sword. The clank echoed through the room. That got the monsters above excited.

Animalistic panting sounded from the balcony above as Fitz stumbled backward again, his fingers numb from the vibration. The Juvenile torso was strong, but the Katana blade was stronger. It had chipped a groove into the shield.

The beast pushed to its feet and twirled the shaft above its head, blood dripping from the slash in its thigh. In a quick movement it swiped at Fitz, but this time he ducked beneath the spear. He went down on one knee and lunged with his sword again, striking the monster in the armpit.

He yanked the blade out, a guttural scream reverberating through the room. Fitz struck the shaft of the spear, splintering the wood as the beast struck him in the face with the shield.

Pain lanced up his nose and stars broke across his vision. He slashed with his blade to keep the creature back while he blinked away the fuzz. Bringing a hand up to his face, he felt the warm sticky blood pouring from his nose. It was broken, no doubt about that.

Something hard hit him hard in the chest a moment later, and he crashed to the ground, gasping for air. He blinked again and saw the creature toss the shield away. It used its knee to break through the middle of the spear like a toothpick. Holding the two pieces in each hand, it strode toward Fitz.

"Get up, Fitz!" Rico shouted.

"Come on, sir!" Tanaka said.

Grunting and shouts sounded from the balcony.

Fitz winced and pushed himself up. He sliced through the air with the sword as soon as he was on both of his blades. The sword hit one of the shafts, sticking into the wood, but the beast used the other to smack Fitz in his helmet. The rattle shook his brain, and he backed up, blinking away another flurry of stars and fuzz.

"I'm going to enjoy this," the creature said. It let out a bellowing laugh. In that moment everything froze, and although Fitz couldn't see he could hear the creature preparing to strike.

Blind and desperate, Fitz ducked just as the blade whooshed above his head. Then, with all of his strength, he lunged. The blade cracked through armor, and then sunk into flesh.

Warm liquid peppered his arms, and a scream so loud it hurt his ears followed.

Part human, part monster.

Blinking rapidly, Fitz's vision finally cleared. He had impaled the beast right through the heart.

The other creatures and Team Ghost fell into silence.

Nothing stirred in the massive room.

Fitz winced again, the blood rushing in his ears. He stood and pulled the sword from the beast's chest, a crunching sound echoing. The hybrid man dropped to both armored knees, staring at Fitz with one monster eye and one human. A grin still on its face, the creature crashed to the ground. Blood pooled around the body, spreading toward Fitz's blades. He took a step back and glanced up at the monsters on the balcony.

They continued to glare at their fallen leader as if they expected him to get back up. Rico, Tanaka, and Dohi waited with their weapons at the ready.

A tense moment passed that was shattered by the squawk from a frail female. She let out a pained roar at the team.

Had this creature been the mate of the beast Fitz had killed?

Team Ghost gripped their weapons, ready to raise them and open fire, but Fitz ordered them to stand down as the beasts slowly withdrew through the open doorways, disappearing into the ancient Nazi facility.

"Holy shit, sir," Rico said. "Are you okay?" She lowered her gun and ran over to Fitz with Apollo trotting along.

"I... I think so," Fitz said. A wave of dizziness washed over him and he crouched. "Hurry, get Stevenson and those other men down."

*Keep your head above your heart, man. Don't...*

Fitz closed his eyes and felt the second rush of blood in his ears. His skull pounded like someone was hitting him with a hammer.

He was going to crash. He couldn't get enough air, and his vision was failing.

Something warm brushed his right hand.

Apollo glanced up, his amber eyes stricken with worry.

"Fitzie!" Rico exclaimed as he collapsed. He fell on his stomach; his arms limp at his sides. He tried to talk, tried to move, but he couldn't fight the darkness. The last thing he saw was the listless yellow slitted and blue eye of the monster he had killed staring back at him.

* * *

Fitz woke up on a vibrating floor. His brain felt like applesauce sloshing inside his skull. Ringing echoed in his ears, but there was another noise beyond that, some sort of chopping. And voices. He could hear faint voices.

He struggled to move, wiggling his fingers first, and then his hands. The shades of red and orange framing his vision slowly retreated. All at once, the ringing stopped like the final suck of a vacuum and he heard a soft voice.

"Fitzie. Fitzie, you're back."

He put his hand on his head, but where his helmet should have been he felt soft padding.

"Where am I?"

The *whoosh-whoosh* of helicopter blades answered his question.

The bright colors vanished, and in their place, he saw a dead face. Everything came crashing back, and he remembered the beast back at the facility.

But this was no monster.

It was Mapes. His eyelids were closed, and the ice on his five o'clock shadow was already melting. Team Ghost had retrieved his body. Fitz had kept his promise to the man after all.

A few feet behind Mapes lay Stevenson. Dohi and Tanaka hovered over him and applied bandages to wounds that Fitz couldn't see. Two other bodies, both covered by white sheets were resting near the open door.

"Hang on, Ghost," said Tito over the comms. "I'm getting you the hell out of this frozen shit hole!"

Fitz struggled to sit, but Rico pushed back on his chest. Apollo wedged up to his side, resting his head on Fitz's vest.

"Stay put, Fitzie. You took a beating back there," Rico said with a smile. Her dimples were the best thing Fitz had seen all day. She blew a bubble, and her grin widened now that she had his attention.

"If you're going to blow it, now's the time!" Tito said.

Dohi stood and walked over to the open Black Hawk door with something in his hand.

Below, branches from hundreds of trees reached up toward the chopper like skeletal fingers. The tunnel to the Nazi facility and the pickup truck came into focus.

Dohi looked back at Fitz for orders. With a nod, Fitz gave him the all clear.

Raising the detonator, Dohi pushed it once, then twice, and then a third time. Three concussions thudded in the distance, deep and loud. Fireballs shot out of the tunnel entrance, slamming into the gate and flipping the pickup truck. The flames raced over the snow, plowing into the graveyard of human and Juvenile corpses, and slamming through the forest.

The bluff over the facility sagged, cracked, and caved in, sealing the prison where the military had once again tried to play God. The weapon had ended up not being a vile or tube after all. Like VX-99, the weapon designed here had turned the poor souls that had once lived in the fishing village into monsters.

Fitz watched the rooftops pass below, saying a mental prayer for the innocent civilians that had lost their lives. Some of the hybrid creatures might have escaped the inferno and retreated into the forest, and Fitz secretly hoped they might be able to find some sort of peace.

All that mattered now was that Team Ghost had completed their mission. They had killed the monster and destroyed the old Nazi facility. Somehow, once again, Fitz hadn't lost a man, woman, or dog.

But this time he had come very close. Stevenson wasn't out of the woods yet, either. Fitz crawled over to him and grabbed his hand as Tito flew over the harbor and ocean, returning to the USS *Forrest Sherman* for fresh orders.

Webb, the Crew Chief, sat across the troop hold, incredulous eyes on Fitz.

"What the hell happened out there, Master Sergeant?" he asked.

Team Ghost had one hell of a story, but Fitz wasn't prepared to tell it now. Instead, he tightened his grip on Stevenson's hand. The man cracked his eyelids and focused on Fitz, his lips trembling.

"Hang in there brother," Fitz whispered. "This battle is over, but we're going back to war."